M000312993

Alan Cherchesov, born in 1962, lives in Vladikavkaz, the capital of North Ossetia. A graduate of the North-Ossetian University, he lectures there on world literature and edits a university journal of cultural studies. He is the founder and director of the Institute of Civilization in Vladikavkaz, which provides alternative education in the humanities.

An Ossetian writing in Russian, Cherchesov has two novels and a number of short stories to his name. His novel *Wreath on the Grave of the Wind*, a sequel to *Requiem for the Living*, was awarded the prize of the Russian Academy of Critics, shortlisted for the Russian Booker Prize, and published in German by DVA and dtv. *Requiem for the Living* was published in German by S. Fischer.

GLAS NEW RUSSIAN WRITING

contemporary Russian literature

in English translation

Volume 36

Alan Cherchesov

Requiem
for the Living

a novel

Translated by Subhi Shervell

glas

The Editors of the Glas series:
Natasha Perova & Joanne Turnbull

Contributing editor: Amy Paton Walsh

Publicity director: Peter Tegel
Camera-ready copy: Tatiana Shaposhnikova

Front cover: photograph by Boris Baratov from his book *Paradise Laid Waste*, Lingvist Publishers, Moscow, 1998

GLAS Publishers
tel./fax: +7(095)441-9157
perova@glas.msk.su
www.russianpress.com/glas

Glas is distributed in North America by
NORTHWESTERN UNIVERSITY PRESS
Chicago Distribution Center,
tel: 1-800-621-2736 or (773) 702-7000
fax: 1-800-621-8476 or (773)-702-7212
pubnet@202-5280
www.nupress.northwestern.edu

in the UK and Europe by
INPRESS LIMITED
Tel: 44-020 8832 7464
Fax: 44-020 8832 7465
stephanie@inpressbooks.co.uk
www.inpressbooks.co.uk

ISBN 5-7172-0070-6

In loving memory of my grandfather

PREFACE

Requiem for the Living is the life story of an orphan boy, nicknamed Alone, who grows up alone in a mountain village in North Ossetia. His strange habits and personality rupture the calm of a village community, causing chaos, despair, and resentment among the locals, who then have to cope with the consequences of the events he sets in motion, which cause them to question the nature and the basis of their traditional existence.

Alone first captures his fellow villagers' imagination at the age of ten when he returns one of the horses stolen by his relatives to their owners. As his relatives have since fled to the other side of the mountain pass, the unexpected honesty means he escapes the savage punishment that tradition requires be meted out to anyone from this family. But it also means he can return to the community and occupy the house his relatives abandoned.

Soon Alone, who is too young to toil the land by himself, finds an ingenious way of providing himself with all life's necessities, and practically turns his neighbours into his farmhands. Naturally, the villagers dislike him for being so clever and different and, moreover, being invariably fortunate in all his undertakings.

Increasingly the enterprising boy becomes an intermediary between the ages-old traditions of the village and the alien culture penetrating the village from the nearest Russian town, which they still call a fort. His fellow villagers regard his behaviour with hostility, believing that he is the one poisoning them with greed and the other vices they associate with alien Russian culture.

But no matter how rootless the boy appears to be, human contact and the bonds of love and family prove inescapable and catch up with him in the end. Yet eventually, his luck abandons him and all his attempts to prevent disaster only prompt further mayhem.

The story is related by a descendent of one of the families involved, who is trying to unravel the mysterious crimes committed in the days of his father's youth, which are all connected with this strange boy Alone, their neighbour. The story spans a whole century, dating back to the early 20th century and leading right up to the present day. But as the novel's action does not hinge on the era in which it is set, a powerful effect of timelessness is conjured.

The story unfolds intentionally slowly in the beginning but then explodes with tragic denouements. At moments it reflects meditatively on the meaning and message of various events in the lives of the protagonists. What is loneliness, love, sin, duty, devotion, passion? Cherchesov ponders on these unfashionable questions in the setting of a traditional community. There, Alone's unusual attitudes bring into question the village's time-hallowed laws and customs.

This novel, which critics have likened to Faulkner and Garcia Marquez', is a philosophical parable in which the hero's unique abilities and alienation highlight the distinctive culture and strict code of honour of the Caucasus. However, Cherchesov's portrait of the Caucasus is very different from the familiar descriptions we find in the Russian classics such as Pushkin and Tolstoy, or in contemporary non-fiction and the media. And while Cherchesov's novel abounds in ethnographic detail, it is not meant for the casual tourist or thrill-seeker: it is told from within an endemic culture threatened by the advance of the modern civilization.

Cherchesov's characters value honor above all else. They religiously observe the laws of the clan and community, and treasure their family graves. And it is these traditions that often lead to tragedy, especially when they clash with those from a different culture.

Significantly, the Ossetians come from the Scythians (known as Alans in the 9th-13th centuries) who later embraced Christianity, unlike the neighbouring ethnic minorities of the Caucasus, who mostly turned to Islam. Rooted in Ossetian mythology, Cherchesov's writing was enriched both by classical Russian and 20th century world literature. Even those who found his novel difficult reading have been gripped by its powerful style and original story.

Russian critics wrote about Cherchesov that few writers feel so keenly the inherent tragedy of human existence, always finite and lonely, and yet, within which man strives for the infinite and universal; few deal so bravely with such clichéd concepts as pride, loneliness, love, jealousy, peace and God, and the interconnectedness of all individual stories in a wider world epic. Cherchesov's novels are full of avalanches, floods, raging rivers, forest fires, meaning that fate crops up frequently, laughing at human endeavour, making man wild and unable to distinguish between good and evil. Sin is constant, but there is always the hope of overcoming loneliness through love.

The Editors

REQUIEM

FOR THE LIVING

Perhaps Time as such does not exist at all, and instead there is only an endless web of endless stories, tracing patterns in the deafening silence of Eternity? Perhaps Time is but a means of retelling them and listening to them? Perhaps it is not stories that grow out of Time, but Time that grows out of stories?

Of course I remember. How could I forget? I was fifteen when he left us, and the whole story of his time with us has long since settled in my memory and been smoothed over, like butter in a tub or a cavity in your mouth after the tooth has been extracted. You only start really to appreciate the tooth once it's gone, only then do you realise why it was necessary and your tongue keeps feeling the gap as if it can't believe it and keeps checking whether it's only imagining it, until it tires and reconciles itself to the loss. And for how many days afterwards do you look straight at people's mouths before noticing anything else? Isn't that always the way? That's it. It's like that for everyone. For those, that is, who are normal, ordinary people. Of course, everyone has their quirks, but then again oddities are there to set off the normal. Yet when the normal gets left far behind that's no longer just a few quirks! That is one's nature itself, and not some offshoot of it.

That's what I'm driving at: he certainly wasn't ordinary. Maybe he was for the first ten years of his life or the tiniest bit longer. His father and mother were caught in a mudslide together with his father's brother, who had a narrow escape but lost his voice, and with his voice his mind. They say he lost the use of his legs as well from fear; only I don't know that for sure and can't remember because I was only born twenty odd years later. But, if that's what they say, something of that sort must have happened to the man, the uncle of the boy. Alone. At any rate, when the whole family fled from the aul*, this uncle was trussed to a buffalo back to back because he could not sit on it due to his bulk. He was as fat, they say, as a three-year old pig, ate and ate all the time, as if in place of a voice and a mind the gods had granted him two extra stomachs to add to the one nature had given him, by right, and which worked no worse than anybody else's, and probably much better because, as they say, even with three stomachs you can't grow that fat. And so they strapped his hulk onto the buffalo's hump, seated the afsin** with the women and children in the wagon, while the old man and his two other sons mounted horses, three of the five stolen, the best in the whole gorge. And, so the story goes, when they fled, no one said a word to them for fear of defiling their tongues and ears, they only followed them with their gazes up to the bend in the road, as far as the dim light of the dawn would allow. Then they went their separate ways back to their homes and began to wait. After a few hours, ten horsemen appeared in their yard, five of whom were brothers and who had, in the course of one night, lost their horses and travelled more than a dozen miles on foot and then galloped no less a distance on borrowed mares. It was at that point, I believe, looking at these men and reading doom in their eyes, that everyone envied the thieves. Honest people often envy thieves, particularly successful thieves, but do not admit it, instead

_____

* aul – mountain village

**afsin – the eldest mother in the extended family

substituting this envy for contempt. Except that envy and contempt are just like meat and salt, the best partners. And so when the brothers said that beyond the mountain pass they already had one blood feud, everyone was jealous of the fugitives, for they had turned out to be successful thieves. And if, as Grandfather told me, they had left behind their homes and land, it was but a small sacrifice. For a sacrifice, he said, requires a real loss, and they had only exchanged home for horses, the best in the gorge. Anyhow, their plot of land was tiny – you dropped your cloak and covered their acres. So it was no great loss, and even if it was, its scent had wafted away on the wind. For the wind always blows at the back of thieves.

So said Grandfather. They must have been lucky thieves – that much I worked out for myself.

The villagers came to hate the thieves even more, and that hate was keener than the silence that had accompanied their flight. But it was still not as strong as the hate that looked down at them from those mares, dazed from so many miles covered for nothing, and now witnessed by the villagers in their despondency. And therefore this other hate, silently staring from borrowed mares, was far more dangerous than their own, alleviated by envy and relit by the desire to cover it up, overlook it, reject it – the envy, that is, and disavow it, and at the same time to disassociate themselves from the whole thing, born and now thriving on the land, where none of the locals had ever stolen or even considered you could get away with it until then, and so spectacularly and deftly and with such impunity. So to stop it once and for all, this danger and, moreover, this envy and awareness of it, a step needed to be taken, an action, a word. Something needed to be done, anything that would look if not useless then harmless, if not noble then not cowardly; mainly it should be a step in the right direction. It was at this point that the old man Khandjeri invited them into his home, having fenced himself off from the danger with tradition and thus transformed ten embittered men firstly into ten weary travellers and then into ten becalmed and contented guests.

It should have been over there and then – not for them of course, not for the strangers, but for the aul, who had already paid their dues – because Khandjeri told them at once, those ten, about the land and the house that, he said, by right belonged to the guests, and not at all to the aul nor to the previous owners; though it may not be much land, he said, we are law-abiding and respect justice; those thieves don't even have any relatives here and so no one here is answerable for them, apart from their own walls and their land, and he hoped that the Almighty would punish them and man had to put his trust in Heaven. In sum, he said everything that goes without saying anyway, what had been obvious since the dawn, and now the evening shadows were drawing in. What would happen next, anyone could guess: from the senile old man to the youngest babe, if only the gods had not deprived the former of his memory and had furnished the latter with the power of speech, even I knew it, though I was only born fifteen odd years later, by virtue of being the son of my father and the grandson of my Grandfather, since there flowed in me half the blood of the one and a quarter of the blood of the other – to predict it even a single drop of their blood would have been enough. So now they should have gotten up and left, having declined the invitation to stay the night and having said their thank you's for the food and drink. They should have mounted their borrowed mares – five of them – and made their way back the fifteen miles to their aul, and returned here in the morning with their equipment and bullock-carts so as to load flagstones from the abandoned house, to substitute vengeance for work and keep their hands out of mischief. That is what should have happened, and everyone thought that that was what would happen. And those ten were already getting up to leave and had already declined the offer of staying on, and had already made the last toast, and even emptied their wine-horns, but then it happened.

No, I don't mean to say that someone had forgotten about his being orphaned. They remembered about it the whole time, and that is why, probably, they had forgotten about it since the string of carts with his whole family disappeared in silence beyond the road bend. Now they remembered in a flash, as soon as they saw him in Khandjeri's yard with his hands tied behind his back, covered in roadside dust, not much taller than his own shadow on the trampled earth. The fear in his eyes was far greater than his shadow, and his height, and the bloodshot scar of the sun in the sky where it had been lanced by the mountaintops. When they remembered they did not need it to be explained where he was found or why he had returned. Where else if not by the gravestones and why else he returned save for the same reason. And so it was that the reasons why became clear to all immediately. The only thing to find out was where he had hidden the horse. Even this was soon found out though the boy, they say, never confessed to anything, persisting in his thievery and crazed from fear. When Khandjeri's son found the horse in the dusk beyond the bend in the road and brought it back into the yard saddled and handed over the bridle to the eldest of the ten horsemen, and he mounted this horse that had now been stolen twice in the course of a day, they tied the boy to one of the mares, now freed, and took him to where they swore they would finish him off within three days if four more horses were not added to the one under the elder. Only Khandjeri told them right there and then that that could not be, that such

thieves do not fall into traps and all that, and that the boy was
an orphan, a child, the son of a worthy father, and younger
than his years but cleverer than his own mind, and when all
was said and done, even if unwillingly, one of their five horses
had been returned, and as such they had to let him go. But
the older of the ten did not agree and also took refuge in
tradition, as Khandjeri had himself a few hours before, only
of course, that was another tradition, well known to all. It
seems traditions exist solely so people can shield themselves
with them. So our men did not rescue the boy. Of course,
few believed they would kill him, or, as was the custom, make
an incision on his ear. Most of them were inclined to think
that he would be made their servant or farmhand. Of course
all were certain in their minds that he would remain there
with them – that's what should have happened in any event.
That's the way it should have ended – for our aul and for
those others. But as I've already said, he was by no means
ordinary. If you will, that day the ordinary in him fell away
from him like a ragged old coat. Or like time, grown weary
with age. That's the way it is: you live and breathe, and then
you suddenly feel that the time is gone, has moved off, torn
you away from yourself and even given you the chance to
see yourself from the outside, even though you did not wish
it, but then you look at your former self from the outside and
there's nothing you can do about it. Time has tired and worn
out, receding of its own accord into the past, and new times
have taken its place sniffing you out blindly with greedy
nostrils. And that's how it should be, for each and all, though
it's rarely the same for each and all.

Only three days later that is precisely what happened,
with time, and it stung each and everyone to the quick: three
days later he returned, with a knife in place of a dagger and
a little basket of food, and he settled in the empty house where

even cats no longer strayed. The eldest of the ten brought him back on the same bullock-cart that had done its work so well, carrying off day after day the superstructures and the flagstones. It turns out that he, the eldest, also did not especially believe in miracles, rather, he saw earlier than the others the past peeling off and within three days broke his custom with it, or at least hit upon that newness which arrived in its place. Then one of those two, the boy or the elder, decided to share this newness and harness a mule to the bullock-cart, and make the same journey for the umpteenth time to put between them a distance of many miles so as to have done with it all, and to turn over a new leaf. So for the aul it turned out very differently from how we had expected, and it all began quite differently from how our men had calculated it, observing silently how the boy nodded to them and then unhurriedly went into the empty yard and from there into the empty house, already sprinkled with mould and not ready for him, just like the aul in fact, dumbfounded and vainly clutching at the slippery slice of broken off time. No more than an hour later, everyone gawps at the boy who goes out of his yard and heads for the neighbouring one, ours that is, calls out to my grandfather and speaks to him about a rifle without lead and powder versus the harvest, and my grandfather can only look at him, saying nothing, and then of course, can no longer hold back and asks why, and he, no bigger than his own shadow on my grandfather's boots, frowns and grows angry and threatens to make his proposal to someone more compliant, and Grandfather no longer vacillates, but tries to figure out in his mind – he often spoke of this himself – how much six sevenths of the boy's harvest, not yet collected, would be, but in any case that was already more than an old rifle without powder, and even more than shame for such an uneven bargain; he goes back into our house and brings it out, and he can't even hold it properly but takes it and proudly walks back, once turning his head and without returning the l followed him. The next morning, shortly after sunrise, once again he stops outside our gates and again calls for my grandfather to say that he's made a mistake. An eighth part, he says, I need only an eighth part, and not a seventh, from each threshing, but now there should be also a sheepskin jacket and some mats into the bargain. So Grandfather again goes into our house and brings it out, and he takes them without looking and disappears into his damp walls. Damp, they say, because no smoke was seen from there. There was no smoke for six days, so they say, and the first two days he left the bowl of food untouched on his doorstep, and afterwards it was also left there, but only towards evening and empty. In his eyes, they say, there was neither malice nor warmth. It was already then that they named him Alone, and the name stuck, squeezing out his real name, which few had known: who remembers the name of every little kid? Once normality ends a name is no longer of any use, as names are designed for others, for everyday folk. After six days he made it clear that was not enough. So they thought of another: Man-Child. Because after six days he appeared on the street with his knife at his belt and walked through the aul straight towards the nykhas*; he only stopped once he'd come right up to it. Our people didn't understand a thing at first, and so, they say, he had to greet them three times and tell them about the fire in his newly lit fireplace. (At first they did not notice the smoke rising above his house, but at last they saw it and understood and rose from their places at the nykhas – the most wizened elders in the aul – and accepted him, and

---

* nykhas – literally: conversation. A village forum where the elders discussed village affairs and took important decisions.

cat *custom?*

pointed out his place on the honoured bench; he seated himself, and after that – here's the thing! – only after he had sat down did they return to their seats. Not one of them, they say, burst out laughing: that look in his eyes stopped them, and who knows if they even laughed later.)

So he came to stay – Man-Child. After that our aul had to figure out what had happened. It was figured out at once that he had to have been orphaned, and then waited for six months for his grandfather once removed and his uncles to become horse thieves and set themselves up with the fastest of treasures, so as to then saddle their treasure, and harness their success, and flee with them beyond the mountain pass to where their pursuers already had other blood feuds; they also worked out that the boy himself had to have stolen one of those five horses and galloped on it to the abandoned graves, so as to be trapped there and await death for three days; and after this he had to return and exchange almost all the harvest from his land for an unloaded rifle, sheepskin jacket and some mats. As for the six days, they could not figure them out, so they had to do more thinking.

The old men pondered on the gun and the fire in the hearth – it never occurred to anyone simply to ask, how could they if each of them was at least fifty years older than the boy, and as many times more experienced. It hindered them, their experience, since what had happened did not figure in it. But the new name, Man-Child, had already come into being. Then one of them – perhaps it was Khandjeri or my Grandfather – realized that he could be conveniently divided into two, and the boy could be forgotten for the time being so as to concentrate on the man, the more so since he – the boy, man, mystery – duly came to the nykhas every day and sat next to them on the bench with such an expression on his face that it never occurred to anyone to laugh, joke or protest.

New custom

That's it. He sat there not merely as the owner of a khadzar*
and a plot of land but as the head of an entire household, a
whole clan, of which he was now the only representative. All
the same, for six days he had been waiting for something and
doing something before he lit the fire in the hearth, fastened a
knife to his belt, for want of a dagger, and came to the nykhas.
Then they remembered the graves and thought about the gun,
and they sent to the Blue Road to check; when they had
checked it was confirmed, because there were indeed traces
and the grass was cropped by just as much as a horse would
need – any horse, even the best in the gorge – for a whole
night.

When they figured it all out and their conjectures had
been confirmed, they could easily reconstruct the rest. They
had figured out that not only had the boy been orphaned, not
only had he fled with the thieves and then stolen himself, not
only had he been condemned, then spared, and come back
home, but also that he had waited for six nights in the dark
graveyard with his unloaded rifle until one of the thieves came
for him and believed that the weapon was loaded, and failed
to persuade him, and left that place forever empty-handed,
secretly at sunrise, defeated and resigned to his fate. Only
now could he – the boy, man, mystery – legitimise his solitude
and as a rightful owner light the fire in the cold hearth and
fasten to his belt a knife, for want of a dagger, and get the
elders to look at the rising smoke, acknowledge this smoke
and rise up to accept him. They also figured out the eighth
part of the harvest and that it would not be the last deal he'd
make and, consequently, not the last bargain my Grandfather
would get off him. And so it came to pass that in his tenth
year, or thereabouts – and those years were more the years

---

* khadzar – house

of a man than a child – he set up his own household, a really substantial piece of property, the only individually owned and managed household in the whole aul, as if thievery had played into his hands, as if his solitude were a boon. But it came to pass also that an eighth of the harvest was actually far, far more than had been originally intended for him, only a week previously no one had calculated how much it would be but now they had: that property would have been shared out among one old man, two strong men and another, their stricken brother (a piece of lard swaddled in a jacket, the walking belly with the voracity of a three-year-old boar), as well as all their children and wives, not counting the afsin and those of their clan that had yet to be born. Now there was just him. And as such it came to pass that our family, that had gained much from the deal, had still not gained as much as he, and had in fact even lost.

"He has hired us," Grandfather told me, gazing tiredly at our neighbour's fencing as the sun quietly warmed his brittle shoulders and dried the water in his eyes. "He has done us a favour but he has also exploited us. He has thrown us alms and demanded in return that we feed his solitude. He has made farmhands out of us."

According to the terms of our agreement his part of every threshing went straight to his barn, and all he had to do was open the doors. So he could sit at the village nykhas longer than anyone, even during the heat of the harvest season as if he were the wealthiest of the wealthy and the laziest of the indolent. But he was not lazy. Far from it. That we all understood afterwards, once we realised what he was preparing himself for. But that was later. He left us thirty years later. By that time he had acquired not only a horse and some sheep, not only the finest tools and bullock-cart, but also his own maturity, unlike that of any other, and he would not sacrifice even a drop of the aloneness that had earned him all these.

Yes, aloneness had made him what he was, standing in opposition to all of us and deprived of anyone's love. It made him a stranger to this land where he had been born and where he grew up, where he lived for forty years, having only gone away once for a mere three days, to meet his own death, and returned here as soon as he had escaped it. Only fate prepared him for something quite different, and once he had steeled himself, he set out. Of course I remember how he left. And I remember all that led up to it.

He fooled us yet again, and my grandfather in the first place; it wasn't only him, Grandfather, but also all the others who expected the next bargain from him to fall into our hands, and they were all thinking that it wouldn't be long in coming because, except for the empty khadzar and a patch of land, he had nothing; surely a gun without cartridges and a sheepskin coat for the winter were not much even for a boy of ten. My grandfather was more impatient than most, naturally, tormented by his burden like a woman about to go into labour. He even thought of a little trick to whip him up and force his hand. He set out on his own to the fort with a dozen aurochs' pelts, returning without them; he held fire for a whole week and didn't say a word to anyone. As Grandfather's patience finally broke, he called my father inside and produced from under his bed a thin bundle, and Father understood at once and trembled with hurt, sensing some malign intent as if he felt, he told me, that it would all come to no good, that we would only disgrace ourselves. Grandfather unfolded the bundle and held it out to my father, and Father told me he had never seen anything finer – although he'd seen greater beauty – and never would again (I think maybe he did but never held it in his hands.) Grandfather must have taken something else apart from those pelts, and that something paid for the workmanship and now sparkled so that it hurt Father's eyes, and shame mounted on shame for my father until he had a lump in his throat. Grandfather told him to take off his old dagger, and he took it off, and to fasten on the new one: "Wear it for a while. Let him see it. And him without a dagger too."

Father nodded and left, and when he walked down the street towards the nykhas, he thought the whole way (he told me this himself) about how he wouldn't be able to bear it, and yet at the same time he would of course but that was really tough. He thought (I'm only guessing) that now he too was poisoned, the same as Grandfather, and that from this poison both they and the whole aul would have a hard time healing. Maybe he thought – made himself think – it would all work out, it would all come off and the old man would turn out to be smarter than his sons.

He had to stroll to and fro past the nykhas, Father said, about seven times, but the boy just sat there alone casting his short shadow and staring at Father, frowning and silent, while the sweat cascaded off Father's brow and his boots squelched up to his ankles, while the boy just watched him in silence, as though he were watching some old nag being paraded before him, and Father said he was cursed if he wasn't then a stricken horse, an old one too. Father said that it wasn't that the boy in him was not stirred as he watched, he remained quite cold while before him they were taking out this horse, harnessed with a simple rawhide strap and loaded with a silver sword and scabbard. And so we didn't succeed in the slightest, nothing worked and the old man had to rack his brains again. It was then, said Father, that grandfather remembered about the donkey. He made us rub it clean, scrub it and scrape it as if it were some royal ambler, everything short of anointing it with oil and brushing its teeth. Then each of us brothers, said Father, rode three times a day to the spring for water for the sole purpose of riding past the boy's khadzar and the nykhas where he might be sitting. What the idea with that donkey was I don't know: what use was the donkey when twenty pounds of silver had gone unnoticed?

Then it was the sheep's turn, and we had to hurry because the harvest had almost all been collected, the threshing time was approaching, and it had to be done before then. So the old man picked the sheep out and started to fatten it up and mollycoddle it as if he were preparing it for slaughter. We brought their grass to them in the yard, so they didn't shed any fat while out in pasture. By then the threshing was done and still he didn't appear. Grandfather sent his other son to his house to invite him to dinner. So then, said Father, came his brother's turn to get drenched in sweat. Except that we'd once again been deceived. Uncle returned and related the whole conversation to the old man, word for word. Or rather, not the conversation, more the speech, for he hadn't managed to get a word in edgeways and only now started talking.

"Sheep he'll need in summer. I didn't tell him anything about them; he went off on that track all by himself. Says he'll get hold of them by summer without us. And for now, he says, he doesn't need anything. Then he asks when it's time to open up the barn. I didn't know what to answer so I only looked at him suppressing a yawn. I just stood there and said nothing."

And then, said Father, the old man started to shake. He just sat there and shook in full sight of everyone, and we could all see that he wasn't shaking with laughter. Father thought that the old man was really in bad shape. Looks like some kind of fever. He probably thought that this disease was more dangerous than any fever, and he knew also that it didn't stop with the old man, for he himself and his brother were no less affected, and there was no cure to be had for any of them. In the morning they filled up the sacks and he had only to open the doors of his barn. So he had won again.

They said he would sit for days on end at the nykhas cleaning his fingernails with his knife and silently looking this way and that, leaving the nykhas only to throw some more brushwood on his fire. But at that time there were still those in our aul who believed that he was awake – the boy in him that is. There were doubters, but no one would dare voice their doubts openly. So you just had to wait, given that, as they say, everything comes to those who wait. Just how true this was would be proved to us soon enough, but in a very different way than the one we'd expected. From that time, they say, no one was daft enough to think that he'd ever lose or give in, even if he wanted to. When that morning, stumbling and limping, he made his way to the nykhas, everyone not only heard or knew but saw it also, if you will, how he gave in and surrendered, not especially defending himself, not trying to fight back, how he was beaten up, vanquished and trampled upon, and yet he had the upper hand. They saw how in the middle of the road he was surrounded by their own grandchildren and great-grandchildren and their children, but he still walked on, not slowing his pace and not quickening it, as if he didn't notice; how he was confronted by this living wall, but even then made no move to push it, hit it, or at least protect himself. He didn't cry out once, taking the punches together with their fury and trying with all his might not to fall down. Finally he did fall, collapsed to the ground knocked down by dozens of fists and a hot wave of his assailants' breath. Their breathing grew louder and hotter, the blows missed their target, aiming at his stubborn silence, and their breathing broke off into a scream of frenzied children's voices, frenzied at first from shock, then from malice, and then from fear, and not one of those grown men knew who was what or where in their stupor and sweat, and couldn't utter a word, let alone get close or intercede, for at first it was somehow too early to do so and everyone was waiting, and then suddenly it was too late – it became clear he had again deceived them, all of them: grandsons and old men, sons and fathers, by not having uttered a sound, and not moving to defend himself. When the brawlers had lost their nerve and run off, when he had been left lying in the blackening dust and red twilight, they still needed a bit more time to get a hold of themselves and shake the torpor off their shoulders. But no sooner had they approached him – this filthy little body on the black earth – than they all froze. For he was already back on his feet, and what's more, he was again walking homewards, heavily but evenly, expansively and unbowed, like a buffalo under plough. A tiny little buffalo... It was like a miracle and lasted no more than a moment: first he was sprawled out, then he got up and walked on. Just as if they'd all dreamt it, as if he hadn't really been lying on his back in the middle of the road, and had not even stopped.

Now, watching him the next morning make his way up the street, each of them at the nykhas was hoping that he would keep silent. Only he wasn't silent for long – just for as long as it took him to get his breath back and wipe the sweat from his brow – and this is what they heard:

"That'll be the last time. There will be no more of that."

Then for a long time again nothing was heard, until he said:

"You can tell them, in any crowd there is a leader. He who takes the first step or he who appears to take it. Let them know, the leader, and the other that appears to be one, there will be no more of that. You can tell them that you saw my blade, and I swore on my blade that that would be the last time."

Then they listened to his silence again. They say that on that day and the two that followed not a soul let their children outside. And he, with wounds cleared, and sores dried, walked to the nykhas as before and did nothing else, warming himself in the sun and picking with his blade at his clean fingernails. Every morning, as before, he grabbed the food bowl and jug of ale left for him on his doorstep, and put them back towards evening. He felt no malice, no gratitude, and no contempt.

But towards winter, something changed. He had clearly become bored and restless. One day he came to my grandfather and asked:

"How many cartridges would I get for a hare? Or, really, well, what's the price of a hare in terms of that stuff with which it is killed?"

Grandfather was quiet for a while and then said:

"It varies. Depends on how many times you have to fire."

The boy nodded.

"That's why I'm asking," he says. "It makes sense to work out how many cartridges it would cost to go down into the forest, hunt out a hare, shoot it and bring it back to someone who hadn't gone down there, hadn't hunted it out and shot it and who hadn't spent what it takes to lay his hands on a dead hare, not just the energy, but also the time. Maybe you know?"

Grandfather thought for a bit and answered:

"I may venture a guess."

"What's your guess? Probably quite a bit?" the boy asked.

"Not that much." Grandfather said. "Just that everyone

will work out their price differently, in their own way, and each time they'll give you as many cartridges as the hare will actually be worth."

The boy squinted at Grandfather as if he were estimating how much the old man himself would cost. Only the thing was, as Grandfather told us, you couldn't tell what he was converting me into: hares or cartridges.

Finally the boy nodded and said:

"Agreed. Name your price."

The old man called out one of his sons and ordered him to bring lead and powder for four cartridges, and when he had brought them, Grandfather poured them into the nimble outstretched palm, which then disappeared, and then, as Grandfather said, reappeared, only empty. And Grandfather said:

"If the hare stays in the forest, then there'll be little gain for the one who didn't go down there, didn't go hunting, and didn't even miss it, the one who didn't expend any energy on this or waste any of his time. If the hare remains in the forest, then the one who didn't venture down there will remember at once about the four cartridges and will want something in return. If you will, he will ask for an extra part from the next threshing of the harvest."

"Well I didn't think that a harvest could have so many parts to it," said the boy. "Did you?"

They both were silent for just as long as it took for the young guest's eyes to tire of the old man's craggy face. Then the boy said:

"OK. Deal. Just show me how it's done." *learning*

Grandfather did show him, and told him how to aim, and even greased the rifle with a marrow so that the bargain was all fairly done, for he was almost certain that now he had seized his chance, it would all work out. When a man knows almost for certain that something will work out he feels that everything needs to be fair – albeit only superficially, only from one angle.

When he had gone Grandfather called out to my father and said:

"That'll do. Take it off now. Fasten the old one. It's too good for you. Or have you forgotten?"

Of course Father remembered, he had not forgotten even for a minute, and so fastened the old dagger to his belt without another word, but all the same blushed furiously. "As if he had shaved my moustache off," he said, "as if half my years had been taken away, as if they'd all laughed at me." But Grandfather wasn't interested in the slightest in what Father felt and how he looked at him. For the next two days they took the donkey to the nearest spring as before, but Grandfather took no notice and didn't even look across the neighbouring fence, so little doubt did he have in the eventual outcome.

Only once did he go up to the nykhas and say something to those sitting there, wrapping their old age in their cloaks. As he came back down, he was even more confident and his eye shone with a serene light. Father thought for the first time, as he told me, about kindness and how it might look. Or rather he knew what it looked like, he'd already seen it, but he wasn't used to it. He'd not gotten used to thinking that his eyes could be so endlessly kind and not be embarrassed about it. Only, as Father said, he did not suspect there could be so much kindness in those eyes simply in advance of an expected victory. And so to keep out of harm's way he forbade himself to think about it.

On the third day the old man ordered pies to be cooked for dinner and waited in a good mood outside, gazing at the road and the sleepy sun overhead. By that time everyone knew of those words that he'd composed and then brought to the nykhas to be declaimed to those present so that he could then hold his peace.

He said something like this: when two people strike a deal, the third should stand aside. He simply stands to one side and looks on until they have done it, because this third party, if he's a fellow villager and knows the laws, won't argue with anyone over a purchase, even if he has something to sell as well. He won't begin to get in the way because he's a true fellow villager and envies no one; he is certainly a clever countryman too, and as such he knows that intelligence is always obvious and always valued, especially when both sides are pleased with their bargain and have already shaken hands on it.

He said something to that effect. No more and no less. Then Grandfather sat in the yard and waited for our guest to open the gate and admit for the first time that he had lost. We all waited as well, naturally. And not just us. In the rest of the aul too, there were not a few eyes and ears peeled. When he finally appeared in the distance, those at the nykhas already knew, but the old man didn't even move to get up, so sure was he. But we, Father told me, just stood alongside him in team formation though no one told us to. Each of us also tried not to look at him, but we didn't feel like talking either. Finally, our eyes got the better of us and we turned to look at him. As soon as we saw, we were struck dumb, we just looked from the old man to the road, and from the road back to the old man, who was as yet untouched by doubt. As Father said, he felt nothing but shame and a kind of malicious delight. Only the shame vanished faster, and as the boy approached only the malice remained, because we were all of us poisoned.

He came up to our yard, opened the gate and said to Grandfather:

[handwritten margin note: Try not to look but curious]

"That'll be four more cartridges from you then."

That's all he said – four cartridges from you. Grandfather sat there and with all his might resisted what he was hearing, and was already past shaking as he'd done that time before. Then he silently nodded at my father to take the two hares from the boy's nimble hands. Grandfather nodded once more, and Father went inside for the powder and lead and poured them into his outstretched palm, just as before. Grandfather looked him straight in the eye and made a real effort to say something but the boy spoke instead:

good business

"If you need another couple, you'd better pay right now. If you want to buy two more, give me another eight on top."

The old man gave the signal, and Father again had to go back inside and bring out the advance. Now the boy had lead and powder for a dozen cartridges. That is, if he'd used all four of the previous shots in catching those two hares, only now no one would bet on it.

When a few days later the boy again opened our gate, the old man bought all four new hares he'd paid for, and added to the marked price a further sixteen bullets and a bag of powder. For future hunting expeditions. The boy stood there in front of him, furrowing his brow and biting his lip, counting on his fingers and putting his bounty in his pockets. The old man looked at him, his arms limp at his sides, his head cocked, as if he were searching for something but to no avail, as if he'd forgotten what he was searching for.

Above win

And so it happened that their deal grew and multiplied like the slain hares in our yard, only it grew in the wrong direction. So now it turned out that to achieve his victory, Grandfather would have to buy all the hares in the entire forest and still be capable of putting down an advance for the same amount again; only no extra part from any harvest was worth that amount of lead and powder.

Grandfather knew this perfectly well, but for another fortnight he could not stop himself, all the more since no one else was stopping him. After all, no one had forgotten his speech at the nykhas, they had no wish to forget it. Only the boy himself could stop the old man now. (Or we could have, had the whole family gone off and shot hares from dawn to dusk without missing once. Only then we'd have to exchange all our land bit by bit for the lead and powder he'd accumulated.) Father said it all felt like giant millstones were at work pulverising all our lead and leaving behind hares' ears. No one knew when it would end, and so all we could do was put the world off again.

A fortnight later, however, our waiting took pity on us and let go: the splinter was extracted from our endless days as the boy reappeared.

He looked in towards evening, when the sun had withered and Grandfather was sitting out in the yard on his log bench covered with skins, looking, as was his wont, at the empty sky over the roadside. When he came in the old man didn't stir, didn't blink, as if he were rooted to that log, which we'd used to chop meat and firewood and which was now covered with skins for him every morning. The boy said:

"Alright. I'll give five back for every ram. Only I'll need them come summer."

Grandfather stayed still and didn't nod this time, so the boy had to say it again:

"Fifteen bullets for those three rams that you've fattened up so they're the envy of all the oxen. Bring them to me when it's warm again. But I'll pay you now. You'll find it easier to sell than to buy. What do you need so many hares for anyway?"

Grandfather's gaze was piercing the empty air, and he sat there motionless and silent, as if he hadn't been listening.

The boy beckoned my father with his finger, and he obediently went to him and opened his palms, and then watched the boy shoot off with his shadow gaily leaping after him. Father went back inside, shoved the bag in the corner and drank water from the jug thirstily; it tasted as if he'd just run many miles. Grandfather sat outside, turning his back to the dusk and our pity, and it was as if he were at his own wake, though at that time we hadn't seen one yet. We all realized then that he'd given up and it was hard to see him that way, as if dragging a fully laden ox-cart up a mountain.

All that my father told me. Grandfather said no more. So it must have been from Father that I learned about the cards. It happened a year later, when Alone had gone to the fort for the first time – he borrowed a mare from Khandjeri with a share of his threshing as deposit, although by that time he had other things to deposit: sacks of grain, or eight aurochs hides he acquired that summer, or better still, his place at the nykhas, or, at the very least, his solitude. Because no one liked him, as I've said already. When he returned he had no bundle with him, which was strange and most unlike him – as if he had deceived us all again. Yet the next morning he went up to the nykhas and didn't say a thing to anyone, and of course no one asked him about his trip. But then he slipped his hand inside his quilted jacket and produced a pack of cards. Our people could only watch and wonder, as this object was like the Man-Child himself: diminutive and incomprehensible, fragile and unapproachable, and almost more cunning and deft than anyone else at the nykhas. So they said. Then he opened the pack, took out the cards and laid them on the ground face up. The elders looked at them, their hands behind their backs, perspiring and considering what he wanted to trade them for. No one had any idea what those cards were for. Some of them thought they were new Russian money from the fort, of greater value than anything they'd ever seen or heard of. They might have thought that he'd want to trade them for something greater than even he had managed so far, and they all grew a bit afraid, my father told me, as if an exotic animal or their own ignorance were being flaunted before them. Some sort of a riddle was offered to them, but not explained. There, indeed, exist man-made things, which serve only to be admired in incomprehension, so as to figure out how they could be attached to your coat if they can't be affixed to any human need – it was the first time our aul had ever encountered such wonders. He jabbed his finger at the cards and said: "Everyone pick one. I choose this one." He put a pebble on the card with a red blotch on it. Then Khandjeri chose his, and after him Soslan, and after them Teimuraz, and after them all the others. All except my Grandfather who chose not to choose any, but nor did he choose to look away. Then the boy said:

"Remember them and don't get mixed up." He buried all the cards in the pile, shuffled them and put the pile face down. He nodded to Teimuraz to turn over the top card. All of them in turn turned over a card, all except my Grandfather, all of them until old Aguz cried out: "That one's mine."

The boy nodded and said:

"You have won."

Aguz asked: "What? What have I won?"

The boy shrugged and returned: "Nothing. You've just... won."

They all fell silent, but, Father said, they'd all be damned if they didn't know just what was on Aguz' mind right then. Indeed, old Aguz' suggestion confirmed their guess:

"Why can't each pebble stand for something you can win? The luck could be on anyone's side!"

They all agreed to this and Aguz suggested: "Let it stand for a wineskin of arrack."

Again they all agreed, but the boy piped up: "No, I have no arrack. I'll put down a quarter sack of flour."

They nodded in agreement and let each in turn shuffle the pack and of course placed the boy in the middle to officiate. Only his card all the same would be uncovered first. So then he said:

"Now I'll put down a wineskin of arrack."

Again they mixed up the cards, put the pile at their feet, and told the boy to turn over the first card, which he did, and straight off it was his chosen card, and he drew a line in the earth with his knife. Grandfather sat nearby, swallowing mutely, as his lips hardened into something akin to a smile.

On that day he did not play, but instead looked entranced at the ground where the boy with thick strokes was notching up his lines, and for each of his lines there were never more than half as many for the others. So that same evening people started dashing about from yard to yard with loads on their backs, and some of them even needed to get out their carts, only the boy of course didn't need to carry even the rubbish from his house though his gates stood open longer than the others' and he, as always, needed to do nothing more than simply open up his barn doors when they carried in the sacks for him, and go with them down into his cellar when they dragged in the wineskins.

Nothing more happened for the next few days, and during those days they bided their time, as they thought he'd forgotten, or he'd gotten bored again. But then they mustered the courage to ask him, and he shrugged and brought the cards. They started to play for hardware and iron tools. Only our old man, said Father, the heavens be praised, still stood to one side and only looked on, a pale smile fixed on his face.

That was the second time in the space of a week that he had sat right next to them but had the wisdom not to join in the game. He sat right next to them and followed the boy's eyes in which there was no enthusiasm, only politeness and boredom, even when he notched on the ground his never-ending palisade.

So again they ran about with their loads, and the boy's home started to look like a warehouse. Only he didn't seem especially interested in all this, and for a couple of days he was no longer seen at the nykhas, though the elders still waited, fired up by the game and infected more than ever before. Father said they'd stealthily dispatch their sons to him to inquire after his health, because they didn't have the guts to borrow the pack from him. Then suddenly they all noticed there were no longer any food bowls on his doorstep, nor any jugs of beer, and they couldn't in fact remember when they'd stopped seeing them there. Somehow they couldn't get round to talking about it, treating it like some kind of general loss or common sin; maybe by then they'd almost come to hate him, though not everybody. For Grandfather there must have been something most satisfying and vindicating in all this, as if he'd swapped places with the rest of the aul, as if his turn had come to look on and laugh softly to himself. Well, however you look at it, the old man was certainly cut from the same cloth as the rest of them, and the difference came down only to his self-imposed distancing from them and his wan and wiry smile. (Like his bald head, Father recalled, which the sun saw only the day of his funeral, when his cap lay alongside his coffin and the rain wouldn't stop falling, yes you remember how hard it rained, and only then, said Father, as he walked behind the coffin, did he remember that smile of his, stretching from his collarbones with the veins on his neck quivering from the strain.) That was what the difference came down to and not that his thoughts ran any differently to the rest of them. He thought just like the rest of them, or almost like them, but their minds worked differently to the boy who was winning things off them. In fact so differently that all this while they could never guess his next move, nor his next thought, nor his next wish, and thus as it turned out they were all doomed.

It wasn't at all their bad luck, it was something quite different, deeper and more ancient than simple luck or bad fortune. It was fate.

They knew no other way. They could only move ever closer toward it, ever closer to their doom, overturning every obstacle that stood in their way. They forced him – he was against it and opposed them right up to springtime. He'd refuse them even when they begged him, saying he'd lost the cards. But they of course did not believe him, as they wouldn't believe in the sudden loss of riches that had been brought home and put in your granaries, and that later no one except you had seen.

Yes, their way of thinking was entirely unlike his. So when towards spring it became clear that he wouldn't give in, they drew their own, cut out with their daggers on thin slabs, recreating the designs and drawings from memory, then rubbing the other side with goat's fat. They looked clumsy but perfectly adequate, especially since they had no choice.

Only my Grandfather still did not join in the game. He simply looked on, nodding his head at every winning and not arguing with any of them. As Father said, he was the only old man among them, though Khandjeri and Aguz had been born before him. Now it was different: previously there had only been one winner but now several of them got lucky, and the one who had gone away with nothing yesterday could be a winner today. The one who hated in the morning could be the object of that same hate come evening, hardly giving his malice and envy the time to cool off before it returned the next day, when it was another's turn to win. Now only two of them stayed out of the game, Grandfather and the boy. Grandfather didn't play because he had forgotten how to win, but the boy didn't play because he didn't know how to lose.

They even observed the play differently, Grandfather frowning and nodding, enjoying his indifference or rather whatever it was that allowed him to avoid arguing and not lose, but to watch others lose and be so close to others' good fortune that it fairly made his fingertips tremble. In fact it was for him just like joining in, only not in the same game as the rest of them. He played against himself, with his eyes and nothing more, and each time he won, though he didn't get anything, he gained what the others had lost.

But the boy watched in earnest. At first, as Father said, he was amused to follow the game in which he was not the winner and put himself in the loser's place, though in reality he'd never been in that place. Anyone else, but not him. He could have mentally swapped places with them when he still played himself. It cost him nothing. He grew bored of it all then. But unlike Grandfather he watched in earnest. I don't know how to explain it, just that in his gaze there was more of the loser than the winner. I suppose it wasn't painful for him to watch, more likely it was awkward or unpleasant, for he could hardly avoid it: what else could one do at the nykhas apart from join in the game or look on?

One day he gave in. He arrived early in the morning, hauling wineskins and sacks of grain. When everyone had gathered, he got out his pack of cards to be shuffled. When they had placed their bets, he said he'd wager everything he'd brought with him. They didn't understand this and waited for him to explain but he only waved his hand and asked: "Is it forbidden to bet more than the others? Let the others bet as they did before."

When the others each drew a card but still didn't hit theirs, he decided to forfeit his turn and said he'd roll it over till the next game. No one objected to this and only Grandfather grunted and stopped smiling. Again they drew their cards and Aguz's came up first; and while they reshuffled the deck the boy watched the sweat cascade off Aguz's face as he frowned and calculated something in his head. But all the others looked at him, and no one, apart from Grandfather, could understand what he was up to.

So again they all placed their bets, waited till the boy placed his, wondering how he'd transform his loss, because he used to win from one go but now he had two. And you can call me a cripple if I can't picture all their faces now, the hot sun and the light coming down from the mountains. Call me a cripple if I can't still see the scorching sun that made your eyes hurt so. And I'm no son of my father or grandson of my grandfather if that light didn't blind them and soften their brains, dulled by the excitement. They knew they would lose! They couldn't but lose, and even he couldn't have saved them, the boy, even if he'd promised them manna from heaven, let alone his house, or his family's share of land. They had been blinded by the sun.

But that was not all. Now, the more I think about it, I'm almost certain – it could be no other way. He had suggested that they play by his new rules and they had accepted. He had suggested that they play against his loneliness – all together, except of course Grandfather, who wouldn't even stake his own echo, let alone his grain, ploughs and girth. He wouldn't stop at wagering the whole gorge let alone the small aul! But they agreed. And not because they seriously thought that they could beat him, or that he'd laid before them particularly tasty bait – no! Well not just that – he'd reeled them in on something else, which deceived them in tandem with the hot sun. That's what I think anyway. And so when he told them: "I'm betting my house and the land," they'd almost been expecting it, so long had they craved it, so long had they disliked him, and couldn't forgive him, they were ready because they were scorched by the sun... they were ready because they were all united against him, and for the first time the war was open.

He said to them: "In return for a promise. Just a promise and no more. Only let each man swear." Again no one objected, so he continued. "I want you to forget. Return them to me and forget. Give me a deposit."

Khandjeri pulled some slates out of his quilted jacket and handed them over to him, and then the cards were shuffled. As before, they formed a tight circle, waiting their turn. And he, even when the card he picked wasn't his, didn't turn pale, or shake, or leap up (though the others all did, having earned their extra minute in the game with doom, having given in totally to the sticky fog of hope, which they would nevermore be able to look back upon without disgust). He only put it to one side and said:

"I have one more turn though. I forfeited the last game."

Then he bit his lip and slowly took out the next card (as if waiting for the minute to end) and they could only watch breathlessly, tormented as they were by the heat and light, none of them looking like elders any more, even Grandfather. When he turned it over and showed them he gathered up the deck and put it back in his pocket, and they listened in silence, heads bowed, at the cracking of the slates as they broke and fell at their feet, and at the sound of his receding footsteps.

Not a few more years passed before he left us forever, leaving behind his home and the graves and his land, for the sake of which he'd once returned and almost paid with his life so as later, after his narrow escape, to guard his loneliness here. He hadn't been part of the times that had peeled away into the past from our aul's memory, he was not the one who broke time into pieces and he often shied away from its flow, not wishing to get in its way, only time (and now this is clearer than daylight) checked with him its relentless course, pounded his stubborn patience from all sides as if with large boulders, washing away the ground beneath his loneliness, so as finally to tear him away from our shores and carry him off to where he would have a fresh start, to a place where man had not set foot for three centuries, to a place where his mystery was destined to depart.

But that was all to come later. Much later. At the time no one could have imagined that he could ever lose, and we all thought only that if we couldn't stave him off, then we could at least belittle, if not undermine, then not reconcile ourselves to his eternal gift, or curse, of victory. They had tired of it. But another couple of years would flow past until they rose up against him, and those two years tanned them with sun, drenched them with rains, crushed them under snows and subdued their pride with dust clouds, until it was whetted to such a degree that they were ready to fly into a rage and forget their conscience, to renege on their oaths and trample them into the ground with the hooves of this horse, a haggard mare they had clubbed together to buy for him – one early morning it had appeared tied to the blackened tethering post in his half-empty yard with armfuls of yellow hay under its mug. Yes, they clubbed together to buy him the mare. In return for their promise. Only now there were no more slates, there were flat pebbles from the river, and they played differently to the way he'd taught them before, although the essence of the game remained the same.

And when he came up to the nykhas and saw the arched

line struck through on the ground, when he silently watched how they flung their pebbles with calloused palms and the smooth discs rolled and turned over flashing white, how they measured out a span's distance to a mark in the ground, how they hoarsely croaked out their bets, how they stubbornly failed to notice him, and how the laughter hurt their throats; when he looked upon their backs bent down with excitement and the years clutching at their wrinkles; when he heard their voices, wheezing hoarsely; when he stood before them, suppressing his outcry; when Grandfather squeezed his stick tightly with his quivering hands and was the only one to look up at him; when their eyes met in that frozen moment of time and Grandfather suddenly let out a moan; when the old man threw open his coat to breathe and shakily gasped for the unsaid words; when he turned away and then ran off while the game continued and the pebbles were still clattering against the hardened ground; when his gun fired and the neighing stopped; when my father stood on the threshold and watched the horse fall behind the fence under the rapidly vanishing smoke and his wet face with the light stubble and black eyes; when the women screamed in fright and the thunder clapped; when all this happened and the heavens poured with rain that thrashed the river and flooded our fields and rushed to Soslan's house, tearing off his fence, the shed and half of the house; when fear gripped their souls and made them mutter prayers – only then did they repent and regret.

They did repent and regret, yet only a week later they would not notice the shot in his door and the bullet stuck in the boards, neither would they see the one who fired it though he was not hiding. They didn't see the boy's eyes puffed up from sleeplessness nor the raised cock on his rifle, of which he hadn't let go since the shot was fired, and all the while the drunken Soslan bawled his songs for the entire aul to hear.

However, they did not play any more. And towards winter the boy disappeared, so they heaved a sigh of relief. But then he came back, and the clothes on him barely covered his body and bound up his wounds. Father said he still had not managed to lose, and no one, not even Grandfather, could remember anyone in the aul who'd managed to overcome a bear in their younger years, and no bear had ever been killed by a mere boy, who had not even fury but only a dry weariness and boredom. But that was when he returned, pulling uphill a sled with the skinned bear carcass. So he'd got himself a bearskin, in addition to the meat and bullet in the door. And also a grey streak in his hair.

No wonder they didn't like him.

"You wouldn't believe it," said Father. "He used to go there and chat with them. We saw it often. He sat by the graves, bowing his head and hugging his knees, he would stare at the ground and talk to them. He could sit like that for hours. And we worked away, and every eighth sack from the threshing we filled to the top, as if he'd care to check it. Like his farmhands we were, we filled them right up, and it made us sick. But here's the thing: you couldn't say he was out of his mind – now isn't that strange?"

That's what Father said.

Sometimes Alone borrowed Khandjeri's horse, and rode either to the fort or maybe to visit those who had once lost five horses in a night and then got one back and didn't even draw a drop of blood from the one who'd managed to steal twice and get caught, so that all normality ended in him and went to feed his loneliness. But he didn't stay there for long, and no guests were ever seen at his gate. For a time all was quiet. He went about almost unnoticed and unheard, and was almost forgotten, like an old disease that is remembered only during sudden attacks. Our people hardly ever followed him

when, instead of sitting at the nykhas, he rumma
riverbed silt and poked at the rocks he picked u
knife. They hardly ever watched him as each month he filled
up his hand-made cart with stones and went to Khandjeri for
his mare, and then rattled down the road to the valley. All
because he didn't return with anything special from the fort
except some metal tools and utensils, and these he gave to
Khandjeri in return for his services.

Now not noticing and not hearing had become almost a
habit, even a norm, but then one day he came back on a light
chestnut horse, dressed in a new Circassian jacket with a
silver belt, and fastened to that belt was no longer a knife
with a rough wooden handle but a real Daghestani dagger.
Only his cart was gone. In Khandjeri's yard he dismounted
and got out from under the saddle a rolled up horsecloth,
opened it and threw it on the old mare's back, and then said:
"Thank you. Here's your share."

Our people watched as the most ancient elder in the
aul went up to his old nag, his chin quivering, and probed the
crimson velvet on its back with his hesitant hands. Father
said that at that moment everyone's hands clenched into fists
and their teeth clenched in their mouths, but again something
got stuck there, came off and got carried away, something
burst or broke, time's motion came to a standstill, leaving only
the sight of a crazed man fumbling over a horsecloth, and all
around mouths closed in malice, furrowed brows and an
unhealthy stillness of the air.

Yes I can see them, as if I had been there myself, as if
I had looked upon them with those same eyes bulging with
disbelief. I can see them through the eternal streams of
memory, flowing with our hot blood from generation to
generation; I can't help seeing it, I can't free myself from this
vision, soldered onto our fate, subordinated to it with its

interlocking chain of misfortunes and curses, deaths and births, hopes and despair, names and questions. I see them all in my mind's eye, watching the old man's tormented joy and his guilt, which consisted of no more than lending his horse with no thought of gain or reward or loss or the profit, which had been made on their common ignorance. I can see Khandjeri's frightened doubt clinging to the reins as he pulls the crimson velvet. I see his face and the faces of the onlookers, and the faces of those who weren't there, who were born later, and these faces are like white spots on their doom, only they can't see it yet, but it's there in the silence, in the absence of the wind, hidden in the crowd of faces, in their closed community (I see all of this clearly, as if with my own eyes, with their visual memory, where it's all mixed together: the seen and heard and reconstructed and as yet unthought, but alive and bright like the crimson velvet.) I see them regain their voices, start talking to one another softly, avoiding the subject, and I see how their voices help them make sense of it and get by and then how they give their voices a rest, each within his own four walls, how the nykhas empties out that day and how none of them has the strength to change anything, to break away, slip out of that crowd, which has practically dispersed, but which they can't tear themselves away from, since it's the only thing they can present before the mystery of loneliness, wandering around their land and having no wish to part from it.

They waited for a few days, waited for weeks, waited a month, till Khandjeri overcame the blow, till he repented and said:

"But the land is ours. And the river is ours. And we have our carts."

They grab their spades, stretchers and their words and go down to the river, to the same place where a pit already yawns, so there's no longer any need to search, and they dig and pile up till they get bloody calluses. Or maybe I'm seeing this wrong?

Then they ride along the long broken road to the fort, getting bogged down in the spring with its sticky snow, the downhill stretches of the road hurry them on, running wide towards the precipice; they're driven onwards by their dull, vague greed, and one of them tries to overtake the others, cracking his whip at his mare, and at some point on the slope the carts start rolling down, their wheels vigorously cluttering in unison, until two of them crash on the narrow road and their axle rims become caught in one another. The carts roll on a bit longer, screeching with wood and iron as they furrow the road with their wheels, but then shudder and stop, unable to disengage themselves, as if they had come up against an unheard-of stone that frightened their horses so that splinters of the rocks fly from the bulging sides of the carts. The others tighten their saddle girths, throw their bodies back and spit out curses, they jump from their carts, not letting go of the reins, feverishly burrow through the mud with their cupped hands, block the wheels with stones, glancing all the while at the depth of the ravine crumbling under their gazes; they offer up prayers to the gods and reproaches to the mortals, and then everyone crowds around the two leading carts, offering words of advice in their impatience, and those who turn up in the thick of it all, now flushed crimson with the strain, twisting and arching their shoulders with effort, bear the weight to eventually release the wheels. Then they move on, slowly riding along the precipice, driving their premonitions away. They still believe they're all in it together. At each stopping place they share their food, carefully filling up the time with conversation and laughter – see it's not so scary, there's nothing to fear. And then, it's back to the road before night falls.

At dawn, harnessing their horses, one of them rubs his eyes worn out with sleeplessness, and the other stealthily counts out the carts. They are all still together.

Towards evening they ride into the fort – a long line of carts, rumbling along the street with their stony weight. I think, here for the first time doubt overtakes them, having ridden along at their heels the whole way, only they don't show it, of course. They frown confidently as if they know where to go and all the more knitting themselves together in their awful doubt; the carts rumble along the narrow lanes amidst the uncomprehending gazes of passers-by – what a rattle they make – while the faces on the carts grow pale and swell with passionate determination, but with every passing minute the waiting becomes more unbearable until the first of them gives in and holds back his horse, bringing the whole convoy to a halt in front of iron gates – the only place which looks like it could be it.

"Here, maybe?" he asks and looks round.

Nobody answers, nobody gets down from their carts, and he sees the sweat glistening on their cheeks in the dusk; in their eyes he reads a sense of relief – for now he's their leader. So Soslan (I think it was Soslan, yes, revenge had built up in him more than in the others, as much as his cart could hold; Soslan, yearning to exchange it for money or for a bay horse, or for a rifle that never misses the mark) jumps down, straightens up his shoulders, puffs out his chest and goes to the gates. At the gates, calling the master, he waits as his straight back sweats under the heat of dozens of eyes aimed at his shoulder blades. Before him he sees a handle welded onto the iron gate, behind the gate he hears the wheezing sound of millstones. He is standing ankle-deep in white dust, and his nostrils soon become blocked by its smell – flour he realises, but what use will they have for our stones then? A mill, the others realise, too, only why bring our stones here? The mill's new, Soslan thinks, there was no mill here before, but what was here I can't remember. Try and remember what's where in the valley.

His eyes grope for the handle on the gate, behind which no one has yet appeared. Even in the thickening dusk the handle glistens with yellow copper, so he hesitates to touch it.

"Eh? Whaddaya want?" they hear just at the moment when his hand is outstretched towards the yellow. Turning round he searches confusedly for the voice's owner and for a moment doesn't find it, but the moment's enough for him to get thoroughly soaked in sweat, and then he sees the man right alongside him, not behind him, but to the side and down, there he stands, on the steps in the narrow door opening – and sweat rolls down his brow.

"I... we," Soslan stutters. "Very many... As many as you want..."

The one down there is dressed up so fancifully that only his moustache gives away his manhood, he asks: "But what is it I may want?"

He blows out smoke and squints. Soslan pokes with his whip behind his back and says: "Almost three dozen... isn't that enough?"

The other shrugs and comes up a few steps.

"What have you got there?" he asks.

"Stones. The same ones," Soslan replies.

"What sort of stones?" the miller wonders.

"Ones that cost money. Lots of money."

"What are they, gold?" the miller goes up to Soslan's cart.

"Something like that," he replies hesitantly, a stupid smirk on his face as on everyone else's face, except the miller's – he just puffs at his pipe and runs his fingers over the stones.

"Show me."

"What?" asks Soslan, or whoever is there in his place.

"Gold," the miller raises his brow. "You said it was gold, didn't you?"

Here of course, they have to stay silent. And they do, only their eyes talk, and Soslan's are roving, but they can't run away now, so he has to say something out loud:

"Maybe they're gold."

The miller turns his gaze to the stone in his hand, puffs for some time and Soslan humbly swallows the smoke. Then he shoves the stone back at him.

"Maybe they're not gold?"

"Maybe not," Soslan agrees readily. "Maybe they're not gold. Maybe something else. Uh huh."

He nods happily and those who can't hear, who are standing far back, catch sight of his teeth flashing in a smile and exult with him.

"Only why have you got it into your head that I need this something more than gold?" asks the miller. "Particularly as none of you know what it is. Where did you get that idea?"

Soslan mumbles in confusion but can't hide his grin, and so those at the back remain as joyful as before, they are only slightly worried about the oncoming night. In the dark we may be swindled, they think, in the dark we may be short-changed.

They see Soslan's head diving to one side and then the other, as if he's showing the whole world his grin, and those at the front hear him repeating senselessly: "Almost three dozen... and all to the brim... as much as you want... maybe it's gold, and maybe it's something better, aha... if need be, we'll bring you more... take it!"

The miller just stands there and looks at him, holding his smoking pipe in one hand and a silk handkerchief in the other. He stands and looks, and once again they have to converse with their eyes, only this isn't good enough for the miller, he clears his throat, but all the same says nothing, and those standing nearest think that it's Soslan's head that's in the way: he waits for it to stop diving, and our men wait as well.

Suddenly the noise grows hoarse, and they all hear the dull scraping of millstones behind the gates slowly dying away; now the night becomes more apparent, and they can even make out the jangling of the harnesses as the tired horses shift from one foot to another. The silence becomes chilly, and those who are closest strain their eyes to follow the pale outlines of the two shadows in front.

The gate opens a bit more and before them appears the miller's helper, they can see him clearly: he's dusted with flour, and he's big and broad as one and a half Soslans.

"Master," he says. "All done for today."

"Wait a bit!" the miller bursts out. "We've been brought some new grain here. Thirty cartloads. Such large grain I've never come across in all my born days. True, it reminds me of cobblestones a bit, but these are much bigger."

The helper goes up to the first cart and looks inside, and then asks:

"What use is it to us if it's so big?"

The miller squints, lights a match, and starts smoking again.

"They don't have anything smaller. But we can have as much of this stuff as we want. Ain't that right?"

Soslan has stopped nodding by now. And our men see how carelessly, brazenly, mockingly the fleecy smoke crawls above his drooping hat.

"No," says the miller's helper. "The millstones won't bear them. Let them first exchange their grain in the next street. There on the roadway the stones are smaller."

"Yes, yes," agrees the miller. "If they start now, we'll put them in the millstones by morning."

Darkness has already fallen making more visible the smoke from the miller's pipe, and it's the clearest thing that can be seen, far better than Soslan's hands, but they can hear Soslan's voice:

"I don't know about the others," he croaks, "but I'll do something else. I'll give you a present. You'll like it. Only don't go away, you have to see it."

"Hey!" shouts the miller, clearly addressing his helper. "Hey, stop him!"

But they can't hear any steps, for instead stones rain down on the road, and Soslan helps them with his voice:

"Sorry. You'll have to wait a bit. I have to use my left hand. But I can see in your eyes that you're more interested in what's in my right."

Though our people can't see, they already know what's in his right hand, and, just in case, they've already pulled out their own from the holders and are aiming at where the gates should be, where a thin stream of smoke is rising. And the stones clatter against the roadway at even intervals, and each blow gives them a pang, and our men fight the pain with blunt silence.

"It's heavy work," says Soslan. "We need a rest. But perhaps you'll give me a hand. The present won't be any the less for it. Ain't that right?"

There's no smoke anymore, so those at the back are now aiming from memory.

"We'll wait," the miller calls out. "It's always good to watch others work. We'll wait."

"Uh huh. You wait," Soslan agrees.

And so it continues, only Soslan breaks to rest more often and it goes on ever longer, and the night hugs them so close that they can start counting lights in the windows, and aiming becomes easier. At last the miller loses his patience:

"Go and help him," he says to his helper. "Our guest doesn't have the strength to get the present down from his cart. All his strength is in his other hand, and he needs more strength to run away."

Soslan chuckles softly and nods.

"That's right. Me and my countrymen are dog-tired. Do you think they're less tired than me? Come and see. Ask them to make you a gift as well. They also have something for you."

The miller stays quiet while his helper, so massive that his clothes could cover not only Soslan, but also his cart, his mare and the shafts to boot, furiously flings the rocks to the ground. Some of the villagers also chuckle, some of them climb off their carts and even get to work with them, so now the whole street resounds with the sound of clattering stones, and here and there mounds of black rocks grow.

Only I think not all of them unload, for some of them still believe. They look at the others with crazed eyes but of course they can't do anything and they don't dare rebuke them. Perhaps at that point they get a bit depressed about being together. I don't know what happened to them that night or how two days later they managed to return with no losses and in one body, with not one of them arrested, that's for sure: the memory of the aul doesn't remember any such thing. Since they were not arrested there could be many guesses what happened. For example, you could picture the convoy, unloaded but not entirely – someone still believes – riding out of the fort and climbing a couple of miles into the mountains before stopping for the night. And the next morning, the believers pick out one of the younger men and dispatch him with a leather sack the size of a cow's stomach, and with a thousand instructions as to what to do. Then they all wait, even the unbelievers. Where can they take their unbelief to, after all? They all wait. When he doesn't return before lunch, the unbelievers stay sullenly silent, and the believers chat feverishly and often let out a forced laugh. When the shadows have long since lengthened on the road, they see a rider from afar and this time they are not deceived. You can imagine that once the man gallops up, he unties the string from his sack and without a word pours the rocks onto the ground, and only then dismounts to fall to the river and drink his fill of cool mountain water.

They need no more explanations now, they've stopped believing and sullenly get down to work, throwing out the stones, and the valley soon resounds with the thunder and echoes, and almost simultaneously the edges of the sky are rent asunder by a jagged bolt of lightning, and both thunders merge into a single commotion, whipping with the rain those there together...

Then, holding back their neighing horses and leaning their shoulders into their carts, peppering their prayers with abuse, they see with horror Soslan standing in the middle of the road, in the pouring rain, in the midst of the thunderstorm, pointing his gun at the heavens and swearing some terrible oaths, and then his gun spits a weak flame into the sky. This figure raging before their eyes is like their own insane fear embittered by memories. Only on this occasion they're fortunate, this time nothing happens, three dozen lives don't go to waste, protected by a shroud of common terror. Afterwards when the downpour has stopped, when the vault of heaven has wrung the last drops of rain out of the azure, they set off again, thinking to themselves: did he really shoot it? They don't know which for sure – the rain or heaven? What if it was heaven? And what sort of heaven is that if you can shoot it?

But of course you could picture it all differently. Maybe without the rain. Only the way I see it, there must have been rain, and if there wasn't, it must have fallen shortly after. Without it I can't see so clearly, and if so many years afterwards I imagine the rain, that's the way it was, though I'm not a clairvoyant.

All right, maybe it wasn't like that, maybe I'm overdoing it. But it seems to me that since he'd got the better of them again, Alone that is, they'd have enough time on the road to remember. They'd remember the mare they'd clubbed together to buy him, they'd surely remember the thunder and the shot and also the river washing away part of Soslan's house, and so the downpour did probably happen there after all, but that they all travelled together – that they'd never forget!

Yet their guessing was not good enough. They guessed wrong. Age was no help to our elders, so what chance did the young men have. Their years had failed to make them any wiser, and that got them thinking: if this was what it was like now, wouldn't it just go on getting worse? What would happen when the boy in him disappeared and there remained only a man with his invincible loneliness living among them? When they sat around the fire at night, drowning the dull gloom with arrack, their souls did not rest any easier. When they'd drained the last wineskin and given all the requisite toasts, exalting their gods and hurling abuse at their foes (they never dared pronounce only one name), they sat long in their tight circle illuminated by the flickering flames and listened closely to their numbing feet and the distant voices below. Only none of them heard what they wanted to hear. And their hearts pumped the burden of their thick blood around their strong arteries and veins. And not one of them could guess what was to come more than a day ahead.

In the morning, time went more slowly and unpleasantly,

after the night of drunken dreams, suffocating nightmares and burning thirst. The convoy snaked slowly along the bumpy road until those at its head shouted, and they all looked over to where his finger was pointing. They dismounted and went down the mountain path, and there, where a warm spring flowed out from the ground, they saw before them broken chunks of rock, coloured marks on the pebbles and eggshells scattered around in the ash. Next they examined the painted pebbles, dipped their hands in the bubbling water and understood even less than an hour before. Someone tried to scratch off the paint from a pebble while another tried to wash it off in the warm spring, both showing the others, who nodded their heads and tutted in surprise. How can that be, they thought, and I can hear what must have been said:

"That looks like the sky when there are no clouds."

"And this one here looks like fresh blood."

"If you put these together you could take it for grass."

"Exactly."

"Those eggs he bought from me. And from you too, right, Wari?"

"The secret's in the water, not the eggs."

"The secret's in the whole thing. The eggs too."

"He must have painted them first. First he coloured the stones and then took them over to the fort. Don't you think?"

"Do they smell of anything? Let me try... they smell funny."

"Not really."

"But what did they want painted stones for?"

The silence is audible. Then one pipes up timidly:

"God knows..."

"Perhaps it's one of his new games?"

One of them pokes the crumbling earth with his boot.

"See over here... a sort of stick." They all look at it closely and paw at it. "Feels like hair."

"It is hair."

"Or a brush. Only the bristles have gone, there are only a few left."

"And paint on it too, the stick's been smeared."

"It's no thicker than an arrow. They used to make arrows like this, only longer. Ain't that so, Khandjeri?" They stare fixedly, with growing irritation at the stick and remains of eggshells. Then one of them picks up a rotting wineskin off the ground and holds it out.

"One of them he won at cards. He's never made his own."

"God knows. Maybe he's fluked that one too."

"Have you ever once smelt it on him? Right! He can't even hold a wine horn."

"He just doesn't want to."

"Eh?"

"If he wanted to he'd learn quickly, God knows, he's brighter than most of us. He just has no taste for the stuff."

"So you're saying the wineskin got here all by itself, right? Or did some sheep just spit out its gut and toddle off?"

They laugh eagerly, maybe slightly longer than strictly necessary to decant it all out of their throats. Therefore silence comes too late, and leaves a sickly sweet taste in their mouths, like that of overripe cornel berries. To get rid of this taste, one of them spits out:

"There's something filthy about it."

Another replies: "Yes, paints all over."

The laughter stops: the man realizes he's blundered.

"Well, cheer up if you can't think of anything more sensible to say than that. Except of course he's better at that too – playing jokes."

"Stop it, and take that stick with you. It may come in handy."

None of them, of course, knows what for but they all readily agree: "Yes don't forget it."

"Put it in your holder, it'll stay safer with your gun – you can't lose it there."

"Don't you worry, it won't get lost down his front – he still keeps his sweat from last year's haymaking."

"You liar. The last time he had a scythe in his hands was more than fifteen years back!" Now they again laugh eagerly in chorus, as if filling up on their stocks of laughter for later.

That same evening, on the approaches to the aul, they lash their horses and burst into the village street, that's eagerly awaiting news, whooping and shouting, without as much as a glance in the direction of the nykhas, where he's sitting alone with his lengthening shadow, watching their antics with a puzzled look. That night the drunken spree wanders from house to house, demeaning the night with shouts. The next morning, Alone finds the usual bowl outside his front door, only this time it's been filled with shit.

They see him thinking, knitting his innocent brows, he peers without looking around him, gritting his teeth and biting his lip until it's white, and then, without a word he steps over the bowl and, throwing his head back in pride, walks to the nykhas, but stops halfway, hesitating just for a moment, then turns right around. They see him harness his horse, humming softly under his breath, leap into the saddle and ride out of his gates. Then slowly, very slowly, so slowly that it's almost a strain to watch, he moves up the road.

Here we no longer need to guess and invent, because Father told me what happened, without hiding a thing, maybe just omitting a few bits. For instance, he couldn't recall who put that bowl there, but that's not so important after all. On the other hand, Father said, no one had ever seen anyone ride a horse so slowly, least of all such a fine horse! They had to watch and wait a painfully long time while he crawled up to the nykhas, humming along, and then crawled past the nykhas, where only his place was empty, where conversation had been squeezed out of the crowd sitting shoulder-to-shoulder. And then, said Father, he turned his head and looked intently at all of them there as if searching each face, all the while still riding slowly while their eyes followed him just as slowly; then he smiled and nodded politely in greeting. Once he'd crawled all the way to the end of the street, he turned round and rode back, as slowly as before, and even, as Father said, far more slowly it seemed, because when he reached the other end, by Akhsar's house, and started riding slowly back up, they all understood that he had only just begun. This went on almost till lunchtime, and they reckoned he must have ridden up and down like that maybe a dozen times. Father swore that even Grandfather or Khandjeri could never have gone that slowly, even if all the elders of the aul had to carry all the men downhill to Akhsar's house.

Towards lunch, once he'd again crawled down the road like that, everybody flew from the nykhas as if blown away by the wind. The next day none of them turned up; Alone was the only one there in the middle of the day, and he was there only briefly, since even his patience needed a breather.

The day after, when a thin stream of elders filed out of their yards to the nykhas, he got them all the same. I thought at the time, Father said, what stubbornness it takes to step over that bowl of shit for three days, pretending not to notice it. Moreover, with such stubbornness he really got under their skin! In fact, when he got them all together that day, they heaved a sigh of relief: try waiting that long for him to say something! When it came down to it, said Father, stepping over it was easier than watching him step over it, especially if you were the one that put it there, or if you were close to them, or if you were the prime suspect.

He wasted no efforts in catching them. And when he sat amongst them and cleared his throat, the hearts of many slowed down and the tension eased, as the waiting and guessing games had now come to an end and it only remained for them to listen to what he had on his mind.

"Rotten business," he said. "I'd never have thought... I'd not have believed it if it happened to someone else. Only now," he said, "I have no more doubts, though it still seems strange. Who could have thought that if someone drops something at your doorstep it could make such a stink. Doesn't someone else's always stink more? The gods have made it that way on purpose so that you don't lust after another's property. What do you think?" he asked. "Is it meant like that or is that just chance? You don't know? Shame. I'm also not sure. It's just that tomorrow I'm setting out for the mountains and I'll be gone all day. I'm afraid it'll disappear and the owner may remember and wish to take it back but he won't find it there. He better take it back. Give this message to him and I'll put up with it for another day. Of course, that would be a bit of a bore. I feel badly for him. Perhaps he can't live without that stuff in the bowl. You'd better think of something to help the man. Or else I'll have to pack everything else in and find out who did it. That's tiresome. Moreover, it's easy to get the wrong man, another person would suffer, that'll be asking for trouble," he said. "For some reason tonight I dreamt of blood. I can't remember whose it was... someone's from here. When I remember I'll tell you. If I dream of it again I won't even try to remember. Only by tomorrow evening I have to know for sure. Though of course, I won't need to know if the culprit takes care of it before that. Right?" He got up, only to sit back down again. "And if anyone's interested, please come, I don't mind, come and check and smell, maybe you'll recognise your own smell. Yes, go on, be my guest. In the meantime, you can relax, your honours. We'll say we've come to an arrangement."

He got up and went quickly home, and they saw from above how at his doorstep he held his nose and nimbly stepped over, disappearing inside. There remained for the rest of them enough time, a whole twenty-four hours, to think in peace about his longest speech yet. And a whole twenty-four hours to watch his doorstep on the sly. Or so they thought. Only they'd made a bit of a blunder and in the middle of the night they had to run in a crowd to the fire. In the low ground by the bend in the road a dirty canvas with a few stacks of fresh hay under it was burning. Of course none of them had a clue why anyone would feel the need to burn their hay, but by morning the bowl had gone and Alone could explain:

"Now that's good. That's great the culprit was found. True, he turned out to be a shy man. Because of some bowl of shit he burnt a stack of hay. All for nothing. There was no need to hurry. He could have waited till morning. He turned out to be bashful. He's still silent."

In fact, everyone was silent, only one of them was more deeply silent than the others. So, I think Father really hadn't a clue who was behind it, unless he was involved himself. I think they were all annoyed that there was someone else in the aul who was clever enough to get the better of them having sacrificed only a bunch of hay and an old piece of canvas. It didn't take much intelligence to outwit them.

Only it seems to me it was not just annoyance but relief too, and somehow from that morning on everyone breathed more easily. Now they could forget about that longest of speeches and his dream of blood. They could even be thankful to the coward in question, whose cowardice helped him to correct his stupid action and thus spare everyone else. But now their souls had been poisoned more than before, their spirits were tormented with doubt, and being old became harder than ever.

You see, said Father, being in doubt is hard for anyone, especially when almost all of your past life stays silent behind you and can't suggest anything sensible to you... Have you ever heard of spite and relief going hand in hand, when the whole aul could be so pleased at someone's cowardice, and all those years of experience were suddenly worth so little and the price was now dictated by this youth and some scamp who'd got scared of him? Have you ever heard of its taking so long, unbearably long, for anyone to see what was really going on, and all the while never really believing that the mystery would reveal itself? Have you ever heard of some bearded stick not giving all these elders any peace, so that they'd ask the one, who had it – "Show us... well it doesn't really look like an arrow... but if he used it for smearing, what an idiot he is! Why go smearing with a stick when you can just dip them in paint like onions in soup... Here, take it back." But at the same time, their throats were drying up with emotion. And that little shit won't tell us for the world but just coddle up his bloody loneliness in full view of them all.

Worst of all, we all knew that he couldn't steal, so we couldn't blame him for anything like that, however much we'd like to. That wasn't odd at all, despite the fact that we'd all seen how the elders of his family had stolen horses, the best in the gorge, and that he himself had stolen one back from the thieves, and after he'd been captured he'd managed to survive and come back home, to this land, so as to change its ways.

Since he couldn't have stolen his horse, he must have paid for it, and that meant he must have come by some good money somehow. And yet, he never took anything to sell to the fort. So we came to the conclusion that he must have sold them something that in the aul was no more precious than the air, but earned him so much money that he compelled them first to dig, then load up and carry, then blush, and then get out their arms, then run away, but at dusk send back one of them who'd lost his mind more than most, and then wait in ever growing hope, and then later swallow that hope along with their shame, unload their carts and drag their drooping insides along the bumpy road home, to get drunk that night, and the next afternoon to look in that cloudy warm spring and see that bristled stick, and smell a mixture of those rotten scents, feeling in their nostrils their own wretchedness and the hopelessness of all that they had always regarded as eternal and unshakeable, that was a perfect fit for all of them, like a shepherd's cloak, but from that morning long ago and with every passing day had felt tighter and tighter until it became much too tight. It was all the more amazing because even in their own eyes they were kind of shrinking, gnawed inside by jealousy, by greed, by revenge, and by doubt. However, since everyone was getting petty it wasn't as bad as if they'd been doing so each on their own.

The torment passed, said Father, and was soon replaced by a weak, drowsy acceptance, that always comes when you've no more strength... Just imagine, for instance, that our horse started trotting sideways, completely forgot all of a sudden how to do it properly, you're lashing it with your whip, you prick your heels in, and it gallops in its own queer way just the same, although you know it's against its nature. You just don't get horses galloping sideways – ask anyone and they'll tell you – no chance. Only this devil of a horse doesn't

know that you don't get them and that it can't gallop sideways...
Imagine you see this miracle with your own sober eyes but
still can't believe it. Who'd believe such nonsense! But there
it is, and what can you do about it? Fight it until you've no
more strength and you've lashed your whip till it turns to rags,
and then what? Well, you'd give in, so that one fresh morning
you'd spit on your utter disbelief and get into the barn to make
a new saddle so you don't fall off your horse. When you'd
made it and got used to galloping sideways, would you want
to remember that it's not possible? Maybe you still don't
believe, maybe you'll never do, but you have no reason to get
rid of the horse. You don't have enough reason not to get
used to it, particularly once you set him off and he'll gently
rock you, so gently you'll nearly tear your mouth yawning.
Let the other horses walk normally, as they should, save for
yours, it occurs to you as you stifle a yawn: you've got two
arms and your left, even if you chop it off and attach it to the
other side of your torso, will never be like your right. Even if
you don't quite get why you're having such thoughts, you still
calm down. You don't get excited, and, at least, your old
disbelief has gone. You can disbelieve as much as you want,
yet gallop where you want. Habit is stronger then miracles.
Habit will tame any wonder. It's only a matter of time. That's
what Father said.

In fact, I remember perfectly how he left, Alone, so as
to help us many years later bridle this miracle, long hidden in
the breast of common memory and fermenting in it like magic
wine in the dark. Even now it's too early to drink it. Maybe
even I won't risk it. Maybe it'd be too risky for you, though
you're younger, but then that's for you to decide. There's no
point in force – it'll get to your head.

This is why I'll be telling you slowly, with all the details
and in the right order.

By that summer he was just knocking on sixteen or thereabouts. He wasn't good looking, so our people never anticipated the future misfortune. I mean who'd ever think that anyone's daughter would choose that road for her heart? Who'd imagine that their hate for him was not strong enough to be inherited as immutably as their own blood? Would Soslan ever have thought that his own flesh and blood could deceive him so?

God forbid, said Father, to live through such horror again. They could all see it from the nykhas. They were sitting there listening to Soslan spin his yarns. Alone wasn't there, else he wouldn't have remained alive, that's for sure. He'd have talked at once. Only Alone wasn't there. Soslan was spinning his yarns and laughing first at his own jokes. They hadn't seen him so cheerful for ages.

Your grandfather said: "For you the kuvd* isn't over yet. You must be going on with it on your own."

Soslan replied: "After such a ziu you remember the kuvd for a whole year. I'm just remembering."

Grandfather had a toothache so he was in a foul mood, he said:

"How can we remember so that we're drunk with joy? Tell us."

Soslan replied without a moment's hesitation: "It's easy. You need to first remember how hard we worked at the ziu**."

Everyone burst out laughing, said Father, because Grandfather wasn't at Soslan's ziu, he had a toothache and he sent us instead, his sons. That day was but a week after the whole aul was at Soslan's to rebuild his barn and repair his house. Till then Soslan had to make do with a shack. But

---

* kuvd – village feast

** ziu – collective voluntary labour to help the needy

of course, Grandfather turned up at the kuvd, forgetting all about his toothache.

Now the elders were sunning themselves and laughing good naturedly, waiting for the young ones to return from the hayfield. When they heard cries and saw the women running toward the nykhas they were as unprepared for tragedy as for snow in summer. The women shrieked and waved their arms, stumbling and craning their heads at the heavens, so that Grandfather first thought it was a kite. Then the old men followed their terrifying despair and saw a shadow climbing up the cliffs towards the crag, and they made out in that shadow at first a woman, then a girl, and then a very young girl, and immediately someone screamed out wildly; not taking their eyes off the cliff, not having the strength to turn around, they knew it was Soslan. They all momentarily fell silent, came to a standstill, stopped breathing, and then instead of a cry they heard a bellowing stifled in his chest, and it was more terrible than the most awful howl. The shadow on the cliff climbed on timidly upward, and the women crowding along the road, paying no attention to the frightened whimpering children, screamed again, their screams only being pierced by Soslan's bellowing. They saw the shadow quiver and turn into a drop, the drop flowed down and caught on a cliff ledge, and silence descended once more and grew deafening, while the drop battled with the emptiness below it, but then the drop broke off and started to fall, and when it crashed against the rocks down by the river, a long wail broke forth from all our throats.

You wouldn't wish it on anyone, said Father. I saw her lying there. When they lifted her up her body was limp, not a single bone remained intact. Your Grandfather said that a prettier young girl couldn't be found in the whole aul. They all said it.

REQUIEM FOR THE LIVING / 65

Alone was away right up till the funeral; in all the days leading up to it everyone forgot about him. Only when they were reading the burial service over her did they catch sight of him on the road. He was carrying something in his arms; as he came nearer, we made out a roll of canvas with something sticking out, two sharpened sticks. I remember as well, said Father, that the ends of the sticks were soiled. As he approached, he slowed his pace, and his face was wreathed with worry lines. When he heard her name through the lament, he swayed and opened his mouth, helplessly swallowing the air. Still apart from us, he turned round and stayed to one side, shaking his head, not believing what he was seeing, shaking his head and swaying. Now we could look only at him, swaying and shaking his head. He turned his back to us, squatted down and spread out his canvas before him. But we couldn't see what was on it. Then he stood up and carried the canvas through the crowd, which obediently parted, and he looked over our heads, or through us, I can't remember now. We heard only his steps, nothing else, even the laments died down, though no one took any notice of it. As he approached the body, he looked out for Soslan, nodded to him and asked:

"I'd like to put this in there with her." Only now did he fully open the canvas and we could finally see it, and so beautiful it was that it kept us from grasping the main idea. We looked, standing on tiptoes, and tried to drive out that idea; I don't know how long we kept peering like that, forbidding ourselves to think of it, only he laid it down, and turned it over, covering her dead body with it, leaving only those who stood nearest to see the underside. Then our glances again turned to him and we saw his eyes frozen over with grief; he couldn't tear his eyes from her, as if he'd got entwined in her hair, and then suddenly he turned his head away and hurriedly broke out of the crowd, pushing us out of his way. When he was gone, the wailing timidly resumed, came back to life, so that again we were left with our thoughts. Next to me stood Aguz' grandson, who said to me:

"So lifelike."

I nodded and replied: "Only better. The waterfall looked so real."

"It turns out he was going to the waterfall. I saw his bearded sticks sticking out of his bag."

"Well now we know what they were for. Now it's clear as day what he took up to the fort."

"You could buy a lot with what you'd get for beauty like that." Aguz' grandson said. "Soon he'll have a whole herd of horses."

But I said: "No he won't. He doesn't need a herd."

"What does he need then?"

We couldn't think of an answer and were silent.

Come evening, when the burial service was over, at which Alone didn't appear, we suddenly saw him again, dead drunk, reeling from one side of the road to the other, and playing with his dagger. You would say he was walking, or moving, so unsteady he was, Father said. He was roaming as if he'd gotten lost on the only street of his only land, that remembered him from birth and was the only one able to bear that knot of loneliness with his house and barn, his allotment, his mystery and the horse. He would stop from time to time and look around him, spitting bitterly, threatening the shadows with his finger and crying:

"You don't know anything! You sit in your holes and know ab-sol-ute-ly nothing! Because you're all hiding and you're too scared to find anything out!"

Then he tottered on and, said Father, I'd never seen anyone more drunk in all my days. He was drunk right through, utterly drunk, drunk to exhaustion, drunk from anger that he couldn't drink himself to oblivion.

The next morning, not yet sobered up, he left his house and headed for the mountains; we saw him, stopping every now and then to press the wineskin to his thirsty lips, and his legs stumbling all the more, and they sombrely waited for him to fall to the dust, giving way to all the arrack he'd drunk. They did have to wait a bit, but not too long. They saw him negotiate the street, the bridge, the first of the climbs, and several more spans of the path, but then throw up his hands, spilling the arrack, and collapse to one side, not letting go of the wineskin, becoming still by the cliff edge, motionless. So then the elders ordered him brought back in, and we went and returned him inside his walls as empty as before, and laid him down on the rough mats.

Only the next day off he went again, just the same, with his wineskin, although he applied himself to it less often than before. It was an open secret for us all, said Father, why he was going up there. The real reason, however, we didn't know until later, and I had to be the first to find that out. Then, of course, no one wondered why he did it, and they'd already stopped wondering why she did it. That was a mistake! We could only look and wonder if he'd make it or not. We saw how much effort it took him to make it up the path, how he reached the cliffs, then was lost from view for a long time only to reappear, how he pushed his wineskin to his back and set to climbing up the rocky ridge, how the yellow sun sizzled over him. Even watching him climb turns out to be a far from easy task as we often can't tell if he's climbing or not, for the sun is rising up faster than he is, moving across the sky to its zenith. Whether he climbs or not, the distance to the crag grows ever smaller. Now he crawls past that very spot, and our hands are shaking, and we look round in spite of ourselves, but breathe a sigh of relief remembering that Soslan hasn't emerged from his house today, and then we again anxiously follow his progress and maybe, just maybe, for the first time ever we wish him victory, who knew not how to lose, who had only ever needed two tries to achieve anything, and this was his second.

When he finally conquers the summit and rises to his full height there's a tear in some eyes, visible even in the sunset, which he'd just subdued by stamping his shadow upon it. Only now we remember how hungry we are in fact, having craned our necks at the sight almost the whole day long, so that our necks are numb. But before going our separate ways, we see in the sunset flame his clearly defined silhouette turning its head slightly and pressing something to his face and then holding it out before him with outstretched arms. We see him sit down carefully swinging his legs over the edge of the crag, sitting there a while without moving, and then again falling on his wineskin. And we don't have the strength to watch him making a drunkard out of his ineradicable loneliness, because we'd all simply grown tired, watching him the whole day prove to us his own immortality.

Back then, repeated Father, we didn't yet know what significance that crag had. Only eight months later would I find out, and before I did others could have guessed, all except Soslan who was almost blind by then. For his eyes, once they'd witnessed what you wouldn't wish the Lord to bring down upon your enemies, let the sickness into them and were covered in a white fog. The fog thickened into great white sties shielding the light of the sun, and merciless time imprisoned him in the everlasting cold of his memories. Thus he was the only one who could never know. And that was for the best.

In spring, said Father, as the roads were improving, Grandfather again thought up a way of getting rich. Only

now of course he wasn't going to contend
Something else had fixed itself in his mind.

Once he called me over and said: "G(
Uruzmag's smithy. Just stand there and watch, t ... come
back and tell me what you've seen that's interesting."

At first I didn't understand why he needed my eyes to
go down to watch Uruzmag at his smithy, but it was not for
me to reason why.

And so I went down there and stood for a bit with the
others, and looked at Uruzmag mending Mairbek's ploughshare,
at him straightening his forceps, took note of the iron hooks
hanging on his walls along with the horseshoes and tongs. Just
in case, I counted how many other people there were watching.
Back home I recounted everything in detail; Grandfather listened
and nodded happily, but then squinted and asked: "Is that all?
That's not very much. Go watch some more."

I went back, and this time stayed a little longer, and
took account not only of the people, the hooks and horseshoes,
but also the pins on which they were hanging and there turned
out to be just enough of them for all the hooks and horseshoes,
except that was obvious from the outset. When I returned,
Grandfather chuckled at what I had to say and stroked his
knees. Then he asked with a sly look: "Is that really all? Is
there really nothing more of interest? Go and check and pay
closer attention!"

So now, as you can well understand, I'd pretty much
lost patience, and my joints ached from the shame of it, and it
crossed my mind the old man was having fun at my expense.
Well, let him, I thought, for I can also amuse myself for a few
hours, and his cunning is enough for both of us. I left the yard
seeming obedient, but didn't quite go where I was told. And,
God is my witness, sitting on the riverbank and throwing stones,
I amused myself to my heart's content, imagining the old man's

amusement at home; then I dozed off for a while, giving him time to have his fill of fun, then lingered on till the evening and waited a bit more until he'd tire of his own fun, and a bit more on top to discourage his habit to have fun at my expense. But when I myself had grown bored, I got up and set off home to the old man whose fun had turned into spite.

He barked at me angrily: "Well? Have you seen enough?"

I replied that I had. He asked what I'd found interesting, and I shrugged: "Nothing really, it's all fascinating. The more you watch, the more interesting it gets. Especially this time round. I couldn't take my eyes off it all."

He stared at me so hard, it was clear he suspected something. That was a singular pleasure for me.

"Idiot," he said.

But I didn't even avert my gaze so pleased I was.

"Clearly, the more interesting it gets, the more your brains leak out." He said.

I shrugged and he went on:

"You were smarter this morning, smarter than you are now. I don't know if it's worth sending you any further than our pasture. I have my doubts about you."

I understood that again the old man had outbid me and he still had more tricks up his sleeve in reserve. So I had to think hard and say:

"Maybe it's from the heat. The heat went to my head. I've been standing here and I've cooled down. I can't remember now what was so fascinating there. A forge is a forge. Nothing special."

He turned his back to me, as if he hadn't heard a word I just said, and leaned against a wall and closed his eyes. So I said:

"On the road of course, it's more interesting. And the

air is fresh. There's no heat to melt your brains. You can't compare the road to the smithy."

Grandfather replied slowly, barely moving his lips:

"You don't have to. Call your brother."

"Why get my brother when I can manage myself? It won't hurt to give me a bit of air and a change of scenery after the forge."

Now I had to stand guard there for a whole half hour until his cunning opened its eyes again and he asked:

"So you've been wrong? Is there really so little of interest there?"

Of course I nodded and hurriedly replied:

"That's how it is. To tell you the truth I was almost howling with boredom."

At this Grandfather grunted mirthfully and said:

"It takes you a long time to cool down!"

I thought to myself: I'm not the one to set the time. If I were I'd have hit the road long ago.

He ordered me to harness the horse to the cart at dawn and go to the fort, find a hardware shop, find its owner and invite him to our house, and if he refused, to ask permission to invite his assistant, and apart from the assistant to load up the cart with as many different types of goods as we could fit in it, and then to say to the shopkeeper that he could name his own price, but that we'd take a tenth of it as our cut, every tenth rouble would be ours, and that his assistant would be put up at our place as long as he needed, and would want for nothing, as long as he promptly counted out the roubles and never forgot to give us our due cut, and wouldn't even have to worry when the goods ran out, as then he'd only need write a note to the shopkeeper and send myself or my brother to the town as messengers, and that if the need arose, they could even trade in other areas, all over the place, for the cart was more than up to this task, and there were as many mountain auls as houses in town, and though in each aul you could count the huts with the fingers on both hands, in each one they'd always have something to trade in, and a tenth part of it too of course, and so we'll both profit as will those in the aul.

On my way to the fort, Father continued, I played around with the idea in my head, but all the same couldn't find any holes in his business plan. It seemed that he'd come up with something where everyone was a winner, just like, say, when I'd been down at the river, playing with the pebbles, and having just as much fun as my old man back in the house, not a moment more, and our mutual cunning, not tarnished by any malice, our quiet, sweet cunning would have seasoned this delicious slice of time cut out for the two of us with its delicate spice. As if another watched it, one who would get full satisfaction from it all without cheating anyone. It occurred to me then that he who sees most wins most. Clear as day. And the road was too short for any doubt on the matter to creep in.

In the fort (which already was called a town by then, but fort slipped off our tongues more easily), I didn't take things at too much of a rush, had a good look at all the various shops and stores, and weighed up what would be of use to our aul in them and realised that hardware was only the start, and if the plan came off, then we could sound out some of the other shops, after all, why not, when all around everyone could make a nice little earner out of it?

I had to bide my time in the hardware shop, though, till the shop emptied out a bit, for speaking Russian in front of a crowd of people was almost like stripping naked in public. So I just stood there, in a corner, fingering some nails and rolling the foreign words around in my throat so that when the time came for me to say them out loud they'd roll off my tongue more easily. But of course I felt uneasy, couldn't quite pluck up the courage, and though my eyes seemed to dart about the entire shop they couldn't find anything to rest on. And no wonder, especially if you compared the place to Uruzmag's smithy. It was my bad luck that just as one lot departed another lot appeared before I could even catch my breath to speak. Their devil-may-care chattering with the shopkeeper made me feel hot. As for those nails, I must have examined them over a dozen times and the man at the counter started casting me suspicious looks. I took a few steps towards the centre of the shop: now in front of me were some shiny hinges and latches. After a minute of hesitation I looked right at him, took a deep breath, but before I even started I spluttered because right above him, above his tiny glasses fastened on his nose, right above his very head I saw something I remembered all my life, that I'd known from childhood, something no one could ever take away from me, not for a convoy laden with gold, that no one could ever have seen as fully and clearly, even if they had a hundred eyes, to say nothing of those old grey goggles on his nose, couldn't describe as truthfully and accurately even if his Russian was better than the Tsar's.

While I looked at this wondrous sight, while I muttered something with dry lips, while I tried not to believe what I was seeing, to brush it aside like a mirage, while I could feel only that it was a bad omen, but didn't let it dawn on me because I wouldn't let my thoughts go down that path, all this while, I pointed my finger at it, forgetting the dozens of words that I'd carefully chosen on the road from the meagre store of my memories beyond the aul. I didn't straight away hear and didn't straight away register what his cries were insistently knocking out on the door of my hearing.

"It's not for sale!" he was almost howling at me, bent over his counter. "No, no! Not for sale! Are you thick or something? No! What an idiot... That's not hardware! That's not for sale! This is the stuff we sell!"

He scooped in both hands and poured in front of me those shiny metal latches. But still feeling robbed of the wonderful but terrible vision, suffocating my throat from the low wall (too low for it, so low it missed the point entirely, monstrously low, as if they'd squeezed a whole arm into the space of a nail), I couldn't remember a thing, couldn't ask anything and could only defend myself with the one sound which the man in specs couldn't recognise as a word, and so continued sprinkling the white sparks into the huge box of rattling latches.

"Don't waste your breath. He asks: when?"

Now I saw a man in their clothes, with their look, their arms. He slowly folded them by his back and asked me in our language, but with a Russian voice:

"You want to know when it was bought?"

Tormented by this sweaty, losing battle with latches and glasses, I nodded in gratitude, not venturing to say anything.

"What's it to you?" he asked, and waited long for an answer, looking at me smiling weakly back and convulsively shrugging my shoulders.

"Doesn't matter. Don't tell if you don't want to," he said, and again I stopped understanding, so he had to translate and slowly, even more slowly than he folded his arms behind his back, repeat it back in our language. Obviously he still wanted an answer, for he fell silent. So I said:

"That place. I know it."

"A beautiful spot," he agreed, and it was already dawning on me that he was the owner. So I suddenly remembered Grandfather, my skin flushed and uttered:

"Very beautiful. It awaits you."

His eyebrows rose:

"Me?"

"Yes," I pressed my hand to my heart. "Be our guest."

After a pause, clearly translating this in his head into Russian, he opened the door in the counter, came up to me and asked out of curiosity:

"Where is it?"

"Two days away," I replied. "The road is hard, though not overly. It's normal. I'll take you myself."

"Is that your cart?" he pointed to the yard, but only with his chin. "You've come all this way just to ask me to be your guest?"

I nodded. He came even closer to me and looked me up and down from head to foot, and I stood there, stiff, straight and frozen, like a log in the frost, like a pillar in the middle of his store, surrounded by customers, squeezed by their hot breathing, and I really felt I was a log, and God's my witness, pitied that log, and watched as he sized me, the log, up, just like he was calculating at what point to place his saw.

"Did he send you?"

I understood it was a question, and, of course, understood it was directed at me, but strike me down with thunder if I knew at which point he started sawing me. I stayed silent for as long as I could hold out, but still hadn't a clue what he wanted, and so nodded once more, for to reply in the negative seemed improper, indecorous, rash, and maybe – that's what I really thought – would destroy the conversation we'd fashioned with so much effort.

"Yes," I said. "Yes. My father."

That was proper and polite and also the truth.

"He can't be your father, he's almost a boy."

I thought – so that's it. That's who he's on about. I

thought: he's a boy to you, but for us, he almost never was. I only had to think now about what to say back to him out loud, this puzzled owner of the shop, of the painting, and of our future, so our conversation would not shudder to a halt and so it would be easier from now on not to notice his foreign accent touching our own words.

"He's my neighbour," he said. "I was sent by my father. He has business to offer to you. The picture has nothing to do with it. I'm just surprised how lifelike it is... And only those who don't know him call him a boy."

Now things became easier for me, because now it was his turn to rack his brains thinking up a suitable reply, and it was his fingers now helping him, not me, as they played around in his box of latches, and when they stopped helping him, he came out with:

"But I could well refuse. What then?"

"Then – your assistant. It's no harm that he doesn't know the language. He doesn't need to."

"Is that so?"

"Yes," I replied. "What's important is that we all profit. Even those back in the aul."

To which he chuckled and repeated:

"Is that so?"

Then he turned to the one in the glasses and started telling him something long and fast in their sharp tongue, and the other one kept agreeing and chuckling nastily. As I watched them talk I felt my hands squeeze my dagger, imparting to it the moist heat of my anger, and locking it there, in the dagger and its holder, trying with all my might not to let it out while they, chattering away, didn't even notice it, not noticing me either, they missed the point entirely, so that not to restrain my anger soon became easier for me, as it did for them to save their lives, for which they didn't even fear, happily throwing back and forth peals of carefree laughter, unaware how insulting it was. When they had finished, my anger had shrunk, so that only the tiniest bit was left, and I wiped it off the handle of my dagger with the edge of my coat.

"Listen," said he. "This is all most amusing. First you travel here for two days on mountain roads just to invite me to your home, then you notice this painting and forget everything, and once you catch sight of me you suddenly remember what you came for, but then agree to change your choice of guest if I decline your invitation... How funny! Tell us, what will you do if he refuses too, my assistant? Will you invite any of them?"

Here he pointed to the crowd of customers, who had already stopped being customers and had been transformed into listeners and observers, faces full of curiosity spoiling both their faces and our conversation.

"No," I retort. "He won't refuse. If he refuses you'll order him."

Again he folded his arms behind his back, and proudly looked at me like that, his smile had now changed and become unpleasant. He said more slowly, more carefully than before:

"Then pray tell me, who will make me force him? You?"

"No," says I. "Not me. You will want to. The profit will make you."

Now there was no more laughter, for a long time there wasn't anything at all, until he again opened the door in the counter, took me by the elbow and led me to a tiny little room behind the counter. We both sat down and at last I told him word for word what your Grandfather had ordered me; he chewed it over and asked me to wait, and all by himself he brought us two steaming glasses, sprinkled in them some white powder and stirred. He thought hard while he sipped from it, so I followed suit and sipped after him, and at that time I still had no idea that was called tea, and didn't know that was sugar; he drank and as he took his last mouthful, he twirled the glass round in his fingers, and then as if he wanted to test its firmness, banged it on the table. He leapt up and yelled something in Russian, and then, strangely excited, opened his arms out towards me and I understood: we had come to an agreement.

He asked about my gun, I said I had a rifle; he asked which, and I described it and how it worked, and he tutted and shook his head, then got up from the table and went to a small cupboard in the corner, got something out and said:

"Revolver."

I asked him to translate, but he replied with exactly the same word: revolver, and then explained how to use it. I said it was great and he named his price and I said: oho! But wasn't impressed. He shook his head and said:

"You don't understand. You must buy it."

"I can't. I don't have the money. I have my rifle."

"Your rifle," he said, "is only good for shooting geese and still lose. You need a revolver."

"Some other time. Once we've become rich. I don't hunt so badly with my rifle. I'm used to it."

"Then nothing will come of this. Save up your money, and then we'll talk again."

"You're not coming?"

He said he wouldn't, not he, not his assistant.

Then I understood: "You're afraid of the abreks*?"

But he argued: "It's human greed I'm afraid of."

I said: "So you're about to turn down all this profit."

He opened his arms: "Profit is when your greed overcomes someone else's. But when the reverse happens,

---

* abrek – men banished from their clan and living alone in the mountains

that's called stupidity and madness. It's all very simple. Before you sell your wares, you have to guard them. And to guard them, you have to protect them not just from rust, but also from others' greed. Buy the revolver and we'll talk."

I thought a while and said:

"But you agreed at first. So you trust me? Trust me in this matter, too. Give it to me for free. And then if the business goes well, I'll buy it off you. Word of honour."

Again he laughed, and again it was merry, carefree laughter, just like I'd cracked a joke, though I wasn't joking at all.

"Would you like some more tea?" he asked.

When we again sipped from our glasses, sitting opposite one another, he said:

"Risk. It's all about risk. If you had your revolver, I'd risk a whole cartload of my goods and the life of my assistant. But if I gave you my revolver for free, I'd risk making an ass of myself."

I swallowed and said:

"I see. Just like giving a whip to a horse thief only to watch him drive away on your horse with it. Is that what you meant? See I'm no horse thief though."

"Probably not," said he. "And I'm no ass. Don't get offended. Better buy the revolver."

"Tell me, can't your assistant handle the revolver?"

"That he can," he replied. "But he's got his own."

"Why then," says I. "Do we need another?"

"And why do we need you apart from my assistant?"

"What do you mean?" I say. "I'm no stranger. I've walked the whole gorge up and down, and ridden all over it."

"Alright, alright," he replies. "You're no stranger. So you'll most likely know when you need to shoot and when's best to keep the revolver close to your chest... and then two revolvers are better than one. Eh?"

"That's right. Only somehow not good." I said.

"Of course it's not good. Maybe because it's right, that's why it's not good."

I got thinking and he stayed quiet, and I thought about your grandfather and how it was not going to be funny this time, and that instead he'd have to decide what else he'd have to lose before getting hold of this thing, and with it the right to gain, which would then only become a gain when he paid with this loss and something else on top, maybe, new knowledge about what was right, or even old knowledge, pronounced as law over a glass of tea by a man who had never set eyes on our places, but had managed to buy and hang on his wall their beauty, even before Grandfather appointed him as the master of our future, only how much earlier I didn't yet know and so I asked him when he'd bought it and he said:

"Last summer. He had two of them. This one struck me more. And both were the size of a man. Just right for our low walls."

"A bit smaller," I corrected him.

"Maybe," he agreed.

"In fact, the size of an average boy, or a girl. And the second one was of a waterfall."

"That's right."

"The water could have been real," I said.

"True," he said. " A talented lad."

But I didn't reply, and only finished my tea and put the glass to one side, but when I got up he again touched my shoulder and said:

"Listen, I've had an idea. That painting will more than do it. It's not that it suits me that much, but alright: agree with him as your neighbour – and the revolver's yours."

I shook my head:

"It's gone."

"Shame," he said.

"It is a shame," I confirmed, said goodbye and left. Before leaving I took another look at the wall.

All the way homeward I thought about the crag on the picture, about the doe standing royally atop it; about the hideous death witnessed by almost the entire aul, but which we were powerless to prevent; about Alone and his love, which no one had foreseen and which had been shared only by that unfortunate girl, at the price of her own death; about the price of poverty unable to buy itself a revolver, and about the price of the revolver that turned out to be dearer than everyone's gain; about success and the wild money needed to obtain it; about the knowledge that points the path to riches but knows not how to detach itself from wretchedness; about the old man, who over the course of many long years of poverty had learnt to invent amazing things, that wouldn't have occurred to anyone else, but failed to work them to his own advantage, apart from eternal hope; and about the boy who seemed not to have stepped beyond the bounds of his loneliness but found there within those bounds far greater than your grandfather in his quick-witted resourcefulness. I thought about how both of them were unhappy, and about how the unhappiness of the former, the old man, was almost preferable to the unhappiness of the latter, because the boy was unhappy even in his successes, which he never sought, which were granted him from on high either like a curse or a blessing – they were no different – and these blessed curses did not even allow him to die when he had tried his hardest, when it was the most right thing to do (as I thought then, and this thought was sheer enlightenment to me) so right that he would have passed into legend, having dulled our memory of him and our defeats to him into a beautiful legend of a beautiful love, which had forever sanctified the crag and its unassailability, and sanctified our timid humility before the crag's unassailability, as evidence of heavenly punishment that keeps humans earthbound, but carries the rest off into legend. But providence ruled otherwise...

Providence ruled otherwise because there had been no such love, and if there had been, then only in half measures. I was the first to find this out, said Father, the first in the aul.

Your grandfather did not interrupt me once while I recounted all that had happened to me, he only pulled a pained face, which made him look older and paler, it was painful for him that he could not hide his pain, even though I did what I could to help him by not looking at him. Then he told me to go inside and rest while he continued sitting in the yard, dissolving in the dusk. When his outlines dissolved completely he came back to the house and for a long time afterwards tossed and turned, waiting for sleep, for so long that I almost changed my mind. Finally I heard his snoring, I got up and slipped outside, hurdled myself over the fence, crept up to the door and called out, oh so softly, and in my heart, in all honesty, I was full of doubts: if he hadn't answered, I wouldn't have tried again for anything.

Only he did hear me and opened up; how couldn't he if the last guest here had stopped by for the horse thieves, and others came to him only on business, they came directly to the barn, and that only to put sacks in there, they came into the house only when carrying in his dead drunk body and had stayed here no longer than was needed to lay him down on the weathered mats and cover him with his bearskin. And so, I was the first proper guest, only he was not surprised to see me: he hadn't the strength to be surprised, so drunk he was.

"Come in," he mumbled and tumbled in, but stayed on his feet.

Seated at his empty wooden table, I watch as he fumbles around the floor by his bed trying to find the wineskin, and how he totters, picks it up and brings it over to the table, carefully clutching it with both hands. I watch as he rekindles the fire in his hearth, and then how he fumbles in his travelling bag in search of a bite to eat, but finds nothing save a chunk of cold meat the size of a man's fist and a stale piece of flatbread. I watch as he ponders whether it is not too shameful to offer them to me, and then he thinks no more of it and puts them down in the centre of the table, gets out a drinking horn from a dark corner, takes the wineskin and pulls out the stopper with his teeth and then with great difficulty fills the horn with araka*, and shakes his head in satisfaction seeing he has not spilled a single drop of the stuff, and then offers the horn to me. Before I drink, I pronounce a toast, half a dozen words without which you can't manage at any feast, even the most wretched and distressing, where the host is incoherently drunk, and his guest is so sober that he has no wish to drink, and then through the water welling up in my eyes I see him take up the horn, fill it to the brim, raise his arm and speak, and I hear a muddle of sounds tumble from his mouth (a dry slab of his voice, tradition and duty, as if the words had stumbled in the dark on his teeth and breaking into the open had got caught in the silt of his tongue) and I am already sorry that I came, and I think of how his voice sounds drunk from just the sight of one horn of drink, and dread to think what will happen when he consumes its contents; and this he does – consumes its contents – as slowly as he rode on his horse past the nykhas that day, or about that slow, but he drains it to the end

---

* araka – strong home-made liquor

and then, looking at me, seeks me out with his dim pupils, and soon he manages to find me in what he sees of me, and grins at this success, gently opens his arms wide in an elegant semicircle and returns them to his knees. The stool he is seated on, this I only notice now, is a bare log on three legs, and I am seated on an overturned gnarled bucket, but the wooden table is well crafted, with carved patterns on it, it's light enough to see that he hadn't got round to finding beauty for the stool, he had still not thought up what tracery to carve into it. On the walls there hangs nothing apart from the old rifle, the same one that had cost him, along with the mats, seven eighths of the harvest for half a dozen years now (yes, said Father, that had suited him down to a tee, and every autumn, counting out the sacks full to their brims with grain, he would always say to your grandfather the very same thing – "What do you think, will the next harvest be any better? Well, do your best. Come back in a year." Grandfather would nod his head in agreement and relief, almost as if it were a master's praise for a capable worker). Yes, almost nothing except for that old rifle the price of half-dozen shares of his harvest and our labours for him, almost nothing except that and several aurochs' hides; except for the empty shelves with no plates or dishes. All those that he had were laid out there on the table, and a couple of bowls down there by his bed.

"Eat," he indicates. "Help yourself."

He cuts the meat with his dagger, and I break off a bit from the flatbread, but it tastes no better than the alcohol he reeks of. He pours what's left of the araka into the horn – I hear the stream now turning into drops and think maliciously: so much the better. He frowns sadly: "I've run out."

I don't answer him, so he repeats stubbornly: "I've run out – can you get hold of some round yours?"

"No," I say. "Not now. That's not why I came."

He keeps staring blankly at me, clearly at a loss for words but obstinately trying to think of something to say to me. By now I'm already past believing that he'll manage it, so I say: "I've come a bit too late."

He shrugs his shoulders and goes on chewing the bread. Then he says something to me that in words would be: "Alright. As you wish. I won't keep you."

I get up and make for the door, and hear behind me: "You'll be sorry."

Now he's steady on his feet. "You won't be back. You won't pluck up your courage again."

But he's wrong, and I'm back after an hour, I almost go running back and don't even hesitate anymore at the door – I don't have time to – I have to do this by dawn. I shake his flabby frame, grab him by the chest, hold down the nausea I feel from the unbearable stench of alcohol from his mouth. I start talking in a whisper, but very soon I've almost broken out into a yell and I keep repeating to his vacant face, struggling out of the pit of sleep:

"I was there! I saw everything! I know!" I repeat this until it's almost too painful for him, until his sleepy eyelids begin to crack open. Then I run over to his hearth and turn over the coals that haven't yet gone out under the weight of the ash, then I once more go and shake him by the chest and whisper (or maybe cry, or maybe plead, or maybe beg): "First you painted the crag... then the doe on it. I know! You saw the girl and drew a doe on the crag ... and you hid it from everyone, but one time you couldn't hold back, you lay in wait for her and showed her ... you just unfurled it and showed her. You didn't need to do anything more! Or even say anything. She would have understood. But you told her who this doe was. You told her didn't you? And you poisoned her with your love, but you were frightened of believing in it yourself, and so ran off to the fort in order to sell off your fear – that fear of your loneliness ... or the fear that you couldn't escape it or exchange it, and you knew that Soslan wouldn't have any of it! You were a coward, but didn't admit it to yourself! ... For the first time you were a coward, and you got scared of your cowardice and decided to trust everything to chance, and so you took the other painting to the fort with you – the one with the waterfall – and gave fate the right to choose, and so fate in the shape of some wretched shopkeeper, who'd never even heard of our land before, bought its beauty together with your fear, fate chose the doe on the crag. But you couldn't imagine that it would choose it twice over! You couldn't think how fate could be not only that shopkeeper but the girl too, who believed that she was the doe and wanted to prove it to you, wanted to prove to you that she was a doe more than someone's daughter ... Now I know it all! I tell you the only thing I can't figure out in my head is why you felt you had to tell her that you were going off to the fort? Why did you tell her that you were off there to sell the picture? Tell me why?"

He prises away my fingers and throws me back off him and nods his puffy head. Then he opens his mouth to speak, but can only cough so that his face becomes scarlet and his eyes well up with tears. Hoarsely, he says: "You don't understand a thing. It wasn't me that killed her. It was my lie."

"You lied to her? What did you say to her?"

"No. Not like that," he shakes his head. "I did show it to her but said nothing. I showed her my lie – that painting."

Now I wait. I can't but wait. I wait for a bit, but it still means I wait right up till dawn. At dawn he explains to me that love had nothing to do with it; that it's his eyes that are to blame, eyes that only saw without loving, and he thought up the doe, and created this realm of beauty and felt proud of his creation; but he met her by chance, all three times, and on the second, he'd just finished the painting and she was going down to the river, only at first he didn't see her and only heard the scrunch of pebbles behind him, she was hiding behind a shaky boulder and wanted to spy on him; then he really did show her it and called her a doe too, only nothing like that had been on his mind, she took a look, blushed and ran away – all in a moment, he says; and he says that the third time – when he went off to the fort (this I'd guessed right), they met on the Blue Path, only this time she had been lying in wait for him, that way round – she for him, not the opposite, and he told her that he was off to the fort to show the doe, and here she blushed far more than before, so much that her cheeks caught fire and her forehead came out in red blotches all over, but she stayed on and he heard her voice for the first and the last time and her voice was more tender than beauty itself and he obeyed it and unfurled the painting and she looked at it for a bit longer than a moment, and then asked him whether he would really sell it, and he replied: if he could, she nodded and quietly wandered off into the aul. That was all, he continued on his way; and he says that he himself believed in the lie created by his own hands and wanted others to believe in it too – wanted to confirm his belief (or his lie, to be precise, he corrected himself) through theirs; and he says about himself: may I be cursed; and says he should have painted something else, some mangy dogs even, strewn around our aul, thousands of dogs, worn out with boredom and envy, and he should have painted in such a way as to make it obvious how much they stank, as if they died twice over on one and the same street; or, he says, he should have painted a donkey on that crag; or painted himself with a wineskin of araka and a heart squeezed by fear; or that bowl of shit on his doorstep; or any of his dreams after his drinking bouts; or the old men playing away at cards in the nykhas; or me in the hardware shop, gazing at the 'realm of beauty' from which I'd only just managed to tear myself away and in which I readily believed, forgetting all its monstrosities and anguish; or the silly young beauty, scaling the cliffs just to prove to him that she could be like the doe; and he says: had anyone ever seen a doe alive scrabbling up a cliff? And he says, how stupid could you be, could you imagine anything more stupid? And he says, think about it: is there anything more stupid than to love a dead shadow of a stupid girl? And he says, that no, there's nothing more stupid than to fall in love with her, this shadow, when the girl's no longer with us, falling in love with the stupid but beautiful doe after its death, after its pointless, stupid death; and he says, no there is something: maybe what's even more stupid is telling a bedtime story about this stupidity to an idiot, ready to believe such stupid drunken ravings; and, he says, that's enough, go, or they will see you, I don't want that and neither do you, nor anyone else in our terribly beautiful world of heavenly beauty; and he says, leave me alone, and he says: leave me alone that's all I'm asking; and he says: hurry up, or else you'll be in trouble, and he says: how much can you make a person suffer; and he says: go away, I'm very tired, I want to sleep now; and he says nothing more, only turns to the wall and covers up his head with the bear skin...

I get up from my knees, and only now I realise that I've been down by his bed on my knees ever since I came in, and I go out onto his doorstep and carefully bound over his low fence and I creep back home to my bunk, and manage to get some sleep, manage also to make myself think that the night is over and manage as well to watch morning stretching out its shoulders and hear life rattling buckets in the women's quarters, and I manage to paint a picture in my mind: a doe and her buck on a crag, a doe and a buck standing side by side, standing there in full view but so high that no one can reach them, not even a bullet. Only I had no time to think what time or season it would be in the picture; should it be autumn or winter, dawn or dusk? But I had time enough to remember it for life, and now describe it to you.

So said Father.

And that's how I remembered it: a doe and her buck high on a cliff, unreachable by either bullet or time.

I remembered what was not, what could not even have been, what was born in a daydream in the deeply moved imagination of my father some nine years before my birth and it has not faded up to now, as if he's forgotten his father's death, forgotten all deaths, except that which killed the girl who had been deceived by the pawned-off doe, and thus her grief reconciled love and loneliness and prolonged their lives for two dozen years so they continue to suffer in those four walls permeated with their grief. It was almost as if a painting – a piece of canvas the size of two good patches on some shabby coat – knew how to contain within itself not only that which has never been and could not be, not only that which allowed a stranger to attach our mountains to the low wall of his damned shop, not only the tragic fate of a girl who had fallen in love with a lie, whose death had blinded her own father and turned the head of the one who had first seen the doe on the cliff and made it come alive on the rough canvas, and before selling it showed it to the silly girl, almost a child, whom he prevented from entering the legend, unable to overcome his cursed vitality, and who committed an outrage against the indomitable crag by scaling it in his drunken stubbornness before our very eyes – a picture could contain within itself not just all this, but also the vision that came to me as my inheritance from a time, whose scent I had never tasted, but which I could not shake off, as if the dyes on that painting – not that remembered by the canvas, but that on which the doe stands alongside her buck – as if the dyes were more fragrant and held more fast than those, which, a year later, exactly a year after the girl's death, a year to the very day, went up in flames along with the canvas and the frame, along with the crag and the doe and the purchased beauty in that little shop with the low walls, went up in the flames of a fire sparked by the night itself, flames which, said Father, you couldn't even call a fire: for the plaster just slightly caved in and only a black stain was left on the wall below the nails on which it used to hang, black scorch marks on the low wall, and that was all, unless you counted the broken window; only, I admit, it burnt down entirely, into nothingness, since the lie had been painted on it for a year by this point, and justice was done, at least stopped being a lie, and by this time already several months had passed since my father's heated imagination had painted on a buck to accompany the doe, and so it turned out, the painting burnt down to cinders; its job had already been done, for this fire was only a rite of prayer for the dead, and, as Father said, when he left the aul two days before this funeral, he guessed at once that he had set off for the painting, that he wanted to look upon it once more, as if he wanted to pay tribute to it, and when he came back four days later, my guess was confirmed right, although not entirely, as I only found out about the fire in the shop later. Of course the arsonist was never found, though one of the neighbours managed to catch a glimpse of him from behind in the dark, his Caucasian hat, his swift horse, carrying him away down the road, and then away out of the fort.

"What savages! I just have no idea," repeated the shopkeeper a couple of weeks later, shaking his head, shattered, and looking at my father with a puzzled look. "I just have no idea who could want to do this. What savagery!"

Or pain, Father thought to himself. Or revenge – upon his own hands, his own gift and his own nights. Or the wildness and desperation of waiting, suffering for a whole year in the drunken stupor of memories. Or maybe a longing for flames, a belated sacrifice, the surrender of a mind conquered by delusions... But aloud he said: "Maybe, yes. Maybe savagery. Not everyone is cultured. Someone has to twirl the tails of bulls."

The shopkeeper stopped shaking his head, let the poison flow into his eyes and asked: "Aren't those the same bulls you wanted to exchange for a revolver? It's not like you."

"Not really," agreed Father. "But this is not about bulls. It could be exchanged for something else. And so that one won't part from it."

He watched the shopkeeper's attempts at laughter. In the end he sneered and said:

"So that's how it is. Most curious!"

"Oh yes," Father nodded and got thinking about the wise old man with his dreams of getting rich, and remembered his instructions, word for word. "You can exchange it for something else. Even for my illiteracy."

At first he frowned, then looked at me for a long time and I could see gradually, wrinkle by wrinkle, how the realisation started to dawn on him, and though I never learnt to read, said Father, I could read him like an open book from that moment. When he got the idea he coughed and asked just to make sure:

"How's that?"

"Get some paper and start writing. Write what you want and I'll put a cross below it."

"What use is your cross to me?"

"You know," said Father. "Write what you want, I trust you."

Once more they were silent and the shopkeeper's look grew tight as if his pupils were being squeezed by resentment, but then resentment slowly began to dissolve in cunning, and when it had dissolved entirely his gaze became about as soft and moist as wood chippings, and he said:

"Alright. Have it your way." He opened a desk drawer and got out a sheet of paper. He wrote so quickly and merrily that a slight chill ran through Father's heart, but he drew his cross on the paper just the same, obediently fulfilling Grandfather's orders and marking out both lines of the cross with some effort with the pen. The shopkeeper picked up the signed sheet of paper with two fingers, waved it in front of him, chuckled mirthfully to himself and tore it in two. "Now let's write a new one. A proper one."

Father swallowed and asked:

"You mean that wasn't the real one?"

"Of course not," he answered. "In that one you accepted that you owe me a hundred roubles and you'll pay me back by tomorrow."

"It was a joke then," said Father, wiping the sweat from his brow.

"And a test as well," he nodded and set once more to scratching at a clean sheet of paper. But Father shifted from one foot to another and fidgeted, getting all the more shy and wiping his brow with his sleeve. This time, before signing, he decided to get to the truth and so when the shopkeeper held out the pen to him, he shook his head:

"Read it out first."

The shopkeeper raised his eyebrows, thought a while and then grinned smugly: "But who's to say I'd be reading out what I'd written down here. How would you know?"

"Alright," said Father. "Alright. I trust you."

"You've no choice. Either trust me or go and learn to

read. Put down your cross." He indicated where with his fingernail.

"Just that you've no reason to trick me," said Father. "I have a brother. And now my rifle goes to him."

"I hear you," said the other. "Go and get my assistant..."

So they came to a deal, and the old man turned out to be right: Father had no need to get out their last treasure, which remained with them as a cherished hope and a long time ago failed to be exchanged, though it weighed almost twenty pounds and required for its crafting all the family silver and the family's humiliation to boot, that had vainly tried to receive in return for itself and a dagger of Daghestani crafting an extra piece of another's land that turned them into farmhands and that enriched them just enough for them to see clearly and realise the depths of their own poverty, stirred up by the agitation of their own greed, or shame, or despair, or maybe their belief in the miracle created before their eyes by a lonely boy which they counted on to subordinate to the cunning wisdom of my grandfather. Yes, the old man turned out to be right, and now it only remained to load up the cart with goods and to start to trade, receiving ten kopeks from every rouble made.

And it also remained to dispose of the silver dagger, depositing it as our only capital stock (the word was not even mentioned at the time, and the notion itself did not exist for them yet, and my grandfather never heard it spoken although he would be fully able to understand its meaning) in the mysterious business started by Barysbi, the eldest son of Khandjeri who had passed away in June. I think, awaiting the arrival of the cart, that mystery was no less on the old man's mind than his own plans or his own age, which meant that he was contemplating the fact that Barysbi wouldn't have started his venture while Khandjeri was still alive, but it was so pressing and alluring that they waited only the traditional forty days till the Remembrance Saturday following the wake in Soslan's house that marked the end of the mourning. He thought that in essence Barysbi offered the villagers the same bait as Grandfather himself had, only what was behind it our old man didn't know, just as the others, who had fallen for his bait and had sold him almost all their family valuables and their family savings. This gave the old man no peace for it was too clever even for him, though he had thought up a way of making a profit out of my father's illiteracy while taking care not to waste it; too clever for him to understand how one can buy up others people's money for free, save for a promise in words to return it in precisely a year's time with fifty percent interest on what they had given him. He racked his brains: what can one buy with the villagers' money that he could sell at such profit as to return one and a half times the initial amount to the villagers while still leaving a little something for himself, and that little something was sufficiently weighty and tangible that it could only be gold itself. A lot of gold. A pile of it. And, of course, not a single guess would fit that secret, and Grandfather's concern did not diminish, it even grew, but together with it grew the insatiable desire to insure himself, to divide this sweet bait with the others and finally part with the shameful memory of the dagger by throwing it into the communal kitty (a huge iron barrel in Barysbi's house) and thus renounce it, this silver witness to Grandfather's defeat, for a whole year. Preoccupied with these thoughts in our blazing hot yard the old man gradually grew tired and weary, falling into heavy, vague dreams, but then he'd start suddenly and open his puffy eyes: but why now? Why not Khandjeri, why his son? Why this haste? Where was the catch? Maybe it wasn't so fast and sudden after all? Maybe it was brewing in Barysbi's head for a long time, only Khandjeri had not accepted the idea, or could not possibly accept it, which was the same thing, the difference was only as to whether the son shared it with his old man or not, so as to spare himself from his father's wrath. But whether it was too soon or too late, it was all done extremely hastily, as if Barysbi feared that he'd be forestalled. In fact, there were only two people who could forestall him: my grandfather, dozing in the young sun, ripe with energy, and this youth who had taken to drinking as he safeguarded his pain within the cold sooty walls. Only the former wasn't quick enough on the uptake while the latter wouldn't even spit for the sake of money. As it turned out, if Barysbi had anyone to fear in the whole affair, it was his very self, I mean his own idea: here the choice is between playing at give-away and following the temptation, or sweeping it under the carpet and then for the rest of your life feeling the astringent taste in your mouth from that old temptation unrealised out of cowardice, indecision and scrupulousness. And, of course, in the choice between action and a yearning for it, Barysbi chose to act as it befits the scion of a tribe whose men had always met death in the saddle, on wheels, or under the croup of their horse, be it in war, on the march, a trip to the fort or – if nothing more opportune presented itself – simply on a special trip to the mountains, as if death itself or a premonition of it had driven them out from the family hearth and their warm beds. And so Khandjeri, no great one for going out on horseback, nor for travelling far, nine days before his death put on his white hood and cloak with a patch below the left shoulder darned with black threads, for the first time in his long years of bleak and boring old age, and clambered up onto his horse bedecked in crimson velvet, and moved off slowly downhill along the riverbank, forbidding any of his family to come with him; he only returned towards dusk, and on his suntanned face was written such anger and v that there wasn't a man in the whole aul who ave taken it for a burning envy of the boy who had that hooded cloak and the black patch. The next day, when once more he returned towards evening, this envy was mixed with fury and had tinged his cheekbones an earthy hue, so that afterwards he didn't even appear at his doorstep for three days; but no, he hadn't snapped, as some people decided; however, the next time he also misjudged and on returning from his exhausting ride that had still not killed him he resembled a white shadow against the red sunset while in his now translucent eyes his humility was praying.

It lasted him a further two days and these two days sufficed for Khandjeri to gather the last scraps of his strength and clamber up for one last time onto his half-alive mare, adorned in crimson, and ride her down the road which finally took pity on his feebleness and let him die a mile from home, tumbling head over heels in thick roadside dust, that still clung to the path in a moist scab of dew. The aul did not have to wait till sunset; at midday they sighted the familiar mare first, then a bay horse and what was being carried on its back, then another mare harnessed to a cart, then the cart itself – at first they glimpsed its collar and wheels, but upon closer observation their mouths dropped: it was a cart, the likes of which they'd never seen before, but there it was coming towards them – and then the rider and his load, and then they saw that his load was stained white, but they couldn't make out who the rider was, so they rose to their feet and told their young ones to hurry to the house of the deceased. By the time the cart rode up to the nykhas, they met the cortege standing with bowed heads and to the outburst of the women's wailing. The newcomers' faces, said Father, were so pale and drowsy that our people did not dare disturb them with questions; what's more they were talking in Russian, which was all the more incomprehensible and smooth-flowing, as if their tongues were made of wax. All of a sudden the sky clouded over and a great whirlwind got up – you must have heard of it, Father said, it was the same whirlwind that in later years blind Soslan would compose his song about, you remember? Well, people had no strength to withstand it, the wind blew us off the street, burning our throats with the hot, fusty air and scaring us no end: such a hot dry blast had never happened in these parts before, nor had they ever seen in our skies such strange brown clouds which never shed a single tear nor broke out into a thunderstorm. So, of course, our men at first took these bad omens as a signs of the gods' grief – for Khandjeri worshipped them and brought them sacrificial offerings, generously sharing with them his meagre stores on their feast days. This is why we tried to ignore the fear in Barysbi's eyes – the others were also shaking in their boots – it was more like terror that froze his fiery hot pupils into an ashen grey. For, in truth the sudden whirlwind gave them no time to get a handle on things or to get it straight in their heads what was going on.

The whirlwind stirred those two as well, and even tore the hat off the one, who sat in his saddle lazily chewing on his tobacco, and carried it down to the river. When they finally dismounted, though they should have realised earlier how unseemly it was for guests to sit there looking down on their hosts, they started chatting amongst themselves in loud rapid voices, and up till then they had only stayed put in their saddles and lazily watched us not bothering to show interest, mostly keeping quiet and not paying attention to what was going on. Your uncle, said Father, took hold of the reins and led their horses into our yard, and there we unharnessed them, together with your uncle and the sons of Askhar and the grandson of Dakhtsyko, only he wasn't much good, since scarcely had he uncoupled one of the mares from the cart when it kicked out at him right at his thigh, so, you could say, he was the first to suffer and he limped for a whole month afterwards, swearing through gritted teeth from the pain and arching his shoulder in a peculiar way; though his leg recovered from the blow, this new habit of arching his shoulder stuck with him, and looked like some invisible fingers were giving him no peace and were constantly and forcefully striving to grab a hold of him.

By the time we had taken the horses to the stables and taken a breather, the wind had died down and in the east a bright patch of sky emerged through the clouds; your uncle stroked the cart, taking off a layer of dust from its shiny side, and quietly asked, "Did you understand anything? Tell us. You know some Russian."

I shrugged and replied: "They're strangers. And not even Russians."

To which he burst out laughing and said:

"Ain't that why you went and learned all that Russian, to work that out? I took one look at them and saw this."

Akhsar's middle son nodded: "Me too. Russians don't got carts like this."

"Or them boots. D'you see them boots?" asked your uncle. "Those boots they've got on them? Their heels are like hooves, very tough."

Dakhtsyko's grandson spat at the ground and swore, stroking his swollen leg, but none of us laughed and your uncle asked:

"How did they end up round these parts?"

None of us could offer an answer, Father told me, even if Alone were there with us he would also have been powerless to guess anything. I still had my freedom then, and the villagers' money and valuables still hung on their walls, stood on their shelves and lay hidden in their squalid huts, and the lifeless body of Khandjeri still lay in rest in his house, now under the sway of its new master, who was forced to hold fire for forty days while the soul of his father (the former master) made its peace with this world before passing on for ever more into the heavens.

Suddenly Akhsar's eldest, who hadn't said a thing till this point, pointed to the skies and gasped: "Look up there!"

We raised our heads, watching how greedily and irreversibly the bright patch of the sky was turning crimson and then voraciously swelled up pressing against the milky edges of the brown clouds. Seeing all of this, Dakhtsyko's grandson jerked his shoulder and said softly:

"It doesn't look like blood. Right? Doesn't look like blood at all."

We kept silent, and he added: "Well maybe just a bit..." He had a fit of coughing and hobbled off, dragging his sore leg, and we followed him.

Those two were already in Khandjeri's house, we caught sight of them straight out although the place was overcrowded; they were pushing their way through the crowd with no trouble at all and not caring a jot, using their elbows till they made it out onto the doorstep, and there, looking all around them they started chatting animatedly, like they were having some sort of argument, and one of them, whose jaw looked like a plough, beckoned me to him with his finger, as if I were a little boy, and like a little boy I went up to him obediently and he got out his pocket watch and tapped it with his long fingernail, repeating something about the time and about some kind of "namit", putting his hand up to his throat, saying he needed to see Barysbi at once; he patted me on the shoulder as if I were a little boy to get me going, and I, like a little boy, nodded and went back to the house. I started pushing around till I found him, grabbed hold of him by the sleeve, and he, turning crimson – with anger, I thought, – took me by the elbow, like I was a naughty boy, and dragged me out of the room asking me on the way what they'd been saying to me. Cooling down slightly, he ordered me:

"Now go. I'll deal with the Belgians myself, I don't need no translator."

So he walked resolutely over to them, while I remained in the hallway and savoured the taste of this new word in a whisper on my tongue, wondering when and where he could possibly have heard it, let alone grasp what was meant by it, and then I saw Alone for the first time that day, and was amazed at what I saw, not so much that he was there, nor even that he was standing shakily on his feet, his back leaning against the fence, what really surprised me was that he wasn't drunk.

You see, Father explained, somehow he was too sober. So sober, that it was even terrifying to see. As if everyone else was as drunk as a lord and he was the only sober one there, and yet exhausted by his own sobriety he could hardly keep on his feet. What's more, said Father, it seemed to me then that, although the deceased was lying over there in the house, it was not him but he who was stuck to that fence ought to be buried – his eyes were filled with such death-like anguish. I didn't avert my gaze in time, so that when our eyes met I simply wasn't able to avoid him, and walking towards him with head bowed I felt again like a harassed little boy; as I was walking, I asked myself who had given him the right to order me about and why I'm so eager to oblige. While he, barely noticing me standing at his side, again directed his gaze towards them and mumbled something I couldn't make out. I waited patiently for him to find his voice as I watched the dying wind depositing yellowy dust on our boots. Finally, Alone said hoarsely, hitting my nose with his alcoholic breath:

"Have you seen the sky?"

I wanted to say, you of all people could have come up with something cleverer than that, but instead said aloud: "Poor old Khandjeri."

But his face expressed surprise and he looked me up and down: "So, you're not scared. Haven't you seen the sky? It seems neither of you has seen the sky."

I shrugged and said: "Go and have some sleep. The folk here can manage perfectly well without you, they won't even notice you've gone. Sleep yourself sober."

All the while I was thinking in my mind what nonsense I was saying. And what nonsense he was saying. But here he somehow flagged, rubbed his forehead and squeezed the bridge of his nose with his fingers:

"Maybe you're right. Maybe all of you are in the right. Just why haven't any of you seen the sky?" He waved his hand. "Alright, so be it ... and, well, do you know anything about them?"

"Belgians," I replied. "They picked up Khandjeri on the road."

"And where was the road taking them?" he asked and we both stayed silent. "That's none of our business, isn't it? We have nothing to do with them. We are polite people and love guests: but who, why and where from – it's all the same to us. We are proud people and not inquisitive, right?"

I frowned and said back: "Are you in a quarrelling mood? Just say so rather than beating about the bush."

He shook his head as if he was drunk and I thought he was pretending, but then I saw he was about to fall. It serves him right, I thought. Again I realised why it was that no one liked him, and thought that it was all of no use, as there was no pitying him. Loneliness had clamped itself to him like a vice. He had been corrupted by it. And there's no pitying the corrupt.

He said: "I'm sorry. I took fright."

I couldn't hear any more of this, and boldly replied: "You liar. There's no fear in you at all. You're not afraid of any old sky. All you want is to get all of us frightened."

Again he shook his drooping head, and his knees almost buckled and his back started to slouch and crumple – but no, he didn't fall down: with the back of his head he clung firmly to the fence and, straining to straighten himself up, he loudly demanded:

"Give me a hand."

After he caught his breath he stared at me fiercely, and I'd almost decided that if he started yelling at me again I'd punch him. But the yell only gurgled in his throat and never burst out, which left me frustrated. So he said:

"Alright. Forget it. Don't worry your little head. Brains are not your strong point."

I gritted my teeth and wondered how much more of this I could take. If he wanted a fight he'd get it for sure. Apart from me, there wasn't anyone for him to fight with.

"You play with the edged dagger," I said. "And you can barely stand. See that you don't cut yourself."

He nodded: "You're right. It smacks of cowardice."

"You said it. A man shouldn't be putting on airs. Better go back to swigging away your araka."

"Dead right," he says. "I'm off home. Uh-huh. But you stay put here. You might find something out. I'm not much use today in this state. I'm a bit confused. Can't even tell if he's telling them off or trying to persuade them. Can't make it out from here."

I looked around too and saw them out of the corner of my eye, but Barysbi's words were being chewed up by the wind, and the speech of the other two was smooth and slippery even up close, like your wet pebbles, so that even if you came close you'll slide off them – what hope did I have of making out what they were saying from ten paces away? But you can't stop your eyes from staring, especially if there's something worth looking at. Now I also got suspicious, said Father, because instead of two patches I saw three of them, three pale faces, and they looked just like three reflections, three copies from the same blueprint, reflecting all of us forty days in advance, so that once those forty days had passed they'd be taking all the villagers' money and valuables in return for our failure, in return for a crime that none of us had ever committed, but the receipt for which had been given by my very hand, that feeble cross I'd placed in the corner of that sheet of paper, that now lay in the iron safe stored up for future use many miles away from here.

I too started to get suspicious, said Father, but had no wish to believe and no way of understanding; nor did your grandfather, interrogating me later that evening about the Belgians, Barysbi and Alone, and listening perplexedly to my tale – who was I to vie with him in intelligence? I remember that night my sleep was troubled and I woke up in a cold sweat hearing Alone's last words, the ones he'd gasped out to my turned back before he went away:

"Khandjeri is dead. And we try to ignore the heavens saying to us that we are finished, and from now on we must live differently."

I thought over these words for a long time, sensing in them a prophecy, and after suffering like that over them I forced myself to forget what he'd said, forced myself right up till dawn.

All the next day we didn't see them once, the Belgians, but the day after, led along arm in arm by his nephew, blind old Soslan came and, beside Khandjeri's deathbed, he sang his last song to the accompaniment of his fandyr, the song about the wind and the tears of river sand, about the grieving gods and a hot soul that heated the sun, about his old friend who had set off to the skies to seek out his daughter and be at her side in place of her still living father. Hearing this song your grandfather sobbed like a woman while the women wailed like children in pain. What am I telling you, you've heard this song many a time.

Well, those two came to the funeral and now, on the surface at least, all was proper and fitting: look at them, we said amongst ourselves, they may be strangers, but they abide by our laws. Having said that, they didn't stay long at the funeral feast, and of course, no one forced them to, we would not dare: the look in their eyes seemed to forbid it. But Alone, who hadn't taken his eyes off them all day, whispered into my ear:

"There's something fishy going on here. They haven't said a word to each other."

I thought that every man has a fool up his sleeve, and also that little strokes fell great oaks, meaning that he has become almost like us, but I said instead: "Better drain your drinking horn so as your brains don't dry out."

He replied: "That's where you're mistaken."

I asked: "Where?"

He said quietly, even gently:

"Under your hat. You try kidding yourself all the time and you're pleased as punch when you succeed. Isn't it nice when all you have fits under your hat, eh? There's your problem – come night you have to take your hat off. And that's when you have your troubled sleep and nightmares, don't you?"

As if nothing had happened, he stood up and said a

toast to the soul of the departed, then sat back on the bench and murmured to me under his breath:

"They haven't yet come to a deal. They haven't agreed on a price. But Barysbi's a patient one, like a rug on the wall. He'll wear them out."

I said: "If you're so clever, why don't you get into buying and selling?"

"Because I don't know yet what deal they're getting mixed up in," he said. "And even if I did know, what use would it be to me anyway?"

"If you're so rich why d'you care what they're up to?"

"Not what they're up to," he comes back. "What we're up to... you just don't get it into your head. But if I figure it out, you'll be the first one I'll share it with."

Only he didn't figure it out, said Father, he was late.

At this point in his story Father was silent for a long time, stroking his bald patch and tutting his tongue sorrowfully, then he put on his hat and froze, just sitting there arching his right eyebrow almost to the rim of his cap and moving his fingers on his sinewy knees. Even without his telling me I already knew what happened next, though my father had only once mustered up the strength to get all the way to the end of the story, and that was on the morning when he had barely recovered from a bad chest cold, and for the first time in several days had got up by himself on his trembling legs, and seated his emaciated body on the log covered with skins out in our yard to catch the covetous springtime sun, and didn't budge from there right until dusk, refusing his meals twice over, first his breakfast and then, as the sun poured warmth at its zenith, refusing his lunch, and he didn't allow me back into the house either, angrily explaining that on an empty stomach I'd grasp it all better: an empty stomach makes for a clear head.

He recounted how they turned up at both the Friday memorial wakes for Khandjeri, and that their expressions were now much less aloof but more respectful, far more than they were at the funeral, and that we no longer hesitated to wake them up; and if no one asked them anything that was because they would respond with broad smirks and a quick torrent of their strange guttural speech punctuated now and then by Russian yes's, no's and thankyou's; it was almost all too awkward, too silly, as if we weren't just speaking in a different language but about completely different things, almost as if the Belgians were deaf to boot, since very often the conversation would consist of awkward nods and lengthy handshakes, and it seemed that the idea of it all was only to borrow their broad smirks, made by lips alone, and bashfully let someone else have their turn at making sense of them, if someone else in the crowd was willing to.

Then they were seen on the fortieth day, and already on the forty-first at the nykhas Barysbi came up with his scheme, saying: "You've got ten days to think about it. Ten days is more than enough. And if any of you don't take up the offer, then you've only yourselves to blame."

The same evening the villagers were watching Aguz entering Barysbi's gate, and hurrying after him was his ruddy-cheeked eldest son with a bag over his shoulder. The next morning by that same gate Dakhtsyko and Akhsar bumped right into each other, and you could see from the nykhas how they searched underfoot for the right words to say, and only find a pretext to pass by one another in a narrow village street, and how they parted off in different directions pleading with themselves not to look around. Grandfather took delight in all this, gleefully rubbing his hands and chortling away, and there was so much joy in his laughter that Father was ashamed even to look him straight in the eye, lest the old man choked on his joy borne out of his anger. And Father thought to himself, just wait till it hooks you too. He was right, of course, though not entirely so: it wasn't just malice and glee, and while the villagers were counting on their fingers, Grandfather was waiting patiently, holding steady and turning over again and again in his mind the same thing he'd already contemplated many times before but hadn't yet voiced out loud, as he strained to penetrate what others had already thought out but kept secret from everyone else concerned.

When the count exceeds the fingers of one hand, the old conniver calls in my father and orders him to get the cart ready; they had four days – two there and two back, with one night spare just in case. All that was required of Father was to manage in time and draw his clumsy cross on a piece of paper. All that was asked of him was not to mess up and get back in time (to be on the safe side, because neither he nor Grandfather believed that ten days decided anything: could it be that an extra day would cheapen the silver in daggers that are supposed to grow in value and weight?) All that was wanted of him was to go there and come back, and what could have been easier! But of course they couldn't have known about the rain... How could they? And how could they have known what the rain means...

Whatever the case, on the tenth day towards noon there were still a good half dozen miles to the Blue Road, and the cloak, shared between the two of them, had been soaked right through as they were hunched up in the cart, shoulder to shoulder, two people who had nothing to say to one another, and who didn't even have a common language except gestures and some shreds of broken Russian reduced to a few phrases and a couple of dozen mutually guessed words. My slightly tipsy father, who had modestly helped himself once or twice to his workmate's long-necked flask, wondered to himself good-naturedly what his companion needed those specs for – that's how sizzled he'd become. The fog was so thick he wouldn't distinguish between your eyes and nose. Towards noon of the tenth day, the road had deteriorated completely, and here and there they had to jump down from the cart and help out the mare, and every time Father would carefully check if the sodden tarpaulin was holding firm to the sides of the cart while his travelling companion was at first annoyed by this but then lazily gestured to forget it, what's the point. A couple of miles from their destination, by the Marshy Stream, his companion quietly struck up a discordant sad tune and it flowed from under his glasses in clear rivulets across his wet cheeks, so that Father felt uneasy and even a bit confused; he pulled the reins against his will but then the thunder came to his assistance and the mare, bolting forward with fright, threw off the travelling companion flat onto his back so that he slid from the tarpaulin and tumbled into the mud. While Father struggled with the horse he sat in a puddle groping about for his glasses, finally he recovered them from the thick mud, rinsed them in the dirty water, and re-fixed them to his nose; then he reached into his coat for his flask and emptied the last drops into his throat; having neatly replaced the stopper he put it back under my father's stunned gaze and suddenly broke out into such infectious laughter that soon my father too laughed heartily. Several more rain-sodden moments later the travelling companion got to his feet, opened his arms out wide, raised his face to the skies and cried:

"How glorious! Isn't this just glorious!"

It's as if he attempted to embrace the juicy immensity of the rain, but then, unable to stifle the thirst in the pit of his stomach, he fell to his knees over the bubbling stream and kneaded it with his fists, breaking forth in laughter and splashes while Father, losing all sense of shame and letting the wrinkles smooth out on his face along with his pride, looked upon this madness with tearful eyes, painfully crushing his ribs in an expansive splash of joy in his chest as he joined in with his hoarse throat, his heart pouring out in a groan replete with happiness:

"Glorioushhh! ... A-haa ... Rain, water ... lots and lots glorioushhh!"

His companion even started firing from his revolver into the echo-resounding air; Father made for his, but checked himself as he touched its cold handle, remembering the shopkeeper and the old man who strengthened their mutual gain by this cold steel and appointed two guardians to look after their venture. Father is no longer in the mood for frolics: at first, to outwit himself, he huddles under the rain so as to cool his neck and mind, and then he is aware of the bitterness in his mouth from the caustic aftertaste of vodka; then a revulsion for it and for his aimless joy welled up in him and now he looks at the other traveller, by the stream, with changed eyes, reproachful and rejecting. He turns away to avoid looking at the stranger relieving himself at the edge of the gorge, whistling his peaceful unconcern through the cavity in his teeth. Then he addresses Father:

"Well, now we can consider ourselves engaged. Thanks to the rain!"

But Father stays huddled beneath his cloak, his head pulled in, and wonders: Why is it that when I'm around them one of my years feels like two of theirs? Why do our mountains seem like child's play to them, as if they've grown up here just to give them a nice place for drinking and pissing into the gorge? Where do they get all the strength to bestow their friendship on the first gloomy traveller in this gloomy land under this gloomy sky, covering their road with this tedious cruel rain? Where do they get the strength to make them unaware of all the sweat and pains around them?

When the fellow traveller gives a snort and a gurgle as he rests his temple upon Father's shoulder, trusting his sweet dreams and the weight of his relaxed body to Father's shyness, Father starts thinking with a sense of gloomy satisfaction: What can you expect from him if, apart from their strength, they have nothing to contend with, being so lazy? And their laziness is natural since their strength wears out anyone, let alone this oddball with his blind goggles? For such strength, all shame and caution are like a tight harness for a mare: just a burden. What can you expect from him? Only he is feeling far more than he is capable of expressing in his own words, and he tries not to think of his numb shoulder under the stranger's dream and to ignore the pleasant sensation in his chest, the kind that you get when you crush a viper that's crawled into a bird's nest or when you feed a sick horse out of your hand. It appears that he himself carries a mystery akin to that breathing now into his shoulder, and so the cleverest thing he can do is to wait and follow the road, which is the only way to realise the extent of their similarity (or their difference), for this road, or so he thinks, is destined to stretch out for several months, or possibly several years, if the deal comes off, and that means the wisest thing to do is to arm yourself with patience and think about what's closest to hand, be it the last mile to go before the aul or the old man living in it, who had mapped out this road without leaving his house and in his lifetime had suffered defeat so many times that he had finally learnt how to turn his son's illiteracy into a paper pledge of his success. And Father's thoughts, which now wreathed his lips in a smile, seek out past the turning in the cliffs, through the drizzling fog, the uneven hunk of his home yard before his eyes can see it, and he marvels at

Grandfather's efficiency: the manger has been moved into the corner, and in its place hangs an awning riddled with holes. Now they must be a stone's throw away from their goal – a mere half thousand or so paces along the winding road and across the narrow stone bridge.

There is not any sort of premonition, and nothing can be heard save for the scraping of the wheels on the wet pebbles and the measured breathing of the mare. The two of them, Father and his travelling companion, were as if deafened by the anticipation of warmth and having surrendered themselves to the haven of sleep, huddled under their shared damp cloak. Shared, albeit not evenly, although fairly: for one of them a benumbed shoulder is enough, stiffened under the weight of another's trust, while the other, to attain his peace, had to have his glasses go blind. For now, blinded not only by sleep, not only by the fog and the musings, but also by their shared deafness, the travellers are powerless before disaster as a log before a wielded axe. Even the mare with the wisdom of age, that pricks up its ears and for several minutes that fall on the travellers' deaf ears, calmly flares its nostrils, and then stops completely, refusing to obey either voice or whip, and even the mare is powerless to save them: fate can reckon better than Grandfather. It reckons not in days or hours, it reckons in moments...

Father has jumped down to the ground and is pulling the mare by the bridle, while his sleepy companion wipes his glasses with his fingers, restoring their fragile transparency and muttering with his swollen lips some indistinguishable dampened words.

"Stay put," says Father. "I'll deal with this nag myself. What a naughty nag you are."

Yet the mare has no inkling to budge, and Father can see from its eyes that something's badly wrong, but he is not yet ready to hear: his hearing is geared to the hours, while it's now a matter of moments. He tugs and tugs at the bridle with his left hand (his right hand is filled to the tips of his fingernails with the stranger's slumber); as he scolds the horse for its stubbornness he realises suddenly that it's rather cowardice: out of the corner of his eye he catches sight on the cliff what is troubling her – it's a snake slithering into his tired brain; and not giving him any time to turn round and check, the moment reaches him and bursts out above his head in a peal of thunder and lightning over the summit, and hurls itself at Father with the chest of the maddened mare tearing towards him and whinnying wildly, and he flies back from the blow, splaying his arms out wide like a fallen cross, and now he hears only the wind, torturing him in his flight, which lasts for the whole of this fathomless moment when he sees the mountainside break open by the thunder and lightning and the deluge of rocks flowing forth from its womb, and three large blots are washed away by this torrent, and he sees the triple death hurtling towards the abyss, absurdly mixing in a dense smashed-up stream the animal, the cart and the man awoken by terror (my father will remember his black mouth cracking half of his face and the glint of specs in his hand) in the thick avalanche of crushing stones mixed in with singed dust, which nonetheless spares Father as it hurtles past, hitting his heels with the burning hot wind; and only now he falls on the ground with his back hitting the warm, soft, wonderful native mud. Only then does he realise that the moment has come to an end...

But then while his eyes are still open he senses that the whitish-silver emptiness, which has arisen out of this moment, has easily obliterated his memory; and before closing his eyes, he obligingly thinks that the mud must be delicious. When he comes to and lifts his eyelids, he sees the sky above him oozing with rain and starts to look for his hands, and sees them covered with detritus and a thick, firm layer of pain, and then makes himself use them to shovel off from his breast his crumbling cloak of rocks, at first slowly, awkwardly and hesitantly, and then faster and faster, in an almost feverish haste, as if he's afraid of missing the consciousness that is returning to him, and as the feeling returns in his legs and he remembers the triple death, the three blots, he hurries away from the precipice and sets about scrambling up the only as yet untouched side of the now warped and mangled cliff, and does not turn round until he elbows and forces his way through a narrow crack in a fissure, and presses his stomach to its dry base and once again catches the wondrous smell of the scorched rock dust, and, thus exhausted, says to himself:

"I'll never manage it. I won't last here. I'll rest a while and move on. I'll just catch my breath."

Meanwhile, he watches as down below the fog becomes peopled by a fussing mass, and in it he makes out the sons of Akhsar, and then Dzantemr and Pigu, and his own brother, running across the shaky rope bridge after some shaggy balls, in which Father can make out Aguz' hounds, and he thinks gloomily: "God willing, they won't search this high. The rain hasn't poured out all its water yet. It'll keep raining for a long while yet." Suppressing the tipsy quivering in his feet he thinks: "As long as the old man doesn't find out... My brother wouldn't suspect a thing... No, they won't come searching up here. They're not that smart." Then he thinks: "Look at that: the mill on the river has been swept clean away. The mill's disappeared." He clucks his tongue, feeling as if all the rest had been a dream and there had not been this triple death, not of the mare, nor of his fellow traveller, nor his own (assuming of course he'd been killed with them, along with the cart, its load and the hope harnessed to it two days ago.)

But maybe it's the other way round: he was now peering into the fog from some heavenly outside as was the due right of every soul newly departed from its mortal body.

Whichever it was, the mill carried away by the avalanche occupied his thoughts far more than his own death or the nightmare he'd just lived through, and that's why thinking about that mill was more pleasant for him than finding out if he was alive or dead, and observing the villagers clearing away the blockages and the rubble where their dogs are howling like mad was far easier for him and less taxing than breathing in the scorched smell of the dust mixing in with the damp in his clothes and saturating the air with a sickly-sweet, cloying acridity, and with it savouring the burning taste of the encrusted alcohol in his throat. "Perhaps I shouldn't watch," he suggests to himself. "What use is it to me to watch them? None at all." Only he's suggesting this to himself as if from one side, surreptitiously, unconvincingly, as if he himself can't fully hear himself suggesting it. And as such, he does not do at all what he wishes, and disobeys his desires, and makes himself feel even worse than before. Several times he decides to turn away, and momentarily covers his eyes with his hands, with his soaked palms (blood, imagines someone hiding behind his thoughts, but this someone or other stays distant, and my father tiredly obeys and resigns himself to the aloofness of this fleeting stranger, sheltering from the light and the rain in his refuge and pretending to be him) but then shakes them and dips them into the dust, and rubs them against each other to make the blood cake, but it doesn't work, so he has to repeat this again and again, until he becomes convinced that he's moulded his hands anew and that the new mould has set. Instead of the voices he can only hear the lisping cough of an echo and remarks to himself that this is for the best: he won't hear the old man, and if he persuades himself not to look over there then he won't see his strained attempts to outstand his last renunciation – of life sacrificed by him for a desecrated hope, and of hope, buried by thunder on the way to his house of suffering, that had been preparing all day since that morning to welcome its guests, but instead had turned as silent as the grave in the premonition of a torrent of impending grief.

Only Father's fears are in vain: soon the fog congeals in the rain, covering the gorge with dirty patches and licking clean the wounds in the cliffs. Now Father hears intermittently someone's pitiful groans, and he is ashamed for the invisible stranger, although he doesn't think it possible to insult him with his remarks and decides to be tolerant: the most important thing is not to doze off, for the groans at once grow louder and can give them both away to those down below, and that must never be allowed to happen; so it's better to keep his eyes wide open. He keeps himself busy with trying not to close them and not to blink, so much so that it seems as if the moon has settled in his eyes as unblinking reflections of its sleeplessness; it's not at all difficult, even comfortable, he muses in his sleep and sweet torpor, but when he once more opens his eyelids, he sees lights wandering in the untidy yellowish mist and to his amazement he tries to find his bearings in time: "Dusk. Torches. The barking almost died down. They must have already dug the others out. Now it's my turn. Only they won't make it up here. Now that it's getting dark they won't even try!"

He watches the flames below flickering in the murky abyss, as if they play some uncomplicated game, and he can tell from the persistent thickness of the echoes that the rain has now ended. Then one flame burns a brighter yellow than the others, judders apart, moving closer to the fissure in a shaky, uncertain arc and Father's face grows numb beneath its cold mask of blood and sweat; a fire now bursts bright yellow from the flickering flame, then it sticks to the branch of the torch, out of which instantly grows a bent hand like smoke from a pipe, and soon after, the shaky outline of a face, a torso, legs...

"Who else would it be if not him," Father understands. For some reason he now counts Alone's steps, and when only a couple of dozen are left to be counted, Alone freezes and stares straight ahead, inclining the flame slightly towards the fissure, so that Father thinks: "He's made it. Now he'll cry out and the others will come running. May the devil curse you."

But he doesn't cry out. He doesn't cry out for so long that doubt wells up in Father's mind: "Surely I'm not dreaming this? There's no way I can check. Unless I raise my voice..." But he decides against it, cleverly reasoning that if he sleeps, then it'd be like teasing a dog, especially if his breath gives him away and comes out too loudly, and if he really sees him, let him give his voice first, that's why he climbed up here.

Except that Alone keeps silent, and stays stock still, and Father sees how the dusk visibly turns into dark, with only its middle sticking out into the wind, as a tireless flame thrust on a branch held in a transparent hand illuminates Father's strange dream – he is now certain that he's asleep and dreaming – and then the flame draws out a semicircle in the bedraggled foggy gloom and steps crumble it in the dark as they are dying away and it gradually resumes its former submissive small yellowness; and soon Father again sinks into a heavy, sticky slumber, he groans quietly from the pain in his ribs and tries to stop his shivering. He hugs himself more tightly, tucks up his knees to his chest and through his flabby, anxious sleep he listens to the rumbling of the wind through the night sky, scraping with its cold edge against the brittle jaws of the fissure. Chunk after chunk the night lazily peels off into the void through the gap-toothed aperture in the cliff that stands watch over his every waking movement, and in a resonant instant he recovers from his disorderly, nagging fever so as once again – like ever-increasing concentric circles emanating out of a stone thrown into placid waters of a spring – to be filled in with chaotic and juddering fantasies.

At this moment, entering our gate for the first time in long years of our family's defeats, Alone urges Grandfather to wait with his mourning.

"Believe me," he repeats, catching his eye as if trying to support Grandfather with his gaze. "The mare, yes, the stranger, yes, the cart, that too, but your son was not there. Even in your heart you mustn't bury him so as not to bring misfortune."

Grandfather only mumbles soundlessly and impatiently presses his elbows, not letting his stick fall from his fingers, and then Alone says back:

"All right then, if you can't be convinced, then may I ask something of you? Give me a week, and I'll prove it to you. Seven days, starting from tomorrow..." Looking into Grandfather's eyes he sees a new hope awakened in them – or could it be suspicion, he couldn't tell – he hurriedly adds: "No, no. You don't understand. I don't know anything. I don't know, but I can feel it... Just one week. No one will begrudge you that, right? I'll set off in the morning."

Seeing how Grandfather half-shakes or half-nods his head, uneasily and askew, down and to one side, as if stuck halfway between a yes and a no, he announces with feigned relief:

"We're in agreement then. See you in seven days... So long! God help us both..."

Leaving the hut, he spots my uncle in the crowd and nods to him:

"The old man's calling you. Better let the neighbours go, your family has no one to bury yet."

He heads back to his own place, and straight to his cellar to gather up some food in a satchel and fill his wineskin with araka.

But that night he does not drink. He puts a steel in his satchel, sprinkles into his hand copper and silver from a flat leather purse and, having counted them, puts them back, then hangs the purse on his chest. Then he goes into the stable to put hay out for his horse and afterwards, bridling him, fits his torch into the saddle. He works carefully and calmly. In these confident, measured movements he whiles away the time, then he goes to the churchyard, leaving the horse tied up to its post outside and omitting to take his flame with him. His feet slide and get mired in the path as he passes the nykhas, and I have no clue what his thoughts are when he kneels at the gravestones. I don't know what his hands and his silence are saying to them, but that hardly matters to a soul, except probably to the one that's following his shadow from its shelter, his face under a black hood, hiding behind one of the tombstones and listening in the crumbling quiet of the cemetery. I don't know if Alone can sense his frightened proximity, at any rate he doesn't show it if he does; on this night he takes a silent council from the graves, and so he should: what use are words here? It's enough that his heart kneels before them.

Later he takes his leave and sets off down the path. On the road – in case it has ears – he says as if in warning to someone:

"It's easy to miss in the dark, but in anger I may just as easily hit the target. I won't forget to take my gun with me... Something around here stinks of carrion."

He has everything ready at home for the journey. He rolls up his cloak into a bundle, picks up his satchel and his gun, takes out his horse by the bridle and leads him to the rope bridge, as the stone bridge is half-destroyed. Having crossed the river they go along the roadway as far as the rock fall. Here again he leaves his horse, takes out his torch from the pommel and ties it in a loop round his shoulder. His satchel and his cloak are also strapped behind his back. He spits on his palms, wipes them dry on the hems of his jacket, and tries for a second time (I'm almost sure it was a second time: otherwise he wouldn't have managed to find the cleft before sunup. It's not just me with the benefit of hindsight, after so many years, but he himself had long realised that it takes at least two attempts to win) to scramble up the cliff. After a good fifty paces he spots a tiny even ledge under the waning moon, he straightens himself and, taking a look down into the dense fog, he lights up his torch without caution. A further ten minutes later, his light touching upon Father's sleep, he thrusts the torch into a chink in the rock and covers it over with stones just to be sure, squeezes into the cleft and shakes Father by the shoulder:

"Wake up ... it's time to eat."

Throwing his cloak underfoot, he opens the satchel and gets out some flatbread, a little cheese and some mutton on the ribs. Father stares, his teeth chattering from the cold, and tries to answer him. Alone understands and nods his head, he pulls out the stopper and puts the wineskin up to Father's lips listening as Father greedily and eagerly swallows. Then he pulls away, giving Father time to breathe, and again holds out the wineskin, only this time Father grasps it in his own hands and drinks from it more slowly, and for longer.

"Now eat!" orders Alone, and so as not to embarrass him, turns away to the torch. Father squats and starts to chew away. He chews furiously, frenziedly, like he's trying to crush his hunger and wipe from his throat the taste of scorched dust. Having eaten, he speaks in a voice thinned out from long silence:

"May the gods bless you for your kindness."

Alone puts his hand on Father's shoulder and answers:

"It's nothing... We have so little time. Tell me now, have you changed your mind?"

Father shakes his head: "I can't. It's better to die than return home. The old man won't forgive me."

"But he won't say that aloud."

"Yes, that's why I won't be able to bear it."

Pondering this, Alone nods in agreement:

"All right. Do you feel it's better for you to wander in the mountains..."

"Maybe it is," says Father. "Only I can never do that either. I named our aul to that man in the fort, you see. Nothing will work out now. Otherwise the old man will have to answer for everything..."

"Have you really told everything to that man in the ironmonger's shop?"

"And how," says Father. "Take a look."

He gets out the revolver from his bosom.

"And in return he's left with a piece of paper. Now that paper is mightier than the revolver. What do you think?"

Alone offers no reply, and his face gives no clue to his inner thoughts. Then he says:

"Listen. Soon it'll be sunrise. My horse's down there. Just you know that the owner will turn up here with a search party, and then you'll end up behind bars."

"Oho yes," Father again agrees. "Behind bars, exactly. That means they won't bother the old man."

He calms down visibly, and he's glad that everything's now going well so he sounds as if this has been his only concern throughout this terrible, nauseating day.

"The thing is that you're not at all guilty," Alone says softly, and Father, stunned by his words, at first repeats them in disbelief, rolling them over his tongue, repeats them several times, as if he wants to get used to their unforgiving, coarse, forbidden, righteous indignation, which from now on replaces his lucidity and his peace of mind – he hears them now in his momentarily vanquished heart that has quickened its pulse in despair. Swallowing his saliva he asks Alone:

"Tell me what to do. I see you don't know either?"

Alone just grins bitterly:

"I don't even know what was written on that sheet of paper. I don't know what was going through your old man's mind. I don't know how many years you may spend in jail: I don't know what prison is like, I don't know whom they'll bury, apart from the Russian, if you turn up in the aul tomorrow, because I don't know how two men can stay under the same roof after they first got rich, and then suddenly lost everything, particularly after one of them loses a son and then gets him back again within the same day, and the other at first dies, and rises again at dawn so as to wait gloomily for weeks and months for the soldiers to come for him and take him off to jail. I don't know how he'll explain and get it into their heads that it was not his fault, because living side by side with his father ruined by despair, he himself will forget that he's not guilty. None of this I know, I can only guess..."

"So even you can't think of anything, can you?" says Father. "What point are you making? It seems you agree that I need to go back to the fort?"

Alone replies: "My horse's waiting out there on the road. Waiting for the sunrise, what's there to understand?" Going quiet for a while he then starts to whistle softly, examining my father's face. "Your nose is swollen up like a kneecap. When we go down into the aul, don't forget to wash off the blood, or else you'll look like an abrek. Like a failed abrek. The sort you meet on the road, follow with your eyes and chuckle behind his back."

"I don't get what you mean. I'll be damned if I do."

"Don't you start bristling up," Alone calms him down. "Better drink some more while I think about the lightning."

"What about it? Think out loud and I'll listen," says Father and takes again to the wineskin.

"I haven't made up my mind yet," says Alone. "Just here's what I find curious. When, for instance, you're wandering through the forest in winter, on a warm day, all around you icicles hang off the trees. So many icicles as there are droplets in the melting snow, but yet not a single one hits you. They fall and fall, and not a single one drops on you."

"So?" asks Father, already frowning now.

"Well, doesn't that surprise you? Isn't it strange the way it works, that you go through the entire forest and not a single icicle gets you, but yet it can also happen that you travel for two days, and get caught in the rain, and the sky is so immense and all around there are so many mountains, but yet, in a flash of lightning, the very cliff right above your head is hit and the rocks fall on the only horse for many miles around... Right?"

Now my father is wheezing and asks in a muted, bubbly voice:

"And so what?"

"Well, that's so strange and odd that one wants to make sense of all this..."

Once more he falls quiet, but Father, his eyes inflamed, anxiously awaits an explanation, and when he realises that there won't be any, again persists with his question: "What's your point? What's your idea?" and again a minute later: "What's your point, I'm asking. What are you driving at?"

Alone just shrugs and says:

"I don't understand it myself. I swear I'm not lying... Look, it seems like it's already started to get light, eh?"

Father reluctantly replies:

"Yes, it's time... So you've stirred me up for nothing? Take your wineskin and I'll carry your torch. So it's all to no avail?"

"Look over there, where the wall is like a bulge in the ridge, pressed into the cliff ... there, over there... no, to your right... there you are. Look for the cornice. It's easier on the legs and you won't fall off it. Get to the north side: it'll lead you straight there. I'll meet you there on the road. All the same we'll have to take a roundabout route, there is no way we can get through the blockage."

"Agreed," says Father through clenched teeth. "See you don't lose your wineskin."

After another half an hour, during which he, sticking close to the wall and almost hanging over the precipice, carefully edges along the sloping cornice, breathing hotly into the cliff face and feeling his breath rebounding on his hot cheeks, listening to the meek flame in his hand as he follows the strip of soot on the stone and his intense gaze discerns the signs of the elusive dawn on the smooth rocks; he is drenched in sweat, aware how long he's been thus crawling, and how long he's had no time to think: the words have piled up in the pit of his stomach, rolling on waves of the araka he's drunk. After half an hour he can make out the firm shallow bottom through the lilac shadows of the early morning mist and catches sight of a rider out of the corner of his eye. With a sigh of relief he jumps on the ground and rubbing his stomach he says:

"I didn't spill anything. Are we off, then?"

Taking hold of the arm stretched out to him, he vaults

onto the horse, takes a tight hold of Alone, and turns back to look once more at his aul. He sees the dawn break out over it, and little does he know that he'll have to carry that dawn with him for a whole eight years.

After they pass the neighbouring aul and leave it far behind, Alone leads his horse down to a spring and says to Father:

"Now wash, freshen up and get ready to tell me everything as it happened."

When they get on the road again Father begins his tale, and at first the words stick in his throat, but Alone never once interrupts him, and only now and then nods to encourage him, or occasionally goes into detail:

"Illiteracy, you say? Well it seems a revolver is no price for that. You've all miscalculated there – the shopkeeper, you and your old man ... but most of all, as it turned out, your travelling companion."

"You're right," says Father, hanging his head.

"And he paid for it once and for all," continued Alone. "With you it's more complicated. But do go on!"

He listens, tilting his head slightly to one side, in his own fashion, squinting his shrewd eyes as if he saw another's past secret, which was still unknown to he who had experienced that past, who had barely survived it, who had fled through the rain and fog to hide from the truth of this past in the cleft among the stones, so as the next morning to wash its bitterness down with some bitter araka and leave it behind on a roundabout road to the mysterious unknown.

"What? A snake?" Alone pricks his ears. "Where did you get a snake in the rain?"

"It must have sensed the coming lightning in good time, snakes are smarter than people, you know. Or maybe I only imagined it... No. Hardly. I couldn't have. Why did our mare rear up then? That mare of ours – may her mare's soul flutter like a butterfly in the other world – though she wasn't especially sharp, nor was she the most stupid of their breed. She probably wouldn't have frozen like that just for anything, I say."

"Well, exactly," Alone doesn't argue. "By God, she was crippled with fear, and that's why she reared. Was she a timid horse, shy, yes? Or am I getting this wrong?"

"Not at all," says Father, surprised. "She's been scalded with fire from her youngest days. You were still a youngster when my younger brother – he was a good four years older than you were – set fire to a haystack in our field, so this mare and I have to scatter the hay to put out the fire, and then a burning clump falls off the top and catches her right in the mug. She took fright, of course. It's just, see, it may be bad and it may be the opposite. Maybe her fearfulness saved my life."

"Well, maybe," Alone replies. "You go on with your story. Don't get distracted."

But then he interrupts again: "No, better tell me about that snake again, all the rest is pretty obvious."

"What about it? It's a viper like any other, only just a bit longer. Or maybe it wasn't, maybe it was shorter... But what does it matter? As I say, I didn't manage to take a good look because just then it blew up! After that I wasn't up to any snakes ... Do you fancy a drop?"

"No."

"As you wish. I do though."

"No you don't."

"How d'you know?"

"Who's gonna know, but me? ... All right then, have a drink. You won't admit it anyway even if it tastes worse than worms. I know what I'm talking about."

"To hell with you. If you know anything don't discourage

others," Father declaims in anger, and then Alone hears the sound of heavy gurgling and smirks to himself. Afterwards Father continues:

"As I was saying, there was the lightning and then the cliff got split in two just like it had been sliced through with a knife.

"That's enough for now," Alone repeats. "Take a breather."

"I don't want to," Father sulks. "I want to go on telling you the rest."

"All right," says Alone. "I'm listening. What's with you now?"

"Maybe I don't want to," says Father drunkenly offended, and Alone hears how Father's suppressing a yawn. "You've spoiled everything."

"I'm sorry if I have," says Alone.

They stay silent, and Father suddenly realises that keeping quiet now comes far more easily to him than rolling around his stiff and tired tongue, but shutting his eyes to the light is still not possible: he has to keep gripping on to this slender back in front of him with the clump of grey hair sticking out from beneath the felt hat, or else he'll be jolted off. So he clings on with his dimming sight to this back and the grey lock in the black hair, and then his eyes seek out some rest on the sly, and he follows them to preserve their rest from his disobedient and wakening fingers, catching anxiety on that Circassian coat. Alone looks at the nervous, stubborn fingers, carefully pulls out his jacket from behind his back and ties Father's drooping body to his own. His eyes squint as before, and I can guess what he's thinking about, but I won't be in a hurry so as not to prevent you from working it out for yourself. And I won't tire you with the bumpy, rain-sodden road to the fort, nor the two halts

Comment by narrator to reader

for the night (it's now for seven nights in a row that Father had slept out under the changeable summer sky and, spreading out Alone's cloak on the grass, he said to himself: "Tomorrow they're sure to put you on a prison bunk. Tomorrow's the deadline mentioned in that paper..."), nor the reiteration of a few words and phrases that meant little ("At least our people are at home now." "Oh yes." "We don't bump into anyone." Or "When you return that dagger to my old man, say something like, well your son hasn't lost everything, say, he's not lost his honour." "All right." "Say that when he gets out of jail, he'll be wiser in future. Let the old man invent other ways to get rich quick. He'll strike some kind of a deal with Barysbi over that dagger won't he now? What difference does a week make one way or another?" or "Where did they decide to bury the Russian?" "In the main cemetery next to your family's graves." "That's good. That's the right thing to do." "What was he like?" "He wore these specs on his nose. He laughed a lot... He's not guilty either, is he? I mean he's even less to blame in all this than I am. And me, in what way am I guilty? Why is it that it falls to the least guilty to suffer God's punishment first? What can you say to that?" "I don't know. Maybe the really guilty ones are judged by people. I can't tell." "I don't get you." "Maybe, it's all about memory. I don't know. But probably, yes, memory."

The shopkeeper recognised him at once, but refrained from showing joy or surprise at his appearance: their faces and listless arms fenced off from his words with grief. First he was silent, then he opened his mouth to speak and started coughing until he turned red; he went into the back room, they heard his ladling out water, and when the shopkeeper had drunk his fill and returned, none of them raised their eyes, only he got hold of himself and from his breathing you could hear how he was egging on his belated fury in his voice, hoarse with cold:

"Where? ... How come? ... And how dare you, you blockhead... I could shoot you ... Well, just, you watch out!"

My father, feeling utterly embarrassed, placed his right hand on his heart, oppressed by that whisper full of spittle, bearing down on him in that hateful moment; he almost joyfully submitted himself to the shopkeeper's shrill screaming and retreated to one side. But Alone roughly grabs his sleeve and says:

"Just you wait," and Father understands from his eyes that his words aren't addressed to him, but to the shopkeeper ("He just caught me in his fist like a puppy. God's my witness, it made me breathe a bit more easily and I was thankful to him for it," Father told me.) "You can always go and get the police. See we've come to you to apologise. Give him back the revolver."

Father doesn't realise right away that the last sentence is addressed to him, he blushes as he fumbles in his coat, his fingers slide over the handle, and just as he's getting it out to hand it over, he clumsily and stupidly drops the weapon on the floor with such a crash that had he fired it there would have been less noise. The revolver rolls flatly on the floor along the smooth planks and freezes by Alone's feet like a mouse. Alone also puts his hand into his coat and produces another revolver (looking at the peeling paint and the sharp dent in the plump side of the barrel, Father understands that they found it: I'd totally forgotten, I was thinking about my own gun all the way, and about his, my travelling companion's, I'd completely forgotten. A piece of iron is just a piece of iron, after all – you can't eat it. It's not a human being... Just a piece of iron..." He repeats this to himself several times with insincere and frightened contempt.) Alone picks up the other gun off the floor and puts them both on the counter. Suddenly a quick nasty thought occurs to Father as he casts a sidelong look at the shopkeeper with the two crimson blotches on his cheeks and a droplet of water hanging off his chin, that now the shopkeeper was, if you like, worse off than anyone else. He's on his own, but there are two of us. Alone has already gone over to the door and locked it, fixing it with a bar; he returns and suggests in an even tone:

"You'd best invite us into your back room, at least we can have a seat there."

The shopkeeper drills him with a hurtful look, drills him for as long as he is able to overcome the burning in his bloodshot bulging eyes, and then he grabs a wet handkerchief from his trouser pocket and loudly sneezes with a sob, and once he's blown his nose, stuffs it back in his pocket, and turns his gaze to the counter and gathers up the pistols laid on it – Father's first and then the one sharply dented inwards, with the scratch on its barrel bearing witness to the death of its owner. He turns his back to them and goes off to the back room while Father and Alone look at each other and in their rush to follow him, nudge each other with their shoulders. On entering the room, the shopkeeper sits at the table and places one of the revolvers on it, but the other, the one Father got in exchange for his illiteracy five days previously, the other he examines and takes to pieces, laying its separate parts out on the tablecloth, and frowning firmly while both Father and Alone follow sullenly from beneath their brows as the shopkeeper tames his agitated fingers with this work. Once more he picks up the revolver, loads it, and cocks the trigger, and only now, resting his elbows on the table, points the pistol at each of their chests in turn and orders them to their seats.

They sit obediently and wait for him to lower the gun, but he, the Russian, only moves its empty, hungry eye from one to the other. In the silence, Father again slips up: he loudly swallows the lump in his throat and feels ashamed; he turns to the window watching the hens clucking in the neighbouring yard. They rake around in the lazy, warm dust and carefully, so as not to disturb the midday slumber, settle their rears on the small holes they have dug up. Father's throat now tickles madly but he doesn't dare to clear it just now.

"Very well then," says Alone, "if this makes it easier for you to handle..."

But the shopkeeper only squints and makes Alone look into the eye of the barrel. Father clears his throat and the gaping barrel immediately shifts to him and freezes, sticking its blackness into Father's profusely sweating forehead.

"He says you've got a certain sheet of paper." Alone's voice stabs at Father's heart. The shopkeeper's left arm gropes for the drawer and gets a written sheet out of it. They see Father's cross, and his efforts not to fall under the words muted into beads of Russian letters.

"We're prepared to exchange it," says Alone while the barrel seeks out his mouth and points straight to it, and Father notices in his terror that the finger on the trigger is white with tension right down to its nail. "Let's say for two revolvers, a silver dagger with its silver sheath, and a story..."

The shopkeeper doesn't respond and only suffers with his lips stretched into a narrow open wound, and almost forgets about his finger on the cocked trigger, the finger growing ever whiter with strain, and filling Father's eyes with the power of its whiteness.

"Maybe we can add something else as well," continues Alone, paying no attention to the gun and the finger. "Maybe we can add several years, a painting and a new paper."

The shopkeeper's face is now contorted as if his leg had just been crushed by a cartwheel, his wide open eyes reveal red veins on the whites, his teeth are tightly gritted, but then he tries to gulp in more air and lets out a wet, deafening sneeze.

"You misfired," says Alone quietly. "So we're in luck."

Only then does my father see that the finger has moved to the handle and the trigger has been released, and the last person to realise this is the shopkeeper – the white retreats from under his fingernails and after a few moments appears on his taut cheekbones; only then does he look down to study his palm and moves it away from his body as if it's been mired in filth, he pushes the gun away into the corner of the table in disgust. He breathes heavily and frequently blinks, his bewilderment is obvious so that my father thinks: we've driven him into a corner, he can't forgive himself that he didn't call out the police. But now Alone speaks:

"So far so good. Maybe we can start with the story? If you don't mind I'll begin..."

After a slight hesitation (my father breathes out all the tightness in his chest with relief, the shopkeeper sniffs, clasps his hands and nervously shifts them to his knees, the table, his belly, back to the table, but Alone does nothing, just straightens his angular shoulders and, casting a sidelong look at my father, resembles for an instant that which he has never really been, or at least hasn't been for those who had known him at all closely, including himself, by the way: for a tiny grain of an instant he resembles a sixteen-year-old youth with fluff on his cheeks and a thin swarthy neck, and Father barely has time to think that he's completely forgotten his name when...) Alone plunges into his story that was not his story at all but, Father said, was mine and the shopkeeper's, and that of the three deaths, but may my tongue fall off, swore Father, if I could ever have told that story so well. You see, Father told me, it was like I was seeing myself from the outside, from the side and from above. I saw again those two days, the rain, the snake, and only now did I get a good look at it as I should have done then, and the lightning, and the rocks raining down. I saw my mouth unstitched in terror, and the mare carried off by the rockslide, and the old man tired of his life, and the cave and the night, and the fog, and the hunger, and the ledge in the cliff; I saw with sober eyes the drunk and doleful road, and the wineskin empty by the morning. And for the first time I saw clearly and completely just how guiltless I was, but saw at the same time how much less guilty than me was the shopkeeper's assistant and my unfortunate old man, and again it dawned on me that when the heavens are guilty, on earth that guilt is assumed by the least guilty, so that when they die they can return this guilt to heaven as their immortal souls; that's why the guiltless who are still alive cease to be entirely guiltless, because the heavens, enraged by this returned guilt, poison the air breathed by the living with yet more guilt, and maybe it can't be any other way. I saw so much that at first I didn't see the tears in my own eyes, and I no longer saw the shopkeeper clearly though he was sitting right opposite me dissolving into a spot before my eyes. By the time I realised this Alone had already finished his story. I brushed the tears from my eyes with my fist while the shopkeeper's head fell to the table, his back was shaking, and then his whole body broke into convulsions. I thought he was crying, but I was wrong because we heard his laughter – it turned out he was shaking with laughter, and I thought: laughter can be bitterer than any tears. It was strange and even frightening.

So said my father, remembering all this.

Alone grew pale from this laughter, he got up and went to find the water pail in the corner, lifted the lid, scooped some water with a ladle and brought it over to the shopkeeper, who drank it up, diluting his woeful laughter in it, and Alone said:

"Give us back the paper. Give it back and you'll feel better."

The man shook his head, choked, and almost burst out into laughter again, but he restrained his quivering and said:

"You think I'm going to cry over him? I couldn't care less for him! I spit on that four-eyed pig! Maybe I'm even glad that it's turned out like this! How do you know what I'm feeling deep down? Maybe my heart is happy now. So happy, that I don't care about the damages! And I spit on you. I couldn't care less about you two. So much so that I'll give this paper right back to you for nothing! Aha! Guess what? I can. You don't believe me? What are you gawping at? You don't bee-lie-ve me! Since you don't believe me then I won't give it back to you. You're right – what need have I to do that? I'd best hand it over to the police and say that this boy, I'll say, tried to bribe me – so that they'll cart the two of you to jail straight away, or even better, straight off to the camps, to Siberia! D'you hear that, you oafs? In Siberia the snow comes right up to your knees! And who said that he was any friend of mine? I spit on friendship – yes I spit on that as well! I don't believe in anything called friendship. I don't want friendship! It's not my fault that he went and got married! Here's me that's waited till my hair's grown grey and my brains have grown empty, and I'm still not married. But he got hot pants... Now you make me laugh! Have you decided that this bit of paper is important? Who needs it anyway? A thousand papers wouldn't stop me from sending him away! If I didn't need to cover over my cheating, like my privy parts, with this bit of paper! And look at you now, you've got this idea of how important you are, but you're really just shits. Little shits..."

Here Alone leaps to his feet and throws what's left of the water into the shopkeeper's face, grabs him by his front and hisses at him. And my father, who hadn't really grasped what the shopkeeper had been swearing about, sees how in a flash Alone puts his dagger to the shopkeeper's throat. Father reaches out to him, saying something and pulling Alone away from the archly grinning wet shopkeeper when suddenly there's a knocking at the door from outside, and they all freeze and listen. The knocking starts up again, pauses for a while and starts up in earnest, so the shopkeeper quietly says, careful not to move his dripping head:

"She won't go away. She's probably noticed us from her yard."

"She? Who is she?" Alone asks.

"His wife," replies the shopkeeper, and Alone, considering all this for a bit, resheathes his dagger and says:

"Open up."

"Just not in front of her..." pleads the shopkeeper, shaking the water off his shirt. His chin is shaking, and his arms are feeling around his body. "She... I ought to prepare her... I'll tell her myself ... later ... well?"

"All right," says Alone. "We'll continue afterwards."

"Of course, yes! Of course, afterwards," the shopkeeper babbles in a sickeningly, somehow, ugly manner as he wipes his head with the towel he rips off the hook; Father is amazed to see fear which hasn't been in the Russian before, even when the dagger was thrust right at his throat – no fear even then, and that knock was enough for him to start fawning. What was all this?

Now he sees the loose pale blue blouse with open sleeves and the unbuttoned collar opening onto the hot, free breasts submitting to her every step. The woman approaches them with a sure pace, her strong legs shod in men's boots covered with a crust of caked mud, and a yellow straw is stuck to her skirt. Her eyes are large and blue, so blue that Father admits to himself he has never known what real blueness is up until then.

"Good day to you," she says in greeting, not embarrassed in the slightest in front of the strangers, and they both mutter something indistinguishable in reply. "Do they understand Russian?" asks the woman of the shopkeeper as he fusses about her, guarding her shoulders with his hands, as if he doesn't dare to touch her, and he quickly jabbers back at her:

"Yes... they understand... They're just a bit embarrassed ... Don't pay any attention to them! I mean, no, sorry, quite the reverse! Allow me to introduce my friends to you ... this is ... Damn, I've quite forgotten... And this one over here is ... errrrr... We're in no rush for all that, it can wait... so you... ah-tchoooo! ... This bloody cold... but I wasn't expecting you, that's why I thought I could have a bit of spring cleaning here as it were, that's why I shut the door. And you could have, you know, just tapped on the window, and we here would have ... well it's worked out awkwardly..."

"Is it awkward that I'm here?" asks the woman, raising her brows.

"What do you mean? Not at all! Be my guest, as they say. I mean, it's always a pleasure, so please ... yes, do come in, come in," pours forth the shopkeeper.

"How much further can I come in? Up the wall, you mean?"

"Oh no, ha ha, why up the wall, you don't want to do that. You stay where you are. It works very well. It's fine when you stand there like that... Don't pay them any attention – they're savages, the local aborigines, they don't understand a thing."

"But didn't you just say that..." her eyebrows rise up her high smooth forehead.

"Oh yes, well, my little joke! I wanted to have a laugh. Well the devil knows what they do or don't understand ... maybe not a jot, and maybe they're just being cunning. In short, with them you'd best keep a sharp look out and be on guard. So what do you want? Why are you here?"

"Me?" she cuts in raspingly, and turns away from him looking both strangers up and down, and for the second time today Father recognises a youngster in Alone, and here again meets the blue full on, drowns in it and quietly, selflessly celebrates this eternal blue minute of her audacity. He ponders dimly and dreamily that he's never seen a bolder look than that of a woman belonging to two men at once (of course, that was already in the past, but she doesn't know yet, and so as it is, she still belongs to both of them, even though one of them had two days before been swallowed up by the gorge, and as for the second, well, not even his own tongue belongs to him now) he'd never seen a look like that in anyone before, nor had he seen such pride in anyone before; only what was she so proud about? Surely not her sins? "Well, I don't remember now why I came. You will excuse me that I omitted to announce my arrival at your door. I've learned my lesson for the future. Good day to you," she nods to him, and an angry blush flashes across her cheeks. "Goodbye to you too, native sirs."

"Hee hee, no offence meant. Why grumble? Don't be silly. We're all neighbours here and one big family, no need to cock your nose at it! Aren't you ashamed in front of these strangers? Though they're locals they can also spread gossip... Wait now ... however, no, go ... all right... afterwards ... we'll sort this out afterwards," the shopkeeper jibbers as he shows her to the door, and when he slams the door and clicks the bolt, for a time not a sound is heard, and Father's face is wreathed with anxiety. He looks over at Alone, who transforms from a puny teenager back into his own self again, frowning angrily. They hear a weak, whispering groan and the shuffling of now aged legs.

"Do you want some tea?" asks the shopkeeper, staying in the passage.

They again sit back down at the table and drink hot sweet tea out of transparent glasses, and the shopkeeper says:

"So, well, yes... how shall I put it... Never mind. I blew my top. Please don't be angry. And take the paper if that makes things easier for you. I'm not going anywhere with it."

The revolvers have already been put away in the drawer and apart from the brass samovar and the tea glasses on the table there now lies only the sheet of paper, dotted with little specks, certified at the base by a shaky and clumsy cross. Father gets out the twenty-pound silver dagger and puts it down alongside the sheet of paper:

"Will this do?"

The shopkeeper turns over the dagger in his hands, tutting his tongue, carefully unsheathing the blade from its cover and catching on it a glint of light.

"It's beautiful! Dagestani?"

"Oh yes. Practically new," Father nods.

"Where will you find a new assistant now?" Alone butts in.

"I don't know" replies the shopkeeper and grows gloomy.

"You can't manage without someone to help you. And if you think about it, you've already wasted a week on it."

"How do you mean?" asks the shopkeeper.

"Well, you haven't searched for a new assistant yet. But maybe you don't need to look any further."

They both turn their heads to my father, and he, embarrassed at the suddenness of it all, turns crimson, looks at his golden reflection in the samovar and wags his head.

"What's the point if he doesn't agree?" shrugs the shopkeeper.

"Offer it to him," says Alone.

"What for?" he shoots back. "What good is this unlucky bastard to me? He'll be the ruin of me."

"But with her you're sure to lose your head," Alone fires back, and the room suddenly grows quiet and close. The shopkeeper leans back on his chair and drums his fingers on the table. Father doesn't look up and thinks that surely something will happen now. But the shopkeeper stays quiet and drums and drums and stays quiet, and then gets up, goes to the cupboard with the glass doors, and gets out a bottle and three glasses. Filling them, he knocks his back in one go, and takes a sniff into his shirtsleeve, and then drains the rest of his tea.

"There aren't any snacks with it," he grins. "What are you waiting for?"

"We have our own," says Father and takes the satchel off his shoulder.

"Are you such weaklings that you can't take it straight?" He asks, blinking his inflamed eyes and sneezing into the handkerchief he'd grasped quickly out of his pocket.

After another half an hour Alone unbolts the door and opens the windows, and Father sees the warm evening roll into the widow's yard, and thinks of the woman, who knew two men, and her shameless blue eyes, and her silken loose breasts as she walked and her proud brow, as smooth as this brass samovar.

The shopkeeper stuffs his pipe tight with tobacco and continues his stale confession that's a few days late in coming:

"At that point your friend comes in," he tells Alone, who has topped up their glasses but has stayed more sober than any of them and only once every so often raises the vodka to his lips. "They'd already been married for three months. I'd not been myself all these three months, and it's like I'm breathing fire in my sleep... Well, I think, it looks like fate's lending me a hand. You only know once you've tried it. I listen to your kinsman and a cold blister grows under my heart. He speaks, I reply, I speak, he nods and hurries to show me he's got it, and I listen or chat with him so as not to talk to myself and not hear the voice of my conscience. I was almost ready, had almost made my mind up, so I asked about the revolver just to pretend proper interest, and it worked admirably and neatly. We could even say we struck a bargain... And suddenly, a slight hitch happened with that revolver, and the slight hitch turned into a hesitation, which turned, as it happens, into a snag, the snag turned into a splinter and lodged itself in my brain: I put it down to fate to find its own solution, it'll be easier for fate as it won't have to betray a friendship; but fate has grown stubborn. I see that there's no exit, and I've broken out all in a sweat, so much do I want to prompt it... But I'm ashamed! Ashamed, gentlemen! However, there's a time and a place for shame... and for nights, dry and fiery, also. Now you both probably think that it must be hard betraying this twelve-year friendship (not just any old acquaintance but a true, genuine friendship that's gone through real hard times and that I wouldn't swap for all the money in the world.) I'd like to confess something and you must believe me... But then whether you do or don't is your business... But hear me out and remember what I say, on that I insist! There is no-o-thing easier than betraying a friendship and hating it for it. Admitting it to yourself is more difficult. I probably betrayed it a long time ago, from the very day I first saw her blue eyes... but admit it, that I've only done today. Even when those eyes shone to me at night I still had no desire to bury my old friendship in them. It shames me to the core to admit it, but I even cherished the hope that that friendship would become deeper on account of my sin: repenting and loving, sinning and repenting, through such torments you penetrate the secrets of the human soul! In short, I cherished my hope and also my baseness, I thought there was still time, we'd see. The cart went off fully loaded, it'll take him a long time to sell out everything and return... maybe a month would pass, and in that month all sorts of unexpected things might happen...

Only one thing gnawed me: that she gave herself to me of her own free will (I'll let you in on a secret, I didn't have to go to her myself, come evening I heard a knock at the door, and all I had to do was to unbolt it), and she, well, cried a bit, as is their custom. It happened as I'd imagined it in my dreams, but in fact it worked out differently... Her eyes let me down, they ruined my joy down to the core. After that they didn't change at all, as if it was all the same for her to look at me or at some ant... Even more offensive is that for her eyes it's all the same whether I'm standing before them or her lawful husband. That was the thing! Give me another drink, don't be afraid; it's just a shame that you can't cleanse your insides with vodka, so as to wake up tomorrow with a hangover and wipe off all the scum from your heart with another drink. It's only good for me now to treat my cold... What was I saying? Eh? ... No, not that, don't distract me... yes, the eyes, I remember, the eyes were truly... Only they didn't let me into their blue, and do you know, native gentlemen – pardon, I sound stupid... but I'm blind drunk, so don't take me too much to task, my shaggy brothers – they never really let anyone into their blue and never will! That I can tell you for certain...

Only... tsss... she's not able to love... and she'll never learn either, even if she tries her hardest... yes hmm... the heart is a clever machine, a most clever little ticker... it's not your old hardware. What, you're getting bored? What do you mean I shouldn't bother? Who else am I to talk to so openly, if not to you? You're like brothers to me now, brothers through murder. And there's no need to look at me like that. By god, I mean nothing ill, though you've made me angry. You people don't have enough tact or education. How can you interrupt a man who bares his very soul before you? You'll listen all the same as I haven't reached the most curious part yet. It's about to come right now, I'm getting there, if you please: she infected me! No, I don't mean that way, not in the nasty, dirty sense... I could see a doctor or a pharmacist then. That'd be easy. This is a different kind of infection, stronger and more noble... a ruinous infection... I see you're curious now. Well, I see it from your faces – don't deny it. Well, fine. Maybe out of curiosity you'll strain to some compassion. Though it's not compassion that I need. It is believed that compassion and pity demean, though it's never said why, what's to be done if suddenly one day, let's say in a filthy, boorish piss-up a weak mortal suddenly simply wants to demean himself... Don't be embarrassed, my Mohicans, by my tiresome logic. Although how are you to know what sort of a beast that is? But about the infection I'll explain, with no complications, on my fingers, as they say, to be completely clear: the more I am certain that she doesn't love me... that she'd never love me, I should have said (despite her reassurances that she does, and maybe even quite sincere) the more I go out of my mind. This kind of infection is called passion in books. This kind of book I read to myself in my heart and, frankly, the reading inflames me in a vile way, and this novel disgusts me. I'm so disgusted with myself that it makes me morally puke... And here you are with your lightning! You know, when fate puts its signature under your shame like this treacherous zigzag it all becomes all the more unbearably vile. Like I was looking for an excuse and received a spit in the face. Ye-e-ess... a fat wad of spit from the mouth of a dead man, whom all three of us: myself, fate and this unlucky Mohican sent to his death. In truth, I sent him for his cuckoldry, the Mohican begged him to go for common profit, and fate had a laugh and brought together the shame, the profit and the cuckoldry. Vile... disgusting, loathsome and vile. But despite this filth and vileness, despite my self-loathing and that the dead man will always snuggle between me and her now, it won't change anything! I can't, though I'm disgusted with her as well, maybe more than with anything else. That's passion, if you will! Let's take another drop! And you, young man, why aren't you drinking? Well, yes, of course, for you it's still a bit early, although you have a talent that's simply remarkable for your years. An unmistakable talent, you might say... A gift! A spark from God! By the way, did you notice that your painting got burnt down? Yes, sir! Then he whitewashed the stain on the wall, the deceased painted it over with a brush himself. I feel so sick at heart, brothers! Why is it that vodka makes you feel so good at first, but then unpleasant and then simply horrible? And who would want to do that, go and brazenly burn such a talented painting? There are so many nasty mysteries and misfortunes around..."

"Well maybe that was also down to passion?" asks Alone, and the other two shudder from the sudden interruption of the shopkeeper's outpouring, and Father turns his eyes that had adjusted to the sweaty forehead of the storyteller towards the voice.

"Passion, hmmm, you mean passion for destruction? Could be..." the shopkeeper tuts. "It can be a small distance from love to hate... In fact that exact same thought occurred to me now – see, I feel that in the end I'm going to kill her... first, the hate; second, the passion; and third, the dead man between us: that is, eternal memory and fear. Besides, there's an end to everything. Love must also have its limits. And what then? Nothing, it seems. Murder! That's what I fear most of all. And d'you know why? I myself, right now, as I said it, guessed all of a sudden just why... Because she won't understand why I'm taking her life! She won't understand this simplest, ever so naive mystery! How can I kill her when I know she won't understand why? How will I forget that last blueness of her eyes? That's the rub! Ha-ha-ha! The circle has closed in. We know why we sent away our friend, although on the surface it all worked out like it wasn't us but fate that hurled those rocks at him. With her things won't work out so well! No. Fate won't come to our aid a second time... Isn't that so?"

"Stop it. You're not killing anyone. Why then did you misfire earlier? If that fate of yours wanted to do its bit, you wouldn't have misfired today," says Alone, folding his arms on his chest. "But if you need to be assured, we'll help you. He'll help you," and he gestures with his chin towards my father.

The shopkeeper frowns, bends his head askance and examines my father as if he'd not seen him properly till now. He hems and haws from time to time but they don't see what he's trying to say. Finally he says:

"I get it now. You're a clever chap. As you put it, I'm scared of killing her, and he's afraid of being the death of his old man. You seem to be saying that he won't scramble free of his memories if he goes back home. That's good, that's well said. And so it'll work out that we'll lean on one another to guard our secret. That's clever. Only then we should change something." He takes the piece of paper and carries it off, almost with sure feet, to the safe in the corner of the room. "Let's hide your secret here. Now let's close it and show where we'll put the key..."

"No need," says Alone. "He's already understood. Tell him."

Father says: "How can I not understand? If I open my mouth when I shouldn't, I'll blurt it out."

"There you see," says Alone. "You've got a good assistant over here. Just that..." he searches for the right word.

"Aha," the shopkeeper calls out and puts his hand on the dagger of pure silver. "You mean this? I agree. Take it back. The old man will need some evidence, right?"

Alone nods and takes the dagger, and without looking at it stuffs it into his coat.

"So it's all settled then," he says. "His wages you can decide yourself. That's not his main concern. What matters to him is that he can outwait it here."

"Outwork it here," the shopkeeper corrects him. "And be a capable assistant. At the same time he'll pick up some Russian here."

"Just don't you go making a drunkard out of him," Alone smiles at the shopkeeper, and a lump forms in Father's throat – for a moment he forgets why nobody likes Alone. "He's been soaking for a full three days now."

"Longer," says Father to stifle the frog in his throat. "If you count the rain."

"Stay well," says Alone. "If you don't mind you can see me out?"

Father gets up and follows him to the door. Outside, Alone turns back to him and says:

"If you change your mind, you know the way back. If

you can't stand it here you'll leave on foot. Only, you won't change your mind soon."

Father nods and notices with some irritation how limply his clumsy arms are hanging.

"Don't get those blue eyes into your head. Your work's simple: mind the shop and let your time here heal you. It won't be harder than ours in the aul... It's all to your master's benefit as well; count on our people hurrying over here just to see you behind the counter, and buy some loose nail since they're here... Well, so long!"

"Aye," mumbles Father, unable to unstick his blocked throat. "Ah-ha..."

He waves his hand in the hope that Alone will look back at him before he disappears from view. But Alone only digs his heels into his horse's flanks. Left standing in the narrow town alley, Father feels the surrounding emptiness with his skin and knows that it will soon be filled with a heavy painful sadness which will dull with time and settle upon him as a patient, lazy burden to be endured.

As he wends his way back to the house, a thick, dark blueness follows him with curiosity from behind the neighbouring whitewashed fence. Meeting her gaze he gets hold of himself and lowers his head, but still manages to stumble on the even ground, and, hearing her raucous laughter, grown daring with sin, repeats some cruel, righteous words:

"I will learn to hate her. I will command myself to hate the colour of her eyes. This woman knew two men at the same time. She is no woman. I already hate her. And when I rest and awake I'll hate her even more..."

He crosses the threshold into the silence, transparent in the gathering shadows. The silence is disturbed only by an insistent, tormented snoring, and for the first time that day, in spite of the smell of spirits hanging in the air, his alcohol-dulled nostrils catch the sharp fermentation of foreign smells. He bolts the door and stands there breathing, and then, leaning his back against the door, he sits on his haunches and watches the thin darkness sharpen the gleam of the goods on the shelves. He listens to the wind tirelessly tousling the curtains on the open window and taps at the glass in the window frames. The darkness thickens and the gleam grows sharper until it becomes so sharp that it dazzles Father's eyes. Father lowers his eyelids and dreams of the terrible blue sky over his abandoned aul, but then he remembers that he has abandoned it so as to heal himself with borrowed time. He is not woken by the furtive suppressed shriek from the back room, nor the tired swearing and the tinkling of glasses, nor the hot and heady smell of tobacco smoke percolating through the cold smells. When the shopkeeper throws a sheepskin over him, Father dreams that it's the smoke that is warming him.

That night she doesn't come. And in the morning she'll find out that she's a widow.

"You see," the shopkeeper says to Father, "it'll be enough for her to see you fussing about behind the counter. It'll dawn on her and no words will be needed... The first words are always the worst... Somehow or other, he was a good friend to me. So then you, my friend, go and grab a bite to eat, everything's there on the table, while you were sleeping I went to the butcher. Then you get behind the counter and when a customer comes in, you tap lightly on the wall and I'll deal with him myself."

Father told me it wasn't just that she was unable to love but she couldn't cry either. A fallen woman. Fallen in every way. Instead of tears and laments there was only whining. And I thought: she's worthless. I gnashed my teeth so much I despised her. Only she wasn't ashamed of anyone or anything. She was sick for three days and then she put on black and came over:

"Could you take me to his grave?"

The shopkeeper replied: "Yes, yes, of course."

But I said: "I cannot. It's too soon for me to go back there."

So he says, "Yes, yes, of course. We'll go just the two of us together. You and I."

"Fine," she nods. "Tomorrow?"

"Whatever suits you best," he replies. "Tomorrow's fine. Tomorrow's the best day for it, actually."

"What about the store?" I ask.

"Never mind. Take a rest for four days. And make yourself at home."

"Why's he refusing to join us?" she asks.

"Because..." starts the shopkeeper, "because... by the way, why can't you join us, as a matter of fact? I'd swear to your old man that you serve as my assistant..."

"No," I shook my head. "To forgive, he needs to get used to it."

"Get used to what?"

"To the fact I've run away. See I ran away first and only later was employed as your assistant."

"Very well, you know best..."

They were gone for a whole week, Father told me. And when they returned at night, the shopkeeper had been drinking heavily and confessed:

"You know I didn't even see your old man in the end. I didn't see the grave either. And that cliff I didn't see an' all. As soon as we got out of town she started shaking. No, she says, I can't. Shall we turn back, I ask. Yes, she says, I beg you, don't be angry. See I haven't recovered from the shock yet. All right, I says. We'll go for the forty days' prayer for the dead. Yes, yes exactly, she replies. But when we'd reached the fork in the road she says, stop here. And she presses herself to me and whispers: there's no turning back now, people will start talking! Probably, I think. Then, she says, let's go off to Pyatigorsk together! They say it's the height of the season now. Or aren't we both sinners? Or don't you love me anymore? After all the suffering we've been through, we need to forget. What a bitch, I thinks. The lustful bitch! However, I don't quarrel with her out loud, I turn round again obediently, and in my heart I'm choking with joy! What a bastard I am, I thinks. My heart is delighted in fact. What can you do, I asks myself, what can you do if it's so easy to be a rascal, so simple and joyful? Forgive me, you must be disgusted with all this..."

All through that night, Father told me, I thought about how one day I won't be able to guard her and I won't hear him suffocating her, then I'll leave this place and forget their secret. And, the gods be my witnesses, I hated her so much that the shopkeeper was almost jealous of me, thinking that I might do away with her myself. One time he couldn't hold back and asked me:

"Have you reached your limit, too? Fancy that!"

Only don't ask me what I replied to him. I kept quiet and pretended that I hadn't understood a thing – my Russian was still poor, but all the same he didn't believe me.

"So you loved her?" I asked my father at this point.

"I hated her," he replied.

"But all the same – you loved her?"

He looked angrily at me and said:

"She was a fallen woman."

I didn't say anything but thought to myself: whatever's the case, he didn't kill her, even if he was madly in love with her. He didn't get the chance.

Because a month or two later the leaves began to turn yellow at the edges, thunderstorms gave way to passing morning chills, trade in roofing iron and rivets became more brisk and requests for joinery and carpentry equipment had slightly subsided. Father's tight teeth had slowly adapted to the expansive alien tongue, so that at times they almost didn't notice one another and he spoke and replied almost freely, as if his throat were smarter than his brains: he could hardly think up what to say when his mouth already coped with the customer; fifteen or so fellow villagers came up from the aul, some even came twice, but all of them looked at my father as if they'd never set eyes on him before, as if they'd known someone similar to him but couldn't quite place him, and, said Father, to look at their faces you could in no way say that they found this meeting pleasant at all. He was alert and hard-working during the day but in the evenings he'd sit on the porch and smoke, seriously and with concentration would he smoke his hand-carved pipe with a rough tin handle, botched from a broken latch, and he listened to his sluggish, incomprehensible heart, detached, and grown alien unto himself, pondering something he had never confessed to me; having smoked and pondered his fill, he went off to his bed in the adobe annex. With every day sleep was harder to come: the nights were longer and darker, and waking up after these nights, swollen into full incomprehensibility, was at once uncomfortable and good; but of course, he hardly ever talked with her, and his silence made his hatred towards her more furious and thirsty; but one day she did speak to him:

"And now you take me to the forty day's wake. I can't turn away from my fate with you."

"We'll go as a three," he replied.

"No," she said. "Just us two. Just you and me!"

Father shook his head: "Two is not enough for you, is it? Do you always need two no less?"

He glanced over to her: the blue had thickened in her wrath so that she couldn't stand it herself and her voice quivered:

"A milksop like you won't cope with even one..."

She gained her revenge by not letting either one of them go to the forty day's wake: towards night she fell into a fit, and they sent for the doctor who prescribed her some complex mixture, looking quite concerned, and come morning the shopkeeper persuaded Father to stay:

"If she dies in my arms I'll lose my mind... God willing we'll go on the anniversary. As my assistant you should obey me no matter what. In short, I beg of you to stay here!"

My father, understandably, stayed back there, he couldn't impose his hate on the love of another – even for a few days; and instead of the journey he occupied himself with taking precautionary measures, which didn't cost him anything, since the goods stayed with the master while being put to good use – he put a lock on the door of his adobe annex and locked it from the inside for the night, secretly guarding his hatred. At first he would hide the key under his pillow, only that must have irritated him and bore into his mind since he decided one day not to take it out of its lock, he probably hoped that he would one day forget to return it there, only I didn't ask him anything of the sort, but I suspect that he forgot about the lock more than once, if, of course, he's my own father and I'm his own son. Overall, everything passed peacefully for them, and no one wanted to give up anything, now even she didn't want to give up, so Father's ruse with the lock and caging himself up turned out to be a mindless and pitiful enterprise in the end, beyond which I only see the gaunt, despondent back of hope abandoning him; after that conversation, she wouldn't have come over to him for anything: she took pride in her sin and could not risk it nor debase herself before anyone – a fallen woman can't fall on her knees for fear of being trampled without mercy; so it turned out that for a good three weeks Father fussed with the lock and worried his soul for nothing. Meanwhile, the shopkeeper had almost given up his drinking, and as it were with every passing day grew more frighteningly and irreversibly sober, while she, as Father put it, was obviously asking for trouble: she would come into the shop, ask for a stool and sit at the counter with the shopkeeper carrying on some trivial conversation but all the while staring at me so that I got sticky between the blades, and he would look at her, his sober eyes riveted to her, seeing right through her; he watched her with curiosity and exultation as if he couldn't have enough of a good look at her, and I felt repelled by this leprous love of theirs, repelled enough to spit on them. That's exactly what he told us then: he was repelled and sickened; that's how Father put it, and I pretended to believe him that except for disgust and hatred nothing else tormented him at nights; what troubled him was a lot else besides, such as the dead man that bound them all so tightly with his unseen and constant presence, the short-sighted, conscientious observer of their sins or sinful thoughts – I think my father realised that they were all the same for the dead man, or else you couldn't really call him a dead man, could you? He was the sole and feared judge, whom both of them remembered by face, or by the smell that had gone unnoticed before, but now infiltrated the nocturnal whizzing of their shared time; and maybe my father's lock was yet another sign of fear, or proof of his submissiveness that Father wished to believe in, or simply a premonition of impending doom; and the woman dealt with all of this best of all; my father observed from the side how utterly beyond her was an ability to love, he wondered at her fatal, self-destructive but nonetheless vain desire to overcome her own nature and her fervent wish to learn how to live in a tormenting, anxious, irreversible enjoyment of sin, albeit for an instant; and so she was also proud in her constant defeats, Father repeated to me, while her sin was in no way disparaged, on the contrary, said Father; she was a fallen woman, he would repeat almost too often, I hated her, remember that! A couple of months later, Alone visited the shopkeeper's again...

I sensed something was wrong, Father told me, only at first I didn't attach much importance to it and decided that he was just tired from the journey; he embraced me and said all the proper words, and then we both went inside, and the shopkeeper also cheered up, and even fussed about for some reason; taken by surprise, he was spilling out words unripened by thought, but Alone forced himself into a smile as he rubbed his brow, lined with black dust that settled in his wrinkles. After he had washed, he recounted to us the village news, which was not like him at all, as if it wasn't him doing so but one of our villagers, that is, he told us news that he would never have deemed newsworthy before, as he simply would never have remembered it. What was the use for Alone to remember about someone or other's lamed mare or lost ewe? Maybe he did remember such trifles, but recollect and recount them – that wasn't like him at all. And, you know, said Father, although at the time I didn't understand what was going on, anxiety lay on my heart, a weak inflexible anxiety. Then we all, as was the done thing, sat down at the table for a meal and drinks. Or rather, Alone was drinking while the shopkeeper and I only sipped our vodka, and I thought what the devil was all that: I, truth to tell, have never once sat down with him to celebrate in all the years we've been neighbours. On that day, I must confess, I would have preferred to stay with them a while longer, but I couldn't, work was waiting for me, so I said:

"You'll have to carry on without me. Someone's already at the door."

"All right," said the shopkeeper. "Go. Hold on out there till evening and then we'll make it up to you."

But Alone got up and said: "Wait a bit. I want you to see it too."

He picked up the bundle from his lap, while the shopkeeper licked his lips with his dry tongue, he knew what this bundle was for he'd seen one like that before. Alone unrolled it before his chest and we saw an inflamed crevasse in the cliff, a slimy, dirty rain, an enormous gaping mouth of a horse as big as half the cliff, and the terrifying, hateful, deep blue eyes, piercing the watery sky. At first we looked only at this insane, familiar blue, then the sharp blackness unfolded through it, and then from those eyes our gaze scanned over the rest of the canvas.

I was the first to ask a question:

"What's this hook? This stripe beneath the fire?"

"A snake," replied Alone. "You told me about it yourself." I shrugged.

"What's wrong?" he asked.

"Well, your earlier style was smoother."

He smirked and said: "That's not a napkin for you. It's not for wiping lips with."

"You don't mean to hang this butchery up for all to see?"

"Well, that we'll have to ask the owner."

The shopkeeper at last came to and quickly, fussily shook his head.

"Spare me that, please. No, not on the wall, obviously, you can't hang it on the wall... Amazing that you have all this in you... all this, so much... well, you know, I'm astonished!

You only saw her once, and there you go, you've captured it right there. It makes my flesh creep... Uh-huh. But, of course, it's too strong stuff to hang on the wall. That's a bit too much, my lad. Your painting is a bit bizarre... It gives me the creeps. And why would I want to give my customers the creeps, eh? They'd look at it and after that you wouldn't be able to lure them in here for any bargains. So don't be angry with me..."

"Do you want me to take it away?" Alone broke in and was on the point of folding it up.

"No, no! Not so soon. Why take it away? Don't be silly. What did you paint it for and take it over the hills and far away? You meant it as a gift, right? Or else I'm missing something here! A gift is a sacred thing and one must never refuse a gift. I know it's a deadly insult and such like. However, if it wasn't meant as a gift, then I'll even buy it from you! Although the painting has its eccentricities, its blots and smudges – see! Look there! How can you say that's not a smudge! That's a smudge, and I dare say, an excellent, world-class smudge! An intentional, utterly lifelike, piercingly brilliant smudge! To tell you god's honest truth, I like it better than that other one, your first one. Well, not like exactly... In fact, yes, I do like it! It would be good to show it to her too! What do you think? Now that's a great idea! It's a brilliant idea. You're right, you're a born artist come from the blue. Let's roll it up now, and in the evening we'll light three candles and show it to her! I'll get a kick from watching her shock! Now that'll be a sight!"

"The customers are waiting," I say. I do hate that woman. And I hate the picture too, and I know that I hate it for its vile merciless truth adorned with bright, oily brushstrokes. I hate this man who has given me shelter, and his vengeful cowardice, ready to spy on his own meanness, waiting for it to be reflected as horror in her bottomless blue.

I hurry to get out of there, so as not to abhor the boy who for two months had been closer to me than my own brother and my old father, who had remained an outcast on the same land as them and because of this could learn this land so well that he had taught himself to recreate it from another's recollections with his own hands. I leave so as to open the front door and stand at the counter. From time to time words reach me from the back room, splashes broken off from the stream of murmuring, but I can't make out what secrets they are discussing there in their muffled voices. Nor do I want to eavesdrop. But occasionally the shopkeeper breaks out into a shout, and against my will I have to listen:

"Never! Even for a scoundrel like me, it's too much! Don't you try to talk me into it..."

A little later I heard him cry out: "What a bastard! Bastard of all bastards! Let him rot! He'll finish him off and it'll serve him right!"

They drone on for a long while, verbally sparring with one another and then I hear a loud spit, and the shopkeeper clearly pronounces:

"That's cute! And a year later – there you are! The mistake came to light. I didn't take a good look in the warehouse! That's cute! But all the same I can't agree to it."

The voices again merge in their heated half-whispering; when I open the door of the back room again the two of them look like they've choked on peppers: mouths open, no good for anything apart from rough breathing and lisping wheezes. I think to myself: well, well, turns out the two of you are thick as thieves, and our artist here is after something more serious than my friendship.

Afterwards, that same evening, the conversation is sticky as if the three of us are stamping barefoot on the ice. The painting is there unrolled, blank side up. The woman isn't there. Alone convinced the shopkeeper to hold off showing it to her, and now he's berating himself drunkenly for having agreed.

"My malice is bursting out," the shopkeeper complains now and again with a bitter sneer. Each time Alone retorts with the same words:

"Don't let it out."

The shopkeeper, bulging his eyes, squeezes his gullet, and they break into a strained laughter, casting cautious looks at me. We agree that Alone will stay the night in my annex, and I will sleep here, in the shop, on the long wooden bench. Out of courtesy, Alone tries to argue, but quickly accedes to my exhortations. By now the shopkeeper is three sheets to the wind, and our guest carefully watches that he doesn't blurt anything out. Then the shopkeeper sets off to bed, and between us hangs a damp silence. The shopkeeper returns for the painting; so as no one nicks it, he says, wagging a wise, unbending finger. Alone laughs nervously, and in the dim candlelight he seems to blush. The shopkeeper retires to his room, and we stay silent, cursing the never-ending evening, listening to the thick, cumbersome flow of time in the dusk.

"See now I," says Alone, "didn't just come here because of that painting."

"I know," I say. It comes out a bit sharply, but that's what I want.

"Basically, I'm here as I have to cook something up," he continues. "Maybe it's not a nice thing but it has to be done..."

I frown and say, so as not to flare up later:

"Let's go to bed. You must be tired from all you've been through today. Tell me it all tomorrow."

And I think to myself: that's so you don't think I'm dying to hear about your secrets. I don't give a damn about them...

Seeing his hesitation I stand up decisively and go straight

into the annex. I'd unlocked it earlier, so now I just make up the bed for him. Behind me he says softly:

"I'm sorry if I've offended you."

Out of surprise I can't find anything to say to this and so pretend that I haven't heard him. When we say goodnight, I see sorrow in his eyes and for an instant I feel ashamed.

I lie down on the bench in the shop and think finally night has fallen; I repeat these words to myself as if I want to remember them forever, I repeat them so as not to think about anything else and the grateful night wraps me up in its rich, fluffy darkness.

Come dawn I wake up to see Alone creeping around the room. He stops on his tiptoes in front of the shelves with goods, unfolds his sack and starts putting his loot in it. He moves calmly and unhurriedly. The window is wide open, and I remember that the previous evening it was he who was sitting right beside it. I pretend that I'm still asleep. He stands half turned away from me and I can't shake off the strange and wild feeling that he's noticed my half-open eyes. I don't understand a thing and keep pretending that I'm asleep. He sets about the boxes. Having emptied several of them he strains to lift his sack off the floor, throws it over his shoulder and walks, staggering under his heavy burden, toward the window. He carefully pushes the sack through it and lowers it to the ground. The iron clangs and clatters. It clatters so loudly that from the intolerable shame of it all I feel like bursting into sobs. He clambers onto the windowsill and disappears. I hear the jumbled-up iron come down upon his back with more clatter and for a long time it audibly and distinctly marks out his steps. I finally hear his horse and open my eyes. I stare at the ceiling and then I wait for the morning to pour its light into the room...

Father looks at the ceiling and waits for the morning to

change narrator

pour its light into the room, and meanwhile Alone, having left the sleeping fort, hobbles his horse by the first turning, where the road dives below the hillside, he looks around, and not catching sight of anyone, takes the sack off his saddle and hauls it into a thick juniper bush by the river bank. He hides his booty in a hollow dug earlier and covers it over with the earth dampened by the night. After washing himself in the river, he returns to his horse, spurs him and hurries onward, ever further away from the crime he had arranged, the punishment for which was to be borne by my father.

In the morning the shopkeeper comes down into the shop, and in his heavy-lidded eyes after his drinking bout my father tries to read something of his complicity. He sees him in his awkward confusion try his hardest not to notice the traces of the robbery and instead keeps covering his eyes with his hand, moaning about his headache. Afterwards, he sends Father out to the grocer's for provisions, while he sideways, clumsily makes his way into the back room. Father is tormented with uncertainty, he feels, but does not know for sure, and so has no right to take any risks: maybe, the shopkeeper really hasn't noticed anything, maybe there hasn't been any agreement with Alone.

When he steps across the threshold of the shop again, just past the door, two strapping policemen fall upon him from both sides. Sweating, they tie his arms behind his back and with disgust Father thinks that these two have been gorging themselves on pickled garlic stalks the night before. While this stupid, coarse, entirely redundant and irrelevant tussle goes on, Father almost puts up no resistance, only trying to protect himself from unnecessary pain. The shopkeeper leans against the counter and excitedly explains to the police officer who is nodding his head:

"When I woke up I immediately saw what was missing.

Well I think, the rascal, didn't even try to cover his tracks, I think he can't have hidden it very far. Scarcely had I sent him off to do the shopping than I came straight for you, climbed out of the window in the back room and ran through the backyard."

"Good for you, very smart," replies the police officer in his thick southern accent. "And where did you, you scoundrel, learn to thieve? Never mind, we'll soon teach you a lesson..."

"Just no beating. I insist on that," says the shopkeeper. "I haven't yet sacked him. Maybe he'll confess and repent, and I'll let him man the shop again. But on this I stand firm, no beating. Or else from a thief he'll become a murderer... The natives can't stand beatings."

Before Father is pushed out on the street with good-natured punches, the shopkeeper puts a satchel on Father's shoulder with the flour, salt and spices he'd bought in the grocers:

"You'll swap those for grub with the warden. Now go, you rascal!"

This did not make anything any clearer for Father, and of course it never occurred to him that in the evening the shopkeeper, having got heavily drunk on moonshine, scrambled up onto his horse and set out from the fort to search out in the darkness the sack hidden in the juniper bushes, carry it back to his warehouse, stuff it in the darkest corner and put it behind various other pieces of equipment and rags and rubbish. Then he finishes off his bottle and wanders off, snivelling and spitting towards the neighbouring house.

The woman hears a crunch in the front garden and the sound of a body crashing on the ground. She has to drag him over her threshold, supporting him under his armpits, through the hallway to her bedside, where, utterly exhausted, she gives in and refrains from the effort of laying him on her bed, so she leaves him to doze on the mat and goes on swearing at him with leaden, sullen, masculine curses, and then she falls off to sleep despite his snoring but soon wakes up beneath his rude and frenzied pawing, and he thrusts his pain and anger into her helpless, resisting flesh and torments her to bitter exhaustion, to the utter depletion of his vengeful patience carried away with the battle, and then he wheezes with his throat and pukes onto the floor reeling before his eyes, while she, pouring out her hatred and tears, in her tiredness hammers his back with her fists and curses him to the ends of the earth.

It never occurred to Father that Alone was capable not only of deception but also of self deception, that fate may trick him suddenly, and all of his plans would fall through, just like the burnt down rafters in the shopkeeper's house.

The fire happened on the tenth day. From the barred square hole in the wall of his cell (a foul-smelling room with two dozen bunks, soiled plasterwork, and a permanent atmosphere of stubborn, lonely fury) the prisoners happily observed the brownish-black smoke swirling up into the expansive, grey, autumn sky, throwing about malicious jokes and trying to guess what was burning down out there. At midday, the prison warden brings them news along with their soup: it is the ironmonger's shop. The shopkeeper is dead and some woman's been badly burnt, but seems to be still breathing.

"Then get her over here if she's still breathing! I love hot women," says the towering lop-eared ex-soldier who's been arrested for self-mutilation (in his fourth year of military service, feeling "sick at heart", he had chopped off three fingers of his right hand with an axe, and before he got to the doss-house he was handed over to police by the platoon commander who had spied on his criminal deed.)

Father bears their laughter. He simply pays no attention to them. He lies on his bunk until evening with eyes wide open. At mealtime he tries to eat but can't cope with a bowl of gruel and some stale black bread. He lies on his bunk the rest of the day and when he spies a full round moon in the window, he comes to his senses, quietly crosses the room to the bunk of the joking soldier, and jamming his knee into the wooden rib of his bed he grabs his fat unshaven Adam's apple with his fingers.

Father doesn't manage to strangle him. The others beat him up conscientiously, darkly and unhurriedly. He will always remember the dirty stone floor, wetted to the door by the black sparkle of his own blood, he will always remember the several dozen legs smeared with it and trampling on his prostrated maimed body. Then he is taken out, and on the way, in the resounding prison corridor, he blissfully loses consciousness and returns to it only a day later in the frozen, narrow isolation cell with walls stinking of mould. Another day later he is led with bound hands to the prison chief, a pale, sweaty man, resembling a fingernail, who tells him in a hoarse voice, coughing the while into his thin fist:

"Let it be a lesson to you. And what's more – khh-khh – you must be thankful that we didn't add it to your case, that in our goodness we decided to punish you only with solitary confinement. Attempted murder – khh-khh – is far graver than stealing any hinges, you filthy rat!"

And right there in the office, his eyes riveted to the golden pendulum of the table clock, fascinated by its fragile yet inexhaustible and measured working of the mysterious mechanism, he again loses consciousness and is hauled back once more to his former cell, to his former bunk.

He feels the taste of water on his lips and sees a fingerless palm on his shoulder.

"See, I'll bring you around now, you idiot, but at night you'll again try and strangle me?" asks the lop-eared, and Father quickly closes his eyelids and starts carefully, word for word, to translate this into Ossetian, shielding from his broad smile with his own native tongue that is insensitive to such words. He unwillingly admits to himself that he no longer feels any hatred inside himself towards the lop-eared. Instead there is indifference – to him, and to the whole lot of them and their beastly laughter. From now on, amongst these people, who are prepared to beat a man to death not out of anger, but out of lazy spite, he develops a sense of caution, watching carefully what he says or does.

But this is not because he comes to value his life or gets frightened. Gradually, morning by morning, there will grow in him a sense of his being earmarked for some vague but doubtlessly important higher deed, for the sake of which he must bide his time and think intensely at nights. This deed is so important and carries such great responsibility that for fear of ruining it or letting something out, he decides to consider it calmly and unhurriedly, making his way to its very essence from different and as yet unclear angles. He learns to take things step by step and immerse himself slowly in the blurred outlines of a secret, implanting himself into it, and thus develops a confident wisdom. This wisdom and a feeling of predestination help him to cope with the overwhelming attacks of despair, that seize him in the same way as unbearable heat from somewhere in the pit of his stomach.

Through overheard gossip he learns some details of the disaster.

He learns that according to the recovered woman, who had been permanently disfigured by the fire, the shopkeeper turned up drunk at her house and forced her to follow him back to the shop where he tied her to a chair facing a curtained wall, then he tore off the curtain and showed her some kind of picture. In answer to questions about what the picture was about the woman would only shake her head, close her eyes and howl uncontrollably and then fall into hysterics. When she lowered her eyes he forced her to look up at that satanic picture by slapping her in the face, while he kept on drinking. Towards evening he lit some candles and put them out in a row beneath the canvas so she could see better. When, exhausted by his labours, the shopkeeper dozed off, the woman could take a rest from the torture and look away from the picture that had been affixed to the wall with common nails at its corners. The painting was not framed. The woman had no way of escaping from the room: the sleeping shopkeeper sat right by the door and raised his brows at the slightest rustle of her feet on the floor – and so everything would start all over again. Towards night the shopkeeper fell into a delirium, imagining that someone was trying to break into the house. He locked the door that led into the back room and bolted the front door. He still felt there wasn't enough light, so he decided to light a lamp as well, though, according to her, he already had ten candles burning. He set about filling the lamp with kerosene right to the brim but in doing so spilt a fair amount on the floor; the shopkeeper told her with an arch smile that they'd sit through the night staring at the painting together. The kerosene puddle gave off a pungent smell but he made no effort to mop it up. And therein lay his ruin. At dawn the woman was woken from her dozing by a heartrending howl. The shopkeeper had clearly slid off the chair in his sleep, knocked over the lamp and fallen face down into the kerosene puddle. He staggered around the room like a huge living torch: his face and front were engulfed in flames. The woman screamed with all her might and launched herself backwards on her chair every time the blinded shopkeeper lunged in her direction for help. At last he fell backwards and lifeless on the burning floor, and the woman, hollering from pain, her feet burning, inched her way on the chair to the door and strained to unlock it with her teeth. The painting had also caught fire and blazed above her head, spitting droplets of flame at her hair. A few seconds later the door also had been set aflame. How and when the latch on the door finally gave in the woman could not say and the assembled neighbours gave her no help at all: they simply didn't have time. They saw the burning heap stumble out onto the front steps and roll over to their feet. That morning, few of them thought she would survive her burns.

"It was all the devil's work, and the devil got his revenge," the folk whispered amongst themselves, reproving the widow for not observing her full mourning period and for living with the shopkeeper, and they crossed themselves in righteous satisfaction.

(Twenty-five years later I manage what my father had never dared to do. Leaving him behind with our bags on Market Square to watch the circus, after we had finished our business at the bazaar, I pretend I have stomach ache and take myself away from the crowd to sprint towards the bystreet which my father has been studiously avoiding for what was now almost two decades, since he regained his liberty and the freedom to choose his own path. I don't even have to ask any passers-by where the Witch's House is, I recognise it at once as if I've lost it only yesterday and have now quickly and easily found it in my memory. I drink it in with my eyes, and my heart pounds ecstatically in my chest, yet I quiver like a timid bird. I see the scorch marks on its left wall, abutting the burnt house's skeleton crucified in the thin air; it has not been buried in all these long years. She has bought out the entire patch and has forbidden the local authorities to lay even a finger on it, and they, having seen her ungloved hands a couple of times, don't want to get involved, just making vague warnings periodically. I catch sight of the straw-coloured curtains quavering in the window, and feel my limbs grow numb, then a gloved hand appears in the window beckoning me to it. But on this occasion I run away. I'll need another six months before I realise that nightmares are far worse than any daytime experiences, and when once more I approach her house, it's almost with relief that I open her gate, cross her yard and knock on her unlocked door. "Come in," I hear, and submit myself to an old rasping voice long since having fallen out with speech; she is sitting on a white sofa in a black dress, a black veil and wearing black gloves and I think: just like a rook on snow. "Take a seat if you want. Only you won't be sitting down probably?" I stay standing and she says: "You look like him. I recognised you last time" Silence falls between us and lolls lazily on the painted floor that separates us. I'm waiting for something, the floorboards squeak, and at last she says in a quiet, measured voice: "I knew even then that your father was innocent. That one, the shopkeeper came here and sat writing, a whole pile of papers he got through. He explained everything, as if he could foresee his own end coming. He shoved them in my face but wouldn't let me read them and put them at once in the safe. But I stole them, shortly before the fire. Let me show you – you'll be the first." She gets up and on unbending, maimed legs, shuffles to the bed, lifts the covers, gets out a clothbound bundle and proffers it to me: "Take it. Do you know how to read? Or you can hand them over to your father. That may be best, in fact. There's no point in waiting any longer, he's long ago done his time and paid his dues. "Not his dues," I reply curtly and think wistfully that I can't bring myself to hate her, though we both want that very much. She's quiet for a bit and I decide that she's smiling and that her smile is evil. "So what! It's his dues as far as I'm concerned, all the more as I appointed him his term. So he had time to know what it feels like, what real suffering is and how to live with sin. He was the third in our trio but wanted to stay pure, and he despised me worse than some cheap slut, looking at me as if hurling dirt at me with his eyes. But he probably envied the shopkeeper for coming to me at nights, and gnashed his teeth! Serves him right! And if he didn't gnash his teeth then it serves him right all the more." She roughly thrusts the bundle to me and heavily falls back onto the sofa; it takes her a minute to regain her breath. Then she says in irritation "No. That's not true. From the start I didn't doubt in the slightest that I'd take the papers to the jail, or the court, or wherever... After the fire, while I lay in hospital, I knew that he would never come to see me, even if he were suddenly freed, freed by my mercy – he'd be afraid to stain himself, and I reasoned to myself: why should he suffer more when so much suffering has already happened, when he's suffered endless shame, and two deaths what's more, and my repulsive ugliness." She raises her hands to her face as if splashing water on it. "I knew from my first days in the hospital I'd become a monster. A month or so later I persuaded them to bring me a mirror. That's when it all started. At first, out of anger, I decided to tell my fortune by the mirror. Well, I say to myself, if this scar on my cheek disappears or even gets an eyelash smaller I'll hand over the papers, and get him out of jail, but no earlier. And if not, well, my dear, you'll have to wait... I cried and cried until my chest grew empty but I had to admit it was no use, the devil himself couldn't make me beautiful again and my scars would never fade. Meanwhile I became addicted to this fortune telling and to talking to your father in my mind; sometimes he'd almost calm me down, but other times I'd be angry with him for not trying hard enough, not suffering enough for my burns. Finally I realized that as long as the papers were in my hands I could leaf though his fate and hold it in my hands like some copper coin, but that was as long as he was in jail as a thief. That's how I could come to hate so much of him and be even with him, and then I'd let him free, throw him out as a mangy chicken out of its cage. But I miscalculated: it was indifference, not hate, that brewed in my hardened soul, and my indifference was sustained all these years by only a blunted and sleepy interest – will he come to me or not? When I saw you from my window I thought to myself, there can't be long to wait now. I didn't touch the money," she adds suddenly. "What money?" I ask. "His wages. The shopkeeper thought they'd give him not more than a year. The money's all there with the papers." I nod and she turns away as if ashamed of her face that she keeps hidden beneath the delicate netting of her veil. "And Alone?" I ask her again. "Didn't he show up at all?" "He was here. He kept asking where the sack was hidden. But I didn't tell him a thing. I tell you – you're the first. Now be gone with you."

I move to the door but something holds me back. "Show it to me. Please." I ask. "Show what?" she asks fearfully. "Your face." I notice her quiver, and her body tightens into a taut black string. She says in a stifled chest-voice: "Do you really want me to?" I nod, for I really do. With a timid movement she takes her thoughtful hand to the veil, freezes, and brusquely throws it off her face. I'm not taken aback. I look at her, trying to memorize its monstrous disfigurement and disclose the secret of that in-depth, unfading blueness that no flame could destroy. I say: "No, you're no witch". As I leave I hear: "You are the first... Thank you. Tell him from me..." but I don't catch the rest. The door closes in shame and I walk out of the gate and tread slowly along the street.

I wander through the bazaar aimlessly until I spy a consumptive pauper morosely seated on a stool before a blank canvas stretched out on his easel. He looks at me with moist eyes, sizing me up, and recites his skimpy mantra: "Paintings, portraits, inscribed for eternity. Magic brush, a sure eye, inspired paints, and no cheating! Reality immortalized. Fast, accurate and true to life. Reasonable prices too." He licks his dried lips and repeats conspiratorially. "Cheap even, a real bargain. He chokes, splutters and turns red. "How much?" I ask, and when he replies I open the bundle and count out the banknotes, extract a few and say: "You have a commission – the Witches House. Paint it. Memorialise it. When you finish I'll give you more. But the painting shall remain with you. I'll collect it later, when the lady of the house is dead. The longer she lives, the more you get paid." He gets clingy and with voracious gratitude grabs my hand and hiccups from his sudden good fortune. We take our leave of each other, but at the other end of the row of stalls, when he's caught me up panting, and coughed for an age, he finally utters, "But how will I find you? You didn't say." "No matter," I say. "Remember today's date, I'll return on this day every summer." I don't know why I've said that but my soul resounds with an exalted feeling as in the church, where I've entered four years hence, when I'm twenty, to order a prayer of remembrance for her, and then I head to the graveyard, buying pure white flowers with the remaining money to strew on the orphaned grave by the iron railing. I collect the canvas without a frame. On the way home I start a small campfire and only then study it in detail. I'll wait till sunrise to see it more clearly. Only it's of no use. The painting is poor, resembling the consumptive beggar. Alone should have painted it. This one gave a likeness but he didn't understand. And he couldn't understand let alone eternalise. I tear it in half and throw it on the burning coals so that my memories are not stained, I'm only sorry I didn't spend all my money on flowers. But then, I think, you at least made a consumptive beggar believe that he was an artist, and that's no bad thing. At home I tell my father that she is dead – he shrugs and grits his teeth. "They called her a witch," I say and he shrugs again and leaves in a hurry. When he comes back he says, "That's not what I called her. I called her a fallen woman." I think, it's easier for him to skirt around the truth. All these years. And I think I wasn't wrong to not tell him about the papers, the money and our meeting, as I had no right to sully his pain, not with the despairing revenge of a woman whom he had once loved, nor with the belatedly generous ransoming of her unfortunate lover, nor with my own knowledge of all this, which somehow – and I'm aware of this when I pass in front of her gate, and she watches me go past through her tears, saying her farewells to the phantom she both desired and abhorred for years on end, who she kept detained behind bars as her vengeance for her own suffocating, excruciating, lonely nights, hiding under her feather bed all written evidence about the man she had crippled and who had left her crippled in return; whom she would never have forgiven and yet forgave as soon as his spirit appeared before her and heard out the whole truth and asked her to show her disfigured face. Somehow that knowledge interfered with me being his son and he my father. I say aloud, "Of course, Father, you wouldn't call her anything else..." I think it was simply easier for him to love my mother. Simpler to survive and become a father, so that at some later date he would come out one day with a shaky step to our threshold under a blinding spring sun and pour out the shame in his soul to his grown-up son. Maybe, I think, that was the only way not to let this story die. He would need a son to relate this story to, and for his birth he would need my mother. And fallen women, as I now know but he had known from the start, don't produce sons, only bastards. And that is the end of all history.)

There in the jail, amongst folk who could beat a man to death at the slightest provocation, Father forces himself to be patient, make no haste, and drop by drop amass within himself an inner reserve of calm confidence – preparing for his impending liberation. He educates himself in full indifference to what they think and say about him here, within the walls of the jailhouse, and occupies his soul with what he will do out there, once he's free again, and so completely stops answering their questions, and even stops insisting on his innocence. He discovers to his great surprise, that as a result of his behaviour, their respect towards him grows – not only that of his cellmates, but also that of the tired and ever mournful-looking investigator with the sad eyes, who suffers together with him through three dull and soporific interrogations, finally noting with dispirited satisfaction:

"You've exhausted my patience. Time for you, sir, to go to court. They don't like stubborn ones there. Well, good luck to you..."

Father only sighs with relief and returns to the cell to continue thinking.

During this time he has much to ponder. He thinks about the young man who had grown out of the orphaned kid, who had once stolen back one of the horses stolen by his kinsmen; he did it to stop being a thief himself and to be an orphan to gravestones no more; he had once stolen so that, at the cost of his own childhood, he could become the lord and master of his own boundless loneliness; he had once stolen so as never to steal again – but yet now he had stolen again.

It occurs to Father that Alone stole with some ulterior motive, and obviously not even for his own gain; he must have had some idea, hatched some plan, which Father could not fathom, but which lay there with the answer to the question why Alone had stolen, not bothering to hide even a full sack of ironmonger's wares that he could easily exchange for the painting he'd brought with him? And the more Father thinks about all this the more strongly he is convinced that the person for whose benefit Alone committed his thievery, was his very own self. The more obvious it becomes to him that the sole reason Alone committed his thievery was to make him, my father, a thief, and hide him, like a thief, behind bars. Now it becomes clear to him – insultingly clear, outrageously simple – why he almost didn't hide himself as he noisily clattered his pickings, condemning my bewildered father to a lengthy stubborn silence in the knowledge that he wouldn't betray him for the world and would suffer till the very end. He remembers his "I'm sorry..." of the evening before and the forceful, cheery clattering of his horse's unshod hooves. That's already a fair amount – even if he hasn't got the root of the plan, he's got part of the way, an intermediate link in the chain of thought which led Alone to hide my father behind bars. Hide him for his own good. Only Father still couldn't understand the meaning of it all but he strained, until he sweated blood, to figure out why his freedom would be so terrible for him, why all of a sudden his only salvation could be found in passing him for a thief and landing him up in jail? What was so terrible about it that it forced him to go to the lengths of striking a deal with the shopkeeper, primed for murder – that the deal took place, Father could already be certain – and agree to get rid of a hired guardian, who had obediently guarded his despair for two months, not allowing him to take the ultimate step and stain his conscience with the blood of the woman who had driven him out of his mind and quenched his passion only so far as to stir it up all the more and transform it into a thirst for destruction? What was so terrible about his freedom if this fear found response in the frightened heart of the shopkeeper who himself feared more than anything turning into a murderer?

And then a vague and timid guess, like a little flame, first plunges him into utter amazement, and then throws him into a fury, so that he breaks into cold sweat, and is filled with ominous torpor, like a man who has fallen into an abyss and is stunned by the immensity of the unfairness that has pushed him into this endless fall, that immeasurably cruel force, which had caused his fate to work out so poorly for him. Everything rebels in him, rises and rears up against this impossible guess, but at that time he contrives, on that powerful, proud wave, rising from the depths of his very being, to summon up the will to drive off this nasty suspicion from his wearied thoughts, and he keeps repeating like an incantation: No, that can't be! Something as stupid just isn't possible! I'd never have killed that woman! The shopkeeper was always right there. No, they couldn't have thought such a thing! They wouldn't have dared!

Yet, however little he believed in the groundlessness of this vile suspicion, the very thought that they had made a thief of him only to prevent him from turning into a murderer, was so piercing and poisonous that soon he was seized by the certainty of this ugly, criminal sense of doubt, and although he didn't allow himself to accept this sticky suspicion, even as a working surmise, he could never quite fully detach himself from it. "Well, come to think of it, just look at it this way," he would think to himself, falling for the usual bitter bait, "if I had had a bit more luck then, I would have killed the lop-eared one. I wouldn't have batted an eyelid. But surely it can't be that easy. Could he really be living inside me, a murderer? Is he only biding his time? No..." Beyond this "no" there is the emptiness and the darkness, and he begins to think of other things.

Of how and when, for example, Alone might be planning to come and rescue him from the jail, and what he might try and exchange him for, and how he might wash him clean of thievery. Maybe for the sack of loot, or maybe for another of his paintings, or maybe he'd even turn himself in as exchange? That he would rescue him somehow, Father was completely certain in his mind. How else otherwise, if... if... well, otherwise, that would be unlike Alone. "And the court? I couldn't care less for them. My term has not been set by them. Alone's got it all marked out for me. Maybe I'll get out of here before I have to show up in court..." But then he is seized by a gnawing, flaccid and quivering sense of anxiety. He remembers the dead shopkeeper and his wrongful, accidental death, tangled up in Father's fate like a persistent evil omen, and he sees in his mind's eye this omen clouding his memory with a rancid brown haze.

Then he starts to think about the paintings so as not to think about the woman. A surprising idea occurs to him when he turns his mind to the paintings: all of them, somehow or other, have been associated with death. One was placed in that girl's coffin, another caught fire on her death anniversary, and a third burnt together with its owner. Then Father takes to thinking of the true nature of beauty and why it always walks hand in hand with death. But very soon he gives up these thoughts and puts them off to another time.

Only for him this other time never comes, and as if by inheritance the task of deciding falls to me, so that almost three decades later, seated by the campfire in which I am incinerating the worthless memory-stained daubing of the Witches House, belatedly I think: "This is all in vain. It is not worthy of fire. It is not worthy of death, for it was never even born." Staring at the flames I wait for the truth to ripen in my mind, stirred by the fire but first conceived by my father, and when it forms itself into words and darkness falls once more, I open my lips and let this truth pour forth into the crisp moonlit night, to the very stars: "They are alike – beauty and death. Only they have the power to make life confess. But beauty is stronger than death. How else could I be able to remember those paintings that I had never set eyes on? Yet this pile of ashes I'll forget forever. I've already forgotten it. It is as if it never even was..." When I pour the ashes over coals, lie down and cover myself with my cloak, and look up at the glimmering skies, and breathe in the smell of the fire and the scent of the night breeze, it occurs to me that beauty is stronger than life itself. Except that maybe life is not stronger than death. But on that distant night I don't want to believe that to be so...

Thought of escape doesn't enter my father's mind for a long time, right up to the time of his court hearing. It wouldn't have occurred to him in court either had it not been for fate – for the second time since he landed up in jail – interfering in his hopes by taking apart two events appointed for the same day: the visit to the fort of the archbishop, scheduled for the first Monday in October, and the date of my father's hearing in the courthouse. Fate had arranged it thus that the barristers considered the first event far more important than the second, and so, in order to excuse themselves from the inevitable boredom of sitting in court for half a day when the other towns folk would welcome their reverend guest on the square, decided to take a holiday on that first Monday in October and postpone its cases to the two Mondays either side of it. So my father's hearing was moved forward by a week, and squeezed in alongside five others. On the last Monday in September, in the company of a feeble soldier and his bayonet he walks with hands bound behind his back the few blocks to the courthouse, angered that for lack of room for him, and him alone, on the cart carrying all the other prisoners, he has to burn with shame under the mocking stares of passers-by.

First they put him in a small longish room with benches nailed to the walls, and order him to sit still and not talk to anyone. As it is, persisting with his fastidious and wary indifference to those who make up his surroundings day in day out, he feels no especial desire to chat. Despite the warden's order, after a couple of minutes, the prisoners strike up a hushed but lively conversation, not paying the guard the slightest bit of attention. In all, including Father, there are seven prisoners: two of them are snub-nosed, smiling, buck-toothed twin brothers, who are charged with the gang rape of their own sister. Such cheerful shameless young lads, said Father, the darlings of the ward. Their faces were white as lard, and their eyes clear as droplets of oil. "She had it coming," they gave as their reason for the crime, grinning mischievously, as if they were talking of the most trivial matter, like some delicious jam on the plate. "She put out to Mikhailo the janitor, so why not us? Aren't we her family an' all? ? Look how that snotty shit fattened up eating our grub! Why throw us out to go to the tarts when we've got it right to hand and for free? No mind, tha', no mind, now she's stuffing up Mikhailo, but we're getting a nice long sleep. Lying on bunks doesn't half do in your back. And the nosh here is free too..." You see, said Father, they liked making people laugh. I felt no hatred towards them either. How can you hate swine just for being swine? I shrug in reply, and Father tells me to forget it. I nod, but I don't forget...

So Father doesn't butt in on their conversation, he listens with one ear, absent-mindedly. He waits and thinks his own thoughts. One by one they start calling out prisoners by their surnames and accompanying them into the courtroom. Finally only three of them are left in there, and by the chilly grey-patched sky, curling behind the barred window, Father realises that it's already way past midday; for some reason he is tired of thinking anymore, and he is nauseated to while away the time with his patience. Now he feels hungry and for the first time thinks of the prison gruel without disgust.

Suddenly something vaguely familiar slices through his hearing, he pricks his ears but the word slides past unnoticed and Father decides that he must have imagined it. The twins, lazily and indifferently, carry on a quiet argument punctuated by yawns.

"Nyahhh, that'll never work. Wall here's joined up with cement," says the one. "And then as well, it's a strong, dense stone an'all."

He raps his fist against the wall:

"Y'see? One charge's got nothin' doing on this. You can try all you like picking away at it with your finger, but you're just tickling it."

"What about two of 'em. Two of 'em 'll nail it right through," suggests the other, while the first one tuts and grimaces in doubt, then scratches his ginger nape and says:

"No less than five would do it. Five, you see, would smash it."

"Blow it up to dust. That's dynamite for you..." the other confirms, and Father shivers. The word has come back, and my father's heart beats faster and out of joint.

"What did you say?" he asks.

He nudges his side with his elbow and hoarsely repeats:

"What word's that you just said?"

The twin yawns and smirks good-naturedly as he repeats the word. Father asks about the Belgians.

"Yeah," says the other twin. "There's loads of 'em, 's like they're blowing up every mountain round heres."

Father goes quiet and his heart is riddled up in anxiety, and when he straightens his thoughts, he asks in a frozen half-whisper:

"Tell me, what it's li're?"

"Dynamite, you mean? Everyone knows that. The normal sort. What else?"

"And can you blow up a cliff with the stuff?"

"Sure you can. Why not, if you have to? It's no sweat for the dynamite, so long as you've got a big enough charge."

Father forces himself into thinking: "That's not the whole story. You can never be sure unless you know why they needed to do it in the first place. I don't know why they needed to blow up that cliff." He sees the rain again and remembers the mare rearing up. When they tell him about Bickford fuses, he remembers why he wasn't able to describe the snake – it was neither too short nor long enough for a viper, but he didn't see its whole length, and saw only enough to catch its similarity and its difference to a snake, to glimpse in passing its fleeting disproportion in size with a normal snake, but he failed to understand that it wasn't its length but its thickness that mattered: it was too slight and frail for a viper, like a stream is too slight and frail to be a river.

They call out the twins' names and lead them off into the courtroom, but my father absent-mindedly fixes his gaze on the feeble soldier and his bayonet and it all dawns on him then, as the soldier asks him with cheery caution:

"Why're you chattering your teeth? You scared or you ill? Chatters and chatters like a woodpecker."

But Father hasn't heard him and thinks to himself loudly: the mill! He says out loud:

"We just happened to be there. Barysbi needed the mill..."

"You what? Don't you play a raving nut! When they call you inside there you can rave all you like, but here you sit and be quiet!" shouts the soldier angrily, and Father catches the fear in his voice, but, occupied with his own thoughts, he doesn't lower his gaze. His teeth start to chatter again, but he takes no notice and squeezes his hands behind his back as the strength of his outrage is filling his chest and shoulders. He feels uncomfortable sitting on edge and gets up towards the bayonet pointing at him. He becomes aware of the bayonet's point and obediently sits back on the bench, instantly forgetting about the soldier. He thinks greedily, with every thought joyfully and expansively sliding into this strictly defined and excited new order that has opened up to him like a template as clear-cut as the window panes, with all the links and chains soldered into place with the hardest steel. He's losing time, but then, thinking it through to the end, his heart jolts and he takes a good look at the soldier and the walls, then looks at the door leading into the courtroom and turns to the other door, which opens into the street and the cool evening. He sees how close it really is, and is stunned by his own indecision. Turning his gaze to the guard, he weighs up in his mind how much time he has lost and what it'll cost him. Two paces separate them – a fraction even for a single moment. He must be quick. He takes aim at the midpoint, at the arc under the soldier's shirt, and tightening the muscles on his neck takes a minute to get ready, watching the guard from under his brow all the while. He charges forward and hits the soldier below the belt with his head, and his puny body buckles and slumps down against the wall. To make sure Father hits with his knee as well and hears the clatter of his rifle falling out of his numbed fingers onto the cement floor. He presses his back to the rifle, squats and feels its blade, then locks it into the bench and tries to cut open the rope tightened around his wrists by rubbing them up against its blade. Then he unfastens the blade from the bayonet and uses it to break open the door lock, throws open the door and bursts out into the street. And the whole time Father's been preparing for his escape and running along the street, he doesn't once think about Alone...

Alone, tells me twenty odd years later:

"I miscalculated. I thought I had an extra week. But then it was too late... Again, this stupid, clumsy chance."

And that's what I think myself, but as the years go by I realise that three chance occurrences in a row cannot be explained by chance. More likely it's three pieces of evidence of the same order, three fingerprints left by the same hand, or three clear traces that marked out the winding path towards inevitable fate. When I understand the significance of the three chance occurrences in a row, I start to figure out what is behind those two events if they are also chance occurrences and also happened in a row. I come to the conclusion that the meaning can be what you will, only its price will be the same – doubt. I understand at last what any first chance occurrence can really be pregnant with before it multiplies. I call it a warning and I immediately figure out what was the warning in that distant story, what was suspicion, and what was evidence; all three events – the fire in the shopkeeper's house, the change of the court hearing day, and the conversation about dynamjte – make me forget about chances and look for causes instead.

One of them I find in Alone's confusion, though he keeps quiet about it and shows no sign that he was shocked like a youngster when he heard about the fire and the death of the shopkeeper, for his cunning and beautiful plot had suddenly been thickly stained with blood and festered with the deformity of the unfortunate woman, of whom there only remained –

and I saw this with my own eyes – two poignant lakes of blue on a charred face and an eternal mournful shame. Of course, Alone felt terribly uneasy for this was the first time he received a "warning", while he never gave a thought about fate, assuming that fate had already run its course for him, and had now breathed its last when it ruined the poor girl, made him fall in love with her spirit, and in his drunken bout drove him up the crag that had killed her. He thought he'd already settled his accounts with fate, and to confirm this he had set fire to the painting he'd sold the shopkeeper in his very shop. Once again he set himself free – even more than when he had stolen back the stolen horse or when with an unloaded rifle he had scared off his uncle who had come back for him, so that he could hang a new chain over his hearth and bring it to life with pure fire. He became freer now because he had lost, and now forever, everything except his loneliness hardened by his unending despondency.

But at that time he had no knowledge of what his freedom and loneliness could create if they join forces. And when he stumbled upon this first chance occurrence, I think he was terrified and confused and in the pure mountain air his nostrils caught a non-existent foreign smoke. To intercept it, he wanted to run, but did not dare. Yes, now he could distance himself from it. Show up in the fort, search out the judge and confess all. That would be by far the simplest course of action. Just like leaping off the careering cart into the roadside and letting it fall into the abyss. However, this he did not do. He preferred to remain tangled up in the whole story, despite the fact it had taken a direction he had not anticipated. Not even remotely. Now, after the death of the shopkeeper, there was simply no one to free Father from jail, free him a year to the day later and even prove his full innocence. All sorts of ideas came into Alone's head but none of them seemed right to him, because the nub of his plan consisted of biding his time until one year to the day when he hid the sack with the stolen ironmongers' stuff. But finding that sack was no easier now than raising the shopkeeper from the dead or getting a confession out of the woman who would keep her silence for more than twenty years. Yet finding the sack was of course only half the problem. He had to prove that the goods were the very same and not any other. Even if he coped with this task how could he bring together this unsuccessful crime and the precisely set date a year from then? The date of the court hearing had already been appointed but Alone could do nothing without the shopkeeper: he was supposed to write a petition pleading for the postponement of the law, in pursuance of his right as a victimised Christian, who believes in the forces of good and has no wish to besmirch his soul with sin by sending off a benighted native to hard labour. But it turned out that time had wriggled free from the shackles of Alone's plot nearly a year before and all that he could do now was to grab on to the tip of its tail and go to the fort and confess his guilt.

However, he stubbornly waited for the court hearing, which meant that he still cherished the hope of rescuing the remnants of his plot and taming rebellious time with his patience. Only then, I think, he first felt the heavy, disturbing burden of his own freedom and how little control he had over it.

I just want to make it clear: his delay was not due to fear of landing up in jail or to cowardice, nor even to loneliness. But just that – his freedom! His freedom piled upon him so high that he no longer had the strength to resist it, as if it would now be dishonest to give in to this chilly boundless freedom that he had cultivated in his loneliness. Moreover, he knew in his heart that he was unable to lose and maybe put his trust in it as never before. And so it happened that this inability played a cruel joke upon him, all the more so as he now had to bank upon his own unbridled freedom so as to fight till the last for his own noble plot, which even he, Alone was not able to improve upon. And in trying to redeem his misadventure he took the risk of delaying, and in the end delayed and delayed so much that he was finally too late. That's how it all seems to me now.

Then he went over to see Barysbi and said to him:

"Something's changed now. Forget about what we'd agreed earlier."

"That's not done. You must keep your word," Barysbi replied.

"Of course. I promised you a year, and you'll get it. But you'll have to swap places with him," Alone said.

"You're off your rocker. No. No way. Better death than shame," Barysbi said.

"It's better if it's an ordinary death rather than a shameful death."

Barysbi thought long and hard, bit his moustache, and then asked:

"Is there no other way?"

Alone shook his head. So Barysbi asked:

"What do you want me to do? I'm just curious what you might suggest."

"I'd say so," said Alone. "You must have enough curiosity and some."

"Tell me then," interrupted Barysbi. "Or else I can still say to hell with the whole thing."

"That's just the problem – you can't. What you can do is this. Let's say you buy that sack of ironmonger's stuff – surely you can afford it – and then saddle your horse and ride off to the fort."

"You want me to..."

"Yes, I do," said Alone. "You're going to take the blame upon yourself and take his place in jail. Then maybe he'll forgive you since he knows who's the real thief. Got it? And if you got it, then it's like I didn't steal for him but for you, right? It sounds strange, but it's the only right thing to do... You're more worthy of the jail than either him or me, you know."

Barysbi got it but to keep appearances asked for a day to make up his mind. But then he asked on top for all the days that remained before the court hearing. He was thinking, most likely, how once again everything had turned out all right, even better than before, because now he could come to terms with his absurd freedom and could even see a way of putting it to good use to further his clever scheme. He reckoned on being able to link them – his freedom and his scheme – but more importantly, linking his freedom with what is normally called higher justice, although to be honest, no one will ever really be able to explain to me how this is any different from higher injustice, and here the real question, when you look at it, is how much, in the long run, injustice is fair or if, on the contrary, the celebrated but forever illusory justice is most fitting for the gods. On reflection, both these words are normally only used to justify yourself in hindsight, or at least to assert your ability to be proved right with time – that's the entire difference between those who say with pride, "I did what I had to do" and those who confess with humility, "I was wrong."

When Barysbi agreed, Alone had all the grounds to believe that yet again he'd be unable to lose, while Barysbi, for whom losing was part of his daily life, asked for a small favour:

"What about my son? I'm not asking about the others,

but what about my boy? Surely you're not going to make him answer with shame for your crime? You owe it to me to..."

"No," interrupted Alone. "Owe is a bad word. I don't owe you anything."

"You owe me," stubbornly repeated Barysbi. "Who else but you? You can help him believe that's not true."

On some reflection Alone nodded.

"I'll tell him I stole to save the two of you."

"And that's it?" asked Barysbi.

"Yes. I won't go explaining any more than that to him. You'll be the one to explain to him if you ever have the guts."

On that they settled, and I think, to all the burning hatred that Barysbi felt for Alone was now added an explosive pinch of gratitude. And, most probably, he hated him now more desperately and keenly than a simple mortal could be hated, hated him with abandon as one hates one's miserable lot. He hated him all the more fiercely because he hadn't had the guts to shoot him when he stole after his shadow that memorable night in the cemetery; and when both of them, Barysbi and Alone, were poised for a shot to ring out to add a final peal of thunder to the cursed rain that had already turned Barysbi into a murderer (albeit against his will, but enough to stop him from killing again, and this time intentionally, and so all Barysbi did was to raise his rifle and aim long and hard while Alone talked with the graves, but then not cock the trigger, and return home and listen to his shame with his heart and know that at daybreak his enemy would leave). He had seen Alone saddle up his horse and thought that he was hurrying after the Belgians, but then he went out to see them himself, and in their place in the quarry he found only the furious and anxious foreman who told him that those two had disappeared the night before, having loaded all their things onto a cart without even hiring a driver. Then he realised they saved themselves while at the same time saving him half the money he owed them for their services plus a box of dynamite, and he understood that for his own salvation that sum was pitifully small, for there's not enough money or silver in the world that could save him from Alone and from the knowledge that he was now a murderer. Barysbi asked the foreman how much that cart cost together with the mare, and then he loosened the string on his satchel and counted out the coins.

"Here," he said. "That's how much it costs to be free of debt."

When he returned to the aul, they say, for two or three whole days he took no action, and neither did Alone, who returned from the fort, where he had left my father to watch a foreign sky. But then he could wait no longer, and Barysbi dispatched his younger sons to buy millstones for the new mill, and said to all the villagers:

"Don't interfere. We'll build it ourselves. Me and my family."

For some time afterwards things went on as if there hadn't been any murder, everything went on according to his plan, which only Alone had guessed, but Alone just kept quiet and watched from the nykhas how the new walls of the mill rose up by the river. They were constructed with the funds collected by the same villagers who fell for possible profit, and for almost two weeks on end carried their savings to Barysbi's house as if to a sacrificial altar, and put them in an enormous vessel, paying for his deception with their own hands, and paying for the dynamite and the services of the Belgians who had delivered it to blow up the cliff and bury the old mill beneath it, so that Barysbi could build another and make it his own property this time, and then charge the villagers for each grinding the same silver they had already paid for his deceit, the dynamite and the Belgians, that had already been used to acquire those millstones, which, in Barysbi's mind, would never belong to everyone and would grind alongside their grain, the villagers' money, and then none of them would dare remind him out loud about his debt, if only out of fear of ending up in debt themselves, for the grinding charge would be set by Barysbi, and him alone.

That was his plan, at any rate, about which only he and now Alone knew. At first, everything went smoothly, and even the rain started right on the tenth day – the last date set by Barysbi for the collection of the fruits of their common greed shared by those poor wretches who were promised that in a year's time they would become if not rich at least a quarter less poor. When the first thunderbolt struck, the Belgians were ready as you like, and Barysbi said to them: go ahead. They hid in a shelter and observed the cliff and the rain; one of the Belgians kept looking at his hand, on which was fastened a small glass contraption, which counted out the minutes with an arrow. And then they noticed Grandfather's cart and Grandfather's mare, and Grandfather's son with some stranger, and the Belgian, who was able to see the time from his arrow, yelled out at the top of his voice and covered over his eyes with his forearm, and they all heard the thunder, and everything that happened next was only seen by Barysbi, because the other Belgian buried his head in the rocks and was shuddering convulsively as if someone was scratching him under the ribcage with sharp nails. Then they both disappeared in the rain and Barysbi remained to watch my father scramble up the mountainside. When they searched for the bodies Barysbi didn't let slip a single word, but in Alone's eyes he saw mistrust; he went back home, got out his gun and followed Alone to the cemetery, but then didn't have the guts to shoot him, and when the moment was lost to eternity, he realised that he wouldn't be able to shoot him tomorrow either, nor after that, nor ever. Then he built the mill and waited. Alone also waited. And when they first came to try out the millstones, Alone came down from the nykhas, went up to Barysbi, took him to one side and said:

"Your mill has turned out just wonderfully. But the main thing is that it's free for everyone to use, am I right?"

Barysbi was silent. So Alone nodded and continued:

"For starters you'll return them their money. All that you haven't yet spent. You'll explain to them that you can't bake up a profit out of misfortune."

Barysbi winced in doubt.

"That won't be easy."

"It won't, but you'll manage," said Alone. "All the more so as you're giving them a miller for seven years in advance. That son of yours is no longer a kid, so he'll cope."

Barysbi gritted his teeth and didn't answer for a long time, but then asked:

"And what will I get in return?"

"In return you'll get a year," said Alone. "One year in which you won't be killed."

So Barysbi asked again:

"Where is he?" He had my father in mind.

"In the fort," Alone replied. "He'll be there just precisely as long as it takes you to arrange old Khandjeri's memorial wake."

"And after that? Where's he gonna get to after that?" asked Barysbi, again having in mind my father.

"Not him," said Alone. "Not him, you. That's your concern."

For some reason Barysbi again said:

"So it's turned out that my son will become a miller."

"Or a son of a murderer. A murderer and a thief," said Alone.

That was the conversation they had then. For the time being each kept his word: Barysbi's family gave the aul a miller and returned the unspent money, while Alone set off for the glacier to paint the thunder on canvas, fighting the heaviness in his soul with his paints. And probably, it was then, in the mountains, high up, half breath to the skies, he met the unfortunate simpleton Rakhimat, the daughter of the withered-armed Gappo. Our people didn't even deign to laugh at her out of pity, almost as if out of respect to some divine tragedy of dumbness laid out before them, that had been continuing for over three decades, in the course of which they were to observe first the ugly-eyed baby, then the half-mute child with the twisted little arms caused by a pre-natal disease, and then the young girl with the tight little braids, which never jumped about in the wind, and with a smile untouched by thoughts, and then the young woman with opaque black eyes ugly with insanity, and hands forever convulsed, and those hard lifeless pigtails, a smile that had settled on her subdued face, weathered and coarsened over the years, a smile whose very sight caused even grown women to avert their gazes, also avoiding to look at her expansive and ample bosom, that called out with its dumb, round and blind flesh from beneath the dark folds of her clothes. And if in her smile and her limpid eyes our people saw utter innocence permanently stamped on her dumbness decreed to her by fate for the rest of her allotted days, then the ripe bust of Rakhimat seemed to them to be a monstrous insult both to such innocence and the memory of the woman who had borne Gappo such a daughter but had ceased to be a wife and mother the very day after the child had come into this world: she had died just before dawn, Father told me, and the milk ran in streams down her body, like silent white blood, and our women wiped it off with a white nappy. I of course did not witness any of this myself, said Father, I hadn't yet learned to speak by then, but so the talk went in the aul. Gappo's old mother nursed the child. At the time they had a buffalo. So you can't say at once how many mothers Rakhimat really had, or which of them was the most real, said Father, and as to which one she took after – the gods only know. Gappo had been a huntsman in his youth, and indeed such an inveterate hunter that he would even venture all the way up to the Glassy Hill in the winter. That's where he ruined his arm: one day a wild boar slashed his shoulder and his blood congealed in the frost so that the arm withered. Afterwards he once again took to hunting with relish, but not for much longer, as if his arm had mellowed him. He did not propose to anyone for some half dozen years afterwards, although his years were already beginning to prop him up. For you see, his maimed arm made him shy. But then he married and seemed to start walking the earth with a firmer step. They were childless for some eight years and, indeed, it would have been better had it stayed that way. May the Lord forgive me for saying such words, Father said. Our people said such things after her death, which don't even bear repeating. It was just as if the fear that had been implanted in him by that wild boar had been passed onto the child, and this was why, so they said, she was so wild of eye and her wrists were twisted sideways. Only I, said Father, don't believe in such rubbish. Who did she get that smile from? And who's to say what the gods have in their heads anyway?

In sum, I can just imagine how the villagers suffered from that mix of contempt and pity at this unfortunate creature who had murdered her mother just by being born, who had been suckled by a milch-buffalo and kept smiling senselessly as the time came for her own blind and numb bosom to be filled with a vain strength. Time forgot about Gappo too: like a spade left stuck in the soil, Father said, he took on no rust, bore no damage or weathering, and became ageless. It was as if age in him had forgotten to grow old. He rarely went up to the nykhas, out of shame, most probably, that the advancing years had not taken root in him. So much so that soon him and Rakhimat could be taken for brother and sister. I have no idea, admitted Father, what the secret was, only that it filled him all the more with shame. But she still kept her smile and would wander in the mountains. Many a time our men would find her by the precipice, squat on her haunches and admiring the flowers. Or here's another: she would watch a rainbow by the riverbank for a whole day. One day I myself was witness to this, said Father: I was returning from the fort one night, and, lo and behold, here's a shadow by the Blue Road. She's standing there and gazing at the stars, and so hungrily as if she were trying to taste them. And you know, said Father, it was an unpleasant sight, to tell the truth. Somehow repulsive. As if watching people in the nude from behind a bush. I saw what he meant and I thought that they were bound to meet one another – she and Alone – and their meeting had been predetermined by fate back when he had stolen that horse from his sleeping uncle, deciding that it absolved him from being branded a thief once and for all. When he laid eyes on her, scrambling along that glacier, he knew that he would have to steal once more, and, probably, in that moment it dawned on him just what he would have to do so as to keep his promise and not let my father appear in the aul earlier than the assigned time of one year.

She stood up and watched him etch out the dimness of his soul with his paintbrush, creating this canvas and sowing sparks of a future fire. He anxiously watched how for the first time in his memory her face awakened from its never changing smile and began to grow pale. And then, a yellow cloud of fear enveloped her warm, lazy eyes and she cried out. He jumped to her just in time to grab her by the waist and keep her from falling, while her body convulsed in his arms and she threw up. He helped her to sit down and suddenly caught sight, right there on the ice glowing in the sunlight, of little golden coins. She didn't notice him picking them up, but scarcely catching her breath, she started feeling in her bosom in fright, causing its awesome bulge to ripple, but not noticing his presence at all. He held out his hand to her and she joyfully grabbed the coins in her twisted palm; and now once more that invincible smile reigned over her features, making him recoil involuntarily. And while she tenderly stroked the coins and cooed to herself under her breath, he caught sight of her big belly, thinking: "If my guess is right then I'm the first one to know about this, and that includes her. Only she would never know of this: Gappo would shoot her before she does." He imagined to himself how her immature heart had overflowed with gratitude to the Belgians who had exchanged her innocence for golden glisters, although they had been unable to overcome it with the sperm they had sown in her womb. Probably, he thought, she bore all this because she was stroking in her hand, just as she was now, a worthless coin given to her by one of them while the other exerted himself with this buffalo girl, imagining that he had bought her. And to make it the easier for her, they gave her another coin and swapped places, and she patiently waited for them to finish torturing her numb flesh and give her another amusing, shining fragment of beauty for her to hide in her ample bosom and carry away to her close warm world. Then they ran off, while she diligently and regularly kept returning to the roadway in the vain hope to see their wagon shining in the sun, from which a few months back, on the first Saturday of remembrance for the deceased Khandjeri, a pale foreign hand had, in the sight of the whole aul, thrown her a shining foreign copper coin – payment for her finding the hat by the roadside and returning it to its rightful owner after it had been torn from his head by the fury of the brown wind, when the skies had sent us their eloquent warning of impending doom, and our villagers had taken it as a sign of fellow feeling and had not even armed themselves with suspicion, and as such did not notice, nor realise, nor talk amongst themselves of the dangerous ecstasy of that idiot girl nor the smirks of those men who had first seen the woman in her. But later the sullied flesh began to take its revenge on Rakhimat and encroach upon her close and happy world and her naive soul was forced to seek out the cool and the spacious, and drove her ever upward, right up to the glacier, and there she found me, the first to realise that she was now with child. Me, Alone thought, it fell to me again, even though I had vowed to give up thieving back when I was a thoughtless youth and wanted to be worthy of the graves. But now...

No, he told himself. First, I must finish the painting.

He was duty bound to finish it so as to express through his disturbing colours if not the whole truth, then at least a feel for the truth, for in the fort he would be forced to lie – to my father to whom he had promised to reveal the truth about Barysbi and the Belgians, and from whom he was now compelled to hide this truth in the name of his own and my father's sake, having taken the decision to protect my father from the sin of manslaughter.

He knew that time was short and he had to hurry before rumours of the mill and the sudden disappearance of the foreigners reached the fort, before my father made the connections in his mind between their own shared suspicions and the villagers' gossip he heard in that ironmongers' shop, but most of all, before my father returned home and started to unwind the tangled knot of mysteries that linked the newly installed millstones with the snake hidden in his memory, that had scared his tired horse in the rain and had often returned to him in his dreams in that adobe annexe with the unlocked lock.

Alone also had to hurry because he now knew of the little coins and Rakhimat that had grown with child from them; and so to the cruel truth of the terrible fire that he depicted on his canvas was added his sense of despair, of which he did not dare breathe a word to the shopkeeper – nor to my father, nor to the pregnant idiot girl, who, if she were to remain in the aul, would have left her father with no choice but to shoot her, like one of the wild boars that he hunted, so that she does not desecrate our land with the fruit of her disgrace.

Alone was now forced to steal for real. To abduct her he thought of calling her out before morning on to the Blue Road, and for that he was not required to invent any tricks. I suppose he had some loose change, so that on seeing them she would instantly forget about all that she would leave behind in going away – that is, if she ever remembered anything of it at all, apart from the sensation of the constant thick cosiness, which she always carried with her anyway. He nonetheless went down to the mill and summoned Barysbi through his son, who had been bound to seven-years slavery at the millstones. When he arrived, he said to him:

"I need the money. The more the better."

Barysbi was so taken aback by this that he did not reply at once.

"Curse you," he said. "To hell with you, and to hell with me too if I haven't handed over every last coin."

"Then pay me out of your own pocket," Alone said.

Barysbi waved his arms, spat on the ground and pointed his finger at the mill:

"Out of my own pocket, you say? Everything I have I've put into their service. What the devil else d'you want of me?"

"Not very much at all. You've never had much money to your name anyway. Maybe, if you don't get greedy, with time more will come your way..."

Barysbi stared at him trying to work out what he was getting at. Then he sat on his haunches and started to think. And when he had tired himself out thinking, he said:

"No. I haven't got anything to give you."

Alone burst out laughing:

"I must have made a mistake. Maybe, the miser in you speaks out more loudly than the blood of Khandjeri. Even louder than hate perhaps."

Barysbi only looked away and gritted his teeth. Then he got to his feet and turned on his heels back home. Alone thought to himself:

"Now he'll give over. When again will he have the chance to buy me off?"

And in actual fact, late that same evening there was a knock at his door, and going out on to the threshold he caught sight in the darkness of a straight back, measuredly moving off while on his step he found a thin leather purse.

"Maybe with time more will indeed come your way..."

The back heard him and seemed to sway a little, stumbling and then became enveloped in the shadows, and Alone thought: now it will be easier for Barysbi to hate me. But this will make it all the easier for me to help him.

Towards daybreak he bridled up his horse, rolled up the painting into a tube, gathered all the money that had spent the night at his house and made off for the Blue Road.

"I tied the horse up to a rock and returned to the aul,"

he told me many years later. "I found her at the riverbank and all I had to do was whistle to her and show her the coins. She skipped all the way behind me, like a ewe behind a ram."

When they got back onto the road he again unfurled the painting and spread it inside out over her shoulders, and almost at once, not even giving her time to look at her strange new shawl and take fright, he sat her on his horse and jumped into the saddle.

"She decided I wanted the same thing as the Belgians," he said to me with a bitter chuckle. "That's why, see, for a whole day on the road she kept quiet and only sometimes cast me a skewed glance not understanding when I'd demand something back for those coins she clenched in her happy hot fist. This silly, naive creature... half human, half beast. And just like an animal, she was afraid of the dark, so I had to tie her up when we made it on to the main road, and gag her with a piece pelt. I wrapped her up with a horsehair blanket so that from the passing carts they took her for a lifeless bundle. A fat, senseless bundle, she was issuing suppressed cries at first, then fell silent, and then became contented and trusting which made me suddenly realise what had calmed her, so I even had a lump in my throat and a massive block of sadness in my heart. That night by the campfire her eyes spoke to me of the same thing. Such an idiotic, pitiful creature!"

"She thought that..." I started off, but Alone interrupted me:

"Yes. Precisely. She had decided that I was her bridegroom. Have you ever seen tenderness in the eyes of a buffalo calf? As we lay down to rest for the night she scattered out the coins in front of her and started to divide them out – one by one, and when she'd counted them all out, she pushed towards me a small shiny pile as if to say that now what was hers was mine also... and, you know, such shame overtook me that it was just as if someone was spying on us, even if it was that extra life that lay within her, and out of shame and evil I again bound and rolled her up, tightly tying the strings of the sack, and even did not forget to gag her."

That's what Alone related to me, and I felt that the journey had turned into an ordeal for him, for he had to handle not just a woman or an animal, but a woman and an animal in one and also with that other life inside their common dumb womb, as well as the burden of his own plans which even for Alone had never been so complex in their permutations and, I believe, gave rise to a deep worry in his heart that they would never come to fruition. He also had to cope with the fact that he had stolen, although the kidnapped girl believed herself very nearly a bride of a generous groom, who had lured her with a stream of golden coins. In a way, he had to cope with the past that had sprouted forth its shoots without his knowledge or participation and yet somehow due to his loneliness, his inability to be the loser, which had poisoned our people with envy at his pointless luck, alongside which each of them, and not only my grandfather, who had been filling up his boundless barn with grain every year, but everyone felt to be his farmhands, ploughing the fields of his luck.

And so now he journeyed on to the fort, and slung over the croup of his light-chestnut horse was the body of the woman kidnapped from the aul, made pregnant through our common misfortune, and hence through his fault too; and he probably remembered those other thieves, his blood relatives carting away the body of his half-crazed uncle bundled on the back of an ox. For all the differences between his own flight and that past one he found grains of wicked similarity: robbery, the road, the stifling horsehair, two bodies deprived of reason: one conceived of the human baseness, the other filled with fat fear as a result of the rockslide that had also destroyed Alone's parents. As he hurried on to the fort he remembered his kin with whom he had severed all ties forever, whose messenger he had scared off with an unloaded rifle; and before the graves of his ancestors he had renounced all that he had in common with them, believing that it was only his appearance and not his nature or destiny. And now it had all of a sudden come to pass that he, albeit against his will, was repeating their flight, even if not in full, and practically "backwards". He must have convinced himself there were more differences in his case and it was a mirror reflection of the opposites rather than the shadow of the chain, which tied him with blood relations to his criminal kin, the chain he had never managed to disentangle.

Whatever it was, he was in a bad mood as he entered the town under cover of night after he'd safely made it through the pass and bided his time for several hours outside the town gates; he led his horse down the slippery dark alleyway in search of the house he was looking for, which none of the villagers had up to that time ever visited and about which he had only learnt from rumour. Straying along the road, he caught sight of a dim lantern above its entrance, dismounted and listened in, breathing into his unsullied nostrils the smells of comfort and sinfulness. The horsehair bundle, its edges hanging over the saddle, slept peacefully on the horse's back. The street was deserted. Somewhere off in the distance, voices could be heard, but out of doors all was quiet. He knocked. Then he knocked again, this time more forcefully. He heard the sound of quick steps. They came closer, stopped, something tinkled quietly, and he saw the door awake by its peephole revealing the watching gaze of a round eye. He stepped back under the lantern and waited for a reply. A young girl's voice said:

"No, luv. We don't take your sort in here."

He got out his money and held it out in his open palm so that it caught the light of the lantern. Behind the door there was silence, then he heard a sigh, muttering, and somewhere further inside the house the clicking of a lock.

"I'll open the gates for you – leave that horse of yours out in the yard," ordered the voice, and the peephole slammed shut. He obeyed and found himself in a dark clean yard, where underwear and petticoats hung out to dry fluttered in the light breeze. He'd tied his horse to the post, took down the horsehair bundle and moved inside the open side door.

"Here," he said, laying his load down on the floor and catching his breath. "Now call the madam."

So he said and stared at the red curtains behind which the girl had disappeared. There came a plaintive sad strumming of a guitar, singing of its sorrow in the midst of this house delighting in sin. The brocade of the curtains rustled, and he saw the grim features of the madam.

"What do you want?" she asked rudely, an emaciated woman, worn out from serving sin. Rakhimat woke up, straightened herself out from her dusty blanket, and her eyes ran round the entrance hall. The madam folded her arms in front of her chest and for a long time did not tear her gaze away from her smile. On her brow a stern wrinkle formed at two points.

"I'll give you money," said Alone. "Name your price."

The woman clicked her fingers and alongside her appeared the same girl that had first let them in. She guiltily tugged at her apron.

"Deal with them, and be quick about it," ordered the madam. "Kick this morel out of here, and his idiot girl, if you don't want me to boot you out first."

"No," said Alone. "I'll go, just let her stay here. She's pregnant."

They looked each other right in the eye. Somewhere the guitar groaned. Rakhimat got up off the floor and moved towards the red curtain.

"Don't you dare," screamed the woman and struck her face with a swinging blow. Rakhimat fell to her knees and howled, rubbing her cheek. The guitar sobbed with frightened strings and fell silent.

"She's staying here," Alone repeated. "Or else, I'll set this place on fire. I'll set you on fire, and your house and all your whores. I said, this girl is pregnant..."

In her rage the madam stepped towards him, but stopped short.

"You little shit," she hissed through her teeth. "You dirty sonofabitch."

"You're scared," said Alone. "That's why you're swearing at me. You're right to be scared. Maybe it's best that we strike a bargain?"

"Get the hell out of here!" shrieked the woman.

Alone bent over and helped Rakhimat to get up, and together they pushed past the madam and opened the curtain.

"Let your servant wash her and give her something to eat," he said. "And meanwhile we'll sit down and have a talk."

"Bastard," said the madam. "You're a real bastard you are."

She gave a sign and the servant girl led the resisting Rakhimat away from the entrance hall.

"That's much better," said Alone. "Now calm down. You don't have enough anger in you."

He let her go first and they entered a large salon illuminated by a single lamp under a red lampshade with a fringe. By the far wall a young girl sat on a sofa. On seeing them enter she put her guitar down and got up to go. Once they were left on their own, Alone settled down in an armchair and asked:

"Hear me out before you make a decision."

He was a good talker. Only the madam was also a good listener, and so nothing came of it for Alone: she didn't believe a word. So then he said:

"Fine. You win. I was lying."

"You milksop. You haven't even had it with a girl yet."

He blushed and came back at her:

"What difference is it to you, who made her pregnant, me or somebody else? You're getting paid just the same."

But she leaned forward, burning him with her pupils, and waved her finger right under his nose:

"No sonny, no... We don't take payment for that kind of thing here. Here you pay for whores. And you clearly haven't learnt how to be with one of them yet..."

Now he turned a deeper shade of red, as if the colour from the curtain and lampshade had all flowed into his face. He felt his heart pumping faster in his chest. In the neighbouring room the guitar started up again, burbling quietly, like a spring. He heard the music, and it seemed to him as if it was suffering alongside him. He started up again:

"If you don't take her in, she won't live... Do you want me to paint your portrait? I can. I can make you look good."

She burst out laughing. Her laugh was unexpectedly youthful and sincere, and for a moment he truly believed that with his brush and paints he could discover her goodness on a clean canvas. But she stopped laughing abruptly and squeezed his hand tightly with her bony fingers:

"Good, you say? I've even forgotten what that means! The last time I was good you were in a cradle sucking your mammy's milk. I remember I took this fella in once out of the goodness of my heart, but after a month or two he nearly had my head off with a hot poker, while good ol' me almost choked on her own blood, and he made off with all my miserable money that I'd saved up labouring under all those snoring males. And d'you know how I cured myself of my goodness? As soon as I'd sorted myself back out again, I made up my mind to have my revenge. Only I didn't manage to ever lay eyes on that louse again, and about half a year later this mutt came up to me on the street. Also looking so sad and shabby. So I took it in, and when it started wagging its tail greeting me, I gave it a plateful of poisoned food. I kept watching it lapping up the grub, this loyal, trusting, shaggy dumb old mutt. All the arsenic, which I'd saved up for that bastard, I fed to the dog instead... Keep playing, why've you stopped?" she turned to the wall and when the sound of the guitar resumed obediently she continued: "That's my little tale for you about my goodness. You embarrassed? Go ahead and paint that! Just don't forget to show me what you've done."

Alone shook his head:

"You cried afterwards. I can paint you crying. You did cry, didn't you? And after that you buried it with your own hands somewhere out in the yard, under the flowerbed. Or maybe you didn't plant any flowers there: you were scared of flowers as you were of your own goodness. Or scared that you didn't have enough of it to overcome your anger. Or that you didn't have enough to stop your heart aching... If you want, I'll paint all this... But you won't want me to."

Alone fell silent, while she stared at him – as if she was breathing him in with her very eyes. Then she got up and swept past him down the room.

"Get him a basin of water and wash his hands," she ordered through the wall.

The girl who had been playing the guitar materialised after a minute. Over her shoulder was a cotton towel. She sat where the madam had been, soaped her own palms and set about rubbing Alone's hands with them. Up to this point they hadn't looked at one another, but he felt that these hands were ready to help him, so ready in fact that they were almost ashamed of it.

"Don't stay quiet," said the madam. "You heard everything. Well what? What do you think?"

The girl quickly shrugged her shoulders and simply bent her head lower.

"Eh you..." said the madam and then again: "Eh you..."

She went up to the table and took his hand out of the water.

"He's just a little boy," she said, studying his palm intently. "I hardly believe it myself... Put him up upstairs, in the corner room."

She pushed his hand and it fell back into the water splashing her dress with dirty drops, but the madam did not stop. She left the room in a hurry to hide her face from him.

"For the time being your idiot girl can stay up there with you, we'll decide the rest tomorrow," she said without turning by way of parting.

And the girl didn't utter a word, not to her, nor to him. She got up and moved her chair closer to Alone's, spread the towel in her lap and took his hands into the towel.

He closed his eyes and listened with his fingers as his former self was forgetting itself; in the sweet darkness he remembered some innermost secret that grew out of his own flesh and seemed to grasp its unity with the time given to him in this joyful moment. Then she touched his cheek and he knew that the girl was now looking at him, but he did not open his eyelids so as to enjoy this pleasurable sightlessness a while longer. She tugged gently at his sleeve and he followed her down the dark corridor where a dim gas lamp from the bleached wall guarded the sounds of someone's muffled laughter and loud sighs behind the wall. The staircase was not lit and the girl turned round to take him by the hand once more.

They made it to the top of the creaky stairwell and ended up in front of a long row of doors all painted black. The girl came to a halt in front of the last one, took the key from the chain off her neck and entered, gesturing him to follow in behind her.

"Just don't light any candles," he said. "And don't tell me your name."

She did not argue with this. She calmly took the cover off the bed, puffed up the pillows and undressed – all in one movement, and all he could hear was the rustling of her dress against her skin as it fell at her feet. He took off his hat and looked for somewhere to put it.

"Don't hurry," said the girl, touching his belt with her cool fingers. "I'll do everything myself."

He lay on the mattress and covered his sweating forehead with his forearm. He thought of how much strength there was in him, and how easily she tamed it with her tenderness. At this moment he knew that she was beautiful. Her skin smelled of a river, only which river he had no idea until he embraced her smooth waves and buried his head in her hair. And only then did he realise that the name of this river was right there beside him, on his very lips, and that its name was deception, cry, pain and memory all rolled into one hot battle. And when he, trembling and crucified with pleasure, groaned in the torment of his new discovery, the bitter words plaintively burst forth from his throat:

"My doe..."

Then they lay in bed and caressed, finding a blessed comfort and shelter in the closeness of a barely known but very dear new creature this night.

"You're a good man," said the girl. "I know it. You're a good man."

He was silent and stroked her skin, trying hard not to think that this was not love at all, no, merely an imitation.

"Say something," she asked. "Anything you like."

He thought and said:

"You're beautiful. Like a doe."

"Like a what?" she said in surprise.

He hugged her and frowned: "Just so, as I said it... You're beautiful."

So as not to give her a chance to answer, he started kissing her, submitting this lithe proud body once more to the desire welling up in him.

They met the morning together, and as the dawn gradually won over the expanse of the sky, so they gradually grew ever more distant and strange from one another and tired of each other. The light had conquered the darkness and the peace.

"It's time," said the girl, getting up. He looked at her pale body, it seemed to him thickset and cold. "Like the morning hoar-frost," he thought to himself and turned away. "No, of course this wasn't love. It wasn't even like it."

They got dressed and waited, confused in the light and confusing their words, till the madam called them down. He drank golden tea from a delicate blue cup and thought how beautiful the girl was, only her beauty was not of the sort that he could capture on canvas.

"I don't even know your name," she said all of a sudden.

He looked up from the cup and replied.

"Me too."

"But you don't want to know," the girl exclaimed.

"No," he said. "I don't."

She bit her lip nervously and grinned bitterly:

"So you won't be coming back?"

"I don't know," he replied. "Where's my horse? Has it been fed?"

"I'll look after her," said the girl, paying no attention to his question. "I felt sorry for her yesterday."

"Rakhimat," he said. "Ra-khi-mat."

"The madam won't take any money off you. Not for her, not for me. Nor for the hay they fed your horse. She liked you."

"You mustn't let anyone see her. Let her hide here in the house. You'd best even forget her name."

"Rakhimat? All right, I'll forget it. Will she really have a child? She's lucky."

"Maybe," he said. "She doesn't know what shame is. Probably she is lucky. The lucky ones also perish."

"I understand," said the girl. "No one must know she's here."

The voice of the madam interrupted their conversation. Alone put down his cup and went downstairs.

"So now you're a man," said the madam smiling as he entered the salon. "Sit."

She pointed to the armchair. He looked about him. The room had changed drastically from the previous night. Now it seemed faded and tired, like the morning itself in this house.

"Do you want to say goodbye to her?" asked the madam.

"No," he replied. "She probably won't even remember by now who she came here with."

"She's sorting through the beads on my table," said the madam. "For two hours now. And not bored with it at all."

"Yes," he said. "She's a hardy one."

"It's funny," said the madam, her eyes growing moist. "I'd never have believed I'd be capable of it."

"I'm glad," he said. "In fact, I'm glad you are. I'm very hungry."

"And you can barely keep your eyes open. Are you hurrying off anywhere?"

"No," he said. "Not yet. I can go later. It'd be better if I went later."

"You off back home?"

"Not right away," he replied. "First I need to deceive a certain someone."

"Oho! You've managed to make yourself an enemy here?" she asked.

"More like a friend," he corrected her. "I have to deceive my own friend."

"Well, for that it's well worth to prepare yourself... They're bringing in breakfast now, I'll give orders."

"Thank you," he replied. "And then I'll take a nap, all right? Just a little nap."

The madam smiled, bent towards him and tousled his hair.

"But of course," she said. "You're our guest here. A guest, not a client."

She went out. A short while later a serving girl appeared and put a tray of food before him. He spread his bread with butter, poured the translucent honey over it and ate greedily. Then he poured some milk and drank it up with gusto feeling the sated warmth spread in his stomach. Once he'd eaten his fill, he set off down the corridor to the staircase and went up to the same room where he had been swimming the night before in the tender darkness and pronounced that forbidden name. He knocked but no one answered. He opened the door, checked the room was empty and without undressing flopped down onto the made-up bed.

It was already way past midday when the madam came to wake him. Before she bade him goodbye, she asked:

"When do we expect you back? Should we wait for you?"

He thought for a bit and said:

"Yes, wait. Take this." He stuffed the leather purse of coins into her hand. The madam thrust her hands quickly behind her back and cried angrily:

"How dare you! You and your worthless pennies! Fool!"

"No," he said. "I'm no fool. At least, I'm not so dumb as to buy your goodness. I know it can't be swapped for coins and that it's not for sale. But take the money. It's hers, not yours. Then it'll be for her child."

She took the purse unwillingly, and he moved off to leave, but suddenly she said:

"It'd be better if you left from the back door, the same way you came in. Am I right?"

He nodded.

"The servant will show you out," said the madam. "Farewell, my guest..."

They smiled at one another and he thought: maybe I'll paint her after all. I'll probably paint her old and weary, but with radiance in her eyes. Now I need to get rid of this other picture. It all depends on how I get rid of it. Maybe there won't be any other after it.

He went out into the yard, saddled his horse, and led it through the back yard to the oak gate in the mossy fence to the side and trotted out into the small dirty alleyway. From there he set off to the ironmonger's house.

Three days passed from the time he kidnapped Rakhimat. Toward evening of the first day Gappo became anxious at her absence: first he was aware of a restless hunger, then of the empty cooking pot that had been scrubbed clean of the last meal cooked in it the day before, then of the knowing silence that concealed some disaster, and then of a fear that the normal order of things had suddenly been disrupted, the unquestionable rule of rituals desecrated, which had been observed by them both for no less than two decades (it was the only thing, apart from the weekly routine of washing up that allowed him twice daily – at breakfast and dinner – to feel that he was in some way her father and she his daughter.) He was worried sick by the wild, unthinkable idea that Rakhimat had disappeared since morning. The panting Gappo ran uphill, burst into the nykhas and collapsed onto the stone bench where my grandfather sat, Aguz and blind Soslan.

"Rakhimat," croaked Gappo, eyes bulging. "She's gone!"

The search was taken up at once. In the morning she had been sighted down by the river but where she had got to next nobody knew. Just in case, they combed the entire riverbank. Due to the onset of darkness they decided to put off until the next morning the young men's expedition into the mountains where Rakhimat had loved to roam so as to share with them later her taciturn and clumsy words of joy. However the next day brought with it no results, so then my grandfather, returning in the evening from the nykhas, muttered to Dakhtsyko, who walked alongside him:

"You can't even say about her that her suffering is over. Suffering doesn't apply to her."

"You're right," said Dakhtsyko. "Death for her would just be a continuation of the water she followed. She loved to follow water and perhaps the water beckoned her..."

"And Gappo?" they were both silent, then Grandfather pronounced: "Poor Gappo."

"Yes," returned Dakhtsyko. "One way or another he was her father."

Deep down the villagers no longer doubted that she was dead, and only for good form pretended that they believed the search would find something. Amongst themselves they no longer spoke of her, but of Gappo who in those few days had changed so greatly that hardly a soul would have nicknamed him Withered Arm: his withered arm had at once become less conspicuous and somehow utterly unimportant. Far more conspicuous now was the look in his bulging grey eyes: they seemed stunned that anyone else besides himself could have any need for the life of that creature assigned to him by the cruel whim of fate to be his daughter. Was her life really needed by God? Gappo was too old to accept this without protest: this was not the God he believed in.

Much was said also of Soslan, but my grandfather grew furious at this:

"He's completely lost his mind," he complained to my uncle. "He keeps going on and on about some kind of hidden blood that will cause some disaster. I don't understand a word of it. People should be ashamed. Pah!" He spat, offended not so much by the blind man's confused prophecies, more by his youth: Soslan was Grandfather's junior by some twenty years if a day, and making out as if he was now our village elder, and what angered him most of all was how yesterday's youngster dared go around prophesying and predicting when he was wall-eyed like a mushroom and not yet advanced enough in years to be a prophet! But nonetheless Soslan stood his ground:

"Hidden blood is ripening into disaster," he proclaimed at the nykhas, pointing his finger meaningfully at the skies and seeming to listen in on his own blindness. ("When we looked at him at those moments, we imagined he wasn't blind at all, and that his eyes were just turned in on themselves..." my uncle told me many years later.) "Our land will go through a great pain and quake, and finally will break into pieces... Remember you my words!"

But my grandfather flew into a fury at this and said at the time:

"The man's a lunatic. The full moon's gone and sucked

all the pus out of his wounded brain. He's remembered his dead daughter and it's gone and re-opened his old wounds, and now here's us, sitting and listening to his ravings."

Of course, it wasn't just him that got angry. The other elders got cross at him too: who knows what he's seeing there in that darkness of his, they mused left alone with their doubts... They were seriously disconcerted that he had not until then revealed his gift of foresight and had never challenged their future with his terrible word; and so they couldn't judge the accuracy of his predictions: they did not have any past experience.

To cut a long story short, the disappearance of Rakhimat became an event elevated in significance by the consequences it brought in its train. When they had first heard about it and at once deciding that Gappo's idiot daughter had been carried away by the river, the villagers, for all their sincere compassion for his grief, never even began to think that it would be so strongly reflected on their own lives and make them suddenly sense a forbidding and vague anxiety for their own future, all the more so as in some inexplicable way the very foundations of their everyday existence had irreparably altered: the nykhas had changed, the same nykhas on which the same people had gathered at the same time of day to have the same sort of conversation. Now two of them, Gappo and Soslan, were perceived by the others as almost uninvited guests (Gappo, stunned by the disappearance of his weak-minded buxom daughter, whom for the preceding thirty years he had been unsure whether he had loved, despised or was simply ashamed of, sat there with fish-like bulging eyes, causing anyone to stumble on their words, halting any conversation; and Soslan, blinded for two years by being confronted face to face with the violent death of his daughter whom,

everyone knew, he worshipped and cherished, so much so
that her heart grew suffocated by his love and strove ever
upwards to the very heights of the heavens, but when she
fell from that crag right before his eyes he only went blind,
sanctifying his grief with noble suffering – he lost his sight
but not his reason, as our men supposed amongst themselves
he had done now, when the idiot girl had vanished from the
aul, whom he now tied into his darkness, that suddenly
became the sole subject on his mind, a darkness that he
touched – and whether this is true or not the villagers could
only guess – by those eyes of his that had turned in on
themselves so as to see the threat that hung over the future
of everyone in our aul.)

Yes, the nykhas had changed now, although before it
also witnessed all sorts of things: grief and death, baseness
and luck, stupidity and peace. But from that time on never
more would it be a sacred and proud bastion of wise, patient
agreement, the last resort of hope for the weak or a sacrificial
altar on which the strong would lay out the fruits of their
generosity. Never again would it become the pledge of our
community spirit – and even the pledge of our common
mistakes, which had to be paid for jointly and unquestioningly.
Never again would it be light-hearted and jolly, nor would it
nourish our hearts with joyful memories of carefree youth,
nor commit desperate pranks and indulge in betting, nor
afterwards be filled with a sense of shame before their ancient
dignity and the declining years. Nor would it ever again be
able to escape from the regret at the rift that had taken place
in the aul, nor escape premonition of a stern time of reckoning
for all. There was no escaping the damp shadows of the
disasters that had been prophesied at the nykhas.

"When I watched your grandfather in those days," my
uncle told me, filling up with his memories my father's

enforced eight-year absence from the aul, "when I looked at him sitting at the nykhas, downcast, aged with an extra old age that had caught up with him instead of the ageless Gappo, I read in his brown wrinkles his futile refusal to accept his lot, his disagreement with those painful and tormented speeches, his rebellion against the sun that hung as a stain in the sky over his head and whose acid yellow stung his eyes, his disagreement with the air itself that once united them at the nykhas with time-honoured traditions but now oppressed and suffocated them with insinuations. I almost felt as if the "hidden blood" Soslan was going on about was hidden under those same pockmarked old stones on which they all sat there... You know," said Uncle, "they looked as if they lost something vital to them, some kind of essential smell... Yes, that's right, I think it was a smell. You could call it the smell of the ages. D'you know what I mean?"

I did in fact. But he went on explaining.

"It can probably be explained better, but I'm no past master at such things. I just think it was an ordeal for them to sit there in the open without feeling with the napes of their necks the blue thickness of the skies above. It was as if the nykhas had now been sullied, but how, when and by what, no one knew.

"Hold on," I interrupted. "You've forgotten about Alone..."

"No," replied my uncle. "I haven't forgotten about anyone. He was also there, of course. And he knew, of course, more than anyone else there. But that didn't make things any the easier for him. He was aware of Gappo's ever bulging eyes. And he couldn't help hearing Soslan's prophecies. The thing is how he listened to them... He was all ears! And he took them more seriously than could be expected of him, which made Grandfather all the more furious inside. Grandfather realised more than most that Alone was marked for luck, which meant that going against him was as much use as running up against a wall. Yet I think there was something else that Grandfather was missing in all this; it wasn't the amount of attention Alone gave the rants and ravings of Soslan, but more how it showed on his face."

"How do you mean?" I asked. "How did it show?"

"Hmmm," Uncle shrugged. "The devil only knows... But it showed there for sure. Only I can't explain it ... but then again..." he said for the first time trying to put into words not just for my benefit but for his own too, the essence of the flickering image before his eyes since his youth: "Somehow, the words that are forming on the tip of my tongue are: he was depleted. I mean Alone. That's how it affected him. That's it. He seemed to be running out, slowly but surely, of strength before our very eyes. And we even started to look upon him differently. No, of course, he was still disliked but now more as a person and not as a monster who had sprouted out of that stripling at the price of thieving and who had disturbed our peace and quiet for all those years."

"A monster," said I. "I see. It seems like the monster shrivelled up and became a human being."

"Something like that," Uncle replied. "Just don't forget though that I only know this now. The others I can't answer for."

"But was he really such a monster?" I asked.

"Eh now, eh..." he looked at me disapprovingly, like I'd turned out to be less clever than he'd imagined. "No one knows that even now. I don't know if anyone ever will..."

At this point our conversation stopped but I went on puzzling why Alone should believe in the prophesy. For a long time I could find no answer. I thought about it so doggedly that blisters formed on my brains, and I felt them swell and grow, boring away beneath my skull and making it itch terribly. But then they burst, and suddenly I worked it out: he was waiting for retribution.

Alone was waiting for retribution. First he had attained freedom, then freedom had enslaved him, compelling him to interfere in our lives and challenge the aul's fates; then his freedom was too much for him, it gradually became for him some baleful, hated necessity and he could hardly bear any more this pursuit of it in time, out of time, but more often for and against time itself. He simply felt that there must be an ending, and he'd managed to get up to so many tricks with that freedom of his that this ending could very well take the form of retribution.

He had more grounds, naturally, to guess just what this "hidden blood" was, and even knew where it might be hidden. Only he was probably not sure whose blood Soslan was talking about: if it was blood to be prevented from spilling then there were two answers: Rakhimat's and Barysbi's; if it was blood that had already been spilt then it was Soslan's daughter and the shopkeeper's assistant; and then the reason why this blood was "hidden" was down to the fact that he'd not yet revealed the full truth of those matters to anyone. If Soslan meant blood that would still flow then given the number of possible permutations, whose it was could be anyone's guess. Or maybe Soslan's prophecy was even more cunning, and pointed to blood both already and not yet spilled, hidden in the earth and upon it, earmarked for the future and forgotten in the past. Or maybe it was even more sly than that and he had in mind a certain individual, even himself? After all, what could "hidden blood" be taken to mean? A life saved or a vengeance postponed? Or maybe even postponed vengeance for someone's life already having been saved? Or maybe a vengeance saved only by such a postponement?

Whatever the case, what interested him most in Soslan's words was a foretaste of retribution to come. So it was no accident that my uncle talked of smells that had been lost: he was talking about the whole lot of them, including Alone. It turned out that even he had lost this smell of the ages. Only I think that unlike the others his sense of smell was far more acute: in the strange prophecies of Soslan he could sense an idea, which he reduced to the impending retribution for his deeds. And what is retribution if not a message from eternity? Even if he lost its smell he could at least hear the wise echoes it was sending to the mundane world, and this echo put him on guard. "He was depleted," as my uncle put it. Now I understood that what he had been depleted of was his confidence, his indifference to the fact that he might end up on the losing side. How could it be otherwise if from now on he had to live with the omen sent to him by eternity and with its persistent and disturbing echo threatening to call him to account! It dawned upon him that he had been challenged, and he decided to take up this challenge, in spite of the power and sophistication of his adversary. On the whole, as I saw it, that was the only way left for him to do battle with eternity and fate. Anything else would have made him a fugitive. And flight was no less impossible for him than was defeat.

Now that he'd abducted Rakhimat and hidden her from sure death in a brothel (the only place where it had been possible to hide her from the prying eyes of the villagers, none of whom had the money or the guts to penetrate the walls of that mysterious establishment that served sin, from where he had just returned, having for the first time known a woman there and in the thickness of the night tasted the pungent spices of its beauty), and now that he had deceived his friend, stolen for the second time in three days, ridden out of the fort at dawn and stuffed his ill-gotten gains in the first juniper bush he came across so that in a year's time, when his friend's enemy left the aul alive (which saved my father from becoming a murderer) this same friend would be granted proof of his innocence from theft and this story would get proof of its credibility; now that Alone, who had been twining the multicoloured threads of all these individual lives together in a knot, had returned home, had gone up to the nykhas and heard the prophecy, he interpreted it as testament to the importance of the lives he had saved and in his own way felt a sense of pride that this prophecy promised him revenge for the suffering he had caused and a bad end. But then he remembered that blind Soslan talked about our land and the terrible fate that lay in wait for it, and he felt ill at ease. He probably tried easing his conscience with the thought that prophecies don't always come true and ordinary mortals don't fully comprehend them.

So for this reason or some other, at nights he started visiting the graves of his ancestors more often.

"He sought peace for his heart in them," my uncle told me. "His spirit was disturbed. It even came to my notice, though I never paid much attention to that sort of thing. At that time something quite different was on our minds, it's even shameful to say it out loud..."

Yes, I thought, remembering back: bedbugs.

They came upon the aul suddenly, infesting the whole place and transforming it into one giant stuffy hive of bugs. In the mornings our folk would awake from the rustling of brown pods crushed under their backs, while on bedclothes was traced out a sticky dry map of the previous night's bloodsucking upon their badly bitten bodies. They tried smoking out the bugs, they burned mats and mattresses, fumigated walls, nooks and crannies, but all was in vain. For days on end the women steamed their linen over open fires.

Each night, under its dark cloak, a warm stream of living putrescence would obsequiously flow again, forming in puddles on their bedding. These globules of greed burst open under feet and were instantly overwhelmed by hundreds of new tiny moving bundles.

It continued like this for a month. Only Alone's house was spared their presence.

"This we found out from auntie Dakhtsyko, who was taking care of him," Uncle told me.

When they caught sight of him sprawled by the bridge, the old men merely spat out with contempt and decided that he'd gone back to drinking. They ordered the young'uns to carry him back to his place and let him sleep it off. But when they got hold of him they realised he wasn't drunk but was burning with a fever. So then they sent for wizened old auntie Dakhtsyko. She was somewhere near a thousand years old and she'd lost damn all from her memory, but there was no one like her when it came to illnesses. It was enough for her to come to the patient's bedside, whisper some indecipherable tongue-twister for half an hour to his illness, then she'd nodded in satisfaction, open her fading yellow eyes and order people to bring her this and that, and then, once she'd driven everyone out of the room, cook up remedies for him by her own hand.

But sometimes Anissa, as she was called, froze before the sick with an offended grimace and would utter not a single word, breathing in with disgust the smell of death swirling around the sickroom that had already planted itself in the body but was yet unseen, and then she would squeamishly cock her head and shake her hands, as if getting rid of some cobwebs, and would leave without a word, hunched angrily and shuffling her feet. She had never once been wrong, and so they did not always and rather unwillingly ran to her for her services, out of fear that in place of her spells and charms they would get only her death sentence and would have to wait for it to be carried out – sometimes days, sometimes weeks, sometimes even months – in the closeness of the house entangled in an invisible but vice-like spider's web.

But they called her over to Alone right away, for there was no one there to be spared from the possibility of her eloquent silence or for the simple reason that there was no one else to call for to help him – I won't be the judge of that. And maybe they saved his life that they could not care less for. Once Anissa had taken Alone's fever in hand and he had recovered, all of a sudden all the bedbugs vanished from our aul. A true wonder it was.

As we scarcely came back to our senses and were able to look around again, I saw Alone from our yard: he sat on his porch, huddling up his folded arms to his breast and hanging his head right down to his knees. He stared somewhere out in front of him. And from my angle it was clear that he could make out nothing that was in his line of sight apart from the outer reaches in the far blue yonder shrouded in mist. I could see the mist corroding his eyes and noticed too that he seemed to be shivering in the slightest breeze, though the day was clear and young. "I remember I thought at the time that I'd never seen him sitting there all hunched up like that, anxiously looking out at that clear day," Uncle told me.

"I thought later it must have been the day he'd received news of the shopkeeper's death. On that tranquil day for the rest of the aul he was pondering what to do next. He decided to keep up the fight and went off back to the fort to find out the date of the court hearing. He stayed there for a whole week, trying to figure out where the dead shopkeeper had buried the sack of stolen goods. Only the woman with the deep blue eyes flatly refused to help him, so each evening after their meetings he would make his way over to the house where he had hidden that second blood. He drank hard till his ears rang viciously, chose himself a girl, each time a new one, and bought her for a whole night so as to see out the cold and darkness by her side. Only the one that he'd been with that first time he never ordered again. I think that's the way it must have been."

In my imagination, when he once again knocked on that door with a red lantern and saw the madam again, and when she smiled back at him to say: "Welcome back, guest," he replied:

"Not guest. But you'll get paid tomorrow."

She looked more closely into his dilated eyes and asked: "Oh, that bad, eh? I'll just go fetch..."

"No!" he screamed. "I don't need her. Give me another one. I'll wait till another one is free, but not her, don't call for her. Her I can't buy."

"Is that really necessary?" the madam asked. "You really have to buy one?"

"Yes," he said back. "But you'll only get paid tomorrow."

The next day, waking up by lunchtime with a splitting headache and ordering a shot of vodka, he went back to the hospital to see the shopkeeper's burnt mistress, but that day they didn't even let him near her. So from there he went off to the barracks, called for "one of the chiefs" and without bargaining, sold his horse to them. Then he went on foot to some inn and drank as much vodka there as was needed for him to last out till the onset of evening when he could go back to the whorehouse. There he got out the soggy banknotes from his pocket and divided them up into two unequal piles, the larger of which he handed over to the madam, and wondered:

"Have a look and tell me how many nights does that get?"

She looked at the money and asked gloomily:

"Where's your horse?"

He waved his drunken arm nowhere in particular and said:

"Serving the tsar and the fatherland... So much for him... So how many nights does this lot get?"

"Not many," she replied. "You'd best hand over the rest."

He was surprised, but didn't object and handed over the other pile, asking with some irritation:

"Well?"

"That's only enough for a week," replied the madam.

"No worry," he smirked. "I won't pester you for the change."

The next day the madam invited him to breakfast and said, looking him straight in the eyes:

"These past two days you haven't asked after Rakhimat once. Why's that?"

He seemed to fizzle out at once, and replied after a short silence:

"How should I know... has she... grown?"

His voice was low and soft, as if flattened with guilt.

"Of course she has," said the madam. "She's pregnant. When you're pregnant your tummy grows. Sometimes it happens very quickly. Especially in establishments like this. That's why you brought her here isn't it? You thought she'd be safe here, and we'd look after anyone who was to become a mother. Am I right?"

He nodded.

"But now you have no wish to see her at all. Why?" the madam insisted. "What are you, ashamed or something? Ashamed of her or of yourself? I want to know."

"Of myself," he returned. "And of her. For both of us, if you like."

"That's just it," said the madam. "You're ashamed to look her in the eye, because her eyes have stayed innocent, but yours haven't. For she sinned without knowing what she was doing, but you sinned in the knowledge you were sinning, though you had a drunken head on you at the time. You're ashamed buying girls for the night, but getting one for free fills you with even more shame, and what's most shameful for you is that you have to choose the lesser of these two shames so as not to face yourself in a strange town... Where's your friend? Answer me! Cat got your tongue? Aren't you tired of your silence? You don't say a word about Rakhimat, not a word about yourself, not a word about your deceived friend. So what happened to him?"

He clasped his head in his hands and sat slowly rocking himself in front of her from side to side. Finally he spoke up:

"I've hidden him in jail. There was no choice. Otherwise he'd have killed someone. And even if he didn't he'd never have forgiven himself. Now he's in prison, just don't ask after him any more. Please. I'm not ready for it yet. But Rakhimat I will see. Show me her tomorrow, all right?

"Fine," she agreed. "Now eat and get some rest."

"First I must go," Alone exclaimed. "I've got to get down to work."

He would visit the shopkeeper's mistress in the hospital each morning, and would leave empty-handed. He had no more money for drinking and his spirit was so low that his legs carried him of their own accord down to the riverside, where he would stand for hours on end looking at the raging waters and thinking how easy it would be just to give in and step into the current. One day in broad daylight he got into a fight with a strong tradesman, who rolled his cart past and disturbed his quiet contemplation and enraptured wonder at the onrushing river by swearing at him for not having heard his cry to watch out. Alone threw himself at him with such savage fury that the trader at first forgot his own strength and for a slack-jawed moment didn't raise his fists to the blows raining down on him, till he flew into his own rage in return. The trader's fists were thickset and heavy, like ingots of pig iron, the likes of which Alone had only seen piled up by the back door of a factory when he'd climbed up exploring one of the town's alleyways. The trader panted, pounded him with sweeping hooks and dull unerring punches, smashing him down to the ground and then waiting with fists raised ready for him to get back on his feet. Finally he couldn't get up from the ground that at the start of their fight had been dusty but was now bloodstained and muddy. The trader looked round at the crowd of satisfied onlookers that had formed around them, rolled down the sleeves of his sweat-drenched shirt, picked up his cart and said in an embarrassed bass:

"Well, get out of the way, you tramps... let the strongest man pass. This fella – pah! What a stubborn bastard. It'll be a shame if he goes and dies..."

But of course, he didn't die. When two workmen carried him at twilight to the porch, the madam thrust some five-kopeck pieces their way and ordered the servant girl to wash him and put him to bed; later she went to his bedside and observed in puzzlement a pure and happy smile on his lips as he slept. That's how I imagine it, at any rate. Afterwards he must have come to, and she probably said to him:

"You looked like a child recovering. There was no pain on your face. It's all covered in blood and all swollen up, but it showed no pain."

"That's because I was swimming in the river," he answered. "I imagined it was carrying me away on its waves and I was flying amidst its foam and coolness towards the warm red night... Tell me, is it morning already?"

"Yes," the madam replied. "Only, don't get out on the wrong side of bed. Don't let the pain in."

"I'll do my best," he said, and then added: "Remember I once suggested to you that I paint your portrait, but you didn't fancy it? Today I'm glad it's worked out like that. My daubs only cause people pain."

"Shame," said the madam. "I changed my mind on that one."

"Forgive me," said Alone. "I didn't mean to upset you."

"You'll upset me all the more if you let that pain torture your face. I'm looking at it and I believe less and less that it was like a child's at night."

"A recovering child," he corrected her. "You know I was only ten when people stopped calling me a boy, and a clump of grey hair appeared on the back of my head. I was shocked when the first time we met you called me a milksop."

"Since then you've grown up a lot," she said, stroking his head briskly with her dry hand. "I'll never call you that any more."

"I must go," he said. "I need to get dressed."

"You won't be able to."

"Help me to get up," he said, raising himself up on his elbows. "I can't lose a whole day. I have to try..."

"Try what?" she asked. "What do you have to try?"

"Just help me get up," he shot back, gritting his teeth. His forehead and temples were now shrouded in beads of sweat. "Please!"

She pressed her lips and eyed him up and down. Then she grasped him from behind by his shoulders and helped him sit up, get dressed, pull on his soft boots and get up on his two feet.

"I'll manage," he said. His head was spinning, but he didn't think anything of it. He'd manage.

"Fine," said the madam. "Go manage. But next time you collapse in the mud and good folk come by to help you, best remember faster where I live, right?"

He stepped outside and shuffled to the hospital. While he slowly made his way up the streets, passers-by got out of his way and looked at him with curiosity. He moved to his goal through a twinkling shroud of blinding sunlight, constantly repeating to himself over and over again: If they let me in to see her, I'll say he's on his way to her. I'll promise her that I'll bring him over myself. I'll hide my pity and disgust from her and I'll swap my deceit for that stolen sack. She knows where it's been put. I can tell from her eyes. Her deep blue eyes didn't have it in them to lie to me, only her mouth lied, but her eyes admitted that she knew where it was hidden.

As I imagine it, if he'd managed to see her that day he would have forced her to tell him everything. But since he didn't, it could only mean that he didn't make it as far as the hospital that day. Probably that's it: he didn't make it. Something stopped him on the way. Not his own body, he'd cope with its submitting its suffering to the stubbornness of his will and the groans of his wounded conscience. It must have been something quite different, sudden and overwhelming, like a revelation, something he'd passed by without noticing it before, but now suddenly stumbled up against and stopped in shock. I even think that what he saw on his way was something utterly commonplace, that he hadn't given the slightest bit of notice to the day before but now couldn't... I imagine, I think... To tell the truth, I'm so used to imagining it that I'm almost certain. All the more so as I know the exact street he took up to the hospital, and here it all comes together for me: he sees the Greek butcher carving smoked meat with his enormous cleaver. As I imagine it, Alone comes to a shuddering halt and freezes to the spot, propping his shoulder up against the railing of the public baths located nearby, and watches, without averting his gaze, how from beneath the crumbs of blackened scum the butcher exposes the dead brownish flesh. He feels sick in the stomach, and thinks that he is like that knife, like that butcher. Through his nausea he imagines that the lightning he'd painted on his canvas sparked the fire in the ironmonger's shop. The fire had spread out, devoured the shopkeeper and crippled the woman. I don't want to be no butcher, he thinks. I won't start carving people up... He feels sick and he carefully turns round, not letting go of the wall. Then I see him wander back to the whorehouse.

"What day is it today?" he asks the servant girl who opens the door for him. She replies, and Alone thinks to himself: that makes tomorrow the last day.

"Listen," he says, turning to the girl, "you couldn't agree to do me a little favour, could you? I've fallen slightly ill. But someone has to go down to the town hospital and tell a certain someone that if they suddenly change their mind, they can send me the news down here, but only up till tomorrow evening. What do you think?"

She shrugs and then nods and sticks out her palm to be paid.

"Later," he says. "I'm dry right now."

The girl doesn't believe him, curls her lip in contempt and spits back abruptly:

"Have it your way. But it's no good pinching pennies..."

That's how I imagine it to myself. I know how the story continues and how it all ends, so that enables me to reconstruct the details and the tracery that have been smeared over with silence, and draw out their curves and lines in a firm outline that bears some resemblance to them.

That night the madam sends two of her girls over to his room.

"She's ordered us to tell you that this is for last night as well," said the first as she got undressed. "You idled around yesterday night, so today you have to work for two."

He thinks: "She wants me to be repelled by all this, she wants me to clear off in time. She's afraid I'll go off the rails but doesn't want that to happen right before her eyes."

And come the next morning, when he was left all alone to stare at the bare ceiling, whispering to himself through his teeth: "She got her way. I feel dirty and disgusted. Like I've been gorging myself on wool – it's made me feel sick..." He hears a knock at the door, and answers weakly:

"Come in!"

Rakhimat appeared at the doorway. She came in awkwardly, sideways, her tummy brushing against the doorframe, making her catch hold of her belly from below with hands quivering and shaking in fright. For a minute he looked at her but couldn't find any words to say, then he sat up in his bed, wrapped himself in his blanket and beckoned her to the chair. She understood him and sat down obediently, smoothing out the folds of her new Russian dress as she did so. Her swollen face wore the round arc of that familiar smile. Alone gulped and said hoarsely:

"I see all's well with you..."

She shuddered, and knit her brows, translating what had been said to her – not so much the words as their sounds – into the language of her own form of madness, and nodded in glee; she delved inside her collar and pulled out a clenched up fist; she opened up her fingers and he saw a tiny mother-of-pearl box.

"What's this?" he asked. She got up and without any embarrassment sat down at the edge of his bed; with a glint of pride in her eye she opened the box's fragile lid. Inside it lay a knitted little doll in a miniscule cradle. Looking most pleased with herself, Rakhimat closed back its lid and hid the little box back in her bosom. Then she rested her head on one shoulder and blissfully lowered her eyes, stroking her tummy and murmuring a mute song. Alone paled at this and fidgeted under the bedclothes. Now he wanted more than anything on earth to get up and run away. Rakhimat didn't notice his disquiet in the slightest, however, and continued humming to herself, gently rocking on the edge of the bed, like a domesticated animal.

"Only now she'd been tamed by her pregnancy," Alone told me before he left us forever, and a bitter wrinkle quivered as a dark shadow round his lips as he said this. "Not coins, not beads, but the child growing inside her. I didn't then know who had explained to her about her motherhood. But it was a cruel thing to do, I thought at the time. It seemed very cruel to me. Just like making a hen fly up towards the skies, fooling its head that it's a bird too... Afterwards, of course, it became clear that no one had said a thing to her. And that she'd made the doll herself. She's only asked the madam for the little box and got permission to use her yarns. It turns out her womanly intuition had explained it all to her. And if that's so..."

"If that's so," I continued his sentence for him when he stuttered, "you began to wonder whether all your efforts were really worth it? The escape, the town, the whorehouse? If her intuition could have explained it all to her then she might possibly have been able to come to her own rescue. For instance, she could have run to Soslan and fallen at his feet, crying for mercy. He could have saved her..."

"Yes," said Alone. Then he corrected himself: "No..." then he shook his head and said: "I mean, as for Soslan, you're right. He would have saved her, as he alone knew what it was like to lose a daughter. And Gappo wouldn't have stopped him defending Rakhimat, let alone her unborn child. But that's not the point. Another thing occupied my thoughts: why had her instincts kept silent when she was still back in the aul? Ask your own mother and she'll tell you... Ask if you get the chance, has any woman ever carried a child below her heart and not been the first to know about it? That's what got me. What was happening to our land if a mother could not hear inside herself? If a woman can't feel that she's a mother? Was our land ready to be destroyed mercilessly and could it no longer be saved? But why?"

"Do you know why?" I asked him, once the silence had drawn itself out and the quiet had grown deafening. "Is it any clearer to you now?"

Alone raised his eyes and it occurred to me that this was the look of a dead man when his eyelids are closed for him. And he lives with it. Maybe he'll die with that look. Only who will close his eyes for him? I won't have to. I won't be beside him when his time comes... He said:

"Maybe at some point I'll understand it with my head. But my heart understood it long ago. Back then even. It's often enough to ask a proper question and your heart prompts an answer."

"True," I said. "You're right. That's what's happening to me right now."

He nodded his approval and said:

"You are truly your father's son." I understood that it was meant as praise.

I waited a while and asked: "So then you came back home, right? After your meeting with Rakhimat you journeyed back home. On what?"

He knitted his brows, blushed and replied with some irritation:

"Whatever next! I went back home that same day towards evening..."

"But you didn't tell me how? On that same horse you had before?" I didn't leave him alone.

He clicked his tongue and his shoulders quivered. Then he said:

"All right. As it happens you really do take after your father. You're too like him to forgive me this."

I thought: sometimes it's harder to forgive one without guilt than if he turns out to be guilty. Sometimes the innocent may be guiltier than guilt itself, even if it's not his fault. But when a person destroys himself this innocence becomes worse than the guilt of a death-bearing alien. At least that's what you feel when someone dies before your eyes.

"You mean to say that she got hold of another horse for you," I said out loud. "The madam got hold of a new horse for you, paying with the money you received for your old horse. You might even say the new one was not as sharp, for when you'd sold yours, you'd hardly driven a hard bargain."

"No one knows about that..."

"Of course no one knew about that," I interrupted him. "Though back in the aul they probably noticed that your horse was less sharp than before. I haven't checked up on that. No need to check: if you think about someone hard you learn to see behind his back. I've acquired that skill... So you returned from there on the horse that the madam had got for you. Maybe she only lent it to you – no matter: you knew yourself she wouldn't accept it back. But most likely she gave it to you as a gift, and you can't refuse a gift, so you promised her something in return, say, a painting... Aha! That's more like it. Promising her that, you hopped into saddle, arriving back home in two days, and another couple of days later you went over to Barysbi's and told him that he would have to take my

Narrator prediction / imagination of the jail story

father's place in jail. He'd have to buy on the side that sack of swag, turn up in town on the day of the court hearing and admit to a robbery that he hadn't committed. You told him that'd be fairer because you hadn't stolen for my father, but for him, for Barysbi, and probably you gave him some kind of timeframe to think it over. After his time was up he agreed. For if he didn't agree, where could he hide? I suspect he wasn't so much afraid of my father or his revenge as of what you'd go round saying to everyone. And not so much everyone, as his own son! If you told his dear son about all his mischief, life for Barysbi would be crossed out by the contempt he'd been held in by his own blood, by a single stern wrinkle of a frown in his young brow. When the day of the trial drew near and you had to prepare for your journey, Barysbi came over to you with the sack of goods, and you made your way to the fort together, but there you learnt you were late, you hadn't counted on my father getting right to the bottom of your secrets, especially since he saw for himself who had actually stolen, and knew that the robbery could only be committed for his own good. You hadn't reckoned that my father wouldn't wait for you, especially if he'd suddenly heard some familiar sounds and recognised a certain word in it and asked it to be explained to him. You and Barysbi didn't reckon that there exists in nature such a crafty beast as chance, and this beast simply hates any cunning plots. You didn't reckon on your own compliance and so took to arguing and quarrelling with each other, not knowing what to do next, for now my father would be put on trial not just for a trivial and doubtful robbery but for the attack on his guard and the getaway. You didn't expect you'd made fools of yourselves, one because he'd been deceived by chance, the other because he'd let himself be bossed around by another fool... Only there's one thing I can't grasp: how could you – you! – be so foolish for so insufferably long?"

Alone waved his arms, clicked his tongue meaningfully, jabbed his finger at my chest and smirked bitterly:

"Whatever next! If everything turned out as you'd have it I'd also have not had a clue why. But the fact is that on that day Barysbi wasn't in the fort at all..."

I turned to stone. And when I caught my breath again, I could only ask him:

"He wasn't there?"

"No," said Alone. "Not him. Nor me either."

Then we looked one another in the eye. We stared and stared until my head span. I lowered my eyes and said:

"I can't make up my mind whether you're a know-all genius, the like of whom the world has never seen, or a common traitor who are legion."

"Neither," he replied. "You just raced ahead and never gave me a chance to finish my story. In your rush you ran out of breath, like a borzoi on the hunt getting so pleased with its agility that it loses the trail."

"Where did I go wrong?" I asked.

"From where you started talking about the sack. Barysbi did come over to me three days before the hearing, but he didn't have any sack on him, which of course put me on my guard, but I decided to bide my time and not ask any questions just yet. We chatted about this and that, some trivial nonsense, but then he said to me, and his face, I remember, shone in the dry autumn sun, making it look like a dirty fingernail, "Have you heard about old Gappo"s daughter? The one that's been born an idiot and is surely going to die one? And maybe even won't be able to give birth neither...' At that I turned my back to his shiny forehead and pretended that I was examining the beams in my barn. But he continued: "They"ve all decided she's gone and got drowned in the river. Idiots! But, imagine it, I suddenly had another idea: why shouldn't she instead go and help with the housework at that whorehouse in the fort, while she's expecting her little bastard? Why couldn't she have been made big with child by some local sketcher, and then with his help go into hiding from her father's righteous fury? That's all really clever for an idiot-girl like that – running away to the town and hiding out in a whorehouse, where all the girls are just like her: they also spread their legs for a few coins, but not everyone gets pregnant, and not everyone's an idiot. But then maybe, it dawned on me, it's the best thing for her, they'll look after her more and take pity on her with tears in their eyes. I also got thinking that meanwhile it wouldn't be worth changing our simpletons' minds about it all. Because they'll all immediately flare up, leap straight on their horses and gallop off to take her life, but before they do maybe they'll go and shoot our new young mischief-making daddy, even if it turns out he's not even the real daddy, but who's going to sort it out when the blood in their brains starts boiling over! See, I've decided not to tell a soul, except for you, and not share with anyone for the time being what I started thinking today. Is that all right with you? Or else she'll never give birth, poor wretch. I think, well, let her have her kid! I'm not going over to the fort now so as not to scare her. Or else I might cause her a miscarriage, see... No, honestly! Someone strongly advised me to take a trip to the fort today, but I've decided to stay put. Who was that now? Well, yes, you were the one that gave me that advice! That's right! Now I remember. For some reason you were so keen for us to go over there together. But now don't get angry that I've changed my mind. Sometimes you've got to spare yourself, right? And don't you go over there either. Well what's there to see over there that you haven't seen already? Stay at home and think a bit less about your friend that's over there in prison. Let him go to the dogs! All the more so as our people have no

Barysbi knew he sent her to the whorehouse

idea yet in their heads where he's got to. You even lied to his old man that he's gone over to Russia for some easy money, and I obediently back you up in your lies, and all the while can't work out why I even have to! Somehow you and me share the same little secrets though I can't stand the sight of you. But then none of our lot here likes you, and so the wisest thing you can do is to stay at home watching over your pots and pans and not say a word for ages, because blabbering only causes trouble and pain. So you remember that and keep mum. If you start weaving your web of lies, it won't be nice for them to believe you, even if your honesty would make any truth blush. But they'll believe them only with a heavy heart for they'd much rather believe in something else. Say, for instance, my ideas about Rakhimat, those strange ideas I started thinking today. Now your head's drooped, and you stare at the ground, but before that your eyes were up the roof. It must be hard for you. You've got nothing to say to this. No more trump cards. Now you won't be squealing on me to my son about dynamite and Belgians, not while I've got a trump card like that whorehouse up my sleeve. You won't trade that in for my honour: I'm far too vile for you. My vileness sticks in your throat. But vileness is such a flighty bitch that just as it starts whimpering from fear it's in a hurry to spit on someone else.' Then he squinted and threatened me through his clenched teeth: "I''ll spit on you from top to bottom. I may perish myself but I won't let you live. You and Rakhimat and that little bastard of hers, if she manages to give birth to it at all! And here's another thing, if you leave the aul without my knowledge and my kind permission – you'll stain your proud bloodline, and that, as far as I can make out, is the only thing that really scares you!' And that, said Alone, was the last straw for me – I punched him. I hit his shiny forehead with all my might, like a rampant bull, he swayed on his feet, stayed up for a bit, but then fell flat on his back by my feet. I bent over him, grabbed him by the scruff of his neck, helped him back to his feet and laid into him again. Once he was back on his feet, I whacked him on his shiny pate, so he keeled over and lay there spitting blood, and then looked for something for his eyes to focus on, but the only thing he could fix his dim gaze on was always me; he had to get up over and over again – he was too full of hate, I helped him straighten up and rubbed my fist into that shining patch on his head, which was getting less and less shiny as we went on, it turned into a thick bloody pulp; soon I was punching only blood, which splattered onto my clothes, and my fists kept pummelling his head that had now started hanging down and rocking from side to side, swimming in its thick and greasy blood; and yet I was helpless like a cry coming from my own throat, a cry I heard turn into a drawn-out tearful screech; but then I started to feel blood flowing down my own face and drip down from my chin onto my shirt, drip and drip, and I felt my mouth start to taste bittersweet from swallowing all this blood, my clothes got covered in it, and my hands and aching knuckles were all covered in it, and suddenly I realised that I hadn't even noticed when Barysbi had hit me back in the face, for he hadn't raised his hands to me even once, he just endured my rain of punches and didn't fight back; but then I realised that in fact I'd started bleeding on my own, and as my heart sank I figured that it was a nosebleed, that the blood was flowing out of my nose of its own accord; so then I got down onto the floor alongside him and lay down there on my back to stem the nosebleed and breathe some air into my clogged up nostrils, air heavy with the swirling sickly smell of murder. We lie on the ground there side by side, and I hear him breathing. His deep breaths seemed to cross the huge distance between shame and triumph. And

Barysbi says to me, hardly able to move his tongue around in his swollen mouth: "Now you know I"m not afraid of you. At last I've nothing to be afraid of you. You can't frighten me now for a long time to come. As long as I want... You'll never kill me now.' He started to laugh. And his laugh was most sincere. My nosebleed stopped, but my head was still ringing from the splitting pain. I lay alongside him and couldn't recognise myself. I felt sick. I said: "You were within a hair"s breadth of death. Such a thin little hair's breadth.' "No-oo," he managed to say, drawing out the word into a groan that slumbered in his throat. "Far from it. Didn"t I say you didn't have it in you to get blood on your hands?' I knew he was right. This scoundrel was right," admitted Alone. "So right in fact that I relaxed, and because I relaxed I felt sick again. So then I said: "You"re such scum that there's only one piece of scum worse than you, and that's got your name while that son of yours honours you as his father.' "Shut up," he said. "You know you can"t get me with that anymore. Help me to get up and to wash my face. Or are you getting ready to hit me some more?' he teased. So I replied: "You"re such scum that you dared to lie in wait for me. You were watching out for our escape and followed us right over to the town, and followed at our heels right the way up to the door of that whorehouse itself...' "To the very door," he confirmed. "I need to wash up. And I"m cold. Give us a hand up.' "You waited out there right up till the morning, like a mangy dog, and then you waited for the right moment to strike. You chose it very carefully. And you even held back when I suggested that you ought to change places with him and take the guilt upon yourself. You pretended I had you in the palm of my hand, but like the scum you are you waited for the scummy moment when you could pin me to the wall with your baseness, after you"d taken the life of that pregnant idiot into your scummy hands, the girl who'd been made pregnant through your scummy tricks and your scummy friends...' "Why are you crucifying yourself over it?" he frowned in irritation. "Well why get so hung up about it? I told you first about what a scumbag I was, but you didn''t leave me any other option! So just stop prattling on and help me back to my feet. I'm cold.' "Listen here, I told him. "Do you really think you''re capable of spreading all that about Rakhimat?' Instead of replying he simply wondered: "What do you think yourself?" "I don''t know,' I said. "I''m not sure.' "That''ll do for me – your uncertainty will do for me. You won't take no risks if you're not sure... So lift me up, will you?' I got up and offered him a hand. I'd lifted him to his feet, taken him inside and poured a whole tub of water over him, he sat down on a bench to rest and said: "That's good! Now I feel good. This is the first time I've felt so good since you stuck your nose in my affairs. But you couldn't keep it there. It started to run! I must have really pinched it if it's got caught up in such a scandal! By the way, how old are you now? Seventeen? Eighteen?' "What''s it to you?" I ask back. ""Cos now each next one will feel like five. So that before you're thirty you'll be more worn out than old Aguz.' "Go home," I said. "Go where they respect you as an elder. Go where they once respected your father as an elder. And called him Khandjeri. Or have you forgotten who your father was?" "No," his face darkened. "And I haven''t forgotten what it means to feel ashamed at the charity of some fortunate little stinker who returns to the aul not on the old nag my father'd lent him but on a bay horse, and leads that clapped out old nag into our yard, and covers her back with a red horse-cloth, which in any bazaar they'd fork out twice as much for as the horse itself, now trussed up in red velvet as if its skin had been turned inside out for a joke; and my father taking her by the reins and in the full view of all our good folk drags her home... I haven't forgotten that at all.' I gave it a thought and said: "You"ve kept it in the front of your mind so much that you've devised a way of turning the common mill and common money to the service of your own millstones. That's cunning! You've got a very selective memory there.' "You mean to say you haven"t?' he almost gnashed his teeth: "Weren"t you the one who contrived to create out of common shame your own dignity, which became hateful to all of us even before you killed your first bear and brought its skin back to the aul. Weren't you the one who used the ruins of your own clan to start a fire from their ashes in their deserted hearth? Weren't you that little boy who forced our elders, all to a man, rise to greet you at the nykhas and acknowledge you as the rightful owner of this abandoned home, that is, their equal? Didn't you compel them in their black envy of you to load up their carts with stones only to exchange them for common disgrace at the fort? Just remember: I wasn't the first! And I probably won't be the last... I just didn't have your luck.' "You had more," I said. "Because you"re scum, and I've got to reckon with it from now on. There's nothing I can do. Today I've no choice but to obey a scoundrel, so he's luckier than me. If I were the lucky one, we'd be already on our way to the town by now... Now you tell me, what do you feel when you look at that son of yours? What do you feel when you track two people who are only trying to save the life of an unborn child? What do you feel when you lie in wait all night long outside the walls of a whorehouse? Or when you wallow in your own blood at the feet of your enemy? What do you feel when you destroy an innocent man? Or when you go and visit your father's grave?' He didn't even take a moment to think before answering. He shot back in my face a solitary word, and the look on his face as he said it made it seem as if this word had only come into being to ever be directed towards me: "Hate!" I said to myself: but of course! What other answer had you expected?"

Alone fell silent and with a far off look in his eyes gazed right past me towards the mountains, over which a glint of clear blue sky had emerged through the clouds and was flowing down towards the aul. From that look in his eyes I could tell that he was leaving for good without waiting for the new day to dawn. That new day would dawn for him over foreign skies. I had to hurry.

"So on that occasion you lost. You lost for the first time in your life three days before the trial."

"No," he exclaimed. "Before then."

I thought and nodded:

"The first time was when he followed you both."

"I don't know. Maybe even before that. Or maybe after. There's no understanding that now. But that day even Barysbi miscalculated. Had he known what happened with your Father he'd never have shown his hand so soon. And, of course, he wouldn't have put off our trip to the town, he wouldn't have denied himself the pleasure of watching in glee how cursed fate had its last laugh at me, taking his side. He'd invite me then to go to the whorehouse with him. Only he hadn't a clue that everything was already over."

"I see, neither of you had a clue, but you still didn't go to the town. You couldn't even take the blame upon yourself because Barysbi had no wish to see Father go free, and he held Rakhimat's pregnancy as a hostage against you. Now you couldn't even go over to that lad who's misfortune it was to be the grandson of the dead Khandjeri to tell him the truth about the man who was Khandjeri's eldest son, tell him the whole truth about the Belgians and the mill, and maybe even about your imprisoned friend and that shopkeeper who's been consumed by the flames, nor even about Rakhimat and her little coins, or even about the refuge where she'd knitted her tiny little doll. You couldn't tell him a thing since you were not the only one in the know. The truth is easier to reveal when you're the only blessed with the knowledge and there's no one else to disentangle its knots, and therefore no one can wind them into new loops. So for a long time both of you tormented yourself by not leaving the aul, and each day Barysbi would go over to the nykhas to make sure that you hadn't gone off on your own, and sometimes on purpose, just to spite him, you didn't set foot outside your door, so then he'd have to send down one of his younger boys over to you to make sure that the smoke from your chimney was rising from a fire tended by your own hands and not by those of anyone else who you'd ask to give you this unusual service. So you kept on tormenting yourselves over the roles you'd been locked into by your enmity; and all concerned were prisoners, imprisoned by a prisoner who'd got imprisoned by his own prisoner, and as it must have seemed to you then, it wasn't only the truth that was in jail but my father and the two of you as well, counting the months till the child in the womb impregnated by strangers gathered enough strength to liberate itself from a prison of its own, and you tried to guess where this would lead your captive destinies off to next. You had little left to wait before rumours would waft up to the aul that my father had been tried for robbery, attempted escape and attacking his guard. According to these same rumours he was now far away, very far away, far from you and your secrets, and when you tried to imagine that far-off clime where they'd sent him in heavy chains, you could see in your mind's eye only endless snowy wastes, for that cruel name of Siberia could summon nothing else from the depths of your imagination but bare thick snow...

That year we'd had a lot of snowfall in our mountains as well. The snow covered our land with white, smooth winter with only the black riverbed and the discordant patches of flagstones and gates scattered here and there. So much snow fell that the sun laboured all of March and half of April to trample down its wet body and penetrate the soil with the warmth of its rays. I know about the snow. Uncle told me everything. Snow rotted among the hills and in the ravines until late spring. It was still melting and making the roads a nightmare when you rode on horseback to the fort.

"It took me five days and four nights to get there," said Alone. "Towards evening I once more knocked on that door under the familiar red lantern..."

Towards evening of the fifth day he knocked at the door under the as yet unlit lantern and said to the anxious madam:

"I didn't have anything to eat yesterday, nor today. If you don't feed me now I'll eat the lampshade of your lantern and drink the kerosene from its iron belly."

As he washed himself and ate, she watched him with a forced smile and occasionally hurried over somewhere only to return straight back again. So as not to ask about the main thing, he said:

"I brought you what I promised. It's in my satchel. Go and take it."

The madam untied the strings and pulled out a rolled up canvas, unfurled it and spread it on the table, holding its edges with her hands. Alone said:

"This painting is the smallest one I've done yet. So I hope it'll cause less evil."

She looked at the picture with dry eyes and he appreciated her self-control.

"Maybe you won't like it," he said, once again avoiding

the main question. "At first I thought of painting you as old and tired but with a pure light in your warm eyes. But then I decided to show you as young and unhappy. In the end you split on the canvas into a young-old woman with sadness in your warm eyes. But a pure light still shines in them. Of course, you probably won't like it..."

"I do like it," said the madam. "It's just very painful. Thank you."

He nodded and rolled up the painting, put it to one side and looked the woman straight in the eyes:

"Where are they?" he put his main question and felt a pain in his neck. The madam lifted her chin, which made her look taller, smiled a quivering smile and patted his arm in her familiar way.

"You'll see them," she said and Alone felt a wave of immense joy roll through his chest. Thank God, he thought. I had almost decided that...

The woman left the salon. She was gone for about five minutes. And then he heard an infant's cry, got to his feet but froze as an invisible film spread out from his throat over his pounding heart. The servant girl opened the curtains to let them forward, and Alone saw the madam holding two white fluffy bundles in both arms. She drew closer to him and asked:

"Just look at them!"

With shy fingers he pulled aside the fine lace and revealed their faces.

"The one that's crying is a girl," said the madam. "The boy is the quiet one, and grins most of the time."

Alone looked at them and thought that they were so tiny that you could hardly call them children yet. But their eyes seemed to look right through you. As if they were looking at you from that hidden world from which they had been thrown out with her scream into this one.

"The girl cries so hard as if we've taken something from her," he said out loud. "But the lad's a hard one to offend. What did she christen them?"

The madam did not reply. Alone looked up. The woman did not turn away, but nonetheless gave no answer.

"Hold on," he said, his throat drying up. "Where's Rakhimat?"

The madam turned to the servant girl who took the babies off her, and quickly went out of the salon.

"She didn't make it," said the madam. "The birth killed her. She didn't manage to christen them. You'll do that yourself. I was waiting for you."

She went over to a sideboard with glass doors, got out a dark bottle and put it out in front of him along with two pot-bellied little shot glasses.

"No," he said. "I won't."

He knew that wouldn't help now. He was too sober to get drunk on one bottle of spirits. He was so sober, in fact, that for some time he couldn't bring himself to think about anything and instead let his mind roam about the room noticing most banal, trivial little details: a tiny spot on the tablecloth (one of the guests had probably lit up a cigarette and stubbed out a splintered match head on the table), a thick clump of dust on the bronze horseback of the carriage clock (a servant girl must have missed it), the airy blue dusk outside the acquiescent window (as if time was slipping by his pain with a yawn, having got bored of him long ago), the worn down heels of the madam's boots (she walked awkwardly but firmly, her toes turned out), a fretted green leaf that had fallen on the edge of the rug (someone had given her flowers, but their scent had faded), someone's muffled coughing, angry at themselves, coming from the top floor (she's afraid she won't be able to work today but she's scared of the madam), the aerial flight of spider's web on the ceiling above the window (a draught: the door to the stairway is wide open), the flowing, silky interplay of the light and shades on the madam's dress (her evening dress, carefully selected to excite male lechery), the cold tongue of flame in the lamp (lazily licking at the clear ice of the glass).

The small details concealed her face from him, but it didn't disappear. It stayed there behind their fake, ethereal covering of brilliant white and waited for Alone to come to terms with his forlorn sobriety and start talking. Finally, he stopped measuring out the room with voracious paces.

"Which one?" he asked.

The madam caught on and answered:

"The boy. The girl came out first. He was second. She was in labour with him for more than two hours. But then he appeared, and she died. She was so pale, like all her blood had drained out of her. And she was no longer smiling. She looked a different person. She looked like a saint. Or rather like a woman, a mother..."

"Like her own mother," he said, "a thick stream of warm milk flowed over her body. I know. I've heard this before... Only I never thought that lightning would strike twice. You stood there by the bedside and wiped off the useless white rivulets from her firm breasts. Her body started to stiffen, but milk still flowed, and the girl, born first, howled in fury at the destruction of her mother who'd not even managed to suckle her, but all the while the little boy... What was the boy doing at the time?" he asked the madam.

"Smiling," she said. "He grinned lying at the feet of his dead mother. Have you ever seen a newborn baby grinning?"

"So that means," he stuttered and grabbed her hands in excitement: "So he's her true heir! Just think about it! He inherited from her not just the sin of an accidental murder, but also her grin!"

He started charging round the room again, and in his excitement continued to mutter terrible words that she couldn't comprehend:

"Draining out all her blood while getting out of her belly, and once he'd done in his own mother while death moulded her into a saintly martyr and wiped the smile off her face, he took up this stupid, savage, everlasting grin! Just think about it!" he cried out again. His eyes shone feverishly. When he again clasped her hands, she interrupted him in annoyance:

"What are you on about? What sin of murder? You're talking as if Rakhimat killed someone..."

He quickly nodded back:

"That's the point! He followed right in her tracks. The difference is that Rakhimat's mother passed away the next day, but he finished off his mother then and there, without even tasting the life that flowed out of her breast. No, you don't understand, do you? And you don't know anything about the hidden blood. But he... No sooner had he been born and no sooner had he killed her than he couldn't wait to take over her grin!"

"Stop it!" she cried out in fear. "You've gone mad! They're only babies!"

Alone stopped short and frowned, as if trying to take in her train of thought, but then grabbed his temples and started rocking on his heels. The skin on his face burned like he'd been scalded. Then he shook his head and said:

"Forgive me. I didn't mean it. I don't know what's got into me. I got carried away. Of course, you're right. Of course he's only a baby. Even if he's sent his own mother to the grave... He's not to blame, he's only a baby!"

"There you go again," the madam said reproachfully.

He opened his arms in repentance out to her and repeated:

"Forgive me. I'll stop." Then for a third time he started pacing up and down the room, stopping now and again, abruptly and unexpectedly, like a caged beast only to bang his fist into his open palm. After a while he suddenly suggested:

"Let's call him Rakhim! What do you think?"

She pondered this and asked:

"Was his father a Muslim?"

"No," Alone replied. "But he was no Christian either. He had no faith. The father's got nothing to do with it though. We're naming him after his mother."

The madam stopped short, but thinking it over, agreed:

"All right. The name's not to my taste, but..."

"It suits him," he finished the sentence off her.

"And what will we call the girl?" she asked. "Who shall we name her after?"

"I don't know yet," he said. "The girl can wait... although..." he paused but then said: "If you don't mind let's call her Lana."

The madam curled her lip in puzzlement and frowned.

"After some Lana or other? Lana as in Svetlana, you mean?"

"Hardly," he replied. "The name's after a certain cliff... But that's not important. You can suggest your own name if you want."

"Rakhim and Lana," repeated the madam. "that's a bit strange, somehow. But everything about them is strange. Lana and Rakhim... I agree!"

So that was settled. When he finally reclined into an armchair and half-closed his eyes she began to tell him of how they buried Rakhimat and looked after the twins. They buried her in the back yard so as not to draw attention. Early at dawn the girls dragged out the body, wrapped up in white sheets, out of the back door and laid her in a shallow pit that they'd dug up over the night during breaks between their clients ("How could you stay open that evening!" Alone asked, but she shot him an angry look. "What did you want us to do? To close for the first time in sixteen years on a Sunday and expect no one to start wondering what had happened? Don't ask me stupid questions!"). Over her body they strew all the flowers they could find in the whole house that morning, and then covered her with earth and smoothed over the turf. The mound turned out small and neat, a mound for her quiet memory, she said. "But we didn't put a cross on it," she said.

"No, of course not. A mound for her quiet memory is a lot. Especially for her. Especially in your yard..."

A wet-nurse was found for the babies nearby. She charged a fair price, so the madam didn't have to bargain with her. In the evenings she sent the servant girl over to the address with a laundry-cart, where under a pile of nightshirts, valences and sheets lay two baskets with the twins. The wet-nurse had done all the laundry for the house and could be trusted, all the more so as she'd been paid not only for milk but also for her silence.

Nearer lunchtime, when the girls got up, the servant girl rolled the cart back to the whorehouse, where the girls, who supported themselves with their youth and non-motherhood, fussed over the babies with abandon. They became attached to them, said the madam.

"You'll see for yourself, they become like..."

The madam struggled to find a comparison.

"Like peasant women, like smiles or sunshine," Alone offered. "Like the pure light from the window."

"Maybe, yes," said the madam. "They seem to forget who they are, the nights and why they've ended up here. Only here's the worrying thing: a couple of times one of them drank herself silly. She even slashed her wrists. You know her."

"I do," said Alone. "Only I don't want to know her name..."

In the daytime, while the babies were in the house, they fed them with steaming milk and a drop of honey. The boy drank the more voraciously and grinned in satisfaction.

"Rakhim," said Alone. "Rakhim and Lana."

"I'll keep that money you left for them," said the madam. "My own's enough for us at the moment."

"It seems like they're far luckier than their mother." Alone said. "She had no wet-nurse. Just an ancient grandma, a father with a withered arm and a glum milch-buffalo."

"It seems like she now means more to you than before," said the madam in a quiet voice. "When she was alive, you hardly ever asked about her. When she was still alive, it seemed like you were trying to forget she existed."

"When she was alive," Alone replied. "I had to guard her secret. Now I need to guard her death as well."

"How do you mean?"

"Just that you're right: now Rakhimat really does mean more to me. Isn't that often the way with the dead?"

The madam thought about it and said:

"Maybe. Especially if few people noticed them while they lived."

"Few people noticed her when she was alive. They only really noticed once she'd vanished. They couldn't understand why it had happened. I can't explain it myself."

The next morning he left. He spent the night in the same room that he had the first time, with the girl who had slashed her wrists and who failed to let him know her name. But come morning he went away – before dawn, hiding from the madam so as not to have to answer the question she'd been saving up till today. He had seen that question in her eyes the day before, but didn't want it to be asked. There were too many other things for him to think about first. Like, for instance, what would happen now to the agreement he'd reached with Barysbi, and could he now annul it? And if he could, then would that change anything? He felt like a man who'd been seated for a long time on an uncomfortable bench with hands tied and mouth gagged, but who'd just had his shackles unfettered and was now allowed to speak but his hands had grown numb, his tongue had grown stiff from silence, he had pins and needles in his legs and forgotten how to walk. Now he had a few days' journeying to weigh everything up carefully so as not to make a mistake when he rode back into the aul with his new secret. Was it really worth him sharing it? For Barysbi no longer held Rakhimat's life in his hands, nor her fateful pregnancy. It was almost as if he was once more obliged to fear Alone's revenge and had to follow his every command obediently. I can make him leave our land, contemplated Alone, riding his horse along the slippery, muddy road. I can simply tell him that she's no more, and he'll realise he's lost: now he has no evidence of our escape or the whorehouse. The madam's not dumb and won't allow the truth to come out. She knows the truth of it all is bad and heartless. I've already told so many lies I'll lie again. Even if Gappo believes him Barysbi won't get anything out of it: they're hardly going to shoot the babies. They're more likely to shoot the bringer of bad news. Barysbi must know that. So maybe it works out that he's lost to me fair and square. But what have I won? At the price of a poor idiot girl's death, who died as she became a mother, and earned only a small mound of quiet memory, I can force an unfortunate scumbag to leave our unfortunate land for good, so as to save his poor son? And if I do that won't I legitimise the high price paid for it? How will that make me any different from the one I'm driving away? Only that I'll be defeating him at the cost of someone's death, someone's shame left unexposed leaving two orphans. That's not enough to make us different and too much to bind us together.

Alone rode along and thought about what kind of difference this was that made them so much alike. He remembered how almost a year before, right after the rains which had buried under the landslide the cliff, the mill, the horse, the cart and the man who'd been exiled to our lands by the treachery of those eyes as blue as the abyss, he had gone by night to his family graves to share silently with them the mystery of the new deaths that day. He remembered how he had felt behind him the cold steel of an invisible but very close gun aimed at him through the pitch darkness and how that gun had not lowered its sullen, round eye from him, while it pondered and sweated in someone's uncertain hands and was unwilling to shoot, though nothing prevented it from doing so – he even turned to face it and threatened to take his own gun at daybreak, but the gun stayed put, swallowed the insult and didn't fire, thus losing once and for all the right to kill, but gaining in its place something quite different and most important, so that several months later he himself would try to beat to death the man who had held that gun in his hands and would know from that time on what it meant not to be able to kill a man, and then stubbornly withstand the blows rained down upon him; he showed Alone what it was like not to be able to finish off your enemy when he deserved it and was giving you every chance to do so.

While he rode on his horse through the sticky, muddy roads back to his native aul, going ever deeper into the mountains and ever further from the fort, his resolve hardened, which surprised him, and with every day he grew more certain of his course.

It was harder to deal with the twins than it would be to

deal with Barysbi. More precisely, was it worth providing them with parents, and if so, then who? Telling the villagers the whole truth about them was out of the question. Not because it threatened them with shame and curses: by her death it was as if Rakhimat had freed them from otherwise inevitable humiliation – her death was more powerful than her sin. But even that wouldn't be enough to make the villagers come to terms with their existence, nor their constant presence, just as it wouldn't be enough ever to prevail upon the elders, the men and even the women to recognise the twins as their own, take them in or even find it in themselves to look them in the eye and hide the terrible word "bastards". Not even Gappo would be able to do that.

Nonetheless, there was among the villagers one man who could forgive them their accidental guilt of appearing on this earth out of wedlock, not sanctified by love or passion in the hearts of those who had paid for their appearance with little shining coins. That was Soslan. It was about him that Alone was now thinking, trying to understand for himself, how good the sinful act that he was planning to carry out would be, or just how sinful the good deed would be that he would give as a boon to the blind man who had suddenly grown wise. Yes, he would forgive them any truth, judged Alone. But in doing so he would condemn both them and himself to countless troubles that would emanate from those who could never forgive them that truth. But that wouldn't stop him. And if he could find it in himself to forgive them the truth he would forgive them the absence of truth as well.

On the morning of the fifth day, Alone reached our gorge. He hobbled his horse at the Blue Road and dismounted. He climbed a boulder and looked down from there onto the sleeping aul. Then he turned round and leaned back against the rock. He stood like that until the sun had pierced the shaggy cloud with its angry bright rays and poured its coarse light on the pockmarked rocks. Then he leapt back onto his horse and turned round its nose to the road that had grown hateful to them both...

When he had once more, soaked through, dirty and thin, turned up on the steps of the whorehouse, the first thing he heard was the voice of the madam saying to the servant girl who peered through the peephole in the door: "If that's him, turn him away. If it's him, you can tell him to go to hell!" The peephole closed, and the servant girl cried out from the other side of the door:

"He's all grubby, like he's been lugging cauldrons in hell. I didn't recognise him at first."

He listened as her steps faded into the distance, and all fell quiet. Alone thought sadly: That's what I didn't take into account. Her pride and her stubbornness. She was a stubborn wench, and grew tired of it. She was a stubborn madam to other wenches and grew tired of that too. And now she stubbornly wants to be a mother. He pounded the door with his fists but elicited no response. Then he returned to his horse, led it over to the corner by the back door, tied its reins to the door handle, returned to where he had been standing before and sat down on the steps.

"I'm a stubborn one, too," he said quietly, knowing that they could hear him. "And I have a stubborn horse. And you have stubborn customers. But if that's not enough for you, then more stubborn than all of them is the hunger of two little ones. Sometime or other they'll want to see their wet-nurse again. Unless, of course you've managed to put a cow in one of your rooms."

He sat on the steps and whistled quietly. Time went along slowly but steadily so that soon the shadows started to draw in. Once it had got dark, he almost dozed off and nearly collapsed in as the door opened.

"I still won't give them over to you," said the madam. "I'd better rip up your painting and kick you out."

"You've already tried that," he reminded her. "Only you didn't do it very well."

"This time you'd better be more careful," she warned.

"Fine," he said to calm her down. "I'll be very careful, and in return you'll promise me a sip of water."

Now she won't be able to contain herself and will burst out laughing, he thought. And this she did, and beckoned to the servant girl and gave her orders. They were left on their own together, but didn't know how to start conversation. Alone drank his fill, and filled up another glass of water, emptied half of it again and said:

"You're so sure you'll manage? Or that they'll manage? They'll grow up sometime..."

"So what," she said. "I'll try to be a good mother to them. You painted me as a good person, after all..."

"Will they be happy when they discover who their mother is? Sooner or later they'll ask and you'll have to tell them. Do you think they'll forgive their mother? Or their love for her?"

"So you suppose having an insane mother is better? Better than a woman who runs a whorehouse? Or than a former whore?" she asked, with her arms belligerently akimbo at her thin waist.

"No," he replied quietly. "I've just found them a father."

She came right up to him, put her hands on his shoulders and looked him in the eye:

"You can't mean yourself surely? That means you've found someone else. Is this someone else their real father?"

"Almost," replied Alone as he thought: he couldn't have put it better. "If anyone could be their father, it could only be him. You'd not find another father for them in a hundred years. He used to have a daughter of his own. He was a good father. I saw it myself."

The madam dropped her hands and smoothed the curls on her temples. Her lips quivered. Alone thought that was it, now she would start to cry. But I still don't know what I can do to help her.

"Please," she said. "I never asked you for anything before. But now – please!"

Alone took another sip of water. It tasted like the dust on his clothes. The woman was crying now. Her tears flowed down her face in streams and fell on her chest, but she seemed not to notice.

"You are not telling me the whole truth. I don't understand..." Alone said.

But she didn't let him finish:

"Remember I told you about that scoundrel, who hit me on the head with that poker? Well now I've no option but to explain to you why he suddenly took it into his head to crack open my skull... And don't interrupt me! You've forced me to tell you it all."

She went over to the window, closed the curtains but didn't light the lamps. Now he could see only her angular silhouette and her blurred face. From her even, muffled voice he could guess that she's already recovered from her tears.

"He wasn't really a scoundrel." The madam began. "He was just the only one who talked to me of love. He could talk about it so hotly and often. It came out a bit affectedly but was still beautiful to hear. He liked to talk of it though it wasn't really necessary to sleep with a tart. He'd come to me just before daybreak, always at the same time. He'd usually smell strongly of wine and cigarettes. Many men smell strongly of wine and cigarettes, but only he managed to make them smell nice. And he never laughed, got into fights or raised his voice. Nor did he swear, as if he'd never heard swearwords in all his born days. He wasn't rich but he'd always pay the right amount and discreetly too, bashfully even; he'd leave the money on the edge of the table, covering the notes with the flower from his buttonhole. He'd wear white shirts and have a white flower in his lapel, and as he left he'd put it on top of the banknotes. As if to say he was sorry that he was paying. He said nothing of himself, nor did he ask any questions of me, he spoke only of beauty and love. When I told him I was pregnant he grew pale, like whitewash, got up from the bed, got dressed and stood there in silence so upright and triumphant, like a tailor's dummy in a shop window. I kept repeating that I wanted nothing from him, that he was not obliged to me at all, and that there was no need for him to stand like that and purse his lips into a line, as if he'd choked on his honour. But suddenly he blurted out: "I love you, and I always will love you, and because of this nothing is more unconscionable to me than to refuse to heed my own heart. So I humbly request of you your kind permission for our conjoinment in wedlock!" That's how it flowed out of him! Can you imagine? I remember it word for word, it was imprinted on my heart for all my days as a magical, blissfully sweet moment when he got down on one knee and humbly bowed his head, and I pressed it to my breast and stroked and stroked him, and in my happiness I wanted to whimper and bite like a homeless mongrel that's suddenly been given the gift of eating its fill... Then he got to his feet, bowed to me, and there were two flushes of red playing on his cheeks, like he was consumptive, he kissed my hand and said: regretfully, I have to leave now. I rushed to him to kiss him goodbye but he had turned round and left in a hurry. I heard his heels clatter down the stairs and through the window I saw him run down the street like a man possessed. Even then I got it into my head that we'd never meet again. Though I didn't, as God's my witness, coerce him into anything at all... All day long I cried, didn't leave my room once, and as it grew dark, my tears sent me to sleep. I slept soundly and peacefully – like I was out on a beautiful open clearing in the sunlight. I woke up to see his pale face looking down at me. He seemed like a stranger to me in the way he looked at me, as if his eyes were no longer his own, as if they'd been burned by terror... But then all was as it had been before, only a hundred times better, more free and open, I can't say... Once more he spoke of his love and was so tender as if his arms were singing out to me. He drank my tears of happiness, like the dew on the berries as he went on whispering sweet nothings in my ear. There were so many of them, I could have drowned in them. And towards night I was drowning, falling into the pit of sleep, as if into a well. I fell and fell, and he couldn't get enough of my fall, we never reached the bottom, I was falling and falling down this bottomless cool well, and it felt wonderful, just like I was soaring... But then all fell ominously still and eerie. The silence made me open my eyes. His hand was raised against me... I felt a flash of light explode in me. A terrible, raging flash of light. It pierced my whole body, so that nothing was left for me except the darkness and the pain. And then the pain somehow vanished, leaving only the darkness and peace. But then I tired of lying in them and once more opened my eyes, but that happened much later. After I'd lost everything: both him and the child. That's how it all turned out! He wanted to kill me, but he only killed his child. He made off with all my money to shift the blame to someone else. It probably burnt his hands – he must have thrown it in the river or burnt it. After that he fled the town, afraid that I would recognise him and give him away. I wouldn't do that, of course. My thoughts were busy with something else..."

"The rest I know," said Alone. "You've already told me the rest. All about the arsenic and the mongrel..."

"Hold on," said the madam. "That's not it... I didn't look everywhere for him just to poison him with the arsenic. Something else was more important to me – just to look him straight in the eye, to read the suffering written there and the repentance... You won't believe me," she said, smiling quietly, "but my reserves of pity for him haven't dried up even to this day. There lives on in me the last drop of pity towards him and it pains my heart. And hate lives on inside me too, though it faded with time just like love and revenge. But my anger at him is still alive, for his vile weakness that was at the root of everything. Why couldn't he have been even the slightest bit stronger!"

Yes, thought Alone, that's the irony of it. If he had been, he wouldn't have smelled so nicely of wine. Had he been stronger, he'd never have fallen in love with a whore, let alone sent her head spinning. Had he been stronger, he wouldn't have gone pale and fallen to his knees, made his proposal and run away from his own words so as to come back the next day and melt in his compassion and love for her, babble sweet nothings with eyes aflame, and not know till the very last minute whether he'd kill her or not, and then out of fear bang her on the head with that poker, grab her pennies and run off in a frenzy, flee out of weakness from the crime he had committed, that covered the floor in a pool of blood, and flee from himself, knowing from the very first step that he had doomed himself to everlasting, endless flight from his own past, a feverish pursuit of his present and the complete impossibility of breaking out into the future that would come for him only as a slow death or as a deathly exhaustion – one and the same thing; his only wish was to rid himself of his nightmares, which were his living death, for his life had long been measured out as short halts on the road from one nightmare to the next... Had he been stronger, thought Alone, I'd never have got to know this woman. And she'd never have become a mother...

"I'll give you Rakhim," he said, "but the girl I'll take with me. The girl will go to the father. That's for the best."

Silence fell. They breathed it in and couldn't breathe in enough of it. The woman groaned and threw herself at his breast. She squeezed him in her clawing embraces and quivered.

"That's possibly the most," she whispered. "That's more than anything... even more than what happened in the past..."

"It's over," Alone replied. "He's no more for you. At this moment he no longer exists for you."

"Yes," whispered the madam. "No more and never again. This is more than him."

"And more than the picture," said Alone. "Now it lies, because the woman it speaks of is only in your past."

"No, it doesn't lie," she exclaimed. "She's just grown smaller in the face of something that's greater than her."

"Her happiness?" asked Alone, and the woman nodded. "Then she became as small as a teardrop. Promise me that was your last tear."

"I can't," said the madam. "Only from now on my tears will be different."

In the morning she brought the two baskets out of her bedroom and put them on the table in front of him.

"The cart is already waiting for you," she said. "We've put all you'll need in it. We can say our goodbyes."

He shook his head:

"I don't go round in carts. Just get the milk and the blankets. The rest I don't need."

"But why?" she asked in surprise.

"No other way," he replied. "It's not my cart anyway. I brought no cart with me."

She hemmed in irritation:

"So that's his problem! He doesn't want to be in anyone's debt. Don't be daft. You can return the wagon at some later date."

"It won't work," said Alone. "There won't be a later date. They mustn't see one another again. Rakhim shouldn't find out how he ended up here. Because he shouldn't know me, nor anything about me. You do want to be his real mother, don't you?"

"Yes," she said. "And I will be. But take the cart. You can bring it back before he works out who you are."

"I can't," said Alone. "I'll be followed from now on. They'll watch over me for a long time now. We have no right to take any risks."

He bent down over the basket with the smiling baby and stared into his little eyes, black as tar, kissed his narrow little forehead, said a prayer over him and turned back to the madam:

"May he be a great son to you. Take the place of the mountains and his blood. You can..."

"Thank you," she said. "I'll take the place of his past, like he's taken the place of mine. It'll all work out fine."

She proffered him her hand like a man, and Alone shook it firmly. Then he lifted the girl's basket but stayed rooted to the spot.

"But where...?" he stuttered and didn't finish. The madam came to his aid and replied:

"She's waiting for you in the back yard. God be with you!"

He went out into the hallway, crossed the threshold and

walked round the house. The girl stood near the horse, touching the saddle, to which were tied his satchel and a knapsack with a pitcher of milk inside. He went up to his horse and started tying the basket to the saddle. She watched how dextrously and quickly his fingers went about the work that engrossed them.

"That's a lot of baggage for one horse," said the girl, and he felt that she wanted to say something else entirely. So as not to give her the chance he called back out to her over his shoulder:

"He'll manage. That's just right for him."

Now he wanted to get out of there quickly. Words don't solve anything.

He heard her breathing behind him. It prevented him from jumping in the saddle and riding off.

"Turn round." The girl said. "Don't hide your eyes. You hide your eyes all the time... That's better. I'm trying to keep them in my memory."

He stood there under her gaze, then turned round to the fence and asked:

"What for? I won't be coming back."

"So I gathered," she said. "I understand you much better now..."

He looked at her questioningly, and for a moment their eyes met. Alone looked away first. The girl said:

"I know what you want. You want me to ask you to take me away with you. You want me to take your face in my hands and beg you not to abandon me, and then you'd wrestle for a whole minute with the temptation, suffer and turn away. And then you'll give me your "no!" and leap onto your horse. I know you want to run off, not just leave. You want to make it easier for you... And you finally want my name. Right?"

He didn't reply. His hands fidgeted with his whip. Her eyes followed his hands.

"Give it here," she ordered, and he apologised and held the whip out to her. "See, it's damp. Oho, now you're hiding your hands... and now you've bit your lip so as to hold back and not slap me in the face," she burst out laughing, but on her cheeks there already glimmered two strips of light bathed in tears and fed by the morning's clear chill. "Only you won't take me with you for anything. All that you need is to gallop off and hear my name as you go. All you want, without asking anything of me, are my love and humiliation, which you'll reject there and then. Only it's going to be different... Climb into your saddle!"

In tears, she pushed him in the chest and he stumbled. As he leaped onto his horse he felt a piercing pain in his neck. Then the girl shoved the whip in his face, turned on her heels and ran back into the house. A cry emanated from the basket. "You've probably deserved that," he thought, going out through the gates into the narrow alleyway. "And even if you haven't, maybe it'll be easier for her..." He carefully led his horse down the roadway. Lulled by the horse's steady gait the child in the basket calmed down. When they had passed the last turning and left the town walls, he heard only sleepy snuffling from the basket.

Six days later at dawn the same snuffling awoke the wife of blind Soslan, the mistress of his larder and portly companion of his darkness, Fariza, and made her quickly open her eyes as if she had been slapped in the face. She listened, froze, and then, as was her habit, rummaged around in her breast and felt the small leather purse hanging round her neck on its little strap for some three years now. She pressed it to her lips, whispered a prayer, felt inside it with her fingers and pulled out the small golden lock of hair tied with a thread. Kissing it, she uttered her prayer a second time, but the crying did not abate. Instead it grew more insistent. The house slept. Alongside her in the women's half of the house the wives of Soslan's brothers lay on their rugs with their four daughters-in-law and the latters' children. Fariza decided not to wake them. She threw aside the curtain that partitioned off the room and looked at the front door. Through a crack the grey mist of dawn was streaming. Out of the dawn, right beneath the door, there rose up an insistent plaintive voice. Fariza got up from the bed and as she was, barefoot, slowly went over to where the voice stemmed from. Leaning against the door she pressed her ear to it, listened as the wailing, interrupted by hiccups, inhaled her approaching warmth, and then started a timid, impatient whining, punctuated by half-silences, in which the child was drawing the air into her lungs so as finally to let out a triumphant cry, and then she was met with a heartrending howl that cut like lightning as she pulled the door open. On her threshold writhed a hungry wide-eyed life in a wicker basket. Fariza made a quick step towards it, left the basket on its threshold, but took the life in with her. Barefoot as before, she enters her husband's room and says:

"Wake up! The gods have sent us a daughter! Look at her."

She holds out the child to Soslan, puts it on his knees and helps his hands find his daughter's face.

"See how lovely she is? Our little girl..."

He is silent, his whole body quivering, his eyelids closed over his walled eyes.

"Soslan," says Fariza. "you're not dreaming this! And you're not dead yet. It's not dark for your hands, is it?"

"No. They see everything... They know this is no dream. They can see the light!"

Word of the foundling flew instantaneously through the aul.

"On that day all was very loud, like on a feast day," Uncle told me, "only for a long time we hadn't had such a loud feast day. The women ran around the streets cooking for such an event, and their youngsters, left to their own devices, played in the puddles and snatched treats from trays. The men gathered at the nykhas, joked and chuckled, all the while trying to work out who was behind it all: few there believed in God's direct intervention (perhaps Gappo did, but he had his own reasons: the Lord who had taken away his daughter was capable of anything), but aloud they said quite the opposite, offering up words of praise to the Almighty and thanking him for the miracle. The only absentees were Soslan and Alone: the former was occupied with his new fatherhood and the latter hadn't been seen in the aul for a good half month. Maybe more," said Uncle. "You Grandfather was the first to suspect him and even asked where he'd got to. And Barysbi replied:

"Who are you asking?"

Grandfather gave him a searching look from under his brow and said:

"Who else but you?"

Barysbi blushed and moved nearer him to say ever so quietly:

"Maybe he's somewhere behind your back?"

When they came down from the nykhas that evening to the house of the blind man to sit down at his table to feast, your grandfather stood apart from the others, grabbed Barysbi by the sleeve and asked:

"Behind whose back? Ours or Soslan's?"

But Barysbi smirked and said:

"Is there any difference?"

With that their conversation ended, but Barysbi was unable to hide his agitation that day. "You see," Uncle explained to me, "it was like he'd caught a fever and showed it off to everyone, so those who happened to be beside him at the table, turned away from him as if they were afraid of being infected by it. But late at night, before lying down to sleep, the old man comes and says to me:

"If you don't want to harrow tomorrow, you can bunk off a while. Tonight is warmer than yesterday. Go take a stroll, if you fancy. Just see to it that folk don't see you. They might start thinking, seeing you all of a sudden on our street at night: what's he doing, out by Barysbi's house at such an ungodly hour? So best go take your stroll unnoticed and stealthily. But pay good attention. Especially if you see anything interesting. If you don't want to go for a stroll – that's your business, who'll say a thing if you're that set on harrowing after all!"

He yawned and went off to bed, but I threw his cloak over my shoulders, pulled its black hood over my head and scurried out of the door, went down to the river and followed its bank for a while, then climbed up to the road and hid behind a rock right opposite his house, lay down on my stomach and began to wait."

Uncle began to wait for the night to become interesting and take him soundlessly past the dreams of others to his quarry. A light was still burning somewhere, helping voices find their peace and turn into quiet. Then the silence scraped the glint from the river, and in the night there remained only the murmur of the mighty waters and the lapping of waves against the shore. Uncle wrapped himself up more tightly in Grandfather's cloak and rested his chin on the rock, counting in the dark its fleeting, indistinct patches. Suddenly he took a deep breath and strained to see: on the threshold there had now arisen a shadow, it slowly made its way to the gate and moved along the wattle fencing towards our house. Uncle squatted on his haunches and, crouching down, followed it along the riverbank. When only a short distance was left to our gate, the shadow darted off to one side and vanished. Uncle ran across the street and took up waiting again, pressing himself against the fence. After a few minutes he caught sight of the shadow returning, scaling the fence and jumping down to the ground not five paces from him. After it had gone off he returned home to warm himself in his bed, plunge into sleep with relish and sleep through the sunrise for the first time in many a long year.

Towards lunchtime he stepped into the yard, stretched his arms out wide, and made his way over to Grandfather, seated as ever on the log covered over with leather, and said:

"Are we going out harrowing tomorrow or shall we wait a while longer? Unless I'm mistaken this evening will be even nicer than yesterday. Just right for a stroll."

But Grandfather, without turning his head, tells him:

"That depends on what your stroll turned up yesterday."

Uncle shrugs his shoulders and says slyly:

"You couldn't really call it a stroll. More like tending."

"Aha. And who did you tend all night?"

"Someone," Uncle replies. "Some wretch's shadow."

Grandfather kept silent, chewed his beard and asked:

"Did it find its pasture right next to us?"

"How did you know that?"

"By its tracks," says Grandfather. "The tracks by the neighbouring fence told me all this morning. You were still snoozing, but I was chatting away with them. They told me a great deal about the shepherd and that shadow. Like, for example, that the shepherd boy was too lazy to drive it back to its shelter for the night..."

"Look..."

"Or that it had gone to this pasture in vain," says Grandfather.

"Yes," says Uncle. "It had no one there to bleat at. Just if you're able to see in the morning what mischief it had got up to in the night, then why on earth did I get sent as a shepherd boy?"

Grandfather with a feigned look of surprise raised his eyebrows:

"Shepherd boy? Shep-herd-boy? All I suggested was that you get some fresh air before you went off to bed."

Steam fairly starts to come out of Uncle's ears from his father's teasing, and he digs his toe into the ground a little, and then asks:

"So that means harrowing again tomorrow?"

"Oh yes," Grandfather replies and adds instructively: "Clement weather is not just good for going out, it's also a boon for hard work."

"But not a boon for traces," Uncle says sullenly and goes out of our yard onto the street, then turns round and heads off to Alone's fence, stops beside it, looks closely at the ground but can't find even a spot of mud: it's paved with stones. "What a cheat!" he thinks. "The cunning old crook! It seems like he does need a shepherd. He needs someone to go out in search of night-time secrets and then say yes to him who'd seen nothing, not done any shepherding, not gone out in the cold, but even before he'd gone off to bed he already knew what was going to happen next door to his peaceful sleep. I simply supplied "yes" to his knowledge and added to his pleasure at the expense of my own shame."

And so my grandfather didn't even need to step outside his front door to confirm the thought that had lodged itself in his wise old head that day and received full confirmation the following morning: Alone hadn't reappeared at his place although neither Barysbi nor my grandfather could suspect anyone else. So that meant, as Grandfather saw it, that Barysbi must be scared for some reason, enough to be so stupid as to break into Alone's house in the dead of night. Barysbi was not satisfied with guesswork. More likely, he was even convinced of his suspicions (guesswork alone wouldn't make you break into another's house – you need conviction for that), if he needed immediate proof of Alone's hand behind Soslan's returned fatherhood. But of course, Barysbi didn't find anything, and now my grandfather could wait calmly for Alone to reappear in the aul after another week or two, and it was already clear as day that when he'd finally come back home he'd swear that he'd not heard a thing about any foundlings, and even if not everyone would believe him, then at least no one would dare doubt the veracity of his words, at least not out loud, even Barysbi, as he hadn't been able to find anything to confirm his suspicions while his convictions alone were clearly not enough on their own. So then, thought Grandfather, it would be worth observing the two of them to try and work out just what it was that was making Barysbi so anxious.

Alone did indeed return a week later. Seeing him on the road from his perch at the nykhas, Grandfather must have thought: "There's your proof for you. Except that proof like this is of the kind that proves nothing, only one's desire to prove the indemonstrable." Had he appeared say six days earlier, Grandfather's convictions would have been swayed. But now he was certain. And, looking over at Barysbi, he saw that he was certain too, which was making things even harder for the man.

"Another couple of days later," said Uncle, "your grandfather watched Alone going over to Barysbi's. I was the first to notice and cried out for him to look. The old man nodded and said that meant he had decided not to scare him. Or maybe to scare him to death. I said that maybe he'd decided to show him that he hadn't yet decided whether to scare him to death or not scare him at all. Grandfather thought about it and said, yes, that could also be the case.

And so it was.

Barysbi told his family to leave Alone and him to it and his guest said:

"I've been gone for a month. In that month someone broke into my house. You wouldn't happen to know who that could have been, do you?"

"How on earth should I know?" Barysbi said. "And would you perhaps know who abandoned that kid over at Soslan's?"

"That you'll just have to ask someone else!" Alone replied. "I was nowhere near here at the time. Ask around in the village. People are saying it all came about through the will of God."

Barysbi returned:

"True. That's what they're saying. Only I wonder who gave the gods the idea."

"Of course," said Alone. "We haven't yet learned to read the heavens."

So then Barysbi says:

"I'm just curious if those gods could have got the wrong house, what do you think? Make some kind of mistake in the dark and put down that wicker basket on the wrong doorstep, eh? Let's say that in all fairness they should have made Gappo a grandfather, but in the dark they blessed Soslan by mistake, eh? So that instead of a new grandfather in the aul there's a new daddy and in their blindness they couldn't make out that it was a granddaughter, not a daughter, and what's more one that looked nothing like him. Do you think that might have been the case or not, what's your opinion?"

"Rubbish," said Alone. "Gappo couldn't become a grandfather. His daughter drowned in the river. Or have you forgotten? Just ask anyone."

Barysbi reddened, swore through his teeth and said:

"So that's how it is, is it? In the river, was it, you say, she drowned? So who was it then who was hiding her pot-belly in that whorehouse? Who gave birth to a child that was in such a hurry to leap out of the sky at night in a basket and make it straight for Soslan's front door? And where did Rakhimat's little bastard get to anyway? Or has she managed to keep him in her womb till autumn?"

But Alone sat at the table, cold as a stone, and waited for him to stop screaming, and then said once more:

"I don't understand you. Rakhimat disappeared almost a year ago. Rakhimat's gone. Rakhimat died. Gappo cannot be a grandfather. The dead don't give birth. Rakhimat is dead. She is no more."

Finally it dawned on Barysbi. Alone saw his thick veins inflate like wet maggots and start to swell up as if he'd been bitten. His eyes bulged with fire and blood, while his lower lip hung down in pain. Then they heard the crack. Barysbi unclenched his fist and shards of the broken drinking horn scattered from his hand.

"Oh well!" said Alone. "If I'd only known you'd get so upset... I see that you, for one, in your compassion and your confusion only get stronger. It's a real shame your son couldn't see how you squashed this horn. He'd have really liked it. He'd probably appreciate your strength. All right, I'm off, but as I leave I'll have a little think about whether it's now worth enlightening him."

He got up. Barysbi called out at him:

"Next week it's my father's memorial. You should..."

"Yes, yes, I know. Of course I'll come," Alone interrupted him. "I haven't forgotten."

"Well, eh, what happens then?" asked Barysbi, spitting the words out with some difficulty. It sounded as if his voice had burnt down, so that all that was left of it now was bitter ash. "What then?"

"I don't know yet," said Alone, seeing in Barysbi's eyes that he wanted to believe but was afraid. *That's what I need from him right now, let him be scared and want to believe.*

On that same day Alone heard from the old men at the nykhas that the girl had been christened with a strange name not from our parts.

"They found a little silver nametag attached to her wrist," explained Aguz. "And it had letters carved on it on the inside. Fariza could't read the foreign letters but Soslan could still remember what they looked like. He ran his fingers over the letters, and decided that would be her name."

Alone licked his chapped lips, pulled his cap down his head, drew his dagger from its sheath and started cleaning under his nails with its blade. Out folk watched him and somehow knew he would cut himself. They watched and waited and noticed the blood even before he drew in his blade himself. He hid his dagger, sucked at the wound and asked:

"So what did he read there? What was the word?"

"Lana," said my Grandfather. "Have you ever heard the like?"

"No," replied Alone. "That's not a name... What was it again?"

Aguz said the name again, and Alone meanwhile thought that she hadn't told him about the nametag. *So the name's come back after all. Now it'll stay with her for the rest of her days. If so, I've guessed right, and the word was no accident.*

"Lana," he repeated aloud and smiled. "Could be worse. So, never mind..."

He thought that at least it was a name that contained love. And what's more, a warm and cosy home.

"It's a warm name," he said. "Though not one of ours. But we haven't had any abandoned babies here before either."

He's right, decided the elders. A name's just a name. As long as the father liked it. If Soslan was fated to be a father again, what's wrong if he invented a name with his fingers on that silver tag? They strongly doubted that he had actually read what was written on it: how could their eyes be more dumb than Soslan's fingers! He had never been able to feel out letters with his fingers, even when he could still see! But now – well really! Suddenly the blind man taught himself to read!

"He made it up, all right. If the name lay on his tongue, then it's God's will," my grandfather grumbled. "But why offend people with fictions?"

To cut a long story short, the aul decided that the girl's name appeared not from the curious curves engraved in silver but from some divine inspiration that had whispered its word into Soslan's heart. In fact, they quite liked the idea of possessing something unique that you wouldn't find in the neighbouring auls around the gorge, nor in all of Ossetia, including the Russian town, and the past. It even flattered them to carry on their lips this short good word denoting nothing save a small miracle and the smell of happiness close at hand, coming in waves every time they passed by the house of the blind man who had become aged by his joy and smooth in the face, and who had thankfully slowed down.

"How can I describe him to you?" Uncle bit his lip and clicked his fingers impatiently. "He was kind of big and lumbering... No, that's not right! He was like a new mother, feeling how her breasts were swelling with milk as she moves about. No longer was he blind, and no more was he a prophet. Now he was a father warmed from inside by a clear and steady light. We saw his smile: it wasn't the smile of a blind man, nor was it the smile of a man frightening us with the future. That could only be the smile of someone who was drinking in the present with large gulps and seeing a bright light within.

That's what Uncle told me. I asked him about Grandfather:

"I don't know. He didn't send me out to spy on Alone any more. He had probably decided that it would be no use using my eyes to spy on what his old head couldn't see through the fog. Or maybe he simply no longer wanted to get involved in it all: he'd never particularly trusted Barysbi, and if Barysbi shook with fright at the appearance of the foundling and started hiccupping and fretting at the sight of our neighbour then there was definitely something fishy. Very fishy. So your grandfather was in no hurry to get himself involved in all that muckraking: he'd had more than enough trouble of his own. Ever since he'd found out about your father and Siberia he'd visibly faded. Often he'd suddenly freeze, sitting out in the sun, and only the stick in his hands would shake slightly, and his eyes would glaze over as if he had died inside and his pupils were clouding over. Or at times he'd suddenly grow restless and run about like a rooster all over the yard, and he'd start swearing at us and picking a fight. But more often he'd just sit there quietly, small and pat, like a sparrow on a branch. You'd look at him and feel like yawning. He was a sad sight. Those times I don't remember so well," said Uncle. "We lived like we were on the cusp of what was and what was to come. Betwixt our memories and our prophesies. We lived out those years with a yawn stuck in our throats. I don't know what else to say about them, save that we survived them...

"And when you had finished surviving them," I said, "my father came back... But it wasn't you and Grandfather who saw him first."

Uncle nodded, turned away and said:

"Maybe my brother shouldn't have done that. He broke with tradition. I even think the old man never forgave him for it."

"Is that what you think?"

"Yes," he confirmed. "I may be wrong, but that's how I see it..."

Not then nor later did Father tell a soul what had happened when they met. But that they had met, my uncle would find out that same evening...

In the twilight Father suddenly appeared on our doorstep and Grandma shrieked, taking his shadow to be an enormous jug with human legs.

"Greetings, Mother," he said. "Don't cry."

But she was already weeping and running to him with arms open wide. Grandfather, alarmed by the shriek, came down the stairs and stood in the middle of the room. Then with a single look he ordered my uncle to bring the bench over to him, seated himself down on it, assumed a dignified air, and boomed out:

"Leave him, woman. Go to your room. We'll call you when we've finished."

Grandma stepped back from Father, wiping her tears with her kerchief, and shuffled off obediently to the women's quarters. (She told me later, her eyes warming: "I asked your grandfather to let him breathe in his home. He had lost his hair there. He had even lost his smell. Let him first get his own smell back... But he only looked back at me severely.")

The old man gave her a steely look, and she quickly bowed her head, covered her mouth with her kerchief and scurried off behind the partition.

"What did you wrap yourself up with?" he asked Father, who replied:

"Skins, rags, clay... I smeared them all with clay, so they stuck to me. The road was a long one."

"Are you complaining?" Grandfather asked.

"No," answered Father. "But the road was long."

"You chose it yourself," he exclaimed angrily. "You look like a woman. A fat scruffy woman."

"It's the clay and the mud," said Father. "And I'm not complaining. I came back..."

The old man blinked, wiped a speck of dust from his eyelashes, and then beckoned Father to came up and stand in front of him. Grandfather examined his hands, preparing to ask his questions. But first he sought out a spot on the floor for his stick, planted it down and leant firmly upon it.

"They say you got mixed up in some nasty affair? You took up, I hear, the life of a criminal. You attacked a man. You robbed someone. You brought shame upon your family. Well, are they telling the truth or are they lying? Answer me!"

After a pause Father looked Grandfather in the eyes and said:

"They're lying about the robbery. I did attack a man, but not in anger, only so as not to stay among the thieves. And I've left the place where the criminals are."

The old man groaned, wiping the sweat from his brow and straightening out his clothes, sniffed and blew his nose, once more wiped his brow, then got to his feet and said:

"It's good to have you back. Welcome back, my son!"

Nor at dinnertime did he hold back, and asked:

"So, well, how is it over in Siberia? Must have been heavy going?"

Father straightened up, pushed his plate to one side, put the crust of bread on the table and said:

"Over there it's cold and hot. Sometimes it's hard there and sometimes it couldn't get any harder. There are many human beings there and many inhuman beings, and both perish. But more often than not they both survive and stay there to suffer. There's no such thing as friends there, but sometimes people will save your life, and sometimes they'll beat you to death. They saved my life, but they didn't beat me to death. I saw all sorts there. As it happened, it was terrible there, but it could also be joyful. But more often it was simply miserable. And many troubles there stemmed from misery. Most troubles there stemmed from misery. The rest stemmed from joy. But worst of all there is the time. It's greater there than Siberia itself. I drank my fill of it, down to the last drop. I'm so full of it that don't make me remember it any more."

And remember it he didn't, avoiding any questions or simply refusing to answer them. Father never told us of Siberia and I never pressed – maybe because he carried it within him, in his movements and his look, in his thickset hands as they lay palms down on his knees or on the table, when he had to rest from the full weight of his memories after even the smallest piece of work, and I looked at his hands and thought that they were capable of much. At times it even seemed to me that they were capable of anything. Probably from the day he returned, my grandfather and grandma had realised this, as had my uncle; Father and him lay down to sleep in the guestroom that night. It was late and dark when my uncle sensed that Father couldn't sleep. He sat up in bed, peered in the dark, aware that Father was waiting, and suddenly asked him:

"What are you doing tomorrow?"

His question surprised him because there was an elder in the house who decided everything for everyone, and he slept as head of the family in another room. But there was something in Father's behaviour that troubled Uncle in the pitch dark in the company of a man who was his brother but was now almost a stranger, who had disappeared from his life for a good eight years. And the answer he got was:

"Going hunting with Barysbi."

At this my uncle simply leapt up from the suddenness of the reply and cried out in stunned whisper:

"What?!"

Father sighed in the darkness and asked:

"Have you got a rifle?"

Uncle replied that the old man had.

"So you still don't have one yet," Father concluded and said: "Borrow one off somebody. But not from Alone."

"So you've already met up with Barysbi? You mean you didn't come straight home?"

"Yes," Father replied. "Tomorrow we're off hunting together."

Uncle didn't sleep a wink till morning. And no sooner had it got light than he set off to Gappo for a rifle, reckoning, most probably, that if Father had to go hunting at least he should have a good gun. Gappo's gun was a sure shot. But why go with Barysbi, thought Uncle, why did he have to go to Barysbi before he set foot across his own threshold?

Father was waiting for him by the bend in the road. He squatted looking at the hoarfrost on the grass. It was a cold morning and the brisk walk brought forth clouds of steam from my uncle's mouth. Father turned round at his approach, and Uncle said:

"I got it for you."

Father nodded and, still squatting, put out his hand. He looked over the rifle, checked the breech and put it down on his knees.

"Not a word to the old man," he ordered and gave Uncle a grey cold look.

"I see," said Uncle obediently and squatted down alongside him. Father broke off a blade of grass and cleaned the hoar frost off it with two fingers. Plucking up the courage, Uncle asked: "Who are you going to hunt?"

Father chuckled and placed his hand on Uncle's shoulder:

"A very evil beast. A dangerous animal. It's called the past... Go home."

He squeezed Uncle's shoulder till it started to hurt and Uncle got to his feet.

"Maybe..." he said. "It's cold here... Maybe he won't show. Maybe he'll forget or something? Or he's decided you must have been joking, hey?"

"Go," said Father and turned away from him, putting the blade of grass between his teeth. Uncle went back to the aul, but looked back at the hillock and, seeing Father looking away at the forest, he launched sharply to his right and fell, rolling down the hillock. Catching his breath, he climbed back to its top and cautiously raised his head above it. His eyes didn't have time to focus on Father when he heard a shot and a bullet buzzed past his ear.

"I told you to go back home!" Father said impassively. "You have no respect for your elders. That's not good."

He shot again, and the bullet lodged itself on the outer side of the hillock. Uncle slid off the hillock and ran down to the road but he did not encounter Barysbi.

When Father returned it was already getting dark. He whistled from the street and Uncle ran out, smiling joyfully that he was alive. Father handed over the rifle to him and ordered him to take it straight back to Gappo. Uncle obeyed, but when he got back home he saw that Grandfather and Father had already managed to have a squabble. The old man was grumpily muttering away to himself, but looking at him Uncle guessed that he was more concerned than angry.

"Just look at him," Grandfather turned to his younger son. "His own master! What ever comes into his head, his legs carry him off to it! A huntsman! He's no huntsman – Pah! He came back empty-handed! Maybe now he's come back, my time here is up! You ask him! Maybe he's now the head of the family? Let him come and tell me to my face: go off, old man, and rest. If you want – in your bed, or in your grave! Let him tell me to my face! A hunter with an empty bag! Have you ever seen the like in our family? Pah!"

Uncle slipped out of the house and went into the guests' quarters. Father was lying on a rug, hands behind his head, thinking intently about something. Uncle shut the door, leaned back against it and said:

"He'll rage on for the whole week and you won't talk to each other. But then it'll blow over just the same. You know him..." he fell silent. Father lay still, almost not breathing. Uncle coughed and asked: "So how was the hunt?"

Father answered at once:

"It wasn't," he said. "The hunt was lousy. It ended before it had even begun. Now let me have my nap."

He closed his eyes and Uncle went out quietly, though he knew that Father would be unable to sleep a wink. It was still the height of the evening when he returned to the house. But Grandfather had already left the room. In the yard he bumped into Grandma who told him that the old man had set off to the nykhas.

"So late?" said Uncle in surprise and opened the gate.

In the gathering shadows he couldn't make out the nykhas that was unusually crowded that day, but he suddenly picked up an unmistakeable sharp smell of danger in the sensitive breath of the evening air.

I was about to go back inside to grab something from the larder before dinner, but suddenly I started to shiver, just as if a snake had wrapped itself round my neck, he remembered. I started shivering so madly that I even made the gate creak. I didn't manage to go back inside though, for it was then I caught sight of him.

Just when my father had collapsed on the rug, lost in his thoughts and unable to sleep, and just when my grandfather, trying not to show his anxiety, sat on the bench at the nykhas, just when Uncle was about to scavenge a bite to eat off Grandma, and Grandma stumbled suddenly near the larder, just then by some invisible will the shadows parted and Alone stepped onto our street dragging behind him a heavy load wrapped up in a cloak he had tied to the strap of his rifle. He dragged it from the bend in the road towards the house of Aguz, while our elders looked on, rooted to the spot, and each of them recalled how many years before in just the same way, right before their eyes, the orphaned boy had dragged behind him the skin of the bear he had slaughtered, having placed its fresh meat in it and with rags wrapped up around his body. They recalled his thin, stubborn legs sliding over the snow and how he didn't fall once despite his wounds, the infirmity in his weak step and the unbelievable tiredness in his pale dirty face. He dragged his tiredness all the way to his house and never let the skin slip once from his hands, then lit the fire in his hearth, and in the straight long wisp of smoke that rose over his roof they saw a proud black finger threatening the aul. They recalled this, for now it was like then, only more so – this time it was worse, far worse, and they sensed it at once, as soon as they caught sight of him, as soon as they remembered and compared. Now the burden that he was pulling along the street was no longer the victory over his loneliness, but the fatal inevitability of some disaster, whose approach they had felt in their hearts for many years, only not knowing when its time would strike. And now he, already a man, grown up and strong, with his coat ripped open from effort on his broad back, was carrying it past them down the road caked with hoarfrost through the receding autumn gloom and stumbling over his own tiredness, the same tiredness that hadn't been able to overcome him when it took the form of a slain bear and its skinned carcass, and they watched how he walked painfully, unevenly towards their houses, and waited for them to come to his aid, and now one and all caught their breath at the thought that he would come to a halt and lay down his load in front of their own gates, handing over to them a disaster wrapped up in the cloak and as yet unbeknownst to them. Under their frightened gazes and the cloudy silence from the steam of their open jaws, he passed first the house of Aguz, then that of Batyrbek, then another six houses and finally reached our own, but Uncle, standing at the gate, made no move to meet him, and the tragedy that he pulled past us grew a whole house smaller and by the same amount grew all the greater and more terrible for the five houses that remained. When Alone got past the stretch of road that flanked his own fence, and then passed another three houses and came up to the gates whose owner no one had seen since yesterday evening, then they understood that he would go no further: further was the house of Soslan.

So it was Barysbi, they decided and hurried down from the nykhas. Alone stopped, untied the strings on the cloak, removed the hood covering the face and called out to his son, crying out his name in front of his gates. It was already dark.

When the villagers pressed into a crowd surrounding Alone and Barysbi, it was already so dark that at first they couldn't make out whether he was dead or still alive. They got hold of the cloak, and pushing with too many shoulders, took it inside, where the women had already begun wailing loudly. But through the noise, the panting and the cries, they heard his words:

"He's breathing. Wounded in the head and broken his leg..."

But they were late in turning round to where the voice had come from: Alone fell face downwards onto the cold earth.

Uncle had seen none of all this, and so did not know as yet that Barysbi was still alive. Meanwhile the villagers, bending over Alone and turning him round onto his back, examined his strange face (it had always been strange to them, and hardly a one of them could accurately describe how it looked, for they rarely met him face to face, and usually only watched him stealthily. But now his face appeared strange to them not only in its extreme proximity and size of its features, but also in its total defencelessness before their curiosity, it expressed at the same time an utmost suffering and inmost calm. Faces such as this they saw only on those who had died in pain, exchanging the sweating fire of their suffering for the cool caress of their final departure. It was a moment on that secret border between being and nothingness, that from the bare earth shone pale before them on the face of a man fallen into unconsciousness from his efforts and from tiredness, like an overworked horse falling down onto the grass. They looked at this face and thought that if it awoke, for now and ever more they would imagine on it the shadow of lonely tiredness leaning toward death. If he recovers, they thought, he would have to carry his death with him, just as he did his blood or his belly. Maybe he had been carrying it with him before, only we didn't know it, thought the villagers, not daring to undo his coat and listen to his heartbeat, as if the very touch of his flesh would be an outrage upon his fainting, his suffering and his calm, upon their witnessing of his fall and the silence that reigned over them all. Orders and cries resounded from Barysbi's house, plates clattered and crockery rattled, water splashed, but before its gates all was silent and still, as if the few men standing around in a circle and the fallen body in their midst had formed into a tiny island of time, independent of the general commotion and emerging out of its troubled waves. A minute later Alone would open his eyes, and they'd help him up, and the island would dissipate under their words, but while he lay there, they belonged to the resurrected clever time and Uncle knows nothing of all this. He runs into the house, paying no heed to Grandma groaning near the larder, and hurries in to see my father. Bursting open the door of the guest room, he cries out to his back:

"So that's your hunt! You came back only to shoot him!"

Father turned sharply round, leapt out of bed and grabbed Uncle by the chest:

"You mean Barysbi?? Barysbi's dead?"

"You killed him," says Uncle and pushes Father's hands off his chest. Father takes a step forward and with a groan bashes his head against the wall rocking it from side to side.

"No," he said. "Not me. I gave up waiting for him."

"Liar!" said Uncle, his eyes welling up with tears. "You shot him and now you're lying. Just don't even think of lying to the old man. Or lie so that he believes you. But better go. Run before they come for your blood. Or better still..." here Uncle leaps at him and they fall to the floor, clutching at each other and rolling around the floor. Father is clearly stronger than his brother. He turns away from his frenzied punches, and then aims a couple of precise punches at him, and Uncle lets go of him. His mouth is cut, a red stream of blood flows from the corner of his lips, mixing by his chin with the salty wetness of his tears. Uncle sits on the floor and repeats:

"I waited for you so long and you come back to shoot. Now they'll kill the old man. Because of you now they'll kill the old man to make everything worse. We waited for you and now you've come back and started shooting..."

"Shut up," Father rudely broke in. "I did not kill him. He didn't even show up. I felt it was pointless sitting there any longer and went off into the forest. I didn't kill him. I wandered through the forest so as to not come back down to the village before evening. I had to wait out till evening. I did not want to kill him."

Uncle wipes the blood from his lips with his sleeve and says:

"When I returned the rifle to Gappo there were eight bullets in the bag. This morning there were exactly a dozen. Two of them you fired at me. Where are the other two?"

"I don't know," replies Father. "They must have fallen out on the way."

"Aha," says Uncle. "They just went and fell out. Of course..."

"Go to hell," says Father. Then he asks: "Who found him?"

And even before Uncle replies, he already knows what his answer is:

"Alone," says Uncle, and as he says it Father has already thrown open the door and run out of the room. In the yard he leaps over the fence and for the first time in eight years enters the house of the man who condemned him to prison, so as to prevent him from murder, who put him away for eight years and committed a murder of his own eight years later. So thinks my father as he runs towards Alone's house and appears on his doorstep without knocking. Alone is drinking from a cup of water. The room is dark and full of shadows sliding around the room at the will of the coals flickering in the hearth. Putting aside his cup and hanging it on the wooden pin over the wet jug Alone says:

"I was looking for you all day. I was afraid I wouldn't find you." He offers Father a bench and sits down after him. "I thought you'd come by yesterday night. But instead of a night guest I got a bullet in the door. So you decided to go hunting first..."

He starts to tell him how he pops over to Barysbi's in the morning, but doesn't find him in, and his family doesn't know where he's gone, except that he's gone off hunting; there was no talk of any hunting companion, they probably thought Barysbi had gone off without one, not a word had been said about my Father. Alone grabs his rifle – obtained ages ago from my grandfather in return for seven-eighths of his harvest and yearly exchanged for our hard labour in the fields and sacks filled to the brim – and follows in their tracks, still hoping that he'd catch up with them, that he'd find my father and convince him, but this hope faded with the daylight that nourished it, and then circling the forest he came out onto the Buffalo Path and stopped there hesitant whether he should go back or not. However, right then he felt a cold gust of wind at his back and moved on towards the summit, which he hadn't climbed for such a long time that at the sight of the deep abyss yawning at his feet his jaw cramped up and his knees shook, but he surmounted the abyss and caught back his breath; he continued onward, but in truth, it was a shorter way back: skirting the wide arc of the hill, he was no longer moving away from the aul but drawing closer to it, and when the forest started to thin out he almost did not notice it for the light had faded. Alone worked up such a terrible thirst that his throat grated, to quench it he descended into the ravine and took to turning over the rotting leaves in his attempt to find a stream, only instead of a stream he found Barysbi sprawled in the ravine amongst the rotting leaves and no longer even groaning, his things also smelled of rot, and under his shoulder there spread a puddle of melted water, so Alone realised that he'd been lying there for quite some time, probably since midday, since a shot had been fired. Barysbi's face was smeared with blood and Alone washed it, scooping the water from the puddle; then he wrapped him up in his cloak and dragged him back to the aul down the gentle slope on the west face of the mountain; it took him almost an hour to get to the spot where the incline, coming to its end, opens out into a flat patch of the riverbank, like ice; when he left the forest far behind him he saw not ten paces away from him the slobbering snout of a jackal and threw a stone at him, but the jackal appeared again, then Alone slung the rifle off his arm, aimed and softly pressed the trigger, but after the smoke had cleared, he realised he had missed: he was too tired, his arms were shaky; after another hundred or so metres he stopped, gave them a breather and tried again, but now too he failed, the bullet merely scraped a rock a few feet from his target, throwing up a small fountain of dust; the jackal shook and moved sideways; then he again followed them, and even when Alone reached the pebbly riverbank and stepped out onto the planks of the wooden bridge, the animal stubbornly followed behind, and Alone imagined that the jackal also intended to cross the raging waters on those wooden planks; only when he'd heard a wounded howl did he relax, then turn back and say out loud: "Go find yourself some carrion, you mangy dog, or else you'll get stomach cramps." He laughed out loud; his laughter lifted his spirits, and he again took up his burden, feeling instantly how veins in his forearms bulged and started to ache and gnaw as they prepared themselves for yet more pain. He moved along the shore, the river sprayed water at them and Alone covered Barysbi's face with his hood; on the wet shingle it was easier to pull the body, but several times he slipped and hurt his knees, and then, having rested momentarily, slowly pulled himself up and moved on. A half-hour later he entered the aul and now there only remained for him to surmount the silent street, and that was hardest of all, for they all, said Alone, sat and watched like cowards, and not one of them hurried over to help, they only watched; in their anxiety their Adam's apples trembled, and each of them prayed to the skies that I didn't stop in front of their gates; when I reached yours, your brother also kept silent clutching at the gate, and again you were nowhere to be seen, as if those eight years continued, and I stepped onwards and thought how everything always ends up so badly, even if the end had been postponed by fate for eight years, why you were nowhere to be seen, for you at least should have been stealthily observing us, like the smith does the horse he's shod, or the host watches his guest eating, but you were nowhere, so I started to think: maybe it wasn't you? And then I thought, it couldn't be anyone else. Finally I arrived and called out his son; then I felt tight inside and went spinning, and suddenly it was dark, very dark and warm, I no longer needed to think, and when I once more opened my eyes, they stood over me, and as before no one was prepared to say anything, so they helped me to my feet and let me go home in peace; I came inside and started to drink water, I drank and drank to quench the dryness inside, and then drank savouring every drop, and had almost drunk my fill when I heard footsteps and knew it was you; you arrived to end those eight years; you came, says Alone, to work out what you'd do next and what you should do with me, for you'd grown tired of revenge, you'd lived with its echo for a whole eight years, and then another whole day, not counting that instant at midday when that echo formed itself into a shot, but now again returned to its old self, only now as it grew closer to nightfall it resounded louder so that you were tired of listening to its repulsively repetitive cracking, and then you, says Alone, came here to make your choice, and I won't stand in your way...

He falls silent and gets up, goes deeper into the room and gets a rifle from the wall. Only my father can now decide, ponders Alone, whether the rifle's price should once again come to one eighth of every harvest collected by them from his fields. Pulling aside the breechblock, he checks the bullet, loads the rifle and puts it alongside his guest. Then he sits and looks at Father, who says:

"I didn't kill him. My brother also reckons it was me that killed him, but that's not so."

"Yes," says Alone. "You wounded him. Slashed his cheek and burst his eardrum with your bullet, but he's alive. He fell into the ravine and broke his leg, but that's nothing. He'll recover. You weren't able to kill him."

A small hot lump swims through Father's stomach. When he again starts to speak his teeth are chattering:

"I didn't even shoot at him. Today we didn't even meet. We agreed to meet up by the bend in the road. I sat there all morning, but he didn't show up. I went into the forest, not knowing myself if I wanted to meet him or..."

"Or you were scared," says Alone. But Father continues:

"Yesterday I knew what I wanted but today I didn't. I didn't know right from dawn and still didn't know as I was wandering in the forest. But when I returned home it was too late to rack my brains about it, and I only wanted to last out the night so that morning would reveal to me what I now wanted. Of course, he lost his nerve but I didn't know if that was enough for me or not. Maybe it wasn't. I didn't know what to do even if it was enough because I didn't know what it was or wasn't enough for. But then my brother said that he was dead, and called me a murderer. He didn't want to believe me, and we fought, but I was already thinking about you. I thought that you'd made a blunder when you'd decided to take this sin upon yourself and conclude what you'd been fighting against for so many years. I thought you'd given in and ran here to look at a man, who had realised his defeat and became worthy of nothing but contempt... Only it seems you didn't shoot him either. It seems like neither of us shot him though we followed on his heels with loaded guns. And now we're sitting in your house and you shove me over a loaded rifle, which still smells of gunpowder, and suggest I make a choice, like I'm some kind of poor murderer that's lost his head... You surprise me. To tell you the truth, I still don't know what to think of you. Only, thank God, you're not worthy of contempt. Maybe you're worthy of hate or, worse, adoration. Or maybe even someone's pity. You're probably worthy of death also. But contempt – no. I can't choose the gun. And I don't want to pity you. Nor do I want to believe you, but I have no other choice. What I want is to go home."

Alone looks away, following the play of shadows under his feet. Then he nods and offers his hand, but my father pays no notice. He pushes the door, runs his hand over it and finds a round depression. Sticking his finger inside it, he says:

"It seems last night he sent you a message. He warned you somehow..."

"Yes," says Alone. "Like he was calling for a witness. Or for help. Or he fired out of despair that he couldn't get me."

"Or because he has no desire to go hunting for his past," Father suggests.

"Maybe so. But more likely from all of those things. It's not so easy to work out."

Father leaves. He goes home where Grandfather is already waiting for him, seated on his bench and sternly knitting his brow. Uncle stands beside him. His swollen mouth is half-opened and his eyes are red. Father approaches them and forestalling the old man says in a voice of iron to ward off all questions:

"Here's what I have to say... Listen carefully for I'm repeating it for the last time: I did not shoot at Barysbi. And if you ever doubt that, I swear to God I will go and kill him though I have no especial desire to."

He turns sharply on his heels and goes outside to inhale with his whole chest the black deep air of the evening on which the longest eight years of his life had come to an end...

Alone at this same time is getting the fire going in his hearth. Tending the coals and throwing on more brushwood, he sits on his haunches and looks into the pure young flame, trying to understand what had taken place that day. He reflects on whose shot it must have been that led Barysbi to lose his balance and fall into the gully, if the only two people who held any motive to shoot him did not. He turns over in his mind every one of the villagers, but fails to find any semblance of an answer, even an incorrect one. Nonetheless someone had pressed the trigger and blasted Barysbi's right ear. The bullet scratched his cheek and exited through his ear. The shot must have come from down below. Someone had fired at him from the gully. But why was the gunner too lazy to go and check if he had got his victim or merely grazed his cheek, if his target practically rolled down right to his feet? Something here evidently didn't tie up. Looking at the fire, Alone thinks: "It's like cutting off your own toes to pull on some tight boots." It was utterly pointless to shoot at a man, wait for him to tumble down into the withered leaves, make sure that your bullet only stunned him and head off back home reckoning only that no one would find him here, and that, as had now happened, no one would know who had fired the shot. To do that you'd have to be a madman. Or so cunning as to outwit yourself... Or maybe, he thinks all of a sudden, someone felt obliged to set the whole thing up so as to frame whomever had a good motive? There were two of those: himself and my father. Besides them, and Barysbi obviously, no one to that day suspected anything. It had turned out to be a closed circle. Or more accurately, a triangle: Alone, Father and Barysbi. So it turned out that someone must be lying. And it turned out that it was my father who was lying, for Alone was speaking the truth, and Barysbi wasn't able to utter a word. And it turned out that nothing could be worked out, since my father hadn't been lying to him either, for Alone was the sole person to whom he could tell the truth without having to worry that any kind of proof would be demanded of him. And it turned out that all three of them were in fact not lying, but all the same one of them had pressed the trigger, so that meant that that person must have been lying, only my father, Alone, and Barysbi hadn't told any lies, though one of them had still pressed the trigger that day at midday, despite the fact that none of them was lying, and Barysbi – well, he hadn't even managed to open his mouth, be it to lie or to utter the truth, but two of the three had definitely not been lying, although one of that threesome had pulled the trigger that day at midday, but then had certainly not been lying or was no longer able to lie... All of a sudden Alone understood everything, and when the realisation dawned upon him he even cried out in surprise. He leapt up to his feet and began

Killed by fear ?

to pace the room forgetting all about his tiredness. In his excitement he slapped his sides and swore, banging against the wall with open palms. Now everything seemed to him so simple and natural that he was stunned it hadn't occurred to him before. Now he knew it all came down to fear. The fear of a man, who realised the same as the other two that a shot had to be fired that day, and who had been waiting for this moment for a whole eight years, preparing himself in his dreams for his lot of being the target for that moment, and from the evening before had been appointed to become this target no sooner than the dawn would flicker in the sky; all night long he couldn't sleep a wink, then he got up and went under night cover to the gates of the one who had kept silent for eight years – as if he had been hoping that everything would sort itself out somehow, although for a good seven and a half years he could have driven him out of his homeland any day, but somehow hadn't done so, and kept on being silent all this evening, maybe he didn't even know that the next day it would all be over – and through a crack in the wattle fencing, he fired at his door, and then ran back, lay down in his bed, and still unable to sleep, listened to the life pulsing heavily in his heart, in his groin, in his belly, in his brains, and tried to guess where it would be intercepted the next day and flow out of him as sweet blood. At dawn he washed, cleaned his rifle, slung it over his chest, packed his knapsack with gunpowder and a dozen lead castings, looked around his household and family and set off past the mill, which he had blown up but then rebuilt; he chose the longest and slushiest road to the river bend. Of course he had no desire to die or be a target, but he desired even more: that before his death vengeance would read no sign of fear in his eyes. He chose the longest path so that he would sweat out all his fear and face vengeance with a steady heart and a firm hand. He even hoped to fight it and so loaded his rifle by the first tree in the forest, and probably his rifle started to seem weightier and more significant to him, but his hands were still shaking, so he walked unhurriedly along the very longest path, towards the river bend, he walked more slowly than the morning moved to its zenith, twirling over his head into grey mist and flowing away for good – or so he thought – out of his last ever sky, obeying the chilly vigour of the wind... Then he started to make stops on the road. The nearer he got to the river bend, the more often would he come to a halt. He leant back against tree trunks and inhaled the smell of damp bark, reassuring himself that, no matter, he could wait, it was fine, he'd been waiting far longer already, and so he could bear it a while longer, what difference did an extra few minutes make, none at all... But these extra minutes turned into an hour, and continued to coagulate and coalesce into a small deposit of living time disintegrating before his eyes into shafts and shards of light coming through the sharp twigs of forest trees. Then he told himself that he was thirsty, that he wanted to drink his fill, and convinced himself that he'd never manage to do this by the river bend. He probably convinced himself of all this a hundred paces from the bend, and so turned back to the path leading up to the incline. Now he even quickened his pace, covering the distance almost at a run, telling himself that he'd come straight back, that my father would wait, for now he wouldn't have very long to wait, that this wasn't cowardice, there was no more time for cowardice, this was just thirst; probably his hands really did stop shaking from his brisk haste, and he did, indeed, awaken within himself the resolution worthy of death, and all he needed was a gulp of ice cold water, a taste of fresh spring water. When he fell upon the spring, the water really was as delicious as he remembered and he drank of it eagerly, plunging his face into the spring and delighting in its cool. Then he sat down on a rock and waited for the liquid to flow all through his body and for the heaviness in his breast to vanish. Now I'll get moving, he thought. I'll rest for a while and then I'll go. I've walked such a long way since dawn that my legs have gone numb. I just need to rest for the shortest while. Best I rest a little and collect my strength. That way I'll reach the river bend faster. Let's just hope he hasn't left. Let's just hope he hasn't decided I'm a coward. I'm no coward and now I'll prove it to him. I'm just taking a breather... The sun was already hanging right over his head, and he thinks that soon it will be midday. When he reaches the river bend, it will be midday on the dot. But will he wait till midday? Maybe not. Maybe he'd given up waiting long ago. Maybe I'll come and he'll have gone already. If he decided that I'm a coward, then he'll have left long ago. From then on he forbids himself to think any more and stands up, preparing for the descent down the slope. Maybe he even takes a few steps before stopping once more, in as much as there really are no more remnants of fear inside him, he bravely thinks this thought to its conclusion, and then tells himself bravely and honestly: he's not there. You know he's not there, and you should have been there early in the morning, and now it's close on midday. He's gone, so he's realised you're a coward. You were a coward for too long for him to believe, even, that you had the guts to make it to there. So then why deceive yourself and go down where no one's waiting for you any more? Wouldn't that just be prolonging your cowardice? He stands there meditating on all this and looks at the eternal curve in the path along which he couldn't make it today to his meeting place with that vengeance insulted by deceit. Then he spits into the grass and turns back towards the crest of the hill, though there's by now not a trace of fear in him. At the fork in the road by the Empty Cliff, he elects to take the slippery path that crawls round its steepest slope and skirts round it in a fragile, capricious ribbon. He has fully recovered now from his earlier fear and so, unconsciously, but stubbornly seeks out danger and chooses a path on which he hopes to last out the entire day, and without losing that feeling of a man released from all fears, to make it to the following day painlessly, so that the shot, albeit a full day late, could still be fired. He still doesn't know how he should cope with it, but now he's sure that he would manage to. Now he's so confident that he even allows himself a degree of carelessness when he skirts round sheer cliff faces or jumps across a narrow crevasse. On a path no more than two-hands wide he moves as hurriedly as if it were a paved street, and not two hands' worth of slippery rock. All of this smacks of an escape along a knife blade as his daring has arrived a few hours too late, so that for him it is more of a chase than an escape. A chase after a lost day for his own honour. Whatever the case, he takes a great risk running along the narrow treacherous path to meet the midday sun and trying with all his might not to fear falling over the precipice. Only he is doomed all the same. For the shot is fated to be fired on that day. Maybe, in the depths of his soul he understands that it is not in his power to avert what time has been preparing for a full eight years and was firmly intended for that day. That a few hours' delay is not enough, just as recovering one's daring is not enough to postpone one's fate. Maybe he feels this and even sincerely hopes to meet his enemy as he's running alongside the precipice and has no fear of dying. But then the precipice falls behind him and still nothing has happened and no one has showed up, and he's a bit hurt by this: so much bravery had gone to waste! He stubbornly walks on following the path like a monstrous serpent, whose tail he now tramples with the fury of an ant enraged at its length; he grows dizzy with his fury, he grows careless as a man drunk on his own daring, and the payoff arrives – a dead branch or divot of land in his path. He trips and mechanically tries to grab onto something, finding only the rifle squeezed in his hand and loaded since dawn, and it responds with a blast and eruption of fire, so that he rolls down into the gully that is rotting with its own dampness, thinking, if he hadn't already lost his consciousness, that vengeance turned out to be a joke, a cruel and vile joke on his weakness and his shame. He lies at the bottom of the gully in a pool of melted water, and his body, no longer aided by his detached mind, tries desperately to beckon death as it sniffs around his motionlessness. But a broken leg, a shot through the ear and a lump on the head are a poor bait for death, and so instead of the sensation of winged peace, of which he dreams while he considers himself dead, there awaits him on awakening only a huge and merciless wave of humiliation. It will crash over him the instant he hears once more inside him his accursed life. And then, contemplates Alone, anything may happen. The sense of humiliation may whip at his soul and squeeze out of it its last desire to be honourable. Now no baseness is beyond him. Now he'll attempt to gain his revenge for not being able to die. He'll have no other choice, thinks Alone, for he is Barysbi and he's still alive. When they try to elicit from him who it was that shot at him, he will be choosing between the man waiting for him by the river bend and measuring his cowardice by the sunrise, and the man who did not let him die by pulling out his body from the gully. He would choose between two hatreds, all the more so since now that the shot had been fired, he need no longer fear their exposure for no revelations could change the fact that the shot had rung out and now the time had come to reciprocate. Now that the shot had rung out, no revelations would induce the villagers to hold him more in contempt than had no shot been fired from his own rifle in reply. They would far rather forgive him the mill and all his baseness than shirk away from vengeance. They would forgive him the Belgians and the dynamite only if he ordered his son to take up his rifle and announce the name of his victim. They will forgive him the dead Russian and the mill if his duped son goes off to hunt for his own honour and in his inaptitude receives a bullet in the head. Now they'd forgive Barysbi everything, except inaction and sloth. But most likely of all, Alone pondered, they would not even know that they should be forgiving him anything, if neither of those whom he could point out to his son says a word about anything. So both of them would wait for Barysbi to start talking. They also have no choice. They simply have to wait. Now this turns for them into an obligation before the whole story and their own consciences. For them to start talking now is just as impossible as finishing him off while he lies there wounded, or sharing his humiliation with him. They haven't kept their silence all these years to tell the whole world of their secret now and allow it to encroach into that firm betrothal of mutual obligations and duties forged over the years by the fate of their common destiny that defined the meaning of their existences and made them what they were today so that they could now on their own – and therefore as a three – reach its denouement and not give up their mysterious triangular unity. In other words, to tell was now to betray: their history and their own selves, it meant to fail the test and debase those eight years that every one of them – not just the one in jail who was sent off to Siberia – had lived in the prison of their own silence. All that remains for us now, thinks Alone, is to let this silence unravel a speedy denouement from the threads of his humiliated baseness. He understands this just as well as I do: Alone thinks of my father.

He guessed right: all night long my father can't get out of his head the two bullets that fell out of his knapsack somewhere in the forest and had now lodged themselves firmly in Uncle's brain. To hell with what Barysbi will go and say. Damn it if the others believe him. The only bad thing is that my own younger brother won't forget that pair of accidentally dropped bullets, he tells himself in the strained silence of their painful proximity, listening to the careful breathing from the neighbouring bed and clenching his fists. Whatever he says, today I did not become a murderer, and that's what matters. For so many years I wondered whether I could avoid turning into a killer and today I know that I have succeeded. I've overcome myself and that's the main thing. What's more, Barysbi took fright of a man who was unable to kill him. Now he'll think up all sorts of stories and maybe make the villagers suspect Alone and me, only I think he'll never have the guts to tell anything straight out loud, just as he won't have the guts to take up his gun. But they'll start suspecting us all the same, especially if they find out about my two lost bullets and Alone's two bullets that missed the jackal that nobody saw except him and therefore nobody will believe it existed, for to this day no one had yet erased from their memories how accurately he shot dead all those hares, and exchanged them for gunpowder off our old man. Even the hole in his door won't save us from suspicion. All that's needed for their suspicion is one bullet or a solitary shell. Just as that's all that's needed for one destroyed ear. They'll decide that for two shots you don't need at all to have different huntsmen. They'd decide that one of us fired at the door so that it would be easier to justify ourselves when the nykhas looks into the motif for making an attempt on Barysbi's life and why this all coincided so tightly with my return. Of course, I'll be the first suspect, only then they won't have the slightest inkling as to why the devil I'd have to go hunting after him, and then they'll remember Alone: if there's a mystery who else comes to mind, but him? That he was the one who dragged Barysbi back to the aul won't embarrass them in the slightest, for even that could have been part of some cunning plan of his: for instance, they might decide he'd been trying to frame me if my reappearance was in the way somehow and irksome for him. But then again, no, my father reasons, that's nonsense. All sorts of rubbish clutter my head. Because their thoughts will fall upon me. Unless Barysbi will suddenly point to Alone. Then they'll believe him unquestioningly. And they'll instantly invent hundreds of reasons why he could do it. Then he'll be past helping. Even if I were to stand up before the nykhas and take the blame upon myself. So, as it turns out, Alone is no less at risk than I am... Only Barysbi's not up to that, he's not even up to saying anything out loud. All he's capable of is indulging in hints. Enough of that. That's not the main thing. The main thing is that today I managed not to kill a man. The only bad thing is that those two cartridges got lost. It's rotten when two pathetic little cartridges fall out of your bag at a most inconvenient moment and your own younger brother remembers about them.

So my father's and Alone's train of thought are about the same, though my father is convinced that even in his desperation Barysbi will not dare to slander either of them: hadn't he read fear in Barysbi's eyes the day before when he met him on the Blue Road as he sat propping his back up against a large boulder and gazing over at the new mill – for my father it was still as new as it was for the rest of us the day they set it up with new millstones and raised them to where they had stood before. I don't know how they met there, only there was nowhere else they could have come across one another apart from the Blue Road if their meeting really hadn't been observed by anyone as if it never took place, but if it did take place then it must have been on the Blue Road, by that boulder. I've no idea, naturally, how my father knew for sure that he'd find Barysbi there, but since they agreed to go hunting then Barysbi must have been there on the Blue Road. As it happened Father did not wait in vain, and probably had good reasons for never telling a soul about that meeting – not just about that meeting but about how he arranged it, as if it happened just like that, like a stop for a traveller or washing hands in a spring before drinking. The thing is, I think, that for my father this meeting had for ages become an inevitable reality, say, even eight years previously, and if suddenly for some reason or other it didn't take place this would have surprised him even more than it would a traveller, journeying for a whole eight years to his destination and suddenly realizing that in all these eight terrible years he hadn't moved a step closer to it. That meeting lived in his dreams all those years he stubbornly journeyed towards it, and day after day he would patiently polish it with his imagination until he'd learnt it by heart and was only awaiting the moment when he'd have the chance to reproduce those few words, movements and gestures that he had repeated in his mind for many hundreds of days, evenings and nights and which, no sooner had Barysbi appeared before him, would take up no more than a minute or even less: a minute would more than suffice to utter a handful of words to the face of a petrified man! Such words as, for example: "Now you've found me. And you did good. Because tomorrow at dawn we're going hunting together. Get your gun and come to the river bend." Or simply: "Maybe all's not lost for you yet. If you're as good a hunter as you used to be, come at dawn to the river bend." Or: "It's too late to go hunting today. We'll have to go tomorrow. We'll set off to the forest at dawn. I'll

wait for you at the river bend. Bring your best rifle."
Something of that sort. Few words and much meaning. And
deathly fear in the eyes of his enemy. That was yesterday.
But today, coming to the end of the hardest day of his life, my
father thinks: "I've grown old. I take no joy in my victory.
I've come home but I still feel bad. I've probably grown old.
And tired of myself. Perhaps, old age is when you grow tired
of yourself and there's no getting away from it. The
inescapability of your own self. And that's a nasty old age.
I'm tired of that too..."

My uncle's already asleep, splayed out on the rug, and
his dreams are loud and troubled. His elder brother, who has
forgotten the smell of home, envies him as he stares at the
ceiling, his head resting on his hands capable of much and
even of not killing another man.

And in Alone's hearth the hot coals crackle in the fire,
straining to banish the cold from his stone walls. His house is
dark and chilly. The night seems to be flowing over the coals
in a vain search for comfort and warmth. Here it is cold and
quiet and only the night moves on...

And in Barysbi's house the embers do not die till
morning. Before the maimed body laid out on the bed sits a
sad middle-aged woman guarding her hopes, her dry hands
placed on the blanket that barely stirs under his weak breathing.
The face of her husband seems alien to her, but not from its
bruises or the wound on his cheek. It is too peaceful and
calm. On it there is writ no pain, no suffering. On it is writ
nothing. This face prevents her from recalling the real face
of the man lying before her. The embers glow, and the flame
climbs up above them, throwing out a shadow that freezes on
his skin as a sharp black stain. The woman quietly cries and
sometimes whispers through her tears a simple prayer. She
attempts to remember the face of the man with whom she's

lived almost her entire life, to whom she has borne three daughters and a solitary son, but every time the face slips away from her grasp, and she has to make do with looking at the one lying before her on the fresh sheets and submitting itself uncomplainingly to the procession of black shadows. The woman prays and cries, reproaching herself for the lack of faith in her soul.

In this late and intolerably long moment, this grieving woman over the splayed body turns out to be the wisest of all...

She turns out to be the wisest of all, for her husband will never speak again, and will never regain his former face, even when scabs shroud his wounds, and the huge lump the size of a clove of garlic on his head disappears. He will not die, but he won't remember who he is, just as he won't recognise the woman he married, nor the children she has borne him. He won't even remember his own name, only he will no longer have need of it, for he will totally forget the language which he has spoken since birth and with which he listened to his thoughts. He will not die, but he won't even realise this while his grown-up son would wish he were an orphan, but instead fate has preserved this life and granted it to a senseless creature with indifferent, unfeeling eyes like hooves, eyes that don't change their expression even when sitting on a bench he issues a shameless and abundant stream. He will not die and grow so humble that his household, to whose hands he will uncomplainingly and unquestioningly submit, will avert their gazes so as not to look at him sitting immobile for hours on end out in the yard where they have led him, breathing evenly, as he fixes his gaze on the plough, the wattle fence or the empty bucket. Nevermore will he go up to the nykhas, and not because this is too much for his crippled legs but because he won't even be let out onto the street, and nor does he ask to be: all he will need from now on is merely a bowl of soup and a piece of bread with a smattering of salt twice a day; his youngest daughter feeds him with a spoon watching the slow working of his angular jaws with irritation and thinking: "He doesn't find it either tasty or disgusting. Even animals know what's tasty and what's not. Even sheep. But it's all the same to him. Maybe if you didn't feed him for a couple of days, he might start munching his own finger. And even then he wouldn't find it tasty or disgusting." The woman with the sad hands, who had turned out to be wisest of all, will resign herself earlier than the others and plead with her only son: "Imagine that he's a baby. It'll be easier for you if you imagine that he's only an unthinking baby and he'll stay a baby to his dying day. Console yourself with the fact that he's at peace. Your father has finally found his peace and that means he's fine. Don't allow yourself to insult him even with your thoughts. Be patient. Nobody's asking you to respect him or to love him. Just be patient and imagine that he's a baby. "

"I heard you," her son replies. "Now look, he's wet himself again. Go and change the baby's nappy."

She slaps him in the face, because he's still more of a son to her than the head of the family. She goes off to get a clean change of sheets and threatens him:

"I'll curse you if you ever again even once... I swear it..."

But her son, his cheeks flushing, thinks: "Some time I'll find out the whole truth and I'll kill the man who shot at him. Just give me time and I'll finish him off. For not killing him as well..."

But the old men at the nykhas stubbornly hold their silence in his presence while my father and Alone prefer not to show their faces there at all.

"Alone? He didn't even visit his family's graves in those days," My uncle tells me many years afterwards. "Like he no longer had anything more to discuss with them. More often he'd just sit it out in his room. Drinking, probably, I don't know. I wasn't invited over. Sometimes no one saw him for weeks. He's really gone back on the wagon, we thought, if no one had clapped eyes on him for weeks on end. Only I won't say that for certain, because no one had seen him drunk at all that year. In that year many a strange thing happened..."

He called them "strange things." All that happened to Barysbi, to Alone and my father, who had suddenly decided to find himself a wife.

"I need a fortnight and a horse," he announced to our old man one day. "In two weeks' time I'll come back and tell you where to send the matchmakers. Give me a horse and the coat in which you married my mother, and two weeks."

Grandfather had agreed to this come evening, despite the fact that he was, in principle, against the idea of his son seeking out a bride on the outside. However, on further thought, he did not risk saying so, clearly judging that it was better to nod for once and in less than a year be presented with a grandson than God-knows-how-long to keep admonishing his stubborn son who had got fixed upon the idea of not marrying any of the girls in the aul. So Father, receiving his blessing and breaking the tradition, hit the road on his own that had to lead him and his mare to the house of she whom he'd like sufficiently to choose as my future mother.

And in the space of five days he caught sight of her. At first he heard her laughter and pulled the bridle, then turned back in the saddle and looked over the wattle fence. He approached the gate and knocked at it with his whip. He greeted the master of the household and entered his house. At lunch they spoke little, but the master attentively studied

Marriage - propose

his solid hands. Father hardly ate a bite and only looked round at any rustle. In those five days he had been inside many homes, but in none of them had he heard such a laugh. Now he wanted to look at her who laughed as if she had never known pain or boredom. A good hour later, during which she hadn't even peeped out from the women's quarters, he said:

"I'm looking for a person. I've journeyed round two gorges but haven't met him yet. Today I imagined that I heard him. For the sake of this person I've travelled round two gorges, but heard him only in your house. I have to see him. Call your daughter here."

Grown white with rage the master did not reply at once. For a minute their eyes flashed at each other, and then he said:

"Thank God you are my guest. But remember that you'll scarcely have stepped over my threshold than you'd have turned from a guest into a scoundrel. And with scoundrels, according to custom, you can boot them out by the backside."

To this Father, moving his torso closer to his arms and leaning on the edge of the table, replies:

"You don't think you can frighten me, do you? Or maybe you just want to insult me? See it's not a good idea to insult the man who will become your son-in-law in a month's time. If, of course, he wants to. But for that, he first needs to take a look at her. Call me out your daughter."

Then between them pass waves of tense and suffocating silence, and the longer it lasts, the harder it gets for the master to think of suitable words. But my future father, not blinking, hurries him with his intense look, and something in this look prevents the master from picking a quarrel with him. In the end, he gives in. She comes out to them with head hung low and trembling like a bird trapped in a snare.

"Show me your face," says father, "and look into mine..."

This lasts no longer than a second, then she runs off like a supple young animal disappearing behind the curtain. Father wipes the sweat from his brow and turns back to his host with a changed voice:

"Let's come to a settlement. We'll strike a bargain quickly, like two poor men. All that I have is this dagger and this cloak. And that mare out in your yard. There's also a clump of land – slightly more than you can stuff in your breast. And these hands, ready for any work. I also have a younger brother and an old father, who has never been rich. There is a full house of hungry mouths and a big bundle of firewood for the winter. We always have enough of that. But the one thing I have in abundance is the past. I have so much of it that I can go to any lengths. If I have to, I'll abduct your daughter. So best give her away to me on good terms. Now I'll leave and you start thinking. In a few days' time I'll send out the matchmakers to you."

He thanks the host for his hospitality and leaves his house. Returning to his own, he tells my grandfather:

"I found her... This is where they live. Hold on for ten days and send out the matchmakers."

But the old man asks, well, what's her name. Father says that he is sure to like her.

"What's her name?" grandfather repeats, but when Father again wriggles out of an answer, he explodes: "You weren't even interested in finding out her name!"

"I'll describe her to you," Father defends himself. "She is like..."

"I couldn't give a damn what she's like!" roars the old man. "Even if she's like a hook, like a cob of corn, like a yellow tooth, like a fence, like chimney or a cauldron, even if she's just like you, I couldn't give the slightest damn! If she has no name, I know just whom she's not like. She's not yet like my bride..."

"No," insists father. "She's more like your bride than anyone else. Or else I'm not like your elder son."

So the old man again has to concede defeat. After another couple of weeks they dispatch the matchmakers, but on their return they bring back nothing save for her name. Now the old man gets excited. His beard shakes anxiously under his tightly clenched teeth. He goes into his room, and returns a minute later to his sons standing there dejectedly. He throws down a bundle by their feet and says:

"Feed him this sword, and if he doesn't accept it – eat it up yourselves! The groom will eat the blade and the best man the sheath! Get going! I'm giving you two days."

They hit the road at once, ignoring the darkness and the freezing drizzle. But on the road, Father suddenly reins in his horse, jumps off, orders his brother to wait, and runs back to the aul. He's forgotten something, thinks Uncle, but just what it is he won't know until they arrive. They dismount in the morning at the gate, which had rejected their matchmakers, and enter the house, which hides behind thick curtains the laugh that had so bewitched my father. Sitting down at the table and knocking back the three obligatory wine-horns, they get down to business. Or rather my father get down to it while Uncle only sits quietly and listens as his brother suggests to their host to take a break and accept from them some gifts.

"With all my heart," explains Father, getting out of the bundle twenty pounds of Dagestani silver and watching the host's reaction closely. He's clearly impressed, and his eyes hurt from its bright sparkle, but from his unruffled, proud exterior both guests reach their conclusion despondently that nothing would come of their silver offering, for not even for twenty pounds of silver would he agree to take in such a son-in-law as my future father.

"It's a good sword," the host coldly pronounces and pushes it away so as not to give in to temptation. "Only I have my own, and it serves me faithfully. I wouldn't want to trade it in for anything..."

Uncle thinks it's all over. Now all that remains for him and my father is to share out the blade and the sheath between them, wet them with araka and shove them in their throats.

But father isn't embarrassed by any of this.

"Wait," he says and pulls out from his hood something all too familiar, but which Uncle hadn't seen for so many years that he didn't recognise it, but the moment he did he understands where his elder brother had run off to the night before leaving him alone in the rain. "We have a little something else here. You certainly won't refuse a present like this."

The host turns it over in his hands and asks:

"What sort of a toy is this?"

"Not a toy – a game," Father corrects him.

He begins to demonstrate it, and then as a trial run he suggests they play. The host wins the first game, naturally, then he who has laid this trap and in doing so has taken his first sure step to becoming my father, says:

"Now let's play for the sword. See, a winning is not a gift, right?"

Pondering this and licking his dry lips, the host nods and takes his turn, pulling out a new card from the pack. Understandably, he wins again. But somehow taking the sword so simply, purely by the whim of a painted card, is against his heavy-footed peasant conscience, but oh how he desires that silver treasure, and then he, making his mind up in a second, like one drunk on his reciprocal generosity, puts his hands under the table, gets out his own dagger and puts it, with its metal belt and a pendant on the table transformed into a kitty.

"Now we have a game," Father encourages him. "I'll stake my mare..."

At these words my uncle's eardrums nearly burst.

"Or maybe..." he starts up but the iron hand of his brother grips his knee forbidding him to finish. The host's eyes become pitiful like those of a hound seeing a fleshy bone that hasn't yet been thrown to him. When he pulls out a card his hand is shaking as if he's scared of burning it. Father maintains his composure although he has grown the slightest bit pale and haggard. He draws out a card, opens it and says quietly:

"My card wins."

Shuffling the pack he thinks: twice more. Just another couple of times and we can go home. He puts into the kitty the host's dagger, his own mare and his brother's fury, and his opponent responds with the silver he has just won. They take many turns to draw out cards until the pack is half gone. It's painful to look at the host – so much is he sweating and suffering. My father though is like a stone. A large cold stone with hollows for eyes. It flashes through my uncle's mind that such stones often fall into a precipice under their own weight. Only with this stone I'll have to leap in after him.

But my father wins again, and from their host's chest bursts forth an involuntary moan.

"That's enough," my father says to him, putting the cards back in their box. "The cards are my gift to you... for your hospitality – thank you."

He gets ready to go and Uncle is already tightening their host's belt and his dagger around his waist, and in such a hurry as if Uastyrdzhi is waiting for him outside.

"Wait," asks the host in a hoarse, broken voice. "Let's play once more... Let's play for..."

"No," replies Father and at once, grabbing them out of uncle's arms, throws the belt and the dagger and the pendant down on the table and after them fly down the twenty pounds of silver and a loud whisper: "All of these and the horse. I stake the lot. Call her out..."

The slightest bit more and the host will burst into tears and I'm on the verge of tears, Uncle told me, fixing his gaze through the open door on the mare munching on the hay, a mare he wouldn't have exchanged for any bit of skirt and, moreover, he would never have added two daggers attached to the two sons of their poor old father.

When she came out to us, I didn't see her, Uncle told me. I looked right at her and saw nothing except some kind of skinny monstrosity. Then he again began to shuffle the cards, and I turned away, then moved out into the yard stealthily so that if I heard anything I'd leap up onto the mare's back and gallop off far away from that accursed house. And from my crazy brother measuring out the price of his vanity with those stupid little pictures, while the price of the sword (all our family silver had once gone into its crafting and decoration) that for fifteen years did not get traded in for anything, and the price of this mare that has always been priceless to us that he had now put into the kitty, had all instantly increased in value by the value of the lives of two brothers, though for these, said Uncle, at that moment he wouldn't have given a penny, even if he had one in his pocket, and his life was dearer to him than any customs. So I knew where I was going. As I came up to the mare I stroked her back and whispered a word in her ear so as she stuffed down her hay faster, while our host's homefolks formed up all around and about us, folded their arms on their chests and followed my every move as if it'd take out a moon hidden in my shirt. I watched the goings-on inside the house through the door I had left wide open. I saw the pack of cards in the middle of the table and both their faces. What they were talking about I couldn't hear from that distance but only saw that they were talking instead of drawing out cards from the pack. Soon they grew tired of this, they stiffened their necks and drilled each other with their gazes, forgetting about the cards and about the time, while his homefolks watched me and sullenly demanded the moon. Then our host sighed heavily, opening his mouth and gulping into his lungs all the air inside the building. Then he uttered something and his mouth closed – I gripped the base of the saddle and the homefolks all took a step forward, closing their circle more tightly around me, the mare, and the sopping wet scruff of my neck. Then your father – the man who'd become your daddy in less than a year and her groom in less than six weeks – turned to me and cried out distinctly:

"Everything's fine."

Then he offered him his hand, and our host still had enough strength in him to accompany us to his gate, and there we quickly and clumsily – I was the clumsy one – said our farewells and I dug my heels into the mare's sides. Once we left their gorge behind and were certain that no one was pursuing us, that no one would fire at our backs, and no one was lying in wait to ambush us, and even that no one could hear us, I brought the mare to a halt, sat down on the ground and put my face on my knees. When I stopped shaking I asked:

"What are you laughing about? D'you think it's so funny to win your own horse three times back and not once in all that time feel ashamed that you could have lost her three times?"

By now he wasn't even laughing, he was cackling in a disgusting manner, simply rolling around with his vile laughter. And the stupid mare under him was also gleefully unlocking its jaws and then let out an utterly savage neigh and reared up on its hind legs. I could no longer make out which of them was neighing and which was cackling, so I went up to them, unfurled my whip and whipped her bony croup so that she broke into a gallop, almost throwing her rider to the ground. I again sat on the ground and waited for him to get control of her. They came back and he said:

"Firstly, not three times, but twice. And secondly, don't even think of blabbing any of this out to Father."

The second point I let slip straight in one ear and out the other, but on the subject of his first point I asked:

"So I was right, finally you didn't even play any longer?"

"Oh well. Who do you take me for? Maybe you think I'm the sort of man who'd stake his own bride?"

I lost my temper again. This self-satisfied insolent brother of mine was starting to drive me mad.

"Not her," say I. "You're the sort that stakes our only horse, and as for her, that girl you call your bride, was staked by her own unlucky father. Only I was asking about another thing. How did you manage it?"

"No problem," he replies. "Surely you don't think I'd strike a bargain with a father-in-law capable of gambling his own daughter away at cards?"

"You don't say! Then what would you play for when he called her out?"

"You're exactly right," he nods to me. "Just that at that moment he wasn't yet my father-in-law, nor me yet his son-in-law, nor was she my bride. But the very next minute we came to our senses and reasoned that it was criminal for a future family to gamble away their relatives at pathetic little cards. It's no good."

I turn over in my head what he'd just said, stretching my inflamed brains, I get up off the ground, shake the dirt off my coat, go up to him and clamber up on the mare. For a mile we are riding in complete silence softened by the distance. Then I burst out laughing and say:

"You mean all you needed to do was make her come out and shame him in front of her?"

"Uh-huh," he murmurs behind my back. After another couple of miles I say to him: "The devil take you! For that you twice risked our horse!"

"Did I?" he asks. "I don't remember that I did. Where did you get that idea?"

He yawns sweetly into my back. When the sun is already crawling out behind the mountains he's had a nap and starts talking himself:

"It all comes down to poverty. Had he not been really poor I'd have to kidnap her. But then – we parted amicably. You only have to show a poor man something that glimmers and glistens and give his fingers the slightest touch of that shimmering object and then you can twist him round your little finger."

"Ah-ha," I confirm. "Or put him in a noose. In case he completes his suite of hearts before you draw all your spades."

"There you go harping on again. You're a boring little fellow, you know?" he says. "The mare is once again ours."

"And just look at her! While you had her in your kitty and drew out your cards, she grew a whole arse's length longer! She's like a lizard with hooves. A goner, not a horse! The devil take you both! And to think you'd really stake such a pitiful animal with a bald mane in such a serious game!"

"Just leave it," he smirks. "A mare's a mare. She's cleverer than any lizard by half. And her backside was always longer than eternity. I could never have lost her..."

"How's that?" I wonder maliciously.

"Tell me honestly: can you imagine what would have happened to us if I hadn't drawn out that card when I did?"

"No I can't," I reply. "I can only begin to describe it: two hungry jackals are racing through the frosty forest snapping at each others' tails and one of them no longer wants to get married..."

"There you see," he says, "what utter drivel you get into your head! All I can say is that it would all have worked out too idiotically if he had won instead of me. You don't come across such stupidity in life. So he couldn't possibly win."

He probably thinks he has uttered something incredibly deep and only now do I realise that my brother is head over heels in love. I have the sensation that someone had betrayed someone else, a feeling that at the gaming table that day instead of a silver sword they had accidentally exchanged not any old person but me. I have the feeling that we're travelling in different directions. At least, I told myself, we still have the horse. Our old nag still belongs to us. And in a month or two we'll be celebrating his wedding. On his wedding day I'll fasten to my belt twenty pounds of excellent silver.

That's how Uncle described it all to me. And that's the form in which it has lodged itself in my memory.

The wedding took place a month and a half later. After a further ten I was born and the first thing I heard on my appearance in this world was her laughter. Every time she remembers this, Grandma throws up her hands in joyful surprise: she was in labour pains for half a day till all the blood's fairly drained out of her, and then she laughed in delight before her tears had even dried! In all my living days I've never seen anything like that.

Mother gave birth to me as if she allowed herself an amusing bit of mischief, and the prank was very much to her liking, for in the next twelve years she would give birth almost every spring, giving my father in all three sons and seven daughters.

But with time her laugh grew quieter and shorter, with age it faded entirely, as a star's reflection in a backwater fades in the wind. This was probably all down to the fact that my father cut himself from her, supposing that by cutting himself from others he could escape from his thoughts about the past. Unless I'm mistaken, it was for this same reason that he had decided to get himself a wife then, so as to cut himself off (as it turned out, in a smooth backwater with a merry star in its midst) from the eight years of his life, from that whole story with Barysbi and the involuntary feeling of guilt for being caught up in it. Now he only wanted one thing – to turn a new page, to find a spring in the dry stony depths of his misery, and not allow anyone to come near its rushing waters. Especially not Alone.

Yes, now I can say that my father acted cruelly towards him. But I won't take it upon myself to berate him for that.

It was simply that he was fed up of losing. At first he merely observed my grandfather suffering one defeat after another, succumbing to the temptation to make a nice earner at the expense of a child, who in essence had never even been a child. Then he observed those, who were similarly poisoned and forgot themselves to such an extent that they rushed to load up their carts with river pebbles and cobblestones and took them for sale all the way to the fort, not suspecting that beforehand they would have to strike up a spark of inspired loneliness from them and illuminate a rough canvas with it. If you consider that in the time between these events and immediately following them he observed how the young milksop had dragged into his house the carcass of a bear he had shot or appeared in the aul on a wiry horse, or had for several days in a row stepped out over a bowl of shit on his doorstep, or how he had marked out lines on the earth to count out all the sacks that would later be brought into his barn – if you consider all of that and add to it his inability to die when he had already fully aged, and add to that his pictures, and his intuition that were uncovered by my father when he was hiding in cliffs; if you acknowledge as well that my father had no dearer relative than Alone's loneliness, then it becomes clear why he acted as he did. Nonetheless he would have forgiven him everything, even his own imprisonment. However he couldn't forgive him that starting with what seemed like an accidental blunder he managed for several years to lose so much that finally for weeks and months on end he wouldn't set foot outside his empty house because all of his initiatives and cunning tricks never led to anything good and merely deepened the misfortunes against which they had been directed; because in saving the life of their common enemy for eight years he had saved only his body by rescuing him from rotting in that stinking gully and thus condemning them both to the stifling torments of shame – none of this could Father forgive him. And so he distanced himself, just as our wise old grandfather did in the past. The only difference was that one had no desire to put his success in competition with an established victor, while the other having finally experienced some good fortune when he turned over the right card at the right time, severed his relations with an inveterate loser. Father's distancing was also a sign of his rejection – drawing aside into safety – warding off from himself and his family that dangerous and importunate freedom, into which Alone involved him; but like a fragile, slender stalk seized by a hurricane and thrown into the boundless secrets of oppressive mute expanses; and now that the hurricane had died down, he had fallen out of them and tried to implant himself deeper into the soil with his as yet unwithered roots, filling up with sap increasingly as he procreated, mercilessly and hurriedly expending the laughter he had found in that foreign valley,

Alone because weaker

and then its echo as well, in which he forgot himself as before in the short nights, when he tried to cut himself off from the past and its images and dreamed only of separating himself from the tenacious and intractable nightmares that welled up sometimes out of the gloom.

In sum, Father had almost attained that for which he had been striving. At least, he made himself not look over his neighbour's fence, where there pined a loneliness desecrated by misfortunes but nonetheless proud, stoically continuing to bear the hatred of men, their caution and their dislike, which had gradually, as my uncle told me, been interspersed with an insulted feeling of disgust. He was avoided as plague. Maybe he kept too quiet for too long and didn't do anything that could shock them, or at the very least perplex and puzzle them. And that annoyed them. That annoyed them as much as the nocturnal howling of the wolf that he'd brought home in winter. He tied one end of his scarf round the wolf's neck as a collar and the other end round his injured arm already soaked through with his dark blood. And so they struggled on through the blizzard, a man who had conquered a beast, and a humiliated beast of prey driven insane by the scent of blood, chattering his teeth in his frenzied rage but catching in them only snowy emptiness, unable to reach with his teeth the fist pressed to his ear. Alone put him on a chain out in his yard and set about to tame him.

Only tame isn't quite the right word for what he did. Humble is closer. Or mock. Or humble and mock at the same time.

Often he wouldn't even feed him, but would simply throw any old bone at his snout, not caring to supplement the meagre ration with even a bowl of dirty water. He could go a week without feeding him, but then suddenly chuck him an enormous hunk of fresh meat, which the wolf would guzzle up in his greed so that his intestines, formerly numbed with hunger, would burst in pain. He tortured him as if he were aiming to distil from the wolf the purest, concentrated, intoxicating hatred, and when it seemed to him that the wolf had matured, he would let him off his chain, and the wolf threw himself upon him in savage fury, suffocated by Alone's proximity, aiming his jaws right at his throat and settling his scores once and for all with the offender who had decided not to tame him into an obedient hound, preserving his wolfish spirit so as to exasperate him down to the last seething vein on his tough chest, and then to grapple with him and subdue all that was wolfish in him, squeezing his shaggy throat with his fingers and forcing him to whimper and whine pitifully like a dog, begging for mercy. And then again forget to feed him, infuriating his sensitive nostrils with his own smell even more than with the smell of a meal eaten by the enemy saturating the air. Then to once more deign to give him food on which to gorge himself and watch as the wolf's hunger gives way to the suffering of his sated greed. Then after another few days take him off his chain, enter into his regular skirmish with the leaping crazed hatred, risking his life, and once more choke that gurgling throat with his bare hands and hear him whimper.

All this disgusted the villagers. In my belief, the true cause of this lay not in what they saw but what they undoubtedly sensed: he had grown so weak that he had yielded to the temptation to grapple with his hatred hand to hand. What they saw was a ferocious, repugnant tussle of two crazed creatures in the snow, mud or dust sorting out the degree of their merits as animals – purely as animals, for the man in him seemed almost to have died away at that time – maybe so that they would fight as equals, disdaining all cheating, trickery and cunning, disdaining everything except naked, unadulterated hatred, or because he had always known that no man dared to crush beneath him that many times a wild animal from whose wounded heart the raging anger of all his wolfish race strives towards the enemy's throat. Or maybe the animal had awoken in him so that the human being could take a rest? Be that as it may, the villagers that beheld all that passed between him and the wolf now hated him, disliked him or were wary of him even more zealously than before, and if on the nykhas they felt compassion towards either of the two of them then it was clearly not towards Alone.

In addition to all this, he stopped visiting the graves. Not completely, but almost, so Uncle told me. In other words, he would now go the graveyard just as rarely as those who censured him. Nor did they try to justify his behaviour, and as such they could find no better explanation for it than that he had grown savage. They didn't give a thought to the possible confusion in his heart, for at that point it was not yet common knowledge how much he had lost. My father took no part in their conversations: he had already distanced himself. With all the cruelty of justice he guarded his policy of non-interference and fathered his brood, reckoning on the healing freshness of the backwater that he had created and fenced off from the outside world, and its power to cure him, as he supposed, of the disease of his memories and former shameful kinship with an inveterate loser, who was nonetheless still taken by all the villagers to be a divinely fortunate holy fool, delighting in their hostility towards him and his deafness to it.

The years passed, and he occupied their thoughts less and less, while the wolf occupied his own thoughts less and less. To look at him, Alone gave every appearance of having calmed down. The beastly skirmishes happened ever more infrequently and soon turned into occasional, tired squabbles devoid of passion. The wolf had grown clever and though he hadn't turned his back on revenge he had clearly decided to bide his time, and wait for the right moment, when his enemy would have dropped his guard, to act decisively. Alone had now become too lazy to tease him. On occasion, he would disappear from the aul for a few days, only he wouldn't go to the fort: people hadn't seen him riding on the Blue Road for ages. They often saw him crossing the bridge and going over to the forested mountain where, so they believed, he had found himself some sort of a cave. Only, again, not one of them had seen this with their own eyes, and so no one could advance their guess beyond conjecture. Anyway, no one really took that much interest in him anymore.

Of course, while he was away, there were those who tried to spite him. For example, they attempted to poison his wolf, whose hatred he still needed, although he kept it on a chain for longer periods. But it soon became clear that his wolf was a special case, too. He had some sort of perspicacious devil in him thanks to whose sense of smell he never once touched the bread soaked in poison. But afterwards, one morning after Alone's return, they discovered half a dozen stone-dead chickens in their chicken-coop, and they realised that poisoned bread had the power to turn on those who had created it, and from that time on they ceased their provocations, all the more so as Alone spent that whole day up at the nykhas, as if he wanted all of them to see his self-satisfied grin. That evening they saw him throw enough meat to his wolf to feed a whole pack of them, a pack of wolves a hundred strong. Now they realised that they had made an error in giving Alone the chance to take action in reply to their persistence. So they decided to avenge themselves upon him by being utterly indifferent, at least appearing to be so; they stuck to it one and all, invariably underscored with deliberate politeness in the face of his eternal restlessness. It was no conspiracy, it simply dawned upon all of them at once that that was how they should behave: in the same way as you could hardly regard as conspiracy the first day of the spring ploughing just because the whole aul goes down as one to the fields after each farmer looked up to the skies and breathed in the smells of the earth. So it all happened simply of its own accord, and now even if he wanted by some miracle to escape his loneliness he had no more chance. He must have felt the inevitability of time encroaching upon him from the future and deaf to his suffering, the same as he who was crucified felt it when they hammered the steel nails through his hands into the wooden cross. And so as to sing this inevitability out of his soul he carved himself a reed pipe from a pine branch. He played it in the twilight hours, sounding its lament at the dying of the light, wounded by the reddening gloom, maimed either by its daily attempts at death, or the treachery of the sun sliding beyond the mountains. There was no melody in his music nor artistry, completeness, or any wholeness fit for the ear. It had no beginning or end, only an unceasing burbling and naive lisping scratching on the nerves of all who heard it, that forever failed to reach that infinitesimal moment of culminating in the clear, sonorous, glorious call long maturing in his boundless desolation. On hearing his timid performance that heralded to all of us a prolonged and undeserved period of suffering, (for to have deserved it, you'd have had to commit a multitude of sins and be condemned to pass right through all hell, and only then, as Uncle said, on proof that hell was too good for you, on your own accord you'd have to ask Alone to blow on his pipe, for the cruelty wouldn't exist in hell to deserve such a punishment), my father's younger brother grew distressed:

"If there's anyone or anything I pity more than my own

ears, it's that shaggy old wolf... See what they now do instead of fighting – one howls while the other blows his pipe. And wouldn't you start howling if instead of throttling you to prove your animal weakness, he blows that thing right to your snout, like he was trying to make a mockery of your powerlessness. Poor old wolf! No doubt he's cursing the heavens that he wasn't born deaf..."

So when Alone occasionally kitted himself out for a week in the forest, they were even grateful. They spoke of some sort of cave, though not a one of them had ever seen it.

I dreamed of finding that cave from childhood, impressed by its unusual mysteriousness and sweetly scared by what lay in wait for me inside it. Sometimes, plucking up the courage, I would set out in his tracks but I would invariably lose sight of his back before midday, and then, checking the notches I'd made on the trees as I went along, I would wander back to my father's sullen, disapproving looks and mother's overanxious joy. I repeated my attempts in spite of their stern warnings, and only gave up on them after I had got so lost one day that he suddenly materialised in front of me, stepping out from behind some tree, and tiredly asked me:

"What do you want?"

Caught off guard I took to my heels and fled, tearing my clothes and scratching my face on the branches, not stopping till I got back home. That time I didn't even get a dressing down. But closer to nightfall, I heard voices:

"It seems he must have met him..."

"Now that's behind him. He won't follow him anymore."

And I thought: "She's right. I won't be going after him anymore. The way I had to run from him... He can really go to hell..."

That time I fled from him. But I didn't flee from his question. That wasn't my fault: it was hard to run away from a question like that. Few people could (maybe Barysbi) although many tried. But for a good while I really did stop following him and spying on him. Except for one day at the end of that suffocating summer when, attracted by the spiral of rust coloured smoke, I clambered up onto the fence and caught sight of the three of them – him, the wolf and the campfire lit between them. Alone was sitting with his back to me and was throwing roughly torn up strips of multicoloured canvases onto the flames, and pouring paints into the fire from saucers hewn from thinly sawn logs. The burning paints produced an evil stink. Then he wiped his hands with a rag, threw that too on the fire, took up his reed pipe and, pressing it to his lips, started to play, staring at the flame and charming it higher into the sky with his tiresome, dumb song. The wolf lay in front of him on the ground, his head slightly raised, never once taking his sincere grey eyes off him, but the chain to which he was tied, for the first time, was by now taut. Suddenly, Alone broke off and said:

"Don't go hiding. I won't be turning."

I froze. I remember how my legs grew numb and my shoulders cramped up with fear. But he carried on talking about a burnt painting, about worthless false paints and a foul-smelling smoke, after which there ought to remain nothing but bitter, greasy ashes. I listened to this but didn't have the faintest idea what he was on about, then I clattered down the fence and rushed into our shed. There I quivered for a long time, clenching my useless fists in anger, and at that moment I hated him with all my feverishly beating heart. I hated him, for I felt for the first time in my life that I was unable to run away from him.

I needed time to reconcile myself to this. I needed to grow up a bit more so that the stories about him, begun by my grandfather as simply whims of his memory and later continued by my father (first as proof that he had renounced them, and then out of the paramount need to give voice to them and turn his back on them in actual fact, and then, notably later, out of a faint hope that his own son would find it in himself to disavow them) with vivid details supplied by my uncle, formed themselves into a sequence, however vague, that still demanded on my part a great deal of imagination, spirit, and blood flowing in my veins, before they formed into an actual history of the departure from our lands of the man who had been forestalling its maturation for so unforgivably long, that he had finally trained himself not to heed it, then got unaccustomed to trusting in it and as a result was late to witness its maturity. I was in no hurry. I was right not to be, for in contrast to those who narrated me those stories about him, I started off by distancing myself instead of ending up doing so. And when I had matured a little and grown strong enough to go to the forest on my own, I no longer walked behind his back but followed the alluring scent of our unavoidable meeting, which could now no longer be prevented by the sullen disapproval of my father, wary of forbidding it outright because he didn't wish to acknowledge openly that such an encounter was at all possible. Yes, I continued searching for the cave, but a whole year was yet to pass before Alone allowed me into it...

In that year Grandfather died, having in broad daylight fallen from the leather-covered log upon which he had sunned his restless old age for so many years. He died suddenly, as if he'd been hit full in the chest right in front of my grandmother's eyes who imagined that he jumped up to show her something ever so important, he even pointed his finger, she said, he raised his finger and pointed and was about to shout something but then he was thrust backward and he only threw out his arms and clawed at the earth with his fingers, and then his head fell to one side; he closed his eyes himself so that no one would see the last ray of light fade away in his pupils.

We buried him in the rain – and it was good to bury him in the rain because our tears were less noticeable. Yet after the funeral, having grown a whole death older, we felt estranged from one another for a while and drew back from the almost tangible emptiness that had settled in our home while we got used to our new selves. It was hardest of all for my father upon whom it now fell to decide how we lived and what we were to do so as to pay the debts for the marriage that had already granted him ten children, and how to prepare ourselves to launch into another – after all, Uncle couldn't wait forever to be given permission to marry! It was easiest of all for my mother, so preoccupied she was with the fulminating life of the children surrounding her that she was not seriously affected by the death that had fallen on the house. For Grandmother the blow must have been the most bitter. But she withstood it and held out for many years after that, witnessing the birth of her great-grandchildren, bearing her own senility and patiently confused with the tangled web of our many names. And I – well, I grew up. I aged and matured with the death, the emptiness and the added year.

It was then he showed me the cave.

On that occasion he had brought some sort of sack with him into the forest. Thanks to its faint yet distinct jangling at his every step in the quiet of the forest I could follow him with my eyes closed. I didn't doubt in the slightest that he could hear me following him or feel my presence in his spine, but he did not try to hide, did not vanish nor did he even turn round, almost as if he was wary of scaring me off, so that now I knew for sure that today was the day he would lead me to his cave. We continued like that for three hours or so, changing paths several times before leaving the beaten tracks completely. And the place where the cave was located – it was no more than a small mound covered in lush vegetation and bare inside – was untouched by the light. The mound was encircled by tall pine trees with luxuriant crowns and bathed in deep cool shade. As he approached it, Alone slung the sack off his shoulders and set about raking away the fallen twigs and the loose turf. Then he moved aside a rock and crawled inside. The opening into which he crawled was the size of a big cauldron. I heard him strike up a flint and light his torch. Then he said:

"Come in."

He said it without even looking at me. Gulping the air into my lungs – for a whole moment I couldn't even exhale it again – I followed his voice, bent over double and crawled inside. The cave was the size of an average room. Shelves attached to the walls were cluttered with wooden heads, stone statues and dead branches he'd picked up in the forest. Alone stood on the earthen floor and looked me in the eye. Driven into a chink in one wall the torch beat its flame into the soot-blackened ceiling and cast unfamiliar patterns, shadows and smears on his face. He looked like a strange black bird in his cherished nest, hiding from the shame of its weak wings that hadn't yet learned to fly.

"Have a look round, make yourself at home," he said, moving to the wall.

By the time I had a good look around me he was already busying himself with the iron objects he'd brought with him in his sack.

"Well? Not what you were expecting at all, eh? You thought it would be something different?" inquired Alone and raised his arm. "That one there I made out of a wild boar bone. And this one here from a scorched chunk of wood. Those five I moulded from wax. There's all sorts here. Which one would you choose? In which of them, do you think, is He present the most?"

"Who do you mean?" I didn't understand, but it only took me a second to guess, and then I started to think that he really had gone nuts.

Alone came closer to me and turned my face to the light. Studying it, he seemed surprised and said:

"You know who I mean. At first I searched for Him in people. Then I tried paints. Then I stopped searching, so repulsive had he become to me. Then instead of Him I found this cave and a small stone idol in it. Him over there, laughing at the two of us, right over in that corner. And now I've again fallen into doubt and resumed my search. I've sought Him in the rocks and the trees, searched for him in the tar and the grass, in the water and even in wax, I've carved, moulded, sculpted and hewed, I picked them up from the earth and out of the snow. Now you can see how many of them there are. There are too many of them for there to be one. Maybe, He doesn't really exist? What do you think?"

He spoke evenly and calmly, like a man certain of being understood and knowing they won't lie or cheat. I had almost calmed down myself. And had somehow grown convinced that he had not lost his mind one bit.

"I don't know," I replied and thought: the bird has not learned how to fly and can't forgive itself for it, but if it's a bird it ought to know how to fly, and as it can't, it must be that it's not a bird at all however much it wants to fly – if only it could soar just once – so it builds itself a nest and takes refuge in it with its anguish to ponder the secret of flight.

"Sometimes I imagined," continued Alone, "that I had discovered Him. There were moments like that. But then everything would suddenly take an unbelievable turn for the worse. It would turn out, I realised, that every time it wasn't

Him. It was a werewolf who'd managed to fool me with my paints. Yet when I came across this cave and saw that it was older than the forests, older than our aul and even older than the earth that covered it, I started to think that if there was any sort of solution to the riddle then it lay in the small human figurine, laughing at time. I had to search right here – in the stones, the trees, the honeycombs and the snow, the water, the bad weather, the fire, the flowers, the rocks, and again in the water, the stones and the trees. For all these were created by His own hand, if of course He exists anywhere at all, or at any rate without my participation and without the paints, like werewolves, taking His image. I decided to give it a go. To see Him with my hands or feel Him to the touch if just for a moment. At times it seemed to me I had found Him, or that He had touched me, or that His breath had touched my brow. I attempted to carve Him out of stone and hew him out of wood. Stone never really lives and never dies even if it crumbles to dust. It knows something of eternity. Something very important... But a tree, because it never gives up fighting, even if it is cut down and deprived of its roots, it will feel the quiet coursing of life within itself for a long while yet, until time itself grows weary, or else it burns to the ground, its living warmth bursting into flame. It knows more of life than the others. True, it also turns to dust, but even the shale calls itself a stone. I tried and hoped I would succeed – no, not to sculpt or carve Him – to receive unquestionable proof that He exists and hears me, and I hear Him and know for sure that it is Him and not a werewolf. As you can see, He is going to stay silent till the very end. Assuming, of course, He exists at all... Do you want to sit down? He got out two small benches from a niche. One of them had been knocked together not long before and still smelt of woodchips. He must have specially prepared for this, I thought. He knew I would follow him, and he knew I'd grown up and matured for his frankness that had awaited me for fifteen years and he was now ready, in this cave that he had furnished as a crypt for his loneliness, to reveal to me any secret from his past when he was capable of anything on earth, save preventing the treachery of fate or averting impending doom. I sat down opposite him and clasped my hands together. A bitter wind blowing into my back reached the torch and its flame plunged angrily, tilting towards the wall. Around me the multicoloured images of his stubborn failures stood in uneven rows. I said:

"They have grown greater than the stone and wood from which they emerged."

"You could say so," he reverted. "But that's not enough. They've proved nothing to me."

We were silent. Being silent alongside him was like standing in the pouring rain – at once exciting and uncomfortable. Then I said:

"Tell me about my father..."

"Of course," he nodded. "That's what you came for. Ask away."

I asked about the prison. Then about Barysbi and the mill. And then about

Grandfather and the thieves who had stolen the horses. I even asked him about the graves, and he replied:

"They're more peaceful that way. I don't want to lie to them and I don't want to disturb them. I have no good news for them right now. You understand?"

I asked him about the fort.

"I can't go there. I don't want to disturb her either."

When I looked out of the cave evening was already drawing in. I had to hurry, and said:

"Don't blame my father. He simply..."

"Yes," said Alone. "He simply married at the right time. I don't blame him. It's good when a man does something at the right time."

"Only he won't find out about this..."

"Of course," he smiled. "You'll protect him against this."

I lowered my eyes and caught sight of the metal objects he'd brought in his sack...

"A trap?" I said in surprise. He answered:

"Someone was here recently. Look," and he pointed to a narrow cut in the ground. "It was trampled on yesterday."

"Maybe you're wrong?" I asked and it occurred to me it couldn't be one of the villagers, for then the whole aul would know about his cave. Unless, of course, that someone was my father. As if reading my mind, Alone shook his head:

"You have nothing to worry about. If it was you father he has nothing to fear. He's known me for far too long to fall into my trap. But then, you may be right. It's possible I'm seeing things."

I thought a while and said:

"I understand. You're setting this trap not for a beast or a man... It's for Him, who won't fall into it all the same, but if he wishes he'll trample that line in the ground over again. If He who you seek calls in on you here, that trampled line must be not a trace but a sign, and now you're hiding that trap by the entrance to check if it was a sign or a trace, although you're almost certain that it couldn't be a trace, so you must be counting on Him to confirm that it's His sign, and though the trap will stay empty, the line will again end up trampled..."

"Just don't get it in your head to trick me," said Alone. "Don't even think of doing that instead of Him. I won't forgive you..."

"I won't," I promised.

When we parted, I suddenly thought: he's behaving as

if today's conversation doesn't oblige me in any way. Rather, he doesn't want to deprive me of a choice or confine my conscience.

Finally I said:

"Why don't you let him go? He's got so old that he's only got his impotent rage and shame left in him. And his hatred too, for which he despises himself, for he's doomed to breathe his last tied to a chain at your feet. Let him go. You don't need him any more. He's no dog. Let him die a wolf..."

I held his gaze, and then went out. I ran the whole way back as fast as my legs would carry me, trying to make it back by nightfall. And though the night overtook me, that evening Father pretended he hadn't noticed my absence.

That night I crept out of the sleeping house, clambered up on the fence and saw the glimmer of light from his door left slightly ajar. The wolf had gone from the yard. I suddenly understood what had made me plead for the wolf. It was very dark but I felt I was blushing. Only I still couldn't quite explain why: because I suggested to Alone to take the place of the wolf in his life, or because in suggesting this I had deceived him.

That night, returning to my bed and taken unawares by the warmth of my home, I mentally swore to myself that I would never risk its comfort for the sake of some insane loneliness. Insane – I remember this apt word and its sweet taste on my tongue from finding it and the way it made everything simple and clear.

I placated my conscience with the thought that not disavowing and distancing myself from it would have meant betraying my own father, and maybe my dead grandfather too – for he had distanced himself also – back when he hadn't known a fraction of what had now been confided to his grandson... Towards dawn I had convinced myself. It wasn't difficult: no one had ever liked him in truth. So I distanced myself. And supposed on that day that I had done so forever.

Only a month later everything was turned on its head once more. And soon Alone left...

I'll tell you about it now. There's very little left to tell. I'll tell you of Lana and the earthquake. After that he left...

She was already in her early twenties, but hadn't yet got married. She was not at all ugly, on the contrary, in fact, many of the other girls her age were envious of the white smoothness of her face, her delicate, slender waist, wrapped in a belt barely wide enough to wrap round most other girls' wrists. However, after she had transformed from a melancholy obedient little girl into one of marriageable age, the matchmakers had stubbornly avoided Soslan's house, not counting the one time when they weren't even allowed to come close it.

That happened some three years ago one dank March day. From the crack of dawn the men of our aul, decked out in clean coats and with their daggers (fastidiously scrubbed clean by their sons) showing from beneath their cloaks, spilled out onto the nykhas and after a short council put out sentries on the road, returned to their homes and started their wait, throwing the occasional stern glance at the walls on which hung their rifles carefully polished with grease, ready to be taken up to rebuff any strangers who, mindful of the rumours, now dared to try their luck where not a single one of our lot had the courage to, though Soslan was by no means forbidding them, and more likely than not, would have regarded favourably some ten to the dozen of their attempts to ask for his adopted daughter's hand in marriage, or at least two thirds of them, he would have gladly accepted a good quarter of their proposals. The only snag was that none of them ever even made the least attempt to do so, despite the fact that the girl was good looking and honourably brought up by an honourable father. It might have occurred to an outsider that the reason was in the way she had become his daughter and the mystery of whose offspring she really was, for the one who knew the truth had to abandon her before any memories of its real parents took root. An outsider would probably have been thinking along those lines, but he would only have to lay eyes on her for such conjectures to fall away of their own accord.

For she was unbelievably, impossibly, bewitchingly beautiful. So beautiful, in fact, that a single glance at her – if it were a male glance – was enough to forget about her being a foundling and about her ever being destined to be someone's wife and mother. There wasn't a prettier girl in the whole world, just as there couldn't have been any girl less suitable for wedlock. Less suitable precisely because of her beauty. In short, her beauty not only delighted but also scared off all those who ever looked at her with male eyes, and among those cursed to be her contemporaries, most of whom had already managed to make successful marriages and produce children, she incited no irritation, aroused no envy, but instead she inspired only their pitying compassion and sympathy. Indeed, when it was discovered that matchmakers were being sent over from the neighbouring valley, they decided as one to stand to the defence of the girl whom they had never dared to touch, as if they saw it as something of a common treasure – they decided to come to the defence of her beauty, which it was permitted merely to gaze upon but not to appropriate, and if they couldn't, then they could hardly let some frivolous stranger, scarcely able to appreciate her beauty have the privilege. And that is what offended them most of all – that he wouldn't be able to appreciate her beauty, or else why would the thought even enter his head to wed her. To wed her, in the aul's eyes, was tantamount to the most foul crime or savage lunacy. To desire the hand of Lana in marriage was like wanting to throw a noose over a rainbow, gathering up the stars in your cloak or eating the waterfall alive. And to succeed in wedding her was like spitting at the heavens, suffocating the rainbow or drowning the stars in the waterfall. Wishing to marry Lana was as absurd and impossible as branding all the women on earth with your enduring lust and then destroying the whole race of men as being wholly unwanted. Marrying her meant sullying sanctity, for her beauty was so perfect and complete that every one of us, great and small, read in her the impending doom to which we could never become related as you couldn't a fleeting moment or a sudden lightning in a storm. But to make an attempt on this doom was a disgrace, an unthinkable blasphemy, against which we stood shoulder to shoulder when the sentries' whistles came. We formed a threatening chain along the road, united by common danger and a sense of honour, and halted their wagons with our common silence, not stooping to words nor explanations, so that those strangers who first tried to win us over with their polite cowardice soon took their leave and rode back whence they had came.

On that day we felt so strong that we almost hated the day to follow, for we knew we'd only be this strong the once. Then the weekdays would dawn and we would flounder in our everyday chores. The weekdays would pile up the trivialities and we would bury our heads in petty concerns. Such weekdays last for a long time. Three years for them is nothing.

Three years later a disaster struck and our doomed beauty, whom our strong men had once defended, standing shoulder to shoulder, was carried away by an icy flow.

Well, what can I say? We had simply fallen blind. And

Soslan, who'd fallen blind far earlier – not with his heart but with his walleyes – who'd been blinded by grief, and yet twenty years before had the wisdom to foresee the whole nightmare, who had then been blinded by happiness – a new fatherhood sent to him by the gods so that in his great joy he had forgotten his prophecies – was now just as powerless to predict the tragedy as Gappo, the half-witted old man with the withered arm and the body of a young man, was unable to sense the keening life by his very side, related to him by unwilling blood and by her doom, for the sake of which disaster sought her out for so many years, so as to appear in the aul, stand before the nykhas with his gleeful smile and not even make us prick up our ears, for Alone, the only one able to recognise him, had been blinded by his own loneliness and played his pipe, annoying his half-blind old wolf with its melancholy tune, and exactly a month later he was sleeping off his hangover in his empty walls, not hearing or seeing anything, missing his motherland's cry for help, and the right to live in it from that day on. When the earth, groaning in pain, stirred up beneath the aul and the cracks ran down to the foaming river, and opened up there in a wide yawning gap – in that very place where the girl stood on the bridge – the riverbed broke open and for a moment swallowed up into its yawning belly the raging stream and then, as if choked on the sinful water, spewed it out, pouring out in waves on the shore and covering us with its accursed rage, when the sun filled up with crimson blood and burned with unbearable heat scorching the thundering air, when time caked in black dust fell from the skies in ashen crumbs like dirty snow, to the women's wails and children's cries, when the smell of burning stung our eyes and a dotted thick fog fell concealing the sun and the river, but then it cleared all of a sudden, and there descended upon us a piercing silence, like a scream – Alone knelt before it

and threw up his arms to the sky... He knelt before the
silence and cried soundlessly, for the heavens once more
had not killed him. For some reason all of us, crowded
together in one huge mass of terror in the village street,
pressed close to one another and hearing our great heart
beat in common fear, all of us looked upon his prayer and
saw his complicity, which he did not even hide, though he
did not then know that we had been orphaned of our Lana.
Then he rose to his feet and slowly wandered back home,
and we again heard our own voices and the plangent lament
of the women, in which there sounded now more of an
exultant joy than grief, for it had all been over and nothing
had changed apart from the damp cracked earth covered
with black dust that absorbed the moisture and turned into
muddy soot. When we walked over it, our legs slipped and
slid as on common slush. The river had not succeeded in
breaking our bank and hadn't even washed away the bridge.
The houses stood almost unharmed, having shed here and
there only the odd patch of clay from their walls and a handful
of flagstone. We were alive. We were all alive, and only
Lana was no longer with us.

When we remembered this, the life that bubbled up in
our throats trembled with worry and the women's lament grew
louder, but the woe in it was mixed with angry joy – we were
alive. We quickly, in our haste, dispatched a group of volunteers
to search for her body downstream while the old men gathered
at the nykhas and set off from there towards the house of
Soslan.

He met them at the door, and on his face was written
his blind suffering. They were ashamed to look him in the
face. Maybe because there was too much life in her eyes.
They stood with heads bowed, but couldn't add their breath
to his own. My father was also one amongst them.

When it grew dark I slipped out of the door and clambered over the fence. Alone sat on the floor by his extinguished hearth and turned over in his hands the remains of his crushed reed pipe.

"Did you see any of it?" he asked.

"Yes," I replied. "Everything."

"How did it happen?" he splashed some araka into the wine-horn and passed it over to me. "There you are. Drink and tell all."

I drained it down to the bottom, and felt the liquid pour thickly in my stomach and promise an impending warmth. I felt better and said:

"I couldn't quite understand it. I can't remember which came first – whether she stumbled first or whether the earth shook. Only if she really did stumble, it did not look genuine. False, somehow, like a lie. As if she stumbled deliberately. But I can't say for sure. I couldn't quite understand it."

Alone nodded: "Down some more and start from the beginning."

I drank some more and said:

"She came outside and stopped as if she didn't know where she was going. She was carrying a bag, and the look on her face was such as if she wasn't just going out but leaving for good... Then she noticed me looking at her and quickly moved on down the street, yet a few steps later stopped again, and I thought she was about to cry. She didn't, but turned back and went to the nykhas at a run. But then, before she'd reached it, she stopped for a third time, heard her mother calling her and, as if she had now finally decided, rushed to the bridge. After that I can't say whether what she did was on purpose or not, but it just seemed to me she didn't fall from that bridge but threw herself off it. I couldn't quite understand."

And he said: "Me neither."

He poured out the araka for us both and we drank. I looked at him and said:

"Your whole nape has gone grey."

"That's the light. He answered. "You're imagining it. It's the reflection."

"Your temples have turned grey too. You've gone grey all over today." I said. "Yesterday it was just a patch of grey."

"Really?" he asked, and I realised that he wasn't listening to me, but was fixed intently on his own thoughts. We had another drink. When I looked at him next he was no longer seated but standing by the rug and examining his rifle, which he hadn't managed to change all this time. I said to him:

"Are you going out hunting in the middle of the night?"

He let my words pass and said:

"Try and remember if anyone visited them these past few days?"

"There's nothing to remember. This morning he came again." I answered.

"Who?" yelled Alone, flying at me and scooping me up off the floor with his spare hand so that the sharp lift made me dizzy and I felt nauseous.

"Damn you," I said. "I feel sick. You got me drunk..."

"Who???" he repeated and stuck his rifle into my back: I could scarcely stay on my feet.

"The devil knows!" I screamed. "I've forgotten his name. The same guy who visited them last time, a whole month ago... Let me go, or I'll be sick all over you."

But he didn't obey, and only clasped me more tightly, dragged me to the water pail and sank my head in it several times so as to continue his torture:

"What did he look like?"

"I don't know," I said, snivelling and trembling all over. "Kind of tall, smiling..."

Then he dropped me and I collapsed on the floor. I didn't manage to curse him before he grabbed me by my chest again and with his burning eyes tried to jog the memory in my fast fading eyes.

"Was he called Rakhim?"

"Yes," I said and started to sober up at speed. "That's it. That was his name. And today he came back round theirs. But somehow this time he didn't stay long "cos I saw him go off into the hills... He has an evil smile."

Alone hit me and I collapsed in a heap on his floor again. He bent down over me and slapped me in the face.

"Why did you keep quiet? Why didn't you tell me anything?" he roared in my face, brandishing his mighty fists in front of it. Then he straightened up and in his rage, if only to stifle his cry, bit his teeth into his fist. The blood showed and the tears welled in his eyes. "The fool! The little arrogant fool!" he repeated, rolling his head in despair. "How dare you have kept quiet!"

He froze suddenly, turned to stone over me, looking into the dark, then howled savagely, grabbed his wineskin and began to drink from it; then flung it to one side, picked up his rifle from the ground and rushed to the door.

"Stop!" I cried. "Where are you going?"

When I caught up with him, past the bridge, I repeated my question, and he hissed:

"I must check the trap!"

We ran through the sultry forest in the pitch dark, I could no longer make out the trees nor the path. Alone remembered them by heart and led me along, stuffing into my hand the hem of his scarf wound round his own wrist –

exactly as he had once before, but in the opposite direction, led the wolf that had attacked him.

By dawn we had almost reached our goal. I was exhausted, but didn't let his scarf out of my hand, so that for the last mile, Alone practically dragged me along, pressing his lips firmly together and seeming not to notice the gasping burden behind him. I was only able to mind the path, the grass flowing beneath our steps, and when he suddenly came to a halt, I bumped into him and we both fell.

"Oh God!" I heard and raised my head.

At first I couldn't make out what had shocked him so. I saw the yawning mouth of the cave, the branches strewn about it and the trampled turf with red flowers. Then I realised that those were not flowers and the entrance to the cave was only half open. A very ancient animal with an enormous head, his half-blind eyes blinking, lay there. We moved over to him, Alone didn't aim his rifle. He walked unevenly on numbed legs, shuddering violently and moaning terribly from time to time. I imagined some kind of triumph in the wolf's eyes. Finally I saw that the wolf wasn't lying on the grass but on a corpse caught in the trap with his throat cut by the wolf's fangs.

Alone went right up to him and looked at his face (sweat streamed down his own, mixing with the dirt and blood from the scratches, and for some reason I thought: it's all over for him too; one end breeds another. Now he'll shoot, we'll bury them, and he'll leave us), he cocked the trigger, turned his gaze (turned it like glass, like a sick man) to the animal, raised his rifle, thrust the barrel into the wolf's ear and waited, but the wolf didn't even stir, having already spent all his hate on his final leap. Alone pulled the trigger...

The man we buried right there, in the cave, among the stone heads and wooden idols, and then covered the entrance with earth, branches, turf and more earth, then put some more turf on top. We took a rest and started upon the wolf. We buried him by the foot of the mound and covered him too with earth. Then we slept. When we woke I asked:

"Who was he?"

"Her twin brother. I never thought he'd find her." Alone replied:

"You never told me a thing about them."

"I was wrong," he agreed.

"Tell me now." I asked.

After a pause he said:

"They'll miss you at home. Some other time..."

"No," I said. "Later you'll leave. Now."

He got up, went over to the nearby pine, pulled down a branch and took off a pot stored upon it. Throwing it over in my direction, he explained where to find the spring.

When I returned, having filled the pot with water, Alone had gone. Looking into the forest I sensed the smoke and followed its smell. Half a verst from the mound Alone had started a campfire and was waiting for me, having threaded a plucked partridge on a switch and holding it over the fire. We roasted it in total silence. Being silent alongside him was, as before, exciting and uncomfortable. Then we ate, washing down the meat with water, and he started his tale. The whole time he talked I didn't interrupt him once. Now and then we merely took our turn to sip water from the pot and throw some more brushwood on the fire. The day rolled on past its half-way point and grew a shade cooler. Then our reserves of brushwood that he'd prepared while I had gone for water were exhausted, but neither of us broke off to go and collect some more. He continued to narrate his tale and I to listen to his even mournful voice, in which he made his confession before leaving us for good. The campfire burned down to its last embers, when he fell silent and I discovered his final secret. Then he sprawled on the grass and looked at the stale sky.

"It's time for you to go home," he said. "Think of your father."

"Why don't we go there together?" I said.

But he repeated: "Have pity on your father." But then added, "Go. I'm staying in the forest for a while."

"All right," I said. "If you want..."

"No," he cut in and closed his eyes with the back of his hand. "I'll go there on my own."

He went there the next morning, which meant I had five days to figure out what had happened and how.

After exactly five days, before sunrise, I ran off to the Blue Road, drew an oval with a cross inside on the roadside, deciding that he'd understand my meaning, then scampered back into the house and began to wait. I had to wait first right up until lunch, and then, once he had come back from the fort, right up to nightfall, for I was still forbidden to visit him openly. I wallowed in my impatience till midnight, until our house was entombed in deep sleep while Alone never left my thoughts. At midnight I again clambered over the fence, cut across his yard and, without knocking, opened his rickety door (only now did I notice how creaky and rickety it was, as if its time had also come).

This time he wasn't just awake but sober too although there was no fire alight in his hearth.

"Did you find out?" I asked him and he nodded.

"Wait," I said. "It's best I try to guess on my own. And where I go wrong, you correct me..."

He nodded once more and folding his hands on his chest got ready to listen.

"Basically, well," I stuttered. "Now I'll begin, wait... I

know it's like what happened to Barysbi, only the other way round..."

"Barysbi?" he asked "The other way round?"

"That's the point," I said. "The opposite."

"Opposite?" he repeated. "Aha."

"For one of them was weighed down by his kin while the other could not obtain any. The first one dreamed of releasing himself and taking his revenge for the crimson velvet on the horse's back; he could hardly wait for the mourning to end to collect the money from the villagers, buy dynamite with it and welcome the Belgians, blow up the cliff, bury the mill beneath it, and then erect a new one and start up the millstones, paying off his debts to the ignorance of the cheated neighbours with the dues for milling. Only he didn't succeed. Chance undermined him. Or destiny. Or fate. Or you and your loneliness who figured out his tricks and then ordering him about simply because he had delayed in shooting you. So that from then on he lived only with a thought of revenge, only now a thousand times more burning and obsessive. When he was finally presented with the opportunity to pay you in kind and bully you with your secret (yours and the pregnant idiot girl's who couldn't even understand it was a secret, for she didn't hear her heart nor her own womb, as she wandered the earth where at any moment death at the hand of her own father threatened her, where she was sullied for a couple of shiny copper coins, but didn't even understand that and accepted them without shame and with gratitude, and would have probably accepted more if the givers hadn't disappeared. And there suddenly appeared another one. He lured her to the Blue Road, but then she found herself in a house, where they also gave themselves to men for money, only there they had the concept of sin and, unable to protect their innocence, they looked after hers as their own, providing her with shiny trinkets utterly unselfishly and with a joyful sadness that rose up in their faded souls every time the thought came to them that someone's happiness could be bought so cheaply. She never learnt anything of her secret. Even when her secret grew below her heart so much that it took the shape of a toy cradle with a baby doll made by her own hands. And when she was dying in the pains of childbirth her secret did not matter any more...), you tell him that the secret is no more and never was, and hold your tongue for eight years. He keeps quiet as well though he suspects whose child it is that was abandoned on Soslan's doorstep, and then my father appears and suggests they go hunting, and then Barysbi suffocates within himself and his distant but now revived baseness, he is disgusted and nauseated by his terror and self-contempt, that the shot, intended by my father, rings out nonetheless – but as a joke, you both think and only the wounded knows (rubbish! He can't know – he can only feel – or rather, he can't know or feel anything) that it's not, that the shot is no joke but a deliverance – from everything at once: from himself, his past, his memory, his kin, his age and even his tongue. At last he's free. He's become a nobody, and only his clothes and his name are somehow the same that belonged at one time to a certain Barysbi, of which now he, if you like, knows less than anyone. Less than his horse, less than the chair on which he sits, and less than those who haven't yet been born, because even they will be told at some point... Yes, he's been delivered / saved from himself. He's probably got what he wanted.

"But with the other, everything was completely the opposite. The other one was born unexpectedly: who could have known that two lives grew in her womb. But it was he who inherited her smile, though he wasn't granted to inherit her innocence, for his very appearance in this world was marked by murder, of which at first he knew nothing at all, thinking his mother to be the one that had raised him. He dreamed of finding his long-lost father, of which, so he thought, there remained at home only a strange and mysterious painting and the spirit of secrecy behind his back. But with the passing of time the stamp – that everlasting crooked smile – showed itself ever more clearly so that in the end he read of it in the loving eyes, that were somehow frightened and suspicious and too dissimilar to his own. But as before he did not let himself fall into doubt for he remembered the painting and dreamed of his father, explaining to himself his mother's anxiety and worry by his family resemblance to his vanished father (even though she would tell him from childhood that he was no longer among the living, he never believed her: at first, he didn't want to, and then he was simply convinced that he must be somewhere, that he was alive and could be found. If you will, he dreamed of him so much, that his non-existent father became more real for him than the existing mother – or she who had usurped her role.)

But then something happened that turned all he knew about himself upside down and made him feel sharply his own guilt for the death of she whose name he had only just heard and part of which he had inherited along with his smile. He probably overheard some conversation, maybe between the girls that still worked there, or maybe it was more vulgar and simpler: one of them, losing her temper at the madam, revealed the secret to him on purpose.

"No," said Alone. "Even simpler than that: she revealed it to him herself. She wanted to put an end to falsehood once and for all. She preferred her adopted motherhood to a counterfeit one, dependent on chance circumstances and gossip. She hoped that the truth would help him, and that he would finally stop rambling on about his father, of whom she herself knew nothing and so her chosen son couldn't possibly find out.

"Only she kept quiet about his sister," I continued. "Of course. She didn't say a word about her – that would be the last thread, which he could grasp. Moreover, she was bound by the promise she had given you, and you held yours without reproach. Only she hadn't reckoned on one thing: the persistence of a man trying to find out who he is and where he comes from, and trying to remember the history of his own silent blood so as to feel genuinely, in all its vibrancy, its inner warmth and the voice of his own heart. So then she did not notice that he only pretended to calm down, yet all the while stubbornly and painstakingly seeking the tracks of that primordial day shrouded in the fog of an unknown road that led you to that house. She forgot that your painting was always in front of his eyes."

"That cursed painting," said Alone. "Those cursed paints..."

"But then he found something else. He probably discovered it in one of the little boxes – a metal nametag with a name engraved on it..."

"I don't know," said Alone. "Maybe."

"...and thought it wouldn't be a bad idea to meet up with the man who'd crafted it, to find out from him who had placed the order. And, if you like, he didn't have many craftsmen to choose from, so very soon he laid eyes on the man whose hands had first carved the letters of his name, and for a small bribe the man remembered there'd been a little girl too, for there were two of those nametags. For another bribe he managed to make him draw out of his memory the second name that he'd carved into the metal the same day. So now he knew the name of his sister. Then he sought out one of those who used to work for his adopted mother selling her body for money, but now, grown old and ugly from diseases and drink, was in no state to sell anything, except recollections of how you carried away his sister. But to where – he didn't yet know. He decided to prepare himself. He wandered round the marketplace looking at those who sold pictures, still not understanding that you had sworn to her never to show yourself again in the fort. There in the marketplace he must have found some beggar from whom he bought your language, which he came to accept as his own. He took the lessons without her knowledge..."

"No, he made no secret of it, and she didn't object because she saw nothing suspicious in it. She never foresaw..."

"No, she didn't expect her son to be capable of what he did. But the problem was he was her son less than ever. He must have pretended very well and his smile must have come in handy... But then he thought up a new ruse, on the pretext of some business, I don't know which ("Drawing," prompted Alone. "He convinced her that he enjoyed drawing from nature...") he hired a driver and a cart and travelled around the surrounding auls ("and brought back drawings sketched on the road by some hack, whom he paid to accompany him. I found him three days ago in the marketplace. She didn't know.") This probably went on for a long time ("Two years," said Alone. "He journeyed all over these parts for two whole years.") Finally he caught your trace. After all his enquiries he heard about you and a month or so later got himself ready for the road again and took the right turning ("This time he took no one with him. The hack stayed behind and the driver got paid for not going anywhere, and a deposit for lending him the horse and cart.") But first he went into hiding. He hid in our forest and only twice a day, morning and evening, stole down to the river to gaze at the girls coming down to the river to fill their jugs with water.

"He must have made sure that they, albeit twins, were in no way alike. When he was certain of this (for now he knew which gate she came out from: not for nothing had he stayed beforehand in the neighbouring aul, where he left his horse and cart and where he found out all about the ones who interested him. So before he set foot in our forest he already knew that she was a foundling, Soslan was blind, you were dangerous, and Gappo was their grandfather on his mother's side. He wandered through the forest and heard his own blood, now convinced that he had found his homeland and now stepped on native ground. So he came across the cave and even rested one night there. I think he realised to whom it belonged, but decided not to linger there, not to have his revenge just yet. His revenge he'd set aside for later. He returned to his horse, rode into our aul, stopped at the nykhas, smiling his broad smile, and started speaking in our language (he sounded like he'd scalded his palate), and then within his rights as a guest selected the house of Soslan. He only had to wait for the right moment and stealthily show her the nametag with his name carved on it. He no longer even had to prove that he was her brother. All he had to do was give her a month to think..."

"Yes," said Alone. "And then take away with him her beauty and her sadness and build what he had always been lacking: his own home, a settled family, locked in common grief, common cares, and common half-knowledge."

"And common loneliness," I said. "Only a month later he didn't succeed. When he arrived one early morning and chatted with Soslan about various unimportant matters, he met with her again – probably like the first time in some secluded place, by the river under the precipice or by the Blue Road – she refused him, explaining that she had no need for anyone else. That she had Soslan, and that was enough, that you can't have two fathers, and that she wasn't going anywhere. And he flew into a rage. He realised that everything had fallen apart, he viewed her reply as the most terrible treachery. Then he revealed to her with a smile who her mother was, and named her grandfather, and threatened that if she didn't come to the cave by dusk (here he explained to her how to get there) he, Rakhim, would expose their shared secret to the whole aul and then she would see what fun everyone would have with it. So she had no choice..."

"She had," said Alone. "But one so bad that she would have been better without."

"It was a choice to swap Soslan's blindness for the bulging-eyed Gappo or the menacing smile of this terrible stranger, in whom flowed the same blood as in her. To become related to the man, who would have killed his own daughter, Lana's mother, had she not vanished in time, and thus he would have killed them both as well; to become related to him who had drawn his mother's last breath with his appearance into this world, as if to oblige his unknown grandfather, and was now suggesting to her to run away from the man who was more to her than a father, for he was a father twice over, loving in her not only herself but also the memory of his other daughter; this stranger with the cruel smile was compelling her to become a murderer of the blind man who had always been doting on her. Otherwise he threatened to destroy all concerned with their common shame... And now she didn't even have the time to think straight about it. When the hour came, she flitted around like a bird in a cage, she rushed first out of the house, then down the street to Gappo's house, then to the nykhas where Soslan was sitting, and then, in utter despair, ran to the forest. Ah! If only she'd managed to reach the cave, she would have seen that he was no more, and then, once she'd buried him, she would have come back home, having not said a word to anyone and quietly crying for her fallen brother till the end of her days...

"Yes," said Alone. "If only she'd managed to run there! But on the bridge she had second thoughts..."

"On the bridge she had second thoughts and chose to give in, throwing herself into the river right before our eyes while you were still sleeping..."

"Yes," he said. "Yes. May God curse me!"

"...and went on sleeping and only woke up when the earth started cracking, accepting her into its depth... And your wizened old wolf, gathering up his strength to take his revenge on you, and who for a whole month lay in wait for you by your cave, tormented by your smell that had settled there, tore apart that bastard who had fallen in your trap."

"Yes! May I be cursed. Yes! ... An oval with a cross."

"... who was misfortunate by dint of his guilt and the silence of his own blood, that he was ready to go to any lengths to identify that blood, and with it – his own self – who he was and whence he came. Only you wouldn't even have revealed that to him. For he was hiding from you as well – the man, whom he had taken to be his long-lost father for so many years now that he had learned all the paints in your picture off by heart..."

"Yes. Oh God! Yes. Yes. Yes..."

"And the only salvation for you – and for us too, for with Lana perished our beauty, one beauty for us all – would have been for you to ride off to the fort and reveal yourself to him even the once, to let him, still only a little boy, believe you were his father, however strange it may have seemed when you consider how old his adopted (though a real one at that point) mother was. He would have believed. He longed to believe... Only you went there too late, only now did you go... What did you tell her?"

"Almost the truth," he answered. "I told her they had gone. Both of them..."

"Aha, and she decided that "gone" meant they'd run away, I imagine? So from now on she'll live in hope that they..."

"So much the better," he said. "That was the last time I lied."

"Because come morning you'll leave us. Where are you going?"

"Over the ridge," he answered. "To the poisoned river. Once, a very long time ago, my grandfather pointed it out to me from the summit. My true grandfather, who didn't know how to steal."

Now I understood. He was going off to where no man had set foot for more than two hundred years, since the days when, according to belief, the river poisoned a whole village, so the inhabitants had to build burial vaults for those who had fallen ill to save those who could still be infected. When the plague had scythed through them all indiscriminately, leaving only empty houses and rotting crypts, the river changed its course and began to destroy their buildings. Sometimes they called it the Cursed River. Now he was going off there to start from scratch all over again. I understood. And then others who dared would follow in his wake.

"Haven't you had enough? You want to try all over again?" I said.

"I don't know," he replied. "Maybe I'll have luck there, and find Him... differently than five days ago..."

"Who?" I asked. He was silent, and I guessed. "Now you're going to seek Him in the water?"

"I don't know," he repeated. "I don't know anything yet."

After a pause I said: "They both took after you."

"Who?" he said, surprised.

"Rakhim and Lana."

"How?"

But I didn't attempt to explain.

Dawn came. His stone house was cold and damp. The last week he hadn't lit a fire in his hearth. We had stayed silent to our heart's content, I got up and said:

"I'll look after the graves."

He nodded.

"Will you say goodbye to them?"

"Yes," he said. "Of course. The house I leave to you. And my share of the harvest as well. But my gun I'm taking with me."

"You've turned entirely grey," I said, trying not to cry. "You've gone grey right through..."

"Yes," he said. Yes. May God curse me three times over..."

We said goodbye, and I didn't clamber over his fence but for the first time went out by his front gate. It was quiet in our yard, and only Father was sitting on Grandfather's log watching me come out to meet him.

I went up to him and said:

"He's leaving. Now he's off to the graveyard, and from there straight away to the ridge."

Father turned round and said nothing.

"He's leaving me his house and his eighth part of the harvest..." I added and looked at the back of his head.

At last he said: "He's late this time. And I'm too late to say goodbye to him."

"As you wish," I said. "Only we'll never be able to escape from him."

Then we were silent for a while, and I came right up to him, trying to look him straight in the eye and said:

"Relax now. It's all over. All that can be over now has come to its end. Relax now."

"I'm not crying," he answered solemnly. "I'm watching."

I followed his gaze and saw as well. Soslan was standing on an enormous boulder by the river, and his face was turned to the torrent of seething water and the pale light. He stood tall and proud. And mighty as the disaster that had befallen him. Even from that distance one could see that he was blind. But now it was the blindness of a prophet, breathing in the smell of eternity. I thought: This is the end of the story if it can have an end at all...

Vladikavkaz – Plovdiv

The latest titles from Glas

Strange Soviet Practices, a collection

Nikolai Klimontovich, *The Road to Rome*, a novel

Nina Gabrielyan, *Master of the Grass*, short stories

Nina Lugovskaya, *The Diary of a Soviet Schoolgirl: 1932-37*

NINE of Russia's Foremost Women Writers

Alexander Selin, *The New Romantic,* modern parables

Valery Ronshin, *Living a Life*, Totally Absurd Tales

Andrei Sergeev, *Stamp Album*,
A Collection of People, Things, Relationships and Words

Lev Rubinstein, *Here I Am*, performance poems

Andrei Volos, *Hurramabad*, a novel

A.J.Perry, *Twelve Stories of Russia: a Novel I guess*

The premier showcase for contemporary Russian writing in
English translation, GLAS has been discovering new writers
for over a decade. With some 100 names represented,
GLAS is the most comprehensive English-language source
on Russian letters today — a must for libraries, students
of world literature, and all those who love good writing.
For more information and excerpts see our site:
www.russianpress.com/glas